Praise for *The Repl*

'A modern
impr
the twists are lovely; dark an eep'
The Times

'Golding folds together a folklore-inspired plot with
the modern twists and tension of a police procedural
novel to create a bitingly unnerving story'
Adele Parks, *Platinum* magazine

'Sewing together the many threads of the case, there
is the added folklore that seeps into an atmospheric,
mysterious and horror-struck storyline. Powerful imagery
and captivating characters, this a grabbing book'
Magic Radio Book Club

'The most original book you'll read this year . . . equal
parts detective novel, psychological thriller and family
drama. Full of twists, turns and atmosphere, make sure
you don't accidentally stay up all night devouring it'
Crime Monthly

'Creepy and atmospheric, the author weaves a magical
thread of folklore into this outstanding thriller'
My Weekly

'Chillingly brilliant'
Best

'A psychological thriller with a difference'
H

Melanie Golding took the MA in Creative Writing program at Bath Spa University in 2015-2016, graduating with distinction. She has recently completed work on a PhD, which examines the use of folklore in contemporary thrillers. In recent years she has won and been shortlisted in several local and national short story competitions, which have been chosen to be recorded as podcasts by the Leicester-based festival Story City, and to be performed at both the regular Stroud Short Stories event and their special 'best of' event at Cheltenham Literature Festival.

Melanie has had a varied working life, including working as a teacher in prisons, young offender's units and residential schools for children with special educational needs. She originally trained as a musician and has recently collaborated as a lyricist with award-winning composer Emily Hall on several projects. Her first novel, *Little Darlings*, became an eBook bestseller and won the DragonCon award for Best Horror Novel in 2019. It has also been optioned for screen by Free Range Films, the team behind the adaptation of *My Cousin Rachel*.

Also by Melanie Golding

Little Darlings

THE
REPLACEMENT

MELANIE GOLDING

ONE PLACE. MANY STORIES

HQ
An imprint of HarperCollins*Publishers* Ltd
1 London Bridge Street
London SE1 9GF

www.harpercollins.co.uk

HarperCollins*Publishers*
Macken House, 39/40 Mayor Street Upper,
Dublin 1, D01 C9W8, Ireland

This edition 2023

1
First published in Great Britain by
HQ, an imprint of HarperCollins*Publishers* Ltd 2021

Copyright © Melanie Golding 2021

Melanie Golding asserts the moral right to be
identified as the author of this work.
A catalogue record for this book is
available from the British Library.

ISBN: 978-0-00-829376-5

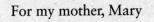

For my mother, Mary

CHAPTER ONE

She steals to the window, and looks at the sand,
And over the sand at the sea;
And her eyes are set in a stare;
And anon there breaks a sigh,
And anon there drops a tear,
From a sorrow-clouded eye,
And a heart sorrow-laden,
A long, long sigh;
For the cold strange eyes of a little Mermaiden
And the gleam of her golden hair.
MATTHEW ARNOLD, 'The Forsaken Merman', 1849

NOW
Leonie

Friday, 21 December

Leonie presses her palm to the outside of the shop window. The glass is cold; the fat little star of her hand leaves an imprint in condensation when she pulls it away. She laughs and slaps her hand back on the window, stamping another and another, a bit like when she does potato printing at the kitchen table, the potatoes soon left aside in favour of dipping her hands straight in the paints. She concentrates on tracing the outlines of the handprints with a fingertip, before they fade away.

'Mamma,' she says. 'Come look. Me do painting.'

Behind her, a handbag stands abandoned on the pavement. She turns around, toddles over, picks up the bag. She looks up and down the street, her whole body turning first one way, then the other. There is no one else there. The chill wind blows in her face, tightening the skin on her cheeks and almost toppling her, almost taking her pink bobble hat from her head. Two bobbles; like a teddy bear's ears.

'Mamma?'

Leonie is still, wearing a small frown. Then, she upends the handbag onto the slabs. Nappies and wipes fall out, nappy bags are whisked up the street by the wind. There is a coin purse, a collection of receipts, a bunch of keys attached to a smooth pebble with a hole in it. Picking up the pebble, she shakes the keys so that they rattle, then drops the lot back on the ground. A fruit bar, half-finished and wound into its torn wrapper is what she reaches for next. She has it in her mouth when she hears the shop bell. The heavy door creaks as it opens, spilling yellow light and warmth onto her fingers, now almost blue with cold, that peep out beyond the cuffs of her coat.

Though it isn't late, it's nearly dark; the shortest day of the year. The girl toddles towards the shop's light, towards the Christmas tree just inside, past the stranger at the door who has stepped aside to let her in, who is saying, 'Where's your mummy?'

Leonie reaches for a bauble, a shiny thing, sparkling.

There's a chocolate bell too and she drops the fruit bar to take it in her hand.

'Whose child is this?' calls the stranger, as the man from behind the counter comes forward, rubbing his hands together, his eyes wide with concern.

'Mamma?' says Leonie to the shopkeeper, recognising nothing but the worry in his expression. Her bottom lip wobbles in uncertainty. Then, her grip on the foil-covered decoration is lost and it hits the floor tiles, smashing into pieces that scatter from the wrapping as it splits. There is stillness as she looks at all the bits in turn, her face registering surprise. This, seemingly, is the most upsetting thing. She shuts her eyes to cry, face to the ceiling, fists clenched, mouth open, revealing eight perfect teeth.

The customer crouches, hovering his hand near the toddler, saying, 'Shh, it's OK, don't worry. We'll find Mamma.'

Both of the adults expect a loud noise, and brace themselves for it. But when the cry comes it is a faint, keening whisper, like distant wind. The child's face is posed in a scream, but there is hardly a sound.

The two men exchange a glance, agreeing that something is wrong, but at this moment there are bigger problems than the strangeness of this cry. The customer starts to pat the toddler on the shoulder, the pads of his fingers barely making contact, and all the time he's glancing around, talking to the shopkeeper, saying, 'Did you see who she was with?' Leonie opens her eyes and screams silently into his face. The soundlessness of it makes it worse, somehow, than if the scream were deafening. The man stands, snatches another chocolate decoration from a branch and gently takes one of the child's trembling fists in his hand. He unpeels the small fingers, places the confection on her upturned palm. Her mouth shuts, and she inspects the red Santa figure, turning it over, searching for how to open it. She hiccups once. Snot runs down her chin.

The bell on the door rings as the shopkeeper yanks it open. He steps outside and looks both ways, then up at the darkening sky and finally down, at the handbag spilling its contents. He walks forwards, nudges the pile of nappies with a toe, notes the keys, the packet of wipes. He's looking for a phone, or a wallet with something like ID in it, but there's nothing. The coin purse contains only cash. He picks up the empty handbag, weighs it in his hand. He finds a pocket at the front and unzips it. Inside is what he thinks is a rock, but on closer inspection is a seashell.

One or two snowflakes swirl in the wind, landing on the concrete and making wet speckles. In the distance, the seals call to each other across the waves, making a sound like human screams, but besides a slight jerk to the head the man doesn't react. If you live here it's a familiar sound, the seal-song, like that of the waves, and the gulls.

The sea sighs as the tide licks the shore, sucking the surface of the beach into new shapes: gentle, curving undulations different from yesterday, that will be different tomorrow, and with every tide that turns.

Just out of sight, a small pile of clothes, buried in haste in the sand, is covered up by the advancing water. Gentle eddies loosen the folds of the fabric, so that a parka slowly unfurls like a flower opening in the darkness. Soon the sea will probe further, uncovering the heel of one boot. Later, the clothes will be completely removed from their rudimentary hiding place by the many strong hands of the currents. Later still they will be scattered on seven different shores. The other boot will remain here, wedging itself between two rocks, unseen by anyone until the litter pickers come in the spring.

CHAPTER TWO

NOW
Bathwater

Friday, 21 December

The water fills the bathtub slowly, over a number of hours. As it does so, the body of the man begins to float, rising with the level of the liquid, the small amount of fat and the air in his body keeping him on the surface, for now. Falling from the tap, the water is clear. As the thin stream enters the tub it mixes with the man's blood, so that the colour of the bathwater varies from pale rose at his feet, to plumes of bright red near his head, where pulse pressure shoots the blood from the wound in regular bursts. It takes a long time, but when the bath is full, the solution finds its way to the overflow, and from there it trickles through the many metres of pipework to the sewers, deep below the block of flats.

In the bathtub, as well as the man and the water and the blood, there is a towel. The towel is drawn towards the overflow, until at last a combination of the man's legs and the bunching of the thick fabric blocks the hole completely. No one is there to turn off the tap; the bath keeps filling, and keeps filling, so that soon, like a bloody version of the magic porridge-pot, it goes over, flooding the bathroom, searching out the edges of the vinyl, breaking through, soaking into the floorboards, pooling in the cavity under the floor. There's a layer of sealant there, and a layer of soundproofing, but the water finds the lowest point. It accumulates, becomes heavier, weakens the plasterboard. It only needs a tiny gap, a pinprick, to break through.

In the flat below, Mrs Stefanidis is preparing to eat her lunch, a small cheese sandwich on white bread. She feels rather than hears something drop, disrupting the air close to her face, but when she places her hands on the tabletop and feels around, there appears to be nothing amiss. After a momentary frown, her fingers find the plate and raise the sandwich to her lips, the macular degeneration that has reduced her vision to a sliver of peripheral preventing her from noticing the spreading pink circle that has wetted the middle of the bread, the droplet of blood-and-bathwater that landed there, that came from the ceiling above. As she opens her mouth, another fat sphere drops and bursts, this time on her hand, and she puts the sandwich down.

Something in the ceiling gives. It starts to come faster, dripping like a broken gutter in the middle of the kitchen table, spattering the walls, flecks of it on the white net curtains, on the clean cups that stand on the draining board. Mrs Stefanidis feels under the sink for the bucket, locates the leak and places the vessel just so, to catch it. She dries her hands on her apron, then reaches into her apron pocket to phone for the maintenance man. Using the specially enlarged buttons on her handset she speed dials Terry's number, listens to it ringing, hopes he won't mind coming to help her; there's no one else to ask. On the table, the bucket is filling, slowly but surely. Soon it will be too heavy for her to lift. The apron she wears is made of crisp cotton. She doesn't see the pinkish prints her fingers have made there.

CHAPTER THREE

NOW
Ruby

Friday, 21 December

When Ruby turned the corner, she knew she was in deep shit. The plan had been perfect, on paper, but of course they'd realised that the timings were tight, with no room for trains being late. Stupid, then, to think the bloody thing would be on time, on this day, of all days. She hurried along the street towards the shop, where blue lights flashed repeatedly from the police car parked outside. If the police were here, it meant that something terrible had happened. What had Constance done, why had they been called? No one was supposed to know about this, a quiet handover of an unknown child on a deserted small-town street, arranged carefully so that the mother could slip away, unnoticed. If the police were involved then it was all over, before they'd even had a chance. Was Constance desperate enough to risk leaving Leonie before Ruby got there? From Constance's state of mind in recent days, Ruby thought she knew the answer to that. Distressing possibilities ran through Ruby's mind: Leonie crushed under the wheels of a car; Leonie drowned trying to follow her mother into the sea. Ten minutes late, that's all it was, and it wasn't her fault, it was the bloody trains.

Ruby's lungs were burning; she'd been running for what seemed like hours. But it was only ten minutes or so. Hardly any time. *Enough time to die*, came the unwanted thought, before she could stop it.

An officer stepped out of the shop, and the sight of the police uniform caused a sickening jolt in Ruby. She thought for a split second that it could be Joanna, before shaking off the notion with logic: Jo lived and worked in Sheffield, fifty miles away. Also, Joanna no longer wore the uniform; as a detective she wasn't on the front line.

'Good evening, madam,' said the officer. 'Can I help you?'

Through the gaps around the flyers in the shop window, Ruby could see inside, where the shopkeeper was lifting Leonie onto the counter.

'Oh, I'm fine,' said Ruby, thinking, *Is she OK? Is she hurt?* And she tried to get past the police officer, reaching a hand to push open the door. The officer moved slightly, to block her.

'I'm afraid you can't go in at the moment. There's been an incident.'

Next to the counter, another police officer held the handbag that Constance used as a changing bag, the one she would have handed to Ruby along with the child. He searched through it, placing the items together in a pile as he took them out one by one. There was no sign, inside or outside the shop, of Constance herself. Ruby became aware of the sound of the waves behind her, wanting to turn and scan the water for the boat that Constance had said was coming to fetch her, not daring to do so. Even if it were there, in the descending dark Ruby might not have seen it: from the stories Constance had told her, family life was very basic. Ruby imagined them like seafaring Amish, without electricity or modern technology, still living in the way they'd been doing a hundred years ago, or more.

There was a strange, almost musical cry from far offshore, whipped away by the wind as soon as she heard it. Might have been a ship's horn. Might have been the wind itself, whistling through a gap in the rocks where the land met the sea.

She glared at the police officer. 'Can you move, please? I need to get inside. That's my baby.' *My baby*, she thought, and in that moment, she realised it was true. Perhaps not biologically, but nevertheless true in the only way that mattered. *She's my baby now.* As the thought settled on her, she stood straighter, feeling proud to claim it.

Ruby craned her neck to see, caught the lost look in Leonie's eyes, and tried to take another step towards the door. The child hadn't noticed her yet, and Ruby so wanted to give her a cuddle, tell her everything was going to be OK. She couldn't get past; the policewoman was still blocking her way.

'You're the mother?' asked the officer.

'Yes,' she said. Ruby's voice was high and quiet, and she worried she'd made her reply sound too much like a question. She cleared her throat. 'Can I go in, please? She'll be scared.' How long had she been in the care of the police? It was only ten minutes. Maybe twenty. No time at all.

The officer moved forwards in a way that made Ruby step back. 'If you could come this way please, madam. There'll be someone along shortly to talk to you.' With arms held out slightly, the officer ushered Ruby away from the shop, towards the patrol car.

'Can't I see her?' said Ruby, trying to see over her shoulder through the glass. 'She's OK, isn't she? Is she safe?' *How to explain it? Even ten minutes was unforgivable.* 'I'm so sorry, I let go of her hand for one second, and she ran off. I lost sight of her.'

The guilt was crushing. Sharp tears formed in the corners of Ruby's eyes, her throat swelled painfully. She glanced at the expressionless face of the police officer, in which she could read nothing at all. No sympathy, no understanding. Then it hit her: it wasn't just the blonde colouring, and the uniform – this person really reminded her of Joanna, and not in a good way. It was the cool, detached attitude, the way she was observing Ruby the way you would observe another species, an insect, or an alien.

'If you wouldn't mind waiting in the back of the vehicle,' said the officer. *If you wouldn't mind.* There was clearly no choice whatsoever.

'Are you arresting me? I haven't done anything wrong. It was a mistake. An accident.'

The officer opened the door of the patrol car and motioned for Ruby to get in. The police radio gave a crackle, and she moved to turn the volume down.

'Do you have children?' said Ruby, but the officer simply repeated,

'If you wouldn't mind.'

It was probably best to do as she was told. Ruby climbed carefully into the back seat of the patrol car and sat there stiffly, pressing her knees together, staring at the headrest in front of her.

'Won't be a moment, madam.'

When the door was shut, the darkness closed her in. The officer walked away, and Ruby scrabbled at the door, checking for an escape route, just in case. The handle slipped from her fingers as she pulled it; the thing was functionless, child-locked. That must have been a mistake. They weren't supposed to keep her prisoner, were they? When she hadn't done anything wrong?

Inside the shop she could see the shopkeeper and the male police officer talking to each other. Like the windows, the glass door was plastered with posters and stickers, so only a sliver of the faces could be seen, quick glimpses of hands gesticulating. When the officer who had put her in the car reached the shop door and opened it, there was a clear view of Leonie, sitting on the counter eating pieces of chocolate from a nest of gold foil that had been placed next to her. A chocolate decoration. Someone must have opened it for her. Leonie was completely absorbed by the process, taking her time choosing a piece and grasping it delicately in her fingers, opening her mouth comically wide to get it in and, even before it was finished, returning her attention to the next selection. Ruby closed her eyes in relief. There were dirty streaks on the little face where she'd been crying, but Leonie was fine. That was really all that mattered. It was going to be OK.

The shop door closed, obscuring most of her view. She could see part of the back of the policewoman as she talked to the other officer, then a slice of the male officer's face as he lifted his radio and spoke into it. His eyes slid towards Ruby, then, though she didn't think he'd be able to see her: the light was in her favour. She smoothed her skirt and applied some lip balm, tried to control her breathing. This was the big test. She never imagined it would come so soon into the journey. Ruby wasn't sure she was ready.

She took a long, slow breath. *I am all that girl has in the world. I have to do this. I have to try.* Outside there was a distant sound, coming from the waves, loud and long, and echoing round the bay. This time she knew what it was. The seals calling. She wondered what exactly they were saying. The lullaby came to mind, the one she learned from Constance, that she often sang to Leonie: *Ionn da, ionn do, ionn da, od-ar da.* Constance had said it was called 'The Seal-Woman's Joy'. The title seemed wrong, now, and in Ruby's head the words sang out in a minor key.

Two cars pulled up: another police car, which parked by the sea wall opposite, and a big black utility vehicle that stopped right behind the car in which she was imprisoned. In the side mirror she saw a woman in a trouser suit exit the black car and go into the shop. After a while this woman came out again, holding Leonie's small hand in hers, leading her away.

Ruby banged on the inside of the window and shouted Leonie's name. The child looked up, perhaps wondering where the banging was coming from. Her mouth formed the word 'Mamma' but she was looking the wrong way, over the wrong shoulder, back towards the shop.

'Here,' Ruby shouted, 'I'm over here, love. In here. Baby girl? Mamma Bee's here.' Her voice faded away as Leonie was pulled out of sight by the suited woman, and put into the black car. *She didn't see me. She thinks she's been abandoned, by both of us.* Ruby's eyes started to sting again with withheld tears. Her nails dug into her palms, leaving deep red crescents. She hardly felt it.

When the roadside passenger door of the police car was opened, Ruby jumped. She hadn't seen anyone approaching. She turned to see the woman in the suit, a large woman with glasses and closely cut curls, who got in, shutting the door behind her. Who was with Leonie? One of the cops, maybe. One thing was for sure: *they* would never leave the child on her own with no one to look after her.

'Hello. I'm Diane, from social services. You're the mother of that little girl, right?'

Ruby nodded.

Diane pulled out a little notepad and pen. 'What's your name, please?'

'Constance.'

The lie came out before she'd really thought it through. But then, once she'd said it, she relaxed. It made sense to be Constance in this moment. After all, Constance was technically the birth mother. More importantly, unlike Ruby, Constance had no official identity, no police record. She'd never paid tax, had a job, or owned a car. Constance was invisible to authority and society, just like Leonie, her unregistered, invisible child.

CHAPTER FOUR

NOW
Joanna

Friday, 21 December

DS Joanna Harper nodded to PC Steve Atkinson, who'd brought the ram. He aimed the front end of the black metal cylinder at the lock with practised precision, just hard enough to break it.

The door to apartment 7 swung wide, and Joanna inhaled cautiously, conscious that the smell of a dead body wasn't one she wanted in her nostrils; once it got up there, that very particular stench took a while to shift. Thankfully, all she caught was a strong odour of damp from the flooded floors. Two paramedics waited outside the flat, along with the caretaker, Terry. She thought of the bucket of bloody water that Terry had shown them and drew a deep breath to steady herself before she stepped inside, her black sneakers squelching on the hall carpet.

Joanna had asked the caretaker what he knew about the owner, a Mr Gregor Franks.

'He's a single guy, I think. Not too short of cash. I think

he's in some kind of sales manager type job. Or stocks and shares, maybe.'

'Age?' asked Jo.

'About thirty, I'd say.'

'When's the last time you saw him?'

Terry had to think hard. 'I don't know. A while now. Two or three years? I only come when I'm called. He never calls.'

'I understand you do have a key to Mr Franks' flat?' said Atkinson. 'But you haven't been inside to check on him since the leak?'

Terry looked pointedly down at the bucket that stood between them on the concrete floor. 'I didn't know what I might find. I'm not good with stuff like that. Sight of blood. You'd need another ambulance, for me, when I hit the floor.'

After they'd climbed the stairs to the seventh floor and Jo tried it in the lock, the key didn't work. Franks must have had it changed. Joanna knocked, and knocked again, and shouted for Gregor to open up, but even as she did so Atkinson dumped the heavy holdall he carried on to the floor and unzipped it, readied the Enforcer to break it down.

Inside the flat, Joanna led the way. With only the leak to go on, and the occupant not known to police, they were keeping an open mind. With that amount of blood there could have been anything happening in the apartment: multiple casualties; dangerous suspects still on scene; a terrible accident. Equally, they might find nothing at all. When Jo was sent to the job, the duty sergeant could only speculate. 'Might not even be blood, could be wood stain or paint, or rust. And if it's blood, could be a domestic accident, where the person has taken themselves off to hospital but left the tap on by mistake.'

'Or, it could be a ritual sacrifice, and the blood belongs to a sheep or something?'

Murray's voice on the radio was without mirth. 'Jo, all we have is a bucket of what is apparently bloody water. No other reports of anything unusual, no body, no one reported at risk or missing or injured. Just go with Steve and check it out for me. If you find anything, I'll divert resources immediately.'

'I'm assuming you're asking me because you don't have anyone else?'

'You'd be right to assume that. I've got so many immediate response jobs on, they're stacking up as we speak. Firearms are at a stabbing in the city centre, all of my other units are out with higher priority stuff. Ambulance will attend but they've stated that the police need to clear the scene before they go in.'

'Understood.'

This close to Christmas, the service always got overloaded. Every year it got worse. A lot of staff took holiday, so that often all they had on duty was a skeleton selection of response officers, half the Control team and a few sergeants, like Murray and Joanna.

'Oh, and Jo? Take a stab vest.'

'Yeah, take a stab vest, it's probably nothing,' muttered Jo as she shrugged on the heavy garment, before walking out of the building and getting in the patrol car with Atkinson. DS Harper enjoyed a good moan, like everyone, but the truth was she secretly loved it when staff shortages meant that she had to get back on front-line work. Joanna made the move to detective because she thought she'd prefer the investigative side of things. She wasn't going to admit it to Murray, but it turned out she was much happier wearing a stab vest and breaking down doors.

'Mr Franks?'

Jo edged along the hallway before pushing open the door to the living room. It was cold and dark in there, the power having been shut off at the same time as the water. By torchlight she could see that the place was mostly tidy and relatively clean. A plate of toast crusts was balanced on the arm of the corner couch, along with an undrunk cup of tea. A box of toys had been put away against the wall.

In the kitchen, a loaf of bread lay open on the counter. She picked up the nearest slice, felt it, gave it a sniff. Slightly stale. A phone was plugged into an outlet. Jo picked it up and swiped the screen, but it was dead. In the wallet lying next to it, she found a driver's licence and pulled it out. A kind face, lightly stubbled, the kind of thick, wavy hair Atkinson had ten years ago.

The next room off the living room contained an unmade double bed and a cot pushed into the corner, the mattress covered in a sheet, an open toddler sleeping bag bunched up on its end, as if the child had just been lifted from it. In the corner, a floral-print summer dress had been tossed, and on top of it lay a single pink baby sock fringed with white lace. Harper quickly scanned the room, then crouched to look under the bed. Nothing there but a collection of seashells in a box.

'Clear,' she called.

There was another bedroom, this one spotlessly neat, not a crease in the duvet cover or a single discarded item on the floor. Joanna opened the cupboards and found meticulously ironed shirts and trousers, all arranged in colour order.

'Clear,' she called again.

Back in the main space the two officers stood in front of the last door. When Atkinson turned the handle, he found that it couldn't be opened.

Joanna banged on the door with a closed fist. 'Mr Franks?' she said. 'Gregor? Can you hear me? My name's Jo. I'm with the police. Can you open the door?'

The silence was the buzzing kind, in which you strain your ears, hoping for a sound, any sound. There was nothing.

'We're going to force the door, Mr Franks,' said Jo. 'Stand back.'

Atkinson picked up the ram. She stepped out of the way as he aimed the front end at the handle and swung.

One great smash and the door was swinging on its hinges. The scene inside was a mess of red and white, blood and tiles, a bath brim-full of bloody water surrounding the pale skin of the man's body. Atkinson coughed, to cover a gasp, probably. The body itself was unmarked, perfectly still and white, hands and feet bluish and mottled, face peaceful, eyes closed. Harper thought of dumplings in beetroot soup, and her stomach rumbled. She'd skipped lunch, saving herself for dinner tonight. Now it looked like she wouldn't be getting any.

'Anything?' called out one of the paramedics.

'There's a body here,' called Jo. She checked behind the door to make absolutely sure there was no one else in the room waiting to attack them, but the action was just routine; she'd known already, copper's instinct, that the man was alone. 'It's safe. You can come through.'

She couldn't see the wrists, only the backs of the man's hands. This was a scene she'd come across a few times in her years as a response officer, and it didn't get any easier to understand. What had made this man do this to himself?

'Is that him, the owner of the flat?' asked Atkinson.

Joanna went back to the kitchen counter for the driver's licence. She compared the dead-looking face in the bath with the living one in the image. She showed the picture to Atkinson, who nodded. 'That's him.'

The two paramedics entered the bathroom gingerly, so as not to slip in the mixture of blood and water on the tiles. One of them knelt by the bath. 'Mr Franks?' he said. 'Can you hear me?' He placed a hand on the man's forehead. Then he turned over the arm nearest to them, exposing the inside of his wrist. Joanna fully expected to see a deep cut there, and perhaps later they would find a razor blade that had slipped underneath the body as he fell unconscious. But there was no damage: the skin on the wrist was intact. The paramedic reached for the left arm: also no cuts.

'Where's the blood coming from?' asked Jo.

'I can't tell at the moment. Somewhere on the back of him.' He placed his fingers at the man's neck, then listened at his chest; his cheek came away wet.

'He's alive.'

This surprised Joanna, who had unwittingly broken the first rule of policing: she had *assumed* Franks was dead, because it had been several hours since the leak was spotted, because it was freezing in the flat, because of the blood and the fact that he was lying in a full tub of water. Mostly because it looked so much like a dead body, and she'd seen more than a few in her time.

The paramedic lifted Gregor's head out of the water. 'Head trauma. That's where he's bleeding.'

Jo spoke into the radio. 'Control, update on the situation in apartment seven in the North block on the New Park estate. We have a casualty, repeat there is one casualty, serious trauma protocol, please – head injury, severe blood loss is evident. Unconscious male, positive for signs of life.'

Over the radio, Sergeant Murray said, 'Copy that, Jo. Any suspects present?'

'No. It's not clear what we're dealing with yet, whether there's anyone else involved. Stand by for update.'

'Received, standing by.'

The paramedic said, 'Gregor, we're going to get you out of the bath now. Can you hear me, Gregor?'

He rolled up a sleeve and pulled the plug in the bath, letting the water out. Then he turned to Atkinson. 'Get some blankets or something. The duvet off the bed. And help us lift him out, would you? Both of you; we'll need all of us to do it safely.'

As the icy pink bathwater swirled away, the two police officers made a soft bed of blankets on the bathroom floor. Harper placed a hand under the man's head as the four of them lifted him out, and was surprised at the sensation of sponginess, an area of skull that should have been smooth and hard but instead felt like wet cake in her palm.

CHAPTER FIVE

NOW
Ruby

Friday, 21 December

Now that she was Constance to the social worker, Ruby thought maybe Diane would make some comment about the name. When Ruby had first met Constance she'd done it herself. It was unusual. Old-fashioned.

Diane noted it down, then returned her cool eyes to Ruby's.

'And your daughter's name?'

'Didn't she tell you?' said Ruby. 'Only, she's not shy, usually. She'll talk to anyone, wander off with anyone. Doesn't see danger. That's how come I lost her. She's quick, too.'

Stay calm, she told herself. All she had to do was get Leonie and run, slip away so quickly that the police and social services had no chance to realise there was anything out of the ordinary happening.

'It didn't take the police long to get here, did it?' said Ruby, in what she hoped was an admiring tone rather than one of criticism. 'The patrol must have been parked up around the corner. Very . . . reassuring.'

Diane blinked. 'What's your daughter's name, please?'

'Oh, sorry! Leonie.' She spelled it. Diane wrote it down.

'Surname?'

'Hers or mine?'

'Both, please.'

There was a hesitation that Ruby wanted to kick herself for. Diane looked up sharply; she'd noticed it too. 'Douglas. We're both Douglas.' Douglas would have to do; she couldn't use her own name, Harper. It would be just her luck that one of the police officers would recognise it and wonder if there was any link to their colleague in Sheffield.

Diane pursed her lips as the pen moved. Then she glanced up.

'What about the father?'

Ruby closed her eyes and saw his face as she sometimes thought of him, that first meeting, the way he smiled shyly and looked away. She shook her head to clear it. Then she glared at Diane.

'Huh,' snapped Ruby. 'That's a bit personal, isn't it?'

The two women locked eyes. Ruby radiated confident outrage, though below the surface she was unsure the act was working. There was a delicate line to be drawn: don't beg, but don't go too far the other way and make this woman angry, or suspicious. After a moment, Ruby lowered her eyes. She dropped the confrontational tone. She said, 'I'm sorry. I've been going out of my mind with worry. I didn't mean to be rude, really. Can I see my daughter, please?'

Diane appeared to consider the question. Her eyes travelled over Ruby, interpreting, judging the outfit: expensive leather boots, the winter skirt, the trendy parka. Ruby knew she looked nice, but she also hoped she looked plausible – the sort of woman who might make a mistake, but never the sort that would make more than one. Never the sort that needed *intervention*. It was crucial, this first impression, these judgements made in seconds, of a person's trustworthiness, her social standing. Diane, from social services, had the power to take Leonie away just like that, if she felt she had justifiable reasons. Ruby prayed that the other woman would decide this wasn't one of those cases.

Diane smiled inscrutably and said, 'I'm sure you'll understand, Ms Douglas, that when a child is found abandoned, alone in a shop, in weather like this, and the police are called, we have to do a certain amount of investigating. It's a child protection issue. One can't be too cautious.' Diane tipped her head to the side, her face blandly apologetic as the weighty words found their target.

Ruby swallowed hard. *Think*. 'There's no need for all that,' she said. 'Just let me explain. She wasn't abandoned. I lost her. We were at the seafront, watching the waves. She's got this idea that it's fun to run off, she does it all the time, all the day long, it's exhausting. So I was buying chips, and I turned round to pay the lady, then when I looked back she'd run off, again! I panicked – she could have gone two different ways and I must have run the wrong way. I've been searching for her ever since I lost her, and it's only been – what? – ten, twenty minutes? I asked loads of people. I was about to call the police myself, and they got here so fast. I would *never* abandon her. There's no child protection issue here. You can tell that by looking at her – she's dressed for the weather, isn't she? She's not undernourished or anything, is she? I just want to see her. I want to say sorry to her. I want to . . .'

A sob broke off the stream of words. Diane offered a tissue. The social worker's expression seemed to have softened somewhat.

'It could have happened to anyone,' said Ruby. She blew her nose. 'I'm not a bad mum.'

Diane put her notepad back in her bag.

'Where do you live, love?'

'Sheffield.'

'So, what are you doing in Cleethorpes? It's a bit chilly for a seaside day trip, isn't it?'

Ruby took a breath before she replied. 'You have to get out, don't you? When you have kids. Can't keep them cooped up all day.'

Diane raised her eyebrows in weary recognition. *She's got kids of her own*, thought Ruby.

The social worker gave her a long look. Then she knocked on the window and someone from outside opened the car door.

'I'm just going to have a word with the police officers, Constance. Then we'll let you see your daughter. OK?'

Ruby tried to say *thanks* but emotion choked her voice and she couldn't get the word out in time. She knew she'd done something right, if they were going to let her see Leonie. *Careful, though,* she told herself. If anything seemed off when the two of them were reunited, that would be it. She might be imprisoned, for attempted child abduction, or providing false details. She might never see Leonie again.

A few minutes later and the door on Ruby's side of the car was opened by the policewoman. Ruby's legs shook as she stepped onto the pavement, pulling her jacket closed against the wind and sleet. A bit further along the road, the big black car also had its door open, and she could see Leonie being lifted out. Ruby wanted to rush over and grab her, take up the child and run, but she was aware of the police and the social worker watching them. She took a step closer and saw the toddler look up, recognise her, try to pull her hand away from Diane's.

'Mamma Bee!' shouted Leonie, struggling against the woman holding her.

Ruby couldn't bear it a moment longer. She ran forward and lifted Leonie up, hugged her tight.

'Mamma's here, baby,' she said, 'I'm so sorry.'

'Mamma,' said Leonie, 'Mamma here. Mamma gone.' Ruby hoped that only she could interpret what Leonie was trying to tell her: *Mamma was here, Mamma's gone.*

'I know, I'm so sorry, my love. I'm back now. I won't let you go again. Not ever.'

She covered Leonie in kisses, then pulled back a little to see the child's face. They smiled at each other. 'Bee,' said Leonie. Or at least, that's what the word *Ruby* sounded like, in Leonie's mouth.

Would they pick up on that? 'She loves insects. Don't you, baby?'

'Mamma Bee,' said Leonie, and giggled. That's what Constance had called Ruby, in front of the baby, almost from day one. *Here's Mamma Ruby, come to give you a cuddle.* As soon as Leonie could speak the words, Ruby was Mamma Bee.

The child still had smears on her face from whatever it was they'd fed her, some sugary crap. The stuff they made those decorations out of didn't even count as chocolate.

'You're all dirty, sweetie, we need to get you a wipe.' She licked a thumb and rubbed at the chubby cheeks. She looked around for a baby wipe to clean her, but couldn't see the changing bag.

The shopkeeper stepped forward. 'Is this yours?'

'Thank you,' said Ruby, taking the bag that Constance had packed that morning with Leonie's things – enough nappies for a day or two, a change of clothes, a couple of toys.

'It was on the pavement, outside the shop.' He frowned slightly, as if he couldn't work out why that might be a strange place for the bag to be.

'She took it when she ran,' said Ruby, a little too quickly. Ruby rummaged inside the bag for the wipes, but Leonie had seen what was coming and was wriggling in her arms to get away. 'No wipe!' she shouted, kicking her legs hard so that Ruby had to put her down. In a split second she'd slipped Ruby's grasp, was running full pelt towards the road. The policewoman said, 'Whoa,' and stepped smoothly into the child's path to catch her.

'I see what you mean about her being a runner,' said Diane, and one of the police officers chuckled.

'Looks like you've got yourself an escapee there, love,' said the female officer, handing the still-struggling Leonie back to Ruby. She abandoned the wipe.

'She's like this all the time. I'm hoping it's a phase.'

'What I'll do, love,' said Diane, 'is I'll send a report to the social worker that covers your area. There'll be a flag on your file, but that's only to help us keep an eye on things. It won't count against you.'

'You're not . . . taking her?'

'No, love. I don't think you need our help at the moment. This is just one of those things. Could have happened to anyone. Your little angel there clearly has a passion for sprinting. Have you thought about one of those backpacks with reins on?'

Ruby nodded. 'I've tried. I bought an expensive one in the shape of a ladybird, but she sits and screams the place down until I take it off her, or I let her hold the end of the reins herself, which kind of defeats the object.'

At the mention of screaming, the shopkeeper made a noise like he was about to say something. Ruby wondered what he'd seen. If Leonie had been crying . . . well. They needed to get going, fast.

'How about a buggy?' said Diane. 'You could strap her in?'

Ruby shook her head wearily. 'She's very keen on being independent.' Leonie was under her arm, still kicking. Ruby crouched down and tried to persuade her to stand on her feet, with little success.

A stern voice spoke then, and Leonie stopped struggling.

'I'm afraid you're going to have to toughen up if you're to keep that little lady safe, madam.' It was the male police officer. 'You need to take charge. Listening to her scream is a lot preferable to the alternative, in a situation like this.'

The child's eyes glazed over. She went limp.

'I know,' said Ruby, picking Leonie up and cuddling her, knowing it was the sound of the man's low voice that she couldn't bear. 'I'm sorry. I'll put her in the buggy from now on.'

'See that you do,' he said. 'Are you going to be safe on the train journey home to Sheffield? Do you have family members who can meet you from the station?'

Ruby felt Leonie's body stiffen as the man kept speaking, and the toddler began to let out an almost imperceptible whining sound.

'Is she OK?' asked Diane.

Ruby exhaled. 'She's just tired, I think.' Turning to the male officer, she said, 'I'll be safe. I won't let her out of my sight. I promise.'

'I could call ahead and have someone escort you home.'

'No, thanks. We'll be totally fine. Won't we, kiddo?' She looked at Diane. 'I've learned my lesson, OK?'

The officer took the social worker aside. When they returned, the man seemed satisfied. He nodded at his colleagues, indicating that they could leave now.

Diane smiled at Leonie, then at Ruby. 'I've got one myself, a bit older,' she said. 'You'd do anything for them, wouldn't you?'

'Yes,' said Ruby, gazing down at the small girl in her arms. 'You would.'

She turned and started to walk in the direction of the train station. Each step she took away from the police was a step into a new life, a new existence for them both. Her heels tapped out a mantra that echoed in the street, *we did it, we're free, we did it, we're free*. She picked up the pace, turned the corner, started to run. There was no going back now. Her only choice was to take Leonie and disappear completely.

CHAPTER SIX

'Farewell, peerie buddo!' said she to the child, and ran out. She rushed to the shore, flung on her skin, and plunged into the sea with a wild cry of joy. A male of the selkie folk there met and greeted her with every token of delight. And that was the last he ever saw of his bonnie wife.

G. F. BLACK, 'The Goodman of Wastness', 1903

ONE HOUR EARLIER
Constance

The water is a living thing. It heaves, the vast surface of it shifting beneath the power of the low-hanging moon, of which only a faint glow can be seen behind thick clouds. At the ocean's edge, a woman stands, her face towards the horizon. Her feet are bare, boots and socks at the bottom of the hastily dug hole in the beach behind her. Where her skin is exposed to it, the offshore wind numbs her. She likes it, the numb feeling. She wants it to envelop her, for it to chill her body entirely, so that she feels nothing at all. Turning back to the hole, she pulls off her parka and drops it in. Then she closes her eyes and takes a long, grateful breath of sea air. The cold salt wind of home.

Although she has stood here – or somewhere very like here – many times before, tonight the beach feels different. For the first time since she stepped ashore so many months ago, freedom is within touching distance. The sand between her toes, the push and pull of the tide; her heart is beating with excitement, with anticipation. She opens her mouth and sings one of the old songs: *Ionn da, ionn do, ionn da, od-ar da*. Her chest resonates with it, the notes blending with the sounds of the wind and the tide. Seals call back, almost as if they are replying. She hears the response, perhaps only in her head, but oh, the joy of it. A chorus of voices singing: *Hi-o dan dao, hi-o dan dao, hi-o dan dao, od-ar da*.

In the fading light, the woman takes a step towards the water, now a blanket of shining black, the waves ready to take her. She longs to submerge herself, to give herself to it, to swim out as far as she can; to sink down; to forget all that she has been and done, all that has been done to her.

Naked now, the woman hesitates: the child is behind her, the other side of the sea wall, by the shop where she left her. She waited as long as she could for Ruby, but her supposed friend didn't come. A flash of anger within: a sacred trust was broken. Ruby said she loved the child, that she loved them both but . . . perhaps she lied. Trust is always a gamble. She won't make that mistake again. She won't need to, after tonight, as it marks the end of all of that, all of this life, and everything attached to it.

She consoles herself that she didn't leave the child entirely alone – there were people inside the shop when she ran. They'll come out and find her; they have to. A small voice says, *but if they don't?* . . . The guilt is heavy on her now, getting heavier with every second. She takes a step away, towards the road. How can she leave, not even knowing if her baby will be safe?

A voice pushes her back in the direction of the water as surely as a hand on her back. *Constance,* it says, or seems to say. The second time she hears it, it sounds like the waves on the shingle. Was it real? Or was the voice an illusion, cast by the strength of her longing? She thought she could hear them, singing out to her, calling for her, but now she's convinced she can't. They're not here for her, it's been too long. They haven't come.

A wave wets her feet. She looks down: they gleam.

Salt tears drop, to join the seawater. She ought to go back to Leonie. Soon, the child will notice that her mother has gone. But if she goes back, she might as well be dead. Whatever the water holds, for however short a time, if she goes in now she'll be free once more.

As she stands there at the cusp of going in, of not going in, she wonders if the knowledge that she has left her will remain with the child forever, a scar running deep, a fear that it was the child's own fault, that the solid fact of her existence was not enough to make her mother stay. She feels the pull of her baby, anchoring her to this place, to this life. But then she hears it again, the song of the seals, and her heart is full. She can't stay. At least under the water, there is a chance she will return to what she was. A chance that she has to take. If it doesn't work, if all she meets is oblivion, even that is better than what she has now. She steps forward, into the water, diving under, letting it take her, deep down, far away.

CHAPTER SEVEN

NOW
Joanna

Friday, 21 December

After the two officers helped the paramedics to haul the man from the tub, together they dried him off as best they could, keeping him warm with the bedding until the stretcher was brought up. They covered Gregor's body in silver space blankets and transported him to the ground floor, where the emergency doctor started administering fluids.

Although still unconscious, the man didn't look quite as dead as he had in the bathroom, which Harper took as a good sign. 'Will he live?' she asked.

One of the paramedics paused to look at her. 'He's alive now. That's all I can tell you.'

The back doors of the ambulance slammed, and a moment later Joanna watched it drive away, slowly at first over the speed bumps, then accelerating, blue lights and sirens blaring the moment they hit the bypass.

Two more patrol cars arrived, with officers on board to help secure the scene. She ordered three of them to guard each of the entrances: one to monitor the lift, one the stairs, and one at the door of apartment 7. She herself stood at the main door to the block, waiting for her superior, Inspector Thrupp, to arrive.

Momentarily alone, Jo stared up at the West block, and thought of Ruby. Which of those tiny windows was hers? Ruby was top floor, like the victim, but the ones in the social housing block didn't get the label 'penthouse'. The seventh floor of the West block was divided into four apartments, each one a quarter of the size of the victim's. She knew this because the last time she'd been here, she'd nearly knocked. She'd got as far as the intercom, looked at the row of buttons, but bottled it at the last second, sent a text message instead. That was a month ago, and there'd been no contact since. That message didn't even really count as contact, since Ruby had never replied. It had been early October when they'd last spoken, shortly after Ruby's birthday when she'd phoned Jo from a payphone, claiming to have run out of credit on her mobile. Jo had known it was a lie: their mother still paid the bill for Ruby's phone. Jo had wanted to meet up then, but Ruby avoided making the arrangement, so that Ruby's birthday present, a silver ring set with her namesake stone, inscribed with a line of Latin, was still in Joanna's pocket.

Jo pulled out her phone and scrolled down to Ruby's icon, pressed to connect. Just like last time, and every time she'd tried for the past six weeks, there was nothing but the recorded message: *The number you have dialled is currently unavailable. Please try again later.* A frustrated sob bubbled up, hard in the base of her throat. She stifled it.

Movement in the corner of her eye made her glance up.

Beyond the patrol cars, youths had started to gather, hoods pulled up against the cold, scarves tucked in around faces, eyes glittering. There were around fifteen of them, she reckoned, dotted here and there in groups of two and three.

'I see the rubberneckers have turned up already,' said Atkinson, appearing behind her.

She pocketed the phone she was still holding. 'They're just interested,' said Joanna. 'Understandable. There hasn't been a big thing on the New Park for a while, has there?'

'Not since that cannabis farm we found at the top of the East block. Oh, and there was that pop-up brothel.'

'All that was before the refurbishment, though. It's a nice area now, Steve.' She arched an eyebrow.

'Well, sure. Shame no one told that lot.' He gestured towards the youngsters, who had mostly retreated to the darker places between the buildings, red pinpricks glowing where they sucked on their cigarettes. 'What's the status of this job, boss? Suspicious circumstances?'

'I'm waiting for that to be made official. New system. We don't get CSIs, or anything, not until it's been signed off by an inspector.'

'Isn't that going to cost the investigation, in terms of time lost?'

'Yes, of course it is. But it's a budget issue. Apparently we need to spread our murders out, or move one or two to the next financial year.'

Atkinson paused. 'Wrongful death? Did Franks not make it?'

'It's touch and go,' said Joanna. 'Let's see what the next few hours bring. If it's not murder then it might as well have been: someone's had a good try at killing the guy. We need to act as if it's murder, get all the details nailed. But we can't start properly until the DI's seen it.'

Jo kept glancing up at the West block, at the window she thought might have been Ruby's.

Atkinson cleared his throat. 'Are you thinking we need to go door to door in that block?'

She snapped her eyes away. 'Let's see what we've got, first,' she said. 'Might not be necessary to knock on everyone's door.'

A shadow of something, suspicion or confusion, crossed his features. Their eyes met briefly, before they turned as one to go back inside.

It was late when Detective Inspector Thrupp finally rolled into the estate in his large black BMW hatchback. He parked in front of the building and got out of the car, the lock giving an audible clunk as he made his way towards Harper in the entrance to the building.

Tall and striking in his shiny leather shoes and grey suit, Thrupp stared hard at the groups of youths lingering in the darkness between the apartment blocks.

'Nothing to see here, ladies and gentlemen,' he boomed. 'Off you go home, now.' The youths responded by retreating further into the shadows.

'All right, Joanna? What have you found? And on the night of the Christmas Party, too. The lads won't thank you for that, now, will they?'

'My missus won't thank me, either,' she said. 'I promised I'd be back at a normal time today.'

'Normal,' said Thrupp. 'Ha ha. She knows what you do for a living, right?'

Just then Joanna's mobile started ringing. She pulled it out, looked at it, then swiped to dismiss the call from Amy. They'd planned to go out to eat tonight, before the party. The 8 p.m. reservation had been hours ago. She really hoped Amy hadn't gone on her own and waited for her.

'You could have taken that,' said the DI. 'I wouldn't object to a quick call from home.'

Jo shook her head. 'That wasn't going to be a quick one. She's got plenty of things to say to me, I'm sure. I'll call her back later. This way, boss.'

CHAPTER EIGHT

Beneath the depths of the ocean, according to these stories,
an atmosphere exists adapted to the respiratory organs
of certain beings, resembling in form the human race,
possessed of surpassing beauty, of limited supernatural
powers, and liable to the incident of death. They dwell
in a wide territory of the globe, far below the region of
fishes, over which the sea, like the cloudy canopy of our
sky, loftily rolls.

GEORGE BRISBANE SCOTT DOUGLAS,
'The Fisherman and the Merman,' 1901

THEN
Ruby

August

Ruby was watching Yoga Man from the safety of the dark.
She was sitting on the draining board, her feet in the sink,
wrapped in a duvet. The routine was familiar; she'd been
watching him without fail, every day, for so long that the
sequences repeated in a pattern she could now predict. Today
was headstand day.

Being awake at 3.30 a.m. was standard for Ruby these

days, now that normal person's things like work hours and a social life were no longer relevant. She dwelled in a permanent half-light; whenever an errant sunbeam edged around the closed curtains and sought her out it felt as if it burned. The only time the curtains were open fully was at night, when she was watching Yoga Man. A guilty pleasure, perhaps even shameful, but in those silent hours, cocooned in the velvet dark and the warmth of the bedcover, she felt more alive than she had in a long time. His movements both soothed and ignited her. When he walked towards her at the end of the routine, to shut the blinds against the approaching dawn, she imagined he was looking at her, acknowledging her. He seemed to gaze straight into her eyes, though where she sat, behind glass, protected by the dark, he could never have seen her.

When it was over, Ruby would get down from her perch and go to bed, tying a scarf over her eyes to block out the light, sleeping until mid-afternoon. Just like Barbara, her boss, had said, after she'd driven Ruby home from work on the day she'd been signed off sick: yoga practice was meant to be good for your mental health. Barbara meant for her to take a class, but perhaps watching someone else do it was equally effective. It was certainly true that once she'd discovered Yoga Man, Ruby felt she was less depressed, and more productive. He was inspirational: when she wasn't watching him, or sleeping, she was working on her music.

Ruby had been spending more and more time playing, perfecting sections from Sibelius's Concerto in D Minor. The piece was fiendishly difficult, and while she played she felt she had a sense of purpose, a hope that she might conquer it, do it justice, as only the best players could. Only when the callouses on the tips of her fingers started to bleed onto the ebony of the fingerboard and her shoulders screamed from the tension of the playing position would she wrap the instrument in its ancient duster and place it safely away. Only then would the bad thoughts seep in, along with the loneliness. She tried to keep playing until it was time to watch Yoga Man, but sometimes it wasn't possible. Thank goodness, then, that in the past few weeks she'd felt a new awakening. She'd started to compose something herself; a piece that, when she was immersed in it, chased away the bad thoughts so completely that she was entirely made of music. It was as if, when she played, she was losing herself in becoming a conduit for Sibelius, or Mozart, or Grieg. But when she sat down to compose, the conduit was something else, not a person. A spirit perhaps, but not a completely nice one. It had personality, this muse of hers.

The melody she was writing had appeared, fully formed, as she watched Yoga Man one night, and she'd scribbled it down, convinced it was something she'd heard before. She hummed it quietly, and its haunting beauty made her think of the ocean at night. The theme began with a tritone – *the Devil's interval* – and in her head the first three notes were played slowly, almost tentatively, on a low flute echoed by a solo viola. Where had she heard it before? It turned out she hadn't. The tune felt so complete, so filmic, and filled with a kind of foreboding. As she went deeper into the composition, it felt less as if someone else had written it, more that it was writing itself. And since then, every time she returned to the manuscript, it seemed like the notes were coming from another place, through her rather than from her. Her fingers held the pen that rested on the paper, and from it the music surged; unexpected, sometimes chilling, and utterly exquisite.

Because of the music, she'd never started the antidepressants that the doctor had given her. More than once she'd picked them up in the packet, taken out the leaflet and read the list of possible side effects, then put them back down again. The doctor had told her the pills would rebalance the chemicals in her brain, but the idea of that was more frightening than the bad thoughts. The pills might dull her creativity, which she already considered to be tenuous, and fleeting. They might take away the desire to compose, and with it the first truly beautiful thing she'd created. It was too much to risk.

The tap dripped on her toe, bringing her back to the room. Across the way, Yoga Man was standing at the window, his hand on the pull for the blind. Ruby stared straight into his eyes, as she usually did. He appeared to be looking at her, and she enjoyed the sensation, the fantasy that he knew she was watching and he was performing it all for her. Then, he cupped his hand over his eyes to shade them, pressed his face to the window. His body language transformed, from relaxed to agitated. He *could* see her. He turned, dashed across to the wall where his light switches were. Suddenly the big window was plunged into darkness.

Ruby scrambled off the drainer, fell heavily on her side and lay there on the tiles, breathing hard. After a minute she crawled towards the bed-sitting room, avoiding the windows in case the man was still standing there in his darkened room, peering out, wondering who it was that was spying on him.

It was impossible to sleep. Instead, as the sun rose, she worked on her composition, adding a movement that became chaotically discordant, spiky and unpleasant. Reaching the final few bars, she decided that she hated every bit of it. She screwed up the new section and tossed it into the bin.

The following day, Ruby practised the Sibelius past the point at which her fingers hurt. She didn't eat all day, so that by the time night fell she was beyond hunger, enjoying the light feeling of nothing in her stomach, her mind a flighty thing, jumping between ideas without fully exploring any single one, forgetting what she'd been thinking about, not really caring either. At the usual time, in the darkness, she parted the curtains and peeked towards Yoga Man's window, hoping to see him there, in yoga pants and nothing else, just like normal. It was planks day today; she loved to see the straightness of his body, his taut backside the only interruption to the perfect line from head to shoulder to heel. Disappointment stung: the blinds were drawn. Her private show was over, all of her fun spoiled. The yoga would go on, but she wasn't privy to it, not any more. Ruby felt nothing but shame, and loss.

Back in the bed-sitting room she opened the manuscript she'd been working on, stared at the hundreds of neatly drawn runs of notes. The work had grown, covering both sides of fifty or more pages, but she suddenly couldn't remember why she'd even started it. The melody she'd been so entranced by, that she'd based the whole thing on, seemed trite, derivative. No one would want to hear this, let alone play it. Not even the Devil; especially not him. There was nothing mischievous or dark there, nothing clever or profound. It was all dull, repetitive, predictable. She got up, dropped the entire sheaf of papers into the recycling chute and climbed into bed. There, in a fit of recklessness, she shook four sleeping pills into her palm and crunched them between her teeth before lying down, closing her eyes and letting the drugs drag her consciousness away.

Waking in the afternoon, Ruby realised she had only half an hour to make her appointment at the GP's. She threw on some clothes and rushed out, hair and teeth unbrushed, bare feet shoved into old trainers. The doctor looked her up and down and briskly signed her off work for another six weeks. He peered at her over the top of his spectacles. 'How are you finding taking the antidepressants?'

Ruby said, 'Oh, fine. I feel much better, actually.'

'No side effects?'

'Nothing significant, no.'

She did not mention that she still had no plans to take even a single one.

The doctor gave her another prescription, which Ruby shoved in a pocket on her way out of the surgery. What would happen, she wondered, if she took all of the pills in one go? Would she die quickly, floating away in a blissful cloud of obliviousness? Or would her liver implode, causing untold pain and suffering? It would be interesting to find out, in a way. At least she would feel something other than shame, or loneliness.

On the tram, exhausted and listless, she stared out of the window, so that at first she didn't notice him: Yoga Man was sitting two rows in front of her. She looked once, then away, wondering, is that really him? She recognised the back of his head, the curve of his neck. Her heart began to pound.

She pressed the button for the tram to stop, got up and went past him, holding on to the rail near the door as the vehicle slowed. *Don't make it too obvious*, she told herself, and allowed herself only a short glance in his direction as she got off. He was staring right at her, a slight frown creasing his forehead. She panicked, then, hurrying out of the doors before they were fully opened, keeping her head down until the tram was out of sight.

Ruby trudged back to the flat in the rain. By the time she got there, she found that a plan had formed, seemingly of its own accord, a bit like the melody had done. There was a quiver of a thrill, that she was being guided by the muse again, but this time not just in music. She made no attempt to resist, or to think it through: she walked in the door and got straight into the shower, turned it up as hot as she could bear it and began to scrub. Soon she'd washed away two weeks of grime, shampooed her hair three times. She shaved her armpits and legs, exfoliated her entire body the way she always used to do. She towelled herself dry, applied lotion, used tweezers to shape her eyebrows. She put make-up on, grabbed a dress out of her wardrobe that she hadn't worn in months. There, she thought, admiring herself in the mirror. I'm unrecognisable. *You're all dressed up with nowhere to go*, said a mean voice inside her head. *I don't have anywhere to go yet*, she said to the voice. *But maybe I will soon.*

That night, she put on a pair of heels, stood in the dark and watched the shadows play on the blinds of his living room, imagining the scene within. It was comforting to know that he was still doing the yoga, even if she couldn't see it. That perfectly muscled body had to be maintained somehow.

Ruby went to bed and slept better than she had in weeks, without any sleeping pills, between clean sheets. The next day she dressed carefully, forced herself to eat a breakfast of scrambled eggs and set off to ride the tram.

There was no sign of him, so she rode all the way to the end of the line and back, getting off in the city centre to sit and watch the crowds for a while. She was gratified to see that several young men noticed her, though she didn't acknowledge their curious glances. Just yesterday, she'd been invisible, a hunched and grubby thing, moving through the press of people without drawing a single eye. Apart from his. He'd looked at her. He'd seen her.

At the market, she bought an apple and ate it while she stood at the tram stop waiting to get on, heading out of town again, only to come back in.

When he wasn't on the next tram either, Ruby couldn't hold back the disappointment. She stopped hoping, but kept riding. There was no reason to go home, really. *See?* Said the mean voice in her head. *I told you.*

The apple core was brown and spindly where she held it between thumb and forefinger, and she was about to admit defeat when suddenly, there he was. Shuffling on board with his head down, after a moment his eyes swept the passengers with a kind of nervousness and paused, she thought, just for a second, on her. Ruby watched him from the side of her vision, her face turned away. Taller than she'd thought, with longish, wavy hair, dressed in a rather ill-fitting suit, Yoga Man had been waiting at the stop nearest the banks. He didn't strike her as a banker, though: too alternative. A bead on a leather string peeped out from below his cuff, so that the impression was of a surfer who'd been to a job interview. As he passed her in the aisle, she looked straight at him, and their eyes met.

He paused. 'Do I know you?'

'I don't think so,' said Ruby, and smiled slightly, shrugging with her eyebrows before turning back to the window.

He didn't move. 'I'm so sure. You look really familiar. Do you ever go to the gym near the bypass?'

'No, not me.'

'Oh, OK.' He sounded disappointed in her answer.

'Wait,' she said, 'are you saying I need to join a gym? That's a bit rude.' Ruby straightened her dress and crossed her arms. She knew she wasn't fat – she was far too thin, if anything, though it was true that she rarely exercised. Maybe he thought she needed to tone up.

'Of course not.' He started to stutter, and a blush rose in his cheeks. 'I only meant that . . . I thought maybe I'd seen you around. My office is near the gym, that's all. I didn't mean . . .'

She watched him for a moment, astounded that anyone would be stumbling over their words because of something she'd said.

He went on, 'I don't even go there, myself. I hate gyms. It's just, I just . . .' For an unsettling moment, she thought he was going to cry.

She placed a hand on his forearm. 'It's OK, I wasn't offended. I was joking with you.'

The movement of the tram yanked his arm away, so that her hand hovered in the air for a beat and they both stared at it before she took it back. He said, 'I'm sorry, I don't usually, I mean I never . . . I'm just not good at talking to girls. I mean women.' He ran a hand through his hair, stared at his shoes, appeared to swallow. 'I'm so sorry, I meant people.' Then he swung his bag onto his shoulder and pressed the bell for the tram to stop. Ruby wanted to grab hold of him, to make him stay exactly where he was.

'Honestly, it was nothing,' she said.

'No, it was a dumb thing to say. But you're kind to say that. I'm really sorry.'

He was edging further away from her.

'Wait,' she said, 'I don't know your name.'

Confusion crossed his face, as if he couldn't work out why she would want to know his name. Then he met her gaze, and the blush rose to his cheeks once more. 'It's Gregor.' He raised his eyebrows in a question.

'Ruby.'

'Like the jewel,' he said, and then cringed as if he'd said something stupid.

The tram was slowing to a stop, people were filling the gap between them as they prepared to get off. Although she wanted to say something clever to make him stay, to make him talk to her some more, to reassure him that he hadn't offended her, all she could manage was,

'See ya.'

The rest of the journey home passed in a blur. She wondered why he'd got off the tram early, whether he'd done it just to get away from her because he was embarrassed, or if he had somewhere else to be. He'd seemed to recognise her, which was both worrying and thrilling. It was possible he knew her from the estate, or from seeing her around the city, in the days before her world shrank to the size of her flat. Perhaps, when she'd still been at work, they'd shared a commute; perhaps she wasn't as invisible as she thought she was.

At her apartment building she had so much nervous energy to burn that she ran up the stairs instead of taking the lift. She'd spoken to Yoga Man! He thought he knew her! He seemed nice! She checked her mailbox and found a letter from Sam, finally. Today was a good day indeed.

At 3 a.m., Ruby was still awake, but feeling almost ready to go to sleep. Her practice had gone really well, she'd mastered some of the more virtuosic sections of the concerto and remembered to stop before her arms started hurting. After that she'd written back to Sam, a slightly manic three-page ramble, that began: *Sam! I think I've met someone. I mean, maybe not met someone, but then maybe that is what I've done. I've made a new friend, anyway, probably? But I have a good feeling about him. You know how sometimes you just know? And I'm composing again, which is a big thing for me. You'll have to hear it when it's done. I think it might be good, and I've never thought that about anything I've written before . . .*

She'd posted the letter, then spent two hours beginning to recreate her composition from the scraps of what she remembered. Despite the difficulty of the task, she eventually concluded that it had been a good thing to throw it out and start again. She had feared that her tricksy muse had gone, that the spirit of Diabolus in Musica had grown bored waiting and left her, but as soon as she started to hum the main theme, it returned, along with her passion. The piece crackled with an urgency that it had lacked in its previous incarnation. In her head she could hear an orchestra playing it; she could even picture herself performing the solo, an image so clear that she could see the exact blue of the dress she would wear, the curve of the stage and the lighting. She could envisage the rapt faces of the audience members, shivers travelling through them and right back to Ruby, on stage. And the applause, washing over her, endless waves of it.

Time was sucked away, and soon the night was almost over. It was just before dawn as she took her make-up off, and Ruby was fizzing with possibility, with positive thoughts of change. She made a pact with herself to start going to bed earlier, to train herself back into normality before she returned to teaching in a few weeks' time. Perhaps she didn't need to stay away so long; she felt so much better. She would ring Barbara and ask to return to work. And she would stop trying to spy on Gregor (she rolled the new name around in her head, relishing the roundness of the vowels, the soft consonants) because that was not normal behaviour, was it? Even as she thought this, she went through to the kitchen and found herself looking over at Gregor's apartment building, hoping to see him there, softly lit by a side lamp, tackling a tricky inversion.

The big window was dark, though this time the blinds were open. She turned the lights off and stood, imagining herself on the other side of the drop, standing in his living room, looking over here. The fantasy was so vivid that she could actually see the outline of herself in his window. She pressed a palm to her own window and gazed at the image of her future self, so content to be inside Gregor's apartment, waiting perhaps to start the yoga routine that they would perform together, now. He would teach her; she would be a good student, and the lessons would calm her anxious mind.

Then, she froze, fear chilling her, running up her spine. She rubbed her eyes, and looked again. The outline she had just imagined had taken shape, become solid, a dark figure forming in front of her eyes as she stared: there really was someone there, standing in the shadowed room, looking out. Not Gregor; it was a woman.

Her panicked brain scrambled for an explanation. She kept darting her eyes away, and looking back, hoping not to see it. Was it a hallucination? Just when she'd started to feel on top of things? *Oh*, she thought, *perhaps it could be a reflection, somehow, of me, standing here*. But when she took her own hand down from the glass, the figure's hand remained, white against the surface of the window. And beyond the hand, looming from the darkness, a pale face like the moon, with dark eyes that stared into her own. The face came closer to the glass, almost pressing up against it, a ghostly vision. Ruby ducked down, trying to hide, even though it was too late, she'd been seen.

Whoever it was – whatever it was – turned and walked away, into the room.

For a while, Ruby stood gazing at the blank eye of the big window, heart pounding, wondering if she was dreaming. No, of course she wasn't, she could feel the cold kitchen floor beneath her feet, the rim of the stainless-steel sink under her fingers. She blinked and the woman was back, standing in the same place, but this time there was a bundle in her arms. It looked like a baby. Holding the child with one arm, the woman placed the other hand on the window, palm out, fingers splayed. With the baby she seemed less like a ghost, more like a human, though Ruby was still afraid; the way she stared, as if in accusation. The way her hands clutched the child, and her eyes, unblinking. Who was this woman to Gregor? His wife? Girlfriend?

Oh, Gregor. Ruby felt the disappointment bodily, the sensation of falling from a height, and gripped the edge of the sink to stop herself stumbling. At the same time she chastised herself: Why was she so upset by this? She hadn't lost anything, not really, because she hadn't had anything to start with, only a glimmer of hope. In a sick kind of a way she was glad to have seen the woman, wife, partner, whatever she was, because it meant that Ruby knew where she stood: back on firm ground, where good things only happened to other people, and all the best men were taken, or not interested. Not that Gregor would have been interested in her. How would she have explained the spying, for a start?

The woman in Gregor's darkened apartment continued to stare across the drop and into Ruby's eyes. After what seemed like a very long time, the woman reached across for the blind cord, and slowly rolled it down, keeping her eyes on Ruby until the very last second.

CHAPTER NINE

NOW
Joanna

Friday, 21 December
Midnight

'So, all the flats in this block are attached to the video-entry system,' said Thrupp.

'Yes,' said Joanna, thinking that it was a shame they didn't have such luxuries in Ruby's block. 'But this one also has a camera here.' She pointed out the CCTV lens embedded in the ceiling near the entrance to Gregor's flat. It was a covert-type camera, flush with the paintwork, but Jo had spotted it immediately. Thrupp paused to consider.

'And have you had a chance to view the footage from either?'

'The entrance system only records when it's activated by the buzzer. The monitor is inside by the door, but there doesn't seem to be anything recorded on this unit since last month. Either there haven't been any visitors, or someone has deleted it.'

'And this one?' he pointed at the tiny lens.

'We don't know where the monitor is for that one. It's probably a phone app.'

Jo took two pairs of blue crime-scene shoe coverings from the packet she kept in her kitbag. After she'd handed some to Thrupp, she led the way into the apartment, where their feet left damp impressions in the carpeting as they walked through to the large living space. Terry, the caretaker, had recently turned the power back on; Jo used a gloved hand to switch on the lights as they approached the open bathroom door.

The bath had a ring of dried blood near the rim, and streaks of red drew the eye to the plughole. On the bathroom floor there was the crumpled duvet, wet and soaked in blood at one end, a wreath of pink surrounding a red-black patch where the man's head had lain.

'The victim was in the tub when we broke the door down,' said Jo. 'It was full of water. He was floating, his head resting at that end.' She pointed to the edge of the bath nearest the wall where blood had pooled.

'Poor bastard. Unconscious and alone, in a bath full of water. Lucky he didn't drown.'

'I don't know how lucky he is, boss. The guy was not in good shape when the paramedics took him away.'

Thrupp turned to inspect the doorframe, where splinters stuck out at odd angles from where Atkinson had broken the lock. 'Could it be self-inflicted? Attempted suicide?'

'Not unless he smashed his own skull in, sir.'

He gave her a sideways scowl. 'Did you photograph the scene before you did anything to it?'

'Nope. We walked all over it, I'm afraid. Paramedics did, too. Have you had any updates from the hospital?'

'The victim is still unconscious, last I heard. That was about an hour ago.'

'Not a murder inquiry then,' said Joanna.

'Not yet.' He looked her in the eye. 'What are you hoping for, resources-wise?'

'We'll need full forensics, a team of investigators, the works.'

'With the room locked from the inside? You don't think it was an accident? He could have fallen over, bashed his head. Maybe he'd stood up to get something from the cupboard.'

Her gut screamed that it wasn't an accident, but her training forced her to consider every option. She cast her professional eye over the scene, searching out possibilities that she might have missed. There was a small mirrored unit on the wall next to the bath. Possible to reach from the bath, but it would have been a stretch, and yes, it was likely that if you tried that, you might slip. One of the doors on the cupboard was open slightly. She could see how it might happen. Yet, that scenario could easily be ruled out: if the man was reaching for the cupboard, he would have fallen out of the bath on to the floor, not backwards into the water.

Joanna considered the velocity of a simple slip-and-fall scenario, if it were the case that he had fallen in the right direction. 'I don't see how a person could injure themselves that badly by falling over in the bath. The water would have broken the fall to some extent.'

Thrupp stepped forward to inspect the rim of the bath. 'I thought the tap was running,' he said. 'That's why the leak happened, and the neighbour was alerted, correct?'

'Yes.'

'So, might have been a dry bath at the time, or only enough water in it to make him lose his footing. Therefore it would have been a harder fall.'

'Do you get in the bath before it's full?' she said. 'I don't. Something hit the guy hard enough to damage the skull, break the skin and cause him to lose consciousness. I'm not sure a fall would do it.' She shuddered at the memory of the place where her hand had supported his head, the cold-porridge feeling of mashed tissue.

On the bathroom tiles, Joanna spotted something that stuck out slightly. Almost the same white as the vinyl, a small triangular piece of something, like a chip from a smashed mug handle.

'What about this?'

Thrupp bent over and squinted at the object. 'I can't tell what that is. A bit of tile that's come off somewhere? Doesn't give us much.'

'Well, that's the point. We can find out, sir, if we have the forensic team. I'm convinced there was someone else here.'

'Based on what? I can't just take your word, Jo. You need something to back it up. Say there was someone else here. How did they get out?'

Above the bath there was a high window. Seven floors up, there was no way an assailant could have used it as an escape route. They turned their attention to the door.

Harper crouched down so that the lock on the door was at eye level. 'This isn't secure. Could have been turned from the outside with a screwdriver. Easy.'

Thrupp said, 'It's still not enough. I need a suspect. Or at the very least, a weapon. This case is borderline, right now.

I could put you and Atkinson on it and be done. Tell me why you need a CSI team.'

Jo darted her eyes around the room once more. With her head close to the bath, she spotted a tiny clump of brown hair clinging to the metal rim of the plughole. It was still attached to a fragment of skin. Nothing about the smooth surface of the bath rim indicated that it could have caused skin to detach; no flaws or sharp edges.

'Here, sir,' she said.

Thrupp came closer. He took out his phone and photographed the fragment. Then he straightened up, nodded to Harper and said, 'You can have everything you need.'

She cleared her throat. 'Thank you, sir.'

After Thrupp had gone, Joanna radioed for Atkinson to come up. More officers were arriving every minute. Soon the place would be crawling with forensic officers, and she wanted to take one last look around before that happened.

When Atkinson appeared in the doorway, Jo noticed that he'd gone slightly green. He kept glancing at his hands, still stained with Gregor Franks' blood.

'You OK?'

'Me? Yep. Sure. Fine.'

Jo knew he wasn't fine. 'There's extra psychological supervision available for this kind of situation, Steve. You want me to arrange that for you?'

'It's not that.'

She looked him in the eye. 'Oh?'

'Well, it is that, sort of. No one likes being covered in someone else's blood, do they?'

'Do you need to take a break?'

He swallowed, stood up straight. 'No. I want to get on with it.'

She gave him a long look, and decided to take him at his word. There wasn't time to do anything else. 'OK. Gather a team to search for a weapon – heavy object, something with sharp corners, I think, though we can have the details narrowed down by Forensics once they've seen the wound.'

Atkinson stepped away to convey the instruction to the other officers on scene. As he adjusted the radio, a streak of red on his hand caused Jo to inspect her own hands. Picking at the dried blood under her nails, she felt nothing much except for a trace of sympathy for her buddy, for the fact that Atkinson had been rattled by what they'd found. All police officers were human. Some, like herself, simply found it easier to detach themselves from the grittier parts of the job. Jo saw this aspect of her personality as a strength, though very occasionally she wondered if other people had something she was missing, something overtly emotional.

Back in the living room, Joanna scanned the floor, and although there were no objects that looked like weapons, there by the skirting was a discarded teaspoon she hadn't noticed before. Atkinson came in and she nodded towards it.

'Shall I bag it, boss?'

'No, wait for the CSIs, they'll need a clean run. Also, you'll need to report your movements, and your account of my movements from when we both entered the flat, for the record.'

'When do you need that report?'

'As soon as possible. Tonight, if you can. What else do you see, Steve?'

He looked around.

'A sofa. A plate. Um. A TV remote?'

'Anything unusual?'

'That box of toys is kind of unusual. The caretaker didn't know there was a kid living here. That doesn't make sense, does it?'

'I don't know. It's a private residence. There's no reason he would know, if he hadn't been told.' She stared through the kitchen door at the fridge, where the child's drawings were held in place by lozenge-shaped magnets. 'OK. Here's a different question. What don't you see?'

'Do you mean, like, what's missing? Well, not much. The TV is still there. There's a posh wireless sound system. If it was a burglary then they didn't take anything obvious. I can't imagine what else might be missing, unless you mean his personal items, wallet, phone?'

'Nope. They're in the kitchen, look. And his car keys. His phone was plugged into a charger, it only ran out because the electricity got turned off. That phone is the latest model. They're like, a thousand pounds.'

'OK,' said Atkinson, 'we can be sure there was no burglar here then, or all of that would have gone. But I don't know. How can we possibly tell what's missing, if we don't know what was here before?'

Joanna narrowed her eyes at her colleague. She gave him another few seconds before she said what was obvious, surely, to anyone, 'There are no photos.'

Atkinson's eyebrows went up. He swept the walls with his eyes. No photos, and no places on the wall where photos might have been. Even in today's digital age people still had family images on the walls. And here in this smart apartment, where a small child had been living – surely the most photographed species of being in the world – there was nothing. No portraits at all.

'Maybe he'll have photos on his phone?'

Harper thought about it. 'Sure, that's possible. But it's still a bit odd, don't you think?'

In her line of work Joanna visited a lot of houses, and where there were babies, there were always baby pictures. Her mother had pictures of her kids everywhere. Grainy baby photos of Joanna, and studio shots of Ruby as a small child. Pride of place above the TV there was a large portrait of the two of them, Joanna in her police cadet uniform and Ruby in her new school uniform, aged eighteen and four respectively, both grinning and standing to attention in front of the fireplace. Here, there were pictures, but none of them had any people in them. Moving around the apartment she realised that every image hung on the wall was a seascape. A photograph of a sweeping beach, a print featuring seabirds, a distant horizon. In the bedroom there were more, paintings of stormy seas, calm seas, sunsets over the ocean. But there was nothing displayed of the people who lived here, nothing to show who they were except the scraps of things they'd left behind. She stood in the bedroom where it looked as if a child had been sleeping. No bed toys, no baby blanket; those things would be with the child, wherever they were now. And whoever had the child would be the one who knew what had happened to Gregor. That was who they needed to find, and quickly.

CHAPTER TEN

THEN
Ruby

September

The apartment seemed too small and dark to stay inside for yet another day, with nothing to do. There were things she *ought* to do: tidying, cleaning, playing her violin, but none of them appealed to her at that moment. The flat was a state, kitchen filthy with grime, but that was usual. What was different was that she hadn't taken her instrument out of its case for many days. It just didn't seem important. Why was she perfecting the Sibelius when she would never perform it? Only a week ago, she'd written to Sam to tell him that things were looking up, that she was composing again, and that she might have met a new friend, finally, though it was early days. She certainly felt stupid for saying that last part. She'd only met someone on a tram and spoken to them for five minutes. Ridiculous to think of Gregor as a 'friend,' she could see that now. Unfortunately she'd posted the letter a few hours before she'd looked across at the window and seen the woman and baby, which had blown the idea of Gregor away like the fantasy it had been all along.

Sam was an *actual* friend, and had been there when she needed him. The only person who had, in fact. If he had a flaw, it would be that he didn't own a mobile phone, but she'd got used to writing letters, even though the fact that he moved around the country meant that he sometimes didn't reply for weeks or months. When she'd had to leave her family home the Christmas before, his narrowboat was the first place she thought of to go, and he'd welcomed her, let her stay until the council found her the flat. There had been five weeks of blissful boat life, no contact with her family, the longest she'd ever gone without speaking to Jo or Marianne. Then, when the flat was secured, she'd decided to get in touch with Joanna.

Shivering in the February cold in the smoker's shelter outside the folk bar, Ruby had hesitated, then pressed Joanna's icon on her phone.

One ring, two. She'd nearly hung up, but then, there she was.

'Ruby?'

For a short while Ruby couldn't speak. Emotion crowded her throat.

'Ruby? Are you there? Is it you? Say something.'

Jo didn't sound angry. If she'd sounded angry then Ruby would have hung up immediately.

'Are you OK? Please, Ruby, just say anything. Tell me you're OK.'

'I'm OK,' said Ruby, her voice thick.

'Thank God,' said Jo. 'We were so worried. Have you spoken to Mum?'

'Don't call her that.'

'Believe me, there's plenty I could call her. I can't believe she said what she said. I didn't speak to her myself for a week.'

'But you're speaking to her now?' Ruby felt betrayed by this. Jo had been there for the fight. She knew how hurtful those words had been.

'I had to. I couldn't let Dad cope with it all on his own. And I would never try to defend what she did but . . .'

'You're about to defend her, aren't you?'

'What do you want me to do, say she's a total bitch? An alcoholic? A failure? We've both had times we've thought those things. And what she said hurt me, too – it was spiteful, and stupid. But she didn't mean it. She's ill, Ruby, and what she said was part of that. It wasn't her speaking, not really. We have to make exceptions sometimes. At the end of the day, she's our mum. She brought you up. She loved you, just the same as she loved me. More, if anything.'

Ruby snorted in disbelief. Marianne did not love Ruby anywhere near as much as she loved Joanna. If it had been Ruby with an unwanted teenage pregnancy, would Marianne have taken the child in and raised it as her own? Of course not. By the time Ruby was thirteen, the same age that Joanna had had her, Marianne wouldn't have been able to hide her little problem for long enough to pass the stringent requirements of the adoption process, the way she had the first time. She would have reeked of booze at the assessment interview.

'Drink makes you more truthful, I've heard.'

'No, it doesn't do that,' said Joanna. 'It makes you self-destruct.'

Ruby felt a pang of sympathy for Marianne, and squashed

it. 'I don't want to get into this, not now. I only called to tell you that I've been fine, I've been staying with a friend. But I won't need to anymore, because I've just been given a council flat.'

'You're not coming home?'

'Coming home? Where do you mean, Marianne's? It's not as if it's your home, not anymore. You moved out years ago.'

She'd told Sam about the fact that Joanna was her biological mother, but in general, Ruby didn't bother to explain to people. She couldn't bear that look in their eyes; the pity, the fascination. Because it was a strange situation, no matter how much their mother tried to normalise it in those early years.

'I always wanted two,' Marianne had said to Ruby, more than once. 'Yes, it was hard when Joanna got into trouble, but to me you were a gift. You were a gift to all of us. Jo finally got the little sister she always wanted.' As she grew up, Ruby thought, *is that really true, that she wanted a sister?* It started to feel like a story they were using to dress up the fact that Jo conveniently got rid of the child she never wanted. Worse than a story: a lie. Marianne wanted another baby, that she believed, but it wasn't Ruby she'd wanted. Ruby was always going to be a poor replacement for the baby Marianne had tried and failed to conceive herself.

Joanna herself was strangely silent on the subject. Since the older of the two left home to train with the police service when Ruby was barely five years old, there had always been a distance between them. To outsiders, school friends and so on, they were sisters, but in the house, it was hard to say it out loud. It was only really Marianne who kept on with the 'sister' thing. When Jo visited, Marianne would say, 'Your sister's home.' Ruby would raise an eyebrow, and Jo would look away. It always felt like they were pretending.

As she'd got older, in describing Jo to other people, the word *sister* seemed completely wrong, but *mother* wasn't right either, not at all. Most of the time, it was easier not to talk about it. And then there was the fight, when Marianne's true feelings were well and truly aired. And that was that, as far as Ruby was concerned. A full stop, but a good one. An end to all of the bullshit.

'So no, Jo. I'm not going *home*. Not after what she said.'

There was a short silence. 'I think that's . . . fine,' said Jo. 'It's wonderful news, actually. You're old enough now to get your own place.'

'That's right. I'm twenty-six. Hardly a babe in arms.'

'Sure. I guess I always think of you as a baby.'

'Well, you would, wouldn't you?'

Joanna made a small choking sound.

'So anyway, you don't need to worry about me being homeless or whatever. You can tell Marianne that. And tell her not to keep on calling me. I'll be in touch, but not until I'm ready.'

'Speak to her for goodness' sake, she's in bits.'

Ruby held the phone away from her ear, ready to end the call. Her mouth hung open slightly. *She's* in bits, she wanted to yell. What about *me*? Jo ought to have been on Ruby's side. Just this once. But no one was on Ruby's side, were they? They were all too busy looking out for themselves, had been from the very beginning. From before she was even born.

The tears were coming quickly now. 'I was OK until I started talking to you. I've got to go. I'll ring again. But not for a while. Sorry.'

She'd ended the call and took the battery out of the phone.

Since moving into the estate, Ruby had answered calls from Joanna maybe one time out of every three. From Marianne, never. The phone had become a thing for playing music on, and not much more.

There was a bench she liked the look of, next to the gardens. The late summer weather was starting to turn, so she pulled on a sweater, took a cup of tea in a travel mug. The buildings rose up in front and behind but the square itself was a little suntrap. She plugged in her earbuds and let the music take her away, felt the beams of light on her face as if they were healing her, and closed her eyes, so that she didn't see Gregor coming out of the North block and walking towards her until he was almost at her side.

'Hello again.' He held up a hand in greeting.

Ruby smiled, took one earbud out. 'Hi.' He was better looking than she remembered, but just as awkward, with a blush already rising to his cheeks.

Gregor stopped a metre from the bench, hovering as if he was unsure whether to sit. 'What are you listening to? I mean, if you don't mind me asking.'

'*Rusalka*,' she said, and waited for his eyes to glaze over, the way most people's did.

'The opera?'

'Yes, do you know it?'

'Of course. I love Dvořák. Though I get a bit sick of Number nine.'

She sat up straighter. Number nine. Most people would call it the *New World Symphony*. No wonder he was awkward: he was as nerdy as she was. Gregor sat on the bench, at the

66

furthest possible distance away. She shifted to the other edge of the bench, maximising the gap between them. She took the other earbud out. The music was distracting her.

'"Song to the Moon",' he said, indicating the tinny stream of music coming from her earbud. 'Beautiful. Though it doesn't end well, if I remember rightly. For either of them.'

In her pocket, Ruby's phone was digging into her leg. She pulled it out, clicked to stop the music. 'These things never do.'

'Never trust a fairy-tale prince, I suppose.'

'Ha,' said Ruby, looking at him sideways, at the way his hair shone gold in the sun. 'There's a rule to live by.'

There was a silence, that got more strained as it went on. Gregor cleared his throat.

'When I saw you on the tram . . .' he trailed off.

Ruby took a sip of tea from her mug. 'Yes?'

'It's just that . . . I think I know where I recognise you from, now.'

Ruby felt her own cheeks begin to burn. She stared at the ground, waiting, wondering if she could simply get up and walk away without saying another word.

'You live in the West block, don't you?' He pointed up to where their windows faced one another. 'Seventh floor, right? Your window is opposite mine.'

Ruby's grip failed her and she dropped her travel mug so that it hit the ground and rolled, some of the tea splashing on his shoes. 'Oh!'

Gregor leaned down to pick up the bamboo cup. He held it out to her.

'Look, I know what you're going to say. You saw me looking at you, didn't you?' She had to get away. Her voice trembled with the tears she was holding back. What must he think of her? 'Well, I'm sorry. I don't know what else to say. It was pathetic. I'm pathetic.'

'Hang on,' said Gregor, a look of confusion crossing his face. 'I don't mind. That's not what I meant. Oh God . . .' his hands flapped, as if he didn't know what to do, how to say what he'd come to say.

'So, what do you mean, you *didn't* see me watching?' The possibility that she'd admitted to something excruciating when she hadn't needed to was somehow worse, in that moment, than the thing itself. Ruby felt a wave of nausea.

'Oh, yeah, I did see you. But . . .'

Panic set in. 'I have to go.'

'Don't.'

Ruby looked down. He'd grabbed her hand.

'It's my fault,' he said. 'I was going to apologise to you. I should draw the blinds. It never occurred to me. I guess I didn't expect anyone to be up at that time in the morning, and your place has the only window that overlooks mine. It's always been empty, so I didn't realise . . .'

She couldn't stop staring at his hand on hers. Anything to avoid looking at his face. He followed her eyes and let go of her then, as if he didn't realise he'd grabbed her in the first place.

'They said when I moved in it had been empty. Some kind of council computer mistake. I haven't been there all that long.'

'When did you move in?' he asked.

She sat down on the edge of the bench. 'A few months ago. But I was working full-time up until recently, so you won't have seen me around during the day.'

His face had a shadow of stubble, not the designer kind, more of the slightly unkempt kind, as if he probably shaved, as a rule, but hadn't for a day or so. Then there was his scent. Soap and citrus, and something almost animal under it all. It reminded her of how her rosin smelled when she applied it to the horsehair of her bow.

'I should be more discreet. I would never have left the blinds up . . . if I knew you were . . .'

Their eyes met and the tension broke. Both of them burst out laughing.

'I shouldn't be awake anyway,' Ruby said. 'But I've been having trouble sleeping, as it goes.'

He studied her face, suddenly serious. 'That's a terrible thing, you know. Not sleeping can really screw with your mental health.'

Don't I know it, she thought. 'Why are *you* awake at that time, then?' she said. 'It was always the early hours of the morning when I saw you.'

He sighed. 'Boring reasons. I go to bed early. I like to do yoga just before the dawn. Not to sound too much like a hippy, but it's . . . magical. The whole world is asleep, even the birds, and there I am, totally at one with body, mind and nature. Oh. I do sound like a total hippy, don't I?'

She laughed a little, then waited. One of them would have to mention it, sooner or later.

'What?' said Gregor.

'Oh, nothing really. I thought you were going to say that the baby woke you up. Your wife must be tired, too . . .'

As she spoke, Gregor's demeanour changed.

'My what?'

'Your . . . wife? Partner? She must have trouble sleeping, too. Because of the baby.'

'You saw Constance?'

'Is that her name? What a lovely name.' What a lovely concept. There were no constants in Ruby's life.

Gregor mumbled what he said next, but Ruby heard every word. 'She's not my wife. We're not a couple.'

'Look, it's really none of my business.'

'No,' he said, 'it's fine. I can see why you would think that. But she's not, we're not . . . I mean, we were. But.'

'What?'

'You know what, it doesn't matter. It's boring, anyway.' He sat there, slumped over slightly. Then, he straightened up and stood, turned towards her with a sad look on his face.

Ruby looked up at him. 'Tell me,' she said, 'I want to know.'

'No, you know what? I only just met you. It wouldn't be fair. Seriously, you don't want to know all the tedious ins and outs.'

'But how can you decide that? You don't know anything about me either, yet.' Yet? What made her say that?

'I know that I like you.' He cringed. 'I mean, in a friendly way. Not like . . . I mean, not that I *wouldn't* . . . oh, shit.'

His cheeks coloured instantly, redder than ever. Ruby looked away, embarrassed for them both.

'I better get back,' said Gregor. 'It was lovely meeting you, Ruby. I hope we'll bump into each other again one day.'

He took a step backwards. He was going to walk away, and she might not see him again. Having wanted to run away herself, Ruby felt suddenly desperate for him to stay. She said, 'Gregor, tell me. I can decide myself if it's boring, right?'

He seemed to think about it. Then he sat down.

'Can I trust you?'

'No, of course not. You only just met me.'

They both laughed.

Gregor said, 'I think I'm a good judge of character. You don't look like a gossip to me.'

'You're right. I am confidentiality personified.'

She mimed zipping her mouth shut.

He let out a long sigh. 'Constance is agoraphobic. We were together, but now we're not. She still lives with me. That's the short version.'

Ruby didn't realise she was holding her breath until she started to speak. 'And the baby?'

He smiled at the mention of the child.

'The baby – she's nearly two now, so not really a baby – was conceived the night we met. It wasn't supposed to happen, I never planned . . . it isn't like me at all. I don't usually do things like that.'

Gregor stole a glance at Ruby. His face was full of regret, embarrassment, hope for understanding.

'These things happen to the best of us,' she said. 'I know that more than most, actually.' He cast a questioning glance at her, but didn't pursue it. She was thinking of her own ignoble origins, but then Ruby's mind flitted briefly to her own indiscretions, which amounted to a string of meaningless encounters during one particularly depressing summer. She tried not to feel bad about it, but the shame sat there, deeply rooted and taking up the space where intimacy should have been. 'Where did you two meet?'

'A beach party, as it happens.'

'Sounds wild.'

'It was fun. And I really liked her. But after she got pregnant so quickly . . . we didn't really know each other, you know? I just couldn't stay in a relationship where we were so different.'

'So, you ended it?'

'Yeah. But I feel bad every day, that I couldn't make it work. The baby. And everything. I have to take the blame, as it was completely my decision to split, but . . . I wish I could love her the way she still loves me.'

'You can't force these things.'

What must it be like for both of them, living together and yet not living together? One of them still holding a candle, and then the baby complicating things. And the agoraphobia must have intensified everything. No wonder he looked so tired. The nocturnal yoga made sense now, too – it was probably the only time the apartment was quiet.

Gregor's eyes took on a faraway look. He stood up. 'I really should get back, now. I only popped out for some milk. Constance gets worried if I take too long.'

Ruby stood up too, and the two of them walked a few steps together. 'Is it that bad for her?'

'It's variable. Sometimes she's fine, seems to be coping OK. Other days, like today, not so much. Thanks for listening, Ruby. Maybe I'll see you around.'

And he was gone, jogging in the direction of the shop before she could say another word.

CHAPTER ELEVEN

He wooed her so earnestly and lovingly, that she put on some woman's clothing which he brought her from his cottage, followed him home, and became his wife.

PATRICK KENNEDY, 'The Silkie Wife', 1891

TWO YEARS AND SIX MONTHS EARLIER
Constance

The Summer Solstice

She sees the rocks from offshore and feels a thrill run through her. The solstice is the night of possibilities, the night things can happen. The sand of the beach is a pale strip against the moving water, the darker cliffs beyond. She cuts through the water smoothly, looping under and around her brother, making him laugh because he didn't see her coming. Others are already on the beach, already lighting the fire. Soon the drums will start, and after that her favourite part, the dancing.

It's her special night tonight, she's been given the blessing from the elders. Normally they don't mix with anyone who isn't from the island but tonight, if she sees an Outsider and she likes the look of him, she can choose him, go with him, give herself to him. Just for one night. It's an ancient rite, practised for centuries, a way of preserving the ways of their people at the same time as strengthening the bloodline. It can only happen now, on this night, because tomorrow is her wedding day. Those babies born nine months from the ceremony are all the more special for it, though it can be hard for the menfolk to accept that this is the way it has to be. Her betrothed hasn't looked in her direction all day. He can't wait for tomorrow, for the ceremony that will tie them together until their deaths. They both know that very occasionally, maybe once in a generation, the girls don't come back. They choose to stay with the Outsider. Constance wants to comfort him, tell him she is his, that she would never leave him. Whatever happens tonight will soon be past, never to be spoken of between the two of them. She can tell he is hurt, but he, like her, must wait until tomorrow. It is the way of their people, and there's nothing either of them can do about it.

They emerge from the sea, slick with seawater. She steps onto the sand with feet that feel newborn, with legs that are unsteady at first after swimming so far. But as she gets closer to the fire she hears the rhythm, the drumming; the beat enters her body so that she starts to move, to dance, to lose herself in this one final night of freedom. She mustn't think of tomorrow, of the boy who sits in the shadows, his heart bruised. Tomorrow is the beginning of a long life together; they have time to mend, to journey, and to bear the children who will carry on the traditions.

When the man comes into the circle of light, their eyes meet and she knows he is the Outsider she's been waiting for. She pushes thoughts of her beloved away so that when he takes her by the hand, she goes willingly.

CHAPTER TWELVE

NOW
Joanna

Saturday, 22 December
Early morning

'Can I call you Sarah?'

The old woman stiffened slightly. 'Well. If you have to.'

Mrs Sarah Stefanidis was sitting in her living room in a high-backed floral armchair, her white stick leaning within reach. On her knees was a tray, where Joanna now placed a mug of tea.

'Careful, it's hot.'

'I hope so too,' said Mrs Stefanidis. 'Nothing worse than a tepid cup of tea.' She slid her hands towards the drink, fingertips fluttering on the surface of the tray. 'There are a lot of you, out there. Up and down the stairs, talking on your radios. Must be serious.'

'The man in the flat upstairs, Mr Franks. We found him unconscious in his bath, taps still running. That's why it leaked through the ceiling. We're treating it as suspicious.'

'You think he was attacked?'

'Yes. I'm sorry. It must be a shock, to hear that something like this has happened in your building.'

'I knew there was something wrong. It was a little worrying, of course, with the water coming down onto the table. But I phoned Terry, and he came straight away, bless him. I thought it was maybe a burst pipe; it's been so cold lately. But after a while . . . I could smell it, just faintly. The blood.' She wrinkled her nose, as if she could still smell it now. Perhaps she could – enough of it had soaked into the kitchen ceiling to cause the plaster to bulge low and stain it rust-red.

'I'm sorry you had to experience that.'

'So, his attacker . . . are they still at large?'

'We're currently trying to identify suspects.'

Mrs Stefanidis rubbed her elbows as if she were chilly. 'You don't think they'll come back? This building isn't secure, not really. People just buzz anyone in, or come in behind you when you open the door. They say they've business here, but who's to know? I don't have anything worth taking, but they don't know that, do they?'

'We don't think it was a burglary. No valuables were taken, or at least, it's not obvious that anything has gone. His wallet was still there, full of cash.'

'Really? So, why? I mean, if they didn't want to rob him? Why would anyone, otherwise?'

'That's what we need to establish.'

'He used to come around, when we first moved in,' said Mrs Stefanidis. 'That was when his mother was still alive, of course.'

'His mother? She lived with him, here?' Jo noted it down.

'Yes, she did. She was a lovely woman, Eva. Only a few

weeks after they came, she disappeared. I haven't thought of her for months. Sweet lady.'

'Disappeared? Was it reported to police?'

'I don't mean disappeared like that. Only, that's what it seemed like to me. She would pop by every other day or so, have a natter, cup of tea. I thought we'd be friends for life. Last time I saw her she said, *See you tomorrow*, but she never came. After a week, I went up and knocked. He answered. *She's dead*, he said. Heart attack. I remember the words, because he sounded so different to how he normally sounded.'

'Different how?'

'I'm not sure. Like he'd been crying, or he had a cold. Also it turned out I'd missed the funeral. Can't complain too much, I hadn't known her long, but it smarted, you know? I didn't really see him at all after that, which was odd, as if he'd forgotten we were once friendly. Grief can do that to a person.'

'So when was the last time you had a conversation with Mr Franks?'

'Probably nearly three years ago, the time when he told me she was dead. Proper mummy's boy, I suppose, must have hit him hard. Can't blame him really. And now this. Such a lot of blood. Not dead, though, that's good news. Quite a relief that he's still with us. Do you think he'll recover quickly?'

'I'm afraid we won't know that until doctors have finished assessing him. We need to find the assailant as soon as we can. And for that we need your help.'

'Well, I don't know how much I'll be able to tell you. Like I say, I don't see him. And I'm almost completely blind, you know. Faces are a particular problem for me.' She frowned.

Throughout the conversation Mrs Stefanidis faced Joanna, the old woman's eyes pointed broadly in the officer's direction but Jo could tell it was only an affectation, perhaps out of habit or courtesy. When Jo moved, the eyes didn't follow. When she spoke they swivelled to approximately the right area. 'Anything you can tell us about the past few days?' said Jo. 'Even if you don't think it's useful. Perhaps you heard something?'

'Just the usual din from her at 6D. When was the attack?'

'This morning, we think. Well, yesterday now, of course. We can't be completely accurate about the time yet. If you don't mind me asking, how is your hearing, on the whole?'

'I'm not deaf, Detective. I wish I were, sometimes. When I open the window I can hear nothing but children shouting from the playground. Everything on the stairs comes through to me, too, stamping and yelling and hollering. Gregor is rather an exception. A very quiet man; I never hear a peep from him, which is more than I can say for the rabble across the hallway, with her screaming back and forth at the kids at all hours. Nothing to complain about with Mr Franks. I suppose it's because he's on his own.'

Joanna thought of the herd of tiny elephants living above her own place.

'Just to be clear. You've never been aware of a child in the penthouse flat, at any point?'

'No. I've not been aware of that.'

'No partner, girlfriends? What about visitors, family members, that kind of thing?'

A silence. 'Well. Now that you mention it. There was something, but it was probably nothing.'

'Please.'

'Last week, I heard a child in the hallway on the floor above. I was going down in the lift to get the post from the lobby. I assumed it was one of the kids from this floor, gone up there to play. The mother at number 6D just seems to open the door and push them out every morning, lets them run around unsupervised on the stairs. Little children, too. They've fallen, in the past, and the ambulance has had to come. Mind you, they fight like rats in a cage, probably pushed each other down.'

'But you remember this incident particularly,' said Jo, gently nudging her to the point, leaving the sentence hanging.

'I suppose I do, yes.' She pointed in the general direction of the door. 'I heard a child's voice, talking to someone at the top of the stairs. When I came up with my post, I couldn't hear it any more. Suppose I forgot about it, until just now.'

'Did you hear what they were saying, get a sense of who it might be?'

'No, no. It was baby talk, couldn't catch it. And whoever the child was talking to was mumbling quietly, so maybe that was why I noticed it. Couldn't have been the woman from 6D, you see. She shouts everything, even when she doesn't need to. I know what they're having for dinner, usually, and whether she's out of cider, or cigs. Which she always is.'

Jo wondered if there would be anything useful to gain from questioning the neighbour any further. She looked around, and something occurred to her. 'You have a really nice apartment, Sarah, do you have much help with things?' The room in which they were sitting was extremely tidy and clean.

'You mean, carers?' Mrs Stefanidis laughed. 'No. I don't need them. I can look after myself. I'm not that old.'

Jo reckoned Mrs Stefanidis was at least eighty if she was a day. 'I meant cleaners, really. Regular domestic help.'

'I do all my own housework. I can't see, but that doesn't mean I'm useless. I can smell things, feel things. The spiders know not to make their webs in here, I go around with a duster every morning.'

'What about shopping? Do you do it online?'

'Online? I wouldn't know where to start. Until recently I used to walk into town, but now there's a girl from the next block who helps me. She says it's no trouble, that she's going herself anyway once a week so we get the tram together. She's great. Plays the violin for me sometimes. Beautiful.'

At the mention of the violin, Joanna became quite still. A memory rose and bloomed, Ruby playing Christmas carols on the fiddle with Marianne accompanying on the piano. This year, on Christmas Day, the piano would probably remain under the embroidered cloth, the way it had all year. They might use it to rest their drinks on, but without Ruby, her mother wouldn't bother. It would stand there in silence like a piece of furniture, or a coffin.

'Beautiful?'

'Yes. Beautiful playing. I don't know what she looks like, of course. She has a beautiful soul, too. That's all that matters, isn't it?'

'What's the name of this person?' but it was as if she knew already, before the old woman pursed her lips to make the sound of it.

'Ruby. Ruby Harper.'

Joanna suddenly noticed the headache she'd been ignoring. It felt like she was being stabbed in the temple.

'What it is, Detective? Are you all right?'

The possibility that Ruby knew something about what had happened to Gregor entered her detective's mind and stuck there, flashing in neon. 'Yes, of course. I'm sorry. I feel a little unwell. I think I might have a cold coming on.'

'I hope not,' said Mrs Stefanidis. 'That's the last thing I need.'

'Do you have anyone who can come and keep you company tonight?'

The old lady shook her head. 'My husband died, oh, ten years ago now. No children.'

'What about friends, other members of your family?'

'Friends apart from Ruby? I'm afraid not. And no family apart from two nieces who never bother.'

'And this Ruby,' said Joanna, breathing mindfully. 'When did you last see her?'

'The day before yesterday. She dropped off some bread and milk.'

'I'll need an address for her, please, and a phone number if you have one.'

Mrs Stefanidis reached into her pocket for her phone handset. 'I have it all stored on here. Feel free to look.'

'Thank you,' said Jo, standing up to take the phone. Scrolling through the contacts, she found Ruby's name and there, under the address she knew by heart, was an entirely different number to the one she had for Ruby. Quickly, she added this new number to her contacts and handed Mrs Stefanidis the handset. She sat down, fiddled with the clipboard she carried, aware that she was supposed to fill in a potential witness contact form with Ruby's details, reasoning that she could easily do that later but also knowing she was deceiving herself; that she was making up excuses not to do it.

'I haven't known her very long, six weeks or so. She saw me struggling with my shopping bag out there, and carried it up for me.' When she said the words *out there*, she waggled a hand towards the window.

Just like Ruby to help an old lady. Just like her to keep on helping, every week, to see someone in need and step in, selflessly.

'Is there anything else I can help you with?' asked Mrs Stefanidis.

'Oh,' said Joanna, realising she'd been staring into space, not speaking. 'Not for now, thank you. I might need to talk to you again. I can have the police liaison officer come and sit with you for a while, if you're feeling shaken?'

'No, thank you. Don't feel sorry for me. I like my own company. I'll be completely fine.'

Harper was almost out of the door when Mrs Stefanidis called her back.

'Leonie,' said Mrs Stefanidis. 'I just remembered. That's what the person said, the mumbling person, to the child upstairs. I couldn't make out anything else but I heard them say the name Leonie. "Leonie, come back here."'

'Does that name mean anything to you?'

'No. None of the children on this floor are called that, from what I hear them yelling. This wasn't a yell, more of a loud whisper. Strange.'

Harper wrote the name *Leonie* on her notes.

'I'll be in touch,' she said, and closed the door.

CHAPTER THIRTEEN

THEN
Ruby

September

Her phone wasn't in any of the usual places. Ruby went through her pockets, then her bag, even looked in her work bag which she hadn't opened since being signed off. It wasn't under the bed, or on it, or in the kitchen. She tried to retrace her steps – she'd definitely had it on the bench, because she remembered Gregor asking her what she was listening to.

There was no sign of it, on or around the bench. The model she had really wasn't worth stealing, and for a moment she considered checking inside the bin to see if someone had thrown it away. Maybe, on his way back from the shop, Gregor had seen it. She walked up to the North block and pressed the button for number seven. There was a click, followed by the sound of static, a channel opening. She looked straight into the camera.

'Hello?' She thought she could hear breathing. 'Gregor? Are you there?'

Another click, and silence.

She pressed the button again. No response to the buzzer, not even the click this time.

He probably didn't have it. It was annoying to lose the phone, but not the end of the world. Sam had lectured her for so long about information safety that she never even accepted cookies. If the phone was gone, it was gone. No one would be able to empty her bank account or anything.

'Would you give me a hand, dear?'

An older woman was approaching the door to the building, struggling with two shopping bags. Ruby took them from her. They cut into her fingers painfully.

'Wow, these are really heavy. Are you going far?'

'Only in there. Sixth floor.' As she took out her key card and opened the door, Ruby noticed the white stick folded and hanging from a belt loop.

Ruby was amazed that the woman, who said her name was Sarah, had been managing alone all this time, what with being elderly and visually impaired. There were no friends or family to help, Sarah explained; she had no choice but to manage.

'I'll help you next time. We can go together.'

'Oh, I couldn't.'

'It's no trouble,' said Ruby. 'I'll be going anyway. It'll be nice to have some company.'

'Well, if you're sure. Give me your phone number, so I can call, and you can call me.'

'Ah. My phone. I can't find it.'

'Oh no! When did you see it last?'

'I was talking to the guy who lives upstairs.'

'Mr Franks? Have you met him, then?' Sarah sounded surprised at that.

'I bumped into him on a tram. Then today he was outside the block, on his way to the corner shop.'

'Nice man, but he's so shy and quiet. Very much a lone wolf these days. Good catch for the right lady. If she can bring him out a bit, you know?'

Yes, thought Ruby, picturing the way Gregor had stumbled over the awkward parts of the conversation. He is shy and quiet. Not really a lone wolf, though, not yet. She was about to say something when she remembered his words: *Can I trust you?*

'Anyway,' said Sarah, 'what's he got to do with your phone?'

'He might have seen it, or seen who picked it up. I can't find it in the flat so I thought I might have left it on a bench out there, when I was chatting to him.'

'Oh, well it could have been anyone who took it, then. People will take whatever they like, in my experience. They'll see a thing they want, and just take it, as if it belongs to them already. Especially round here.'

Ruby said goodbye to Sarah and climbed the stairs to the seventh floor. On the landing there was a single doorway, the door painted shiny black, with a silver number seven at the centre.

Before she could knock, the door opened.

Music swelled, seeming to fill the hallway. Tears sprang to Ruby's eyes. Elgar's Cello Concerto always had that effect on her.

Gregor stood there in an old grey T-shirt with sweat at the armpits, moisture beading on his forehead. At the sight of her, he frowned and smiled at the same time.

'How did you get into the building?'

'How did you know I was here?' Ruby said.

'Slightly embarrassingly, I have motion sensors. On the stairs. They alert me when people are coming up.'

She could barely hear his voice. 'Why are you whispering?'

He beckoned for her to step inside, shut the door behind them.

'It's going to sound paranoid.'

'I can tell that.'

'I had a thing, with one of the downstairs people. A bit of a falling out.'

She couldn't imagine what this unassuming person could have done to annoy anyone in the building. From what Sarah had said, she was hardly even aware of his presence. 'What happened?'

'It was my music. A man came and banged on the door, said it was too loud. He threatened to "fill me in" if I didn't turn it down.'

'Really? But you can't even hear it in the corridor.'

'No, that's right, not any more. I had the entire place soundproofed, after that, to make sure it never happened again. It was really scary. Oh, wow. I'm not making myself sound very manly, am I?'

They both laughed. 'Not really, no. Have you seen the man since then?'

'No, I've been avoiding being seen too much. I don't want to bump into him. Or anyone else I might have unwittingly annoyed, of course.'

'You're so brave.' She laughed again, teasing.

'Well, too late, it's public knowledge, now. I'm a nerd and a chicken and I'm proud.'

'Me too,' she said. 'Someone in my block complained, too, but I was practising in the middle of the night so I can't really blame them.'

'Practising?'

'Yes, I play the violin.'

'Professionally?'

'That was the dream. But no, unfortunately not. I'm a teacher.'

'Huh.' He looked thoughtful.

'I'm not very good.'

He frowned. 'I bet you're amazing.'

'I meant I'm not a very good teacher, actually. I wasn't too bad, as a performer. But a lot of it is down to luck, you know. Whether you get to do it for a living.'

'I'd love to hear you play.'

Ruby went red. 'Um . . .'

'Not in the middle of the night, of course. Though I get why you might do that. Some music sounds better when the world is asleep, doesn't it? And some things, like yoga. They're better too.'

For a moment, they just looked at each other. Ruby felt like her cheeks were on fire. 'So,' he said. 'You never said. How did you get in? Not that I'm not happy to see you, but unless somebody . . .'

'The woman downstairs let me in. Sarah?'

'Mrs Stefanidis? She's a sweet old thing. Sometimes I wonder how she manages, all alone. I'd help her out, but . . .'

'You have enough on your plate, sneaking around and trying not to be beaten up?'

'Well, yeah, that and, the other thing. The . . . family thing.'

She followed his eyes to the door across the hallway. Ruby assumed that was where Constance and the child were, right now.

'I actually did try your doorbell first, but no joy.'

'You buzzed?' Gregor went to the wall by the door, where there was a panel with a video screen. He pressed play on the last recorded footage, and sure enough, there was Ruby, waiting by the entranceway. 'It must have been Constance who answered. Sorry about that, I was working out. In my room.'

Ruby noted the use of the term *my* room. Not *our* room, then. He lived with her, but he wasn't *with* her. She was gathering evidence, still unsure whether to fully believe it.

'Ah yes. You hate gyms. But not exercise, clearly.'

He gave a half-smile. 'Come through, you can meet them.'

The short hallway led to a large, immaculate living room. There, seated on one of the couches was a small woman in a green, skin-tight jumper dress with bare feet, her dark hair plaited in a long rope that coiled over a shoulder and reached almost to her lap. Standing, holding the edge of the couch was a small child in a red sleepsuit, with a cockscomb of black hair, rosy cheeks and pale skin.

'This is Leonie,' said Gregor. 'Say hi to Ruby, baby girl.' He waved a hand at the toddler, who stood completely still and stared at Ruby with huge grey eyes just like her mother's. 'And this is Constance.' To Constance he said, 'Ruby lives in the West block. Remember I told you, we met on the tram, the other day. Ruby plays the violin.'

The woman raised her eyes to Ruby's. The only person smiling was Gregor. When Ruby glanced at him, he made a kind of reassuring-yet-apologetic face and a half-shrug, as if to say, *sorry about them*. Looking back at the mother and daughter, the way they regarded her seemed guarded, almost startled. Wild animals caught in a beam of light, alert to whatever might come next.

'Hiya,' said Ruby, grinning and waving, not knowing whether to try any other kind of greeting. Constance and Leonie continued to stare at her. There was no vibe whatsoever for a hug, or a double-cheek kiss.

The living space was bigger than Ruby's entire apartment. There were two identical couches arranged around a stylish coffee table, facing a very large flatscreen TV affixed to the wall. Floor-to-ceiling blinds concealed the impressive picture window onto the city, and if they had been open she would have seen that it was overlooked by only one window: her own. Four doors led off the main space. The door to the kitchen stood open; the others were shut.

Ruby settled herself on the couch opposite Constance. Gregor took the remote and turned the music down a little. She was grateful for that. It was impossible to concentrate on anything else when music was playing.

'Nice place,' said Ruby. 'How long have you lived here?'

'Two years, three months,' said Constance, her voice dreamy, almost wistful. 'And six days.'

Very precise, thought Ruby. 'We were just talking about the neighbours,' she said. 'Have you met any of them?' Was she babbling, talking too fast? Ruby thought perhaps she hadn't heard, was about to repeat herself when Constance shook her head.

'No.' There was a trace of an accent. 'I don't really go out.'

She looked at the child, at how pale she was, except for

those cheeks. Leonie moved towards her mother without taking her eyes from Ruby, who smiled in a friendly way to try to put everyone at ease.

'I just met the woman who lives underneath you,' said Ruby. 'She seems nice.'

'I don't know her.' Constance narrowed her eyes at Ruby, then glanced at Gregor. 'How do you two know each other, again?' Scottish, that was the accent. But softer, somehow worn at the edges, musical.

'We, er, don't, not really. I bumped into Gregor out there this afternoon, but when I got back to my flat I couldn't find my phone. I'm always leaving it places.' She turned to him. 'I meant to ask, did you happen to see it?'

His eyebrows went up. 'No, sorry. I would have returned it to you if I had. Was it not there when you went back?'

She shook her head, no.

'You could try the police station lost property? Someone might have handed it in.'

The idea of the police station lost property made her feel tired. She wondered if she even needed a phone. She only used it to play music, and to ignore calls from her family. 'I've probably lost it in the flat somewhere. Wouldn't be the first time.' Maybe Sam was right, and life would be simpler and healthier without technology. She could get a record player. The more she thought about it, the less likely it seemed that the phone had been stolen. She should really have checked inside the bin.

Ruby sat down cross-legged on the carpet in front of Leonie.

'Hi,' she said.

The baby dropped to her bottom and shuffled across the room in a sort of travelling lotus position, using her feet to propel her forwards in little bum-hops.

'That's an interesting way of getting around,' said Ruby to Constance.

It seemed as if Constance wasn't going to talk any more, but then she gave a slow blink and said, 'Yep. She doesn't like to crawl. It's not quick enough, apparently. She's a speedy one.'

They heard the kettle being switched on, and the water beginning to boil. Gregor whistled tunelessly as he opened and closed the cupboards and the fridge.

Leonie was heading towards Ruby with a toy lion in her hands. 'Is that for me?' she said when the baby was close to her.

Leonie thrust the toy at her. 'Line,' was what it sounded like.

'Lion! Amazing job, well done! What else you got in there?'

Leonie shuffled off towards the box.

When Ruby turned to Constance she was gazing intently into Ruby's eyes. The kettle was loud. 'You're the girl from over there,' said Constance, pointing at the drapes. 'I saw you.'

Ruby went cold. 'Yes, you're right. I wasn't spying or anything. I've got insomnia, so I'm up at funny hours. Sorry if I . . .'

'And is what he said right? You're a musician?'

'Yes. Do you like music?'

On the stereo, the Elgar reached a crescendo at the same time as the kettle, and Constance leaned in.

'What's he told you, about me and Leonie?' She spoke with

an edge of, what, panic? Desperation? Ruby felt accused, as if she'd been gossiping.

'Nothing, really,' said Ruby.

'Nothing?' Constance made a face indicating that she clearly didn't believe her. 'He didn't say anything about where I came from? About the sea?'

She couldn't tell Constance what he'd said to her about the beach party, and the one-night stand that resulted in the pregnancy – it suddenly seemed so personal.

'We didn't talk for long. He just said that you were together, and now you're not, but you live together for the baby's sake.'

Constance closed her eyes momentarily, as if the revelation pained her somehow. When she opened them they were clear, and full of determination. She reached out a hand and placed it on Ruby's wrist, gripping her, holding her there when she recoiled, tried to pull away. The concerto ended just as the kettle clicked off, so that the only sounds were Leonie dropping wooden bricks from the box on to the floor, and in the other room, the pouring of water from kettle to mug. 'Did you believe him?' Almost a whisper now.

From the kitchen, 'Do you take milk, Ruby?'

Ruby kept her eyes on Constance. *Do you take milk? Did you believe him?*

'Yes,' she said, to both of them, though when Constance's face fell, she wasn't sure any more that it was the right answer.

CHAPTER FOURTEEN

NOW
Joanna

Saturday, 22 December
Early morning

The moment she was out of Mrs Stefanidis's flat, Jo tried Ruby's new number. In the seconds before it connected, hope soared in her breast only to be crushed by the recorded message: *This person's phone is turned off.*

Back in the lobby, she briefed the CSI team, then excused herself and made her way to the West block doors. Part of her knew there wouldn't be a response to Ruby's buzzer, so when there was not, she was only half devastated. But of course, it was party season. There had been a new group of friends, recently, but Jo didn't know the first thing about them, just a passing comment back in October, the last time they'd spoken. 'Any boyfriend potential?' she'd asked. Ruby had made a strange noise and said, 'One of them's a guy, but it's complicated.' Joanna had so many questions about that, but at the time it hadn't been right, somehow, to interrogate her. *Complicated* usually meant bad news. Maybe Ruby was with the new friends now.

Joanna wondered how everything had gone so very wrong. Right up until the day of the fight, she'd thought the family, unconventional though it may have been, was functioning OK. Throughout Ruby's childhood everything was fine. She'd seemed well-adjusted – happy even. It was easier for Jo not to be there, to listen to Ruby call her mother Mum, and not her, but she thought she was making things better for everyone by staying away. She'd missed so much, and hidden how much it hurt, assuming her own issues were the only fallout from the decision taken – while she was still a child herself – with the best intentions for everyone involved. How wrong she'd been, about so many things.

Everything had come to a head on Christmas Day. Jo walked into the living room and found her mother sitting with a glass in her hand.

'Where's Ruby?' Jo asked. Dad was in the kitchen, banging tins and running the tap.

Marianne took a long sip. The glass was full of ice and clear liquid, but Joanna did not assume it was water. She glanced at the clock and saw that it was 11.52. Close enough to lunchtime for a first drink, she supposed.

'She's sulking,' said Marianne, and from her voice Jo knew instantly that the half-finished drink in her mother's hand was far from the first of the day. She walked out of the room to find Ruby sitting on the stairs, her lips set in a thin line.

'She's been drinking since breakfast,' hissed Ruby.

'Did you have a fight?' asked Joanna.

Ruby shook her head. 'I just . . . can't deal with it today.'

She went back up to her room, making it clear she didn't want Joanna to follow.

Later, Dad served lunch, fussing and flitting about, asking everyone three times if they would like more of this or that, if they were sure they didn't, trying to jolly everyone along the way he'd done for years. Ruby had joined them, but declined to pull crackers. She'd barely spoken a word, in fact, until she suddenly interrupted Dad's flow as he tried to push more sprouts on to her plate. Glaring at Marianne, she said,

'You need help.'

Marianne was pouring red wine into her glass, a third refill that saw the bottle emptied. 'What have I done?'

'Ruby,' said Jo, 'it's not the best time—'

'Why, because it's Christmas?

'No, because . . . well, we've all had a drink, haven't we?'

'You haven't. I haven't.' She pointed to their drinks. The wine in their glasses had barely been touched. 'It's never a good time, is it?' She jabbed a finger at Marianne. 'She's drunk all the time. Why does no one ever talk about it?'

In the silence, the question presented a natural response. A trap to fall into.

Dad was the one caught by it. 'Talk about what?' He froze, half-standing with oven mitts raised. He glanced from Marianne, to Joanna, to Ruby. In that moment, they were all thinking the same thing. Not the alcoholism, which they also never talked about. The other thing.

'Your father was a mouthy little shit, too,' said Marianne to Ruby, and Jo stood up, as if to get between them. She wanted to slap a hand over her mother's mouth.

'Roo—'

Dad said, 'What? I was a what?'

'Not you,' said Marianne, reaching for the corkscrew. 'That boy. The one that got Joanna pregnant. Apple doesn't fall far from the tree.' She popped the cork on a new bottle of red and filled her glass to the brim. 'I think he's in prison, now, right Joanna?'

'Mother, stop.' Jo took a step towards Ruby, but she flew out of her chair and over to the doorway, where she hesitated, staring at Joanna. *Do something*, she seemed to say. In a rage, Jo snatched her mother's wineglass as she tried to take a swig so that the deep red liquid splashed across the table, the carpet, the walls. Marianne cried out, as if in pain. Then she placed her palms on the table, head down like a hyena about to strike.

'You're so ungrateful. Both of you. I don't know why we did what we did, Phillip. It wasn't worth it.'

'Marianne, what are you saying?' said Dad. 'Don't listen, girls, she's not herself. We love you, both of you. Why don't you go and have a lie down, darling?' The oven mitts fell to the floor as he tried to wrestle his wife to a standing position.

'Get off me,' shouted Marianne, falling into her chair.

'I'm leaving,' said Ruby.

'Good,' said Marianne. Then, she looked at Jo. 'You should never have had her, Joanna. Would have saved us all a lot of trouble.'

Damage control was impossible this time. As Jo and Dad scrabbled for what to do, how to limit the damage, Ruby turned, walked straight out of the front door and didn't look back. She left all of her things, turned off her phone and disappeared, only days later sending a text to Jo saying to tell Marianne never to call, and that she'd be in touch again when she felt ready. Which wasn't for almost two months, when she rang to tell Jo the news about her council flat on the New Park. However, Jo wasn't to visit, or tell the parents, (in Ruby's mind no longer her parents) where she lived. 'I trust you,' she'd said. 'I'll be ready one day. But not yet.'

'So why give me the address now?'

'Just so you know where I am. If, say, someone dies or something. Otherwise, I'll call you. You're not like her. At least I can rely on you to respect my wishes.'

Since then, she'd spoken to Ruby maybe once a month, and never for very long. Jo felt she was being punished for something, and furthermore, that she deserved it. Most recently, contact had completely dried up. In her day-to-day life, Joanna tried not to dwell on it, especially on her part in the way the family was falling to pieces. Their mother did need help, but Jo wasn't the one to give it. It was up to Dad to get something sorted. As for Ruby, the mantra Jo repeated became: *If you love someone, set them free.* Jo was holding tight to the hope that Ruby would come back eventually, if she was patient; if she didn't push it.

She tried the new number once more, listened to the recorded message almost to the end before hanging up. The words *this person's phone is turned off* at least offered the possibility that it might one day be turned on again. She imagined what Ruby might say to her, if she ever answered. She hoped it would be *I've missed you*, but she knew it would more likely be *I told you not to try to get in touch until I'm ready*. Trying to get in touch was a reflex action, though, and she had little control over it; she almost called the number again as she spun on her heel and jogged towards the North block, just to see if it had been turned on in the last few seconds, but the other cops were watching her approach so she slipped the phone into her pocket instead. She was furious with herself for letting the silence go on for this long, but Ruby could wait a day or two longer; this case couldn't. There was a suspected attempted murder, and zero leads.

Atkinson had just finished briefing another officer in the lobby when Jo walked in.

'Did you get much from the interview with the neighbour?' he asked.

Jo explained that Mrs Stefanidis was visually impaired, but her hearing was perfect. She told him the name that Sarah had heard being said. 'It might be the child that's been living there, though she seemed convinced, like Terry was, that Franks lived alone. Might be worth checking against the names of any children known to be living in the block – can you put someone on that? I'm heading over to the hospital to have a look at the victim, see if anything's changed.'

'Do you want me to come with you?'

'No, you get home, Steve.'

'Really?'

'Sure.' She indicated the PC on door duty. 'PC Box can cover you for this shift. He probably needs the overtime to pay for my Christmas present.'

The young PC laughed, a little nervously.

Atkinson patted his pockets for his phone, probably eager to call his partner. 'Thanks, boss.'

'You make sure you get some sleep. I'll need you nice and fresh in the morning.'

The constable's face fell. 'Tomorrow morning? I've, um, booked it off, ma'am.'

'Sorry, Steve, you might need to unbook it. You're needed on this one, what with being first on scene. I'll warn you now, this case might be a long one. It won't stop until it stops.'

She gave him a steely look, challenging him to start complaining about the sanctity of Christmas, only a few days away. She didn't think he would: people knew what they were signing up for when they entered the service. Goodbye, private life. It shouldn't have come as a surprise that crime continued to occur even on high days and holidays. Imagine if all police officers decided not to bother working at those times.

He seemed about to speak, but then he dropped his eyes. 'Yes, of course. Sorry, it's not me. It's Felicia, she's all set for a day at home.'

'You don't have to work, Steve. I can have another PC replace you on the case. But if you were thinking of moving to CID, a case like this could really give you the edge. It's up to you.'

As she walked towards her car she felt confident that Atkinson would make the right decision. The truth was that Steve was like Jo, when it came down to it: married to the job. Of course he loved his girlfriend, that was clear from the way he was around her. But Felicia was going to need to accept that she was always going to come second in Steve's life to what he cared most about: making the world a better place.

As she drove through the deserted streets, Joanna felt fortunate that Amy wasn't anything like Felicia. Broken dinner dates didn't matter between them, not in the long run, because Jo sometimes needed to prioritise work. Amy understood that.

It was confusing to Jo, then, that as she approached the house she shared with her girlfriend she could see Amy coming out of the door holding a large suitcase, and wearing a decidedly pissed-off expression on her face.

Jo parked up and got out, just as Amy slammed her own car boot shut. It was so full of stuff that the lock wouldn't quite catch. She stood and watched as Amy tried to force it closed.

'What's going on?' asked Jo.

Amy gave one last push and the boot clicked shut. 'What does it look like?' she said, turning and leaning on the car, arms folded.

'Hey, I'm sorry I missed dinner. There was a big case and I had to—'

'I don't care.'

'What?'

'I don't care what it was. For once, I thought you'd be able to keep a promise to me.'

'But Amy, I didn't have a choice—'

'That's bullshit, Jo, and you know it.'

Amy was shivering in the wintry air.

'You're cold. Why don't we go inside, we can talk about it.'

'There's no point. You don't listen to me.'

Jo felt surprised at that. 'I do listen to you.'

'The fact is, Joanna, there's always something. Some little shit has always done something that desperately needs your attention on a Saturday night, or someone's dropped dead, or they've found a haul of drugs. And sure, I understand that the police service needs to respond. But it doesn't always need to be you, does it?'

There was a pause, during which the only sound was the

chattering of Amy's teeth. Joanna was listening, hard. *I do listen to you*, she thought, *see?* She stepped forward to put an arm around Amy, who flinched away, pointed at Jo's trousers.

'Is that blood?'

She looked down at herself. Her coat and the thighs of her jeans were soaked. She looked like a butcher. 'Oh. Yes.'

'What's going on? Is it a murder?'

'Honey, you know I can't tell you anything until the details are made public.'

Amy threw her hands up. 'Oh, for f—'

'Where are you planning on going, anyway?'

'A friend's. What's it to you?'

'I don't want you to go, obviously.'

'I don't want to, either. But I think it's time. I'm too young to be someone's dreary home-sitter. I'm not good at waiting. Or being stood up. I think I'm worth a bit more than that.'

'If I could tell you what I'm working on, you'd understand. It's big.'

'If you could tell me what you were working on,' said Amy, 'maybe we wouldn't be in this mess.'

'What do you mean?'

'When you and I weren't involved, you didn't have to keep everything from me. We were working together. Talking to you was part of my job, a part I liked. Remember when I was a plucky journalist and you were my best cop pal?'

'Yeah, but what we've got now, Amy. It's special. Right?'

'Being a police officer's partner isn't what I thought it would be. I thought I'd get more information, not less.'

'So, that's what it's about? You can't grill me for the details in newsworthy cases anymore, so you want to leave?'

'Don't you think it was more exciting, before we were a couple? When the confidentiality standards didn't apply?'

'They did apply, Amy, but it was different. We had a professional relationship. I can't share details of a live case with my wife.'

'I'm not your wife.'

'You could be.'

She hadn't known she was going to say that, and for a moment she wanted to take it back. Was she proposing?

Amy almost laughed, but then she stopped. 'Are you proposing?'

Perhaps she was. The idea filled Joanna simultaneously with excitement and dread. The last thing she wanted was to lose Amy. The next to last thing she wanted was a wedding. But she'd said it now. And perhaps, if she proposed, it would make her stay. 'Yes? Yes. I am. Will you?'

'Will I what?'

'Marry me?' Even to Joanna it sounded unconvincing. And terrifying.

Amy sighed and pushed her away, not unkindly. She gazed into Jo's eyes and smiled with half of her mouth, the way she did when she was sad. 'You'll be relieved to hear that the answer's no, Joanna. I don't want this life for me. And you don't either.'

Jo could feel her slipping away. 'I can change things at work, if it matters that much. I can move departments . . .'

'No. You won't be happy doing that.'

'You breaking up with me isn't exactly going to make me happy either.'

Amy searched Jo's eyes. A tear slipped from her cheek and fell into the darkness. 'I wouldn't be so sure about that.'

Jo watched as Amy walked to the car without looking back. She made no move to stop Amy from getting into her car and driving away. The hard truth was, Amy was right. It had been better before they moved in together, before Amy had started trying to change the way Jo lived. They'd been playing house, but it wasn't a game either of them liked. Jo knew it wasn't just the work, too: the training was another source of friction. There was a timetable on the wall in the kitchen that clearly set out the hours of cycling, swimming and running Joanna needed to do to keep competition-fit, yet Amy had always seemed surprised and annoyed by Jo's dedication to it. Triathlon was a passion for Joanna, but also a lifeline. It allowed her to process the more stressful parts of the job. It got the anger out, and the frustration. Without it, she would have come undone, and she wouldn't have given it up for anything.

Jo climbed the stairs to the building, her mind a jumble of feelings. She loved Amy, but she also loved being alone. She was sad that her first attempt in years at a proper relationship had failed after less than six months, and then angry that Amy seemed to be more worried about her own job than anything else. Then she thought about their history together, that heady, wonderful few weeks when the friendship had developed into something more; the way Amy looked in the morning, sleep-ruffled and make up free, and she was back to feeling sad again. Finally, as Jo entered the flat and saw that all of Amy's flowery mugs had gone, her stacks of shoes were missing from the hallway, and that terrible painting she'd insisted on hanging pride of place above the fireplace had been removed, she felt something she wasn't proud of, but couldn't deny: a wave of quiet relief.

Jo quickly got changed out of her bloody clothes and into a fresh set of smart jeans, a long-sleeved shirt and warm jacket. She trotted down the stairs and jumped into her car. It was as if a weight she didn't know she'd been carrying had been lifted from her shoulders. When she returned later to grab some sleep before what would inevitably be an early start, an empty bed would be waiting. Jo smiled at the thought of it, then felt guilty for smiling, and wondered where Amy was now, and whether she would be OK.

Work mode kicked in, sweeping aside the feelings, keeping them on ice for later. She started the car and set off for the Royal Infirmary Hospital, where a severely injured man needed her help to find his attacker and bring whoever it was to justice.

CHAPTER FIFTEEN

THEN
Ruby

September

Gregor opened the door before she got there, dressed in a clean T-shirt and jeans. 'You came,' he said. 'And you brought the violin.'

Ruby felt a rush of joy that he was so pleased to see her.

'How did you get in the building, though? Mrs Stefanidis again?'

Ruby nodded. 'I've told her I'll help her with her shopping. You know she's almost blind?'

'You didn't mention Constance to her, did you?'

The door to the living space opened a crack and a tiny girl shouted 'Hi!' as she yanked it completely open, then bum-shuffled towards them before using the doorframe to stand up.

Today, Leonie wore a yellow sun dress, with white sandals on her feet, which she used as levers to get her across the carpet super-fast. 'You look ready to go to the beach, honey,' said Ruby.

'Beach!' shouted Leonie. When Ruby glanced up at Gregor, he winced and made a shivering motion.

'Yeah, your dad's right. It's a bit cold for that today. Hey, why don't you show me the rest of your toys?'

Leonie had spotted the violin case. She dropped to the floor, shuffled across and reached up for it, so that Ruby drew it away instinctively.

Gregor said, 'Oh, don't touch, baby girl. Precious.'

The child's eyes flitted between Ruby and Gregor. Then the little hands reached for the violin again. Gregor squatted and picked her up. 'Ruby's going to play something for you, Leonie. Shall we go in the living room?'

Constance was sitting in the exact same place as before, wearing a blue woollen skirt and a long-sleeved top. She acknowledged Ruby with a small movement of her head, before resuming staring at the big picture on the wall, a large photograph of the ocean during a storm. Her hair was coiled into its rope, gleaming black against her shoulder. The way she stared at the seascape, as if she longed to dive in, suddenly brought to mind a ballet Ruby had played for when she was a student at the conservatoire: *Ondine*. Constance's long limbs, so graceful as she sat there, pointed feet crossed; Ruby could imagine her dancing the character of the water-nymph. It was as if her pose was simply a pause in the choreography, and that at any moment she might rise, wraith-like, from the couch and perform a slow pirouette.

'See,' Gregor said to Constance. 'She's come back. I told you she would. And she's going to play for us.'

'Oh,' said Ruby, 'only if you don't mind.'

Constance looked at them and nodded, almost imperceptibly.

Her expression was hard to read, her eyes glassy. It was past lunchtime but despite her physical poise she looked vacant, as if she'd just woken up.

'What songs do we know?' said Gregor to Leonie. '"Twinkle, Twinkle"?'

'Yay!' said Leonie.

'Can you play that, Ruby?'

Ruby was unfolding her music stand. Twinkle, Twinkle? Maybe she wouldn't need the stand. She took out her instrument and played the tune from memory. While the sound of the nursery rhyme filled the room, only Constance looked away, still focused on the print. The sun streamed through the window, surrounding her in a kind of ethereal glow. It was as if she held herself apart, was only half there in the room. Ruby wondered where the rest of her was, which world her attention had wandered to. Certainly one with a wild sea and a dark, brooding sky.

At the end of the song Leonie applauded wildly. Gregor stared. 'That was so beautiful,' he said.

'What?' laughed Ruby. 'It was only a nursery rhyme.'

'Yes, but the violin. The sound it makes, that you make, it was . . .'

She noticed that Constance had turned her head, was staring at him, her lips pressed together. Ruby suddenly felt acutely aware of the attention Gregor was showing her.

She lowered the instrument.

'Don't stop,' he said. Leonie wriggled in his arms and he put her on the floor, where she bum-shuffled towards the toy box.

Ruby put the violin under her chin, and played 'Twinkle, Twinkle' again. There was a sound coming from the baby, who was turned away from them as she piled up bricks in a stack. This kid was singing. A perfectly clear tone, in tune with the violin.

'Is she . . .'

'Yes,' said Gregor. 'She sings all the time. It's amazing.'

Leonie fell silent, as if she could sense them listening. She turned around. '"Twinkle, Twinkle"?' she said, though it came out *Tingle, tingle?* Ruby began to play again.

This time she played Mozart's variations on the same tune, *Ah vous dirai-je maman*. Leonie picked up bricks and arranged them into piles, all the while humming along in tune. Constance looked like she'd zoned out again, her eyes having returned to the sea scene, but Gregor stood transfixed, watching Ruby. When she'd finished, he was full of questions: how long had she been playing? How much training had she had? What was her conservatoire like? Had she ever wanted to give up as a child?

'I used to play the piano but I gave it up when I was eleven,' said Gregor. 'I thought I knew better, but I regret it now – exactly the way my parents told me I would. I wish I'd listened to them and kept on practising.'

'Well,' said Ruby, 'I wasn't given the option, thankfully, or I might have given up, too. I hated her for it, at the time, but now I can see why she was so strict.'

'Your mother?'

'My . . . yes.' Gregor frowned at her, wanting her to explain the hesitation. She just smiled; it was too soon to go into all of that.

He said, 'I'd love for Leonie to play. You say you started when you were three?'

She nodded. 'My folks were pretty keen. They were a bit like you, gave up playing when they were young, always regretted the decision. You know, you could take it up again now, if you wanted to? I know a few good piano teachers.'

Gregor laughed, as if the notion were ridiculous.

'I'm serious.'

He shook his head, still laughing. 'I was never very good, anyway.'

'Your parents must have thought you were, if they willing to pay for lessons.'

His face darkened, she thought, for a split second. 'I suppose.'

'I was sorry to hear about your mother, by the way. It must have been a shock for you.'

'My mother?' he said, and for an instant she thought he looked angry. Then his face smoothed out into wide-eyed bafflement. 'But how did you . . . oh, yes, of course. Mrs Stefanidis.' He rolled his eyes.

Ruby felt awkward, that she'd admitted she'd been discussing his business behind his back. She knew how he felt about gossip.

'I'm sorry . . .'

'Don't be. It was a long time ago,' he said, in a way that made it clear he didn't want to talk about it. Ruby didn't think three years was very long, but what did she know about grief? In some ways, she felt, she was very lucky indeed.

Gregor said, 'But Leonie, she's got potential. You could teach her, couldn't you? I'd pay you, of course.'

'I could, but she's a bit too little now. When they're little you just need to sing to them. How old is she, exactly?'

Ruby had directed the question to Constance, but the other woman hadn't noticed. She was concentrating on coiling a strand of hair around a finger, watching as it slipped around and back, around and back.

Gregor cleared his throat and said, 'She's not quite two.'

They both looked over at the child, who might have been able to sing in tune, but wasn't even walking yet. Something worried Ruby slightly about that. She vaguely remembered a video of herself, on her first birthday, running across a lawn into her father's arms. She doubted there were any videos of her singing, though, not until much later.

'Next year, then,' he said. 'And it will be worth it, right? What a skill to have, Ruby. I know she'll pick it up quickly, she's got an amazing ear. Like you.' He smiled at her, his eyes full of admiration.

Ruby caught a movement in the corner of her eye, Constance's head turning once more to look at them. All of a sudden, Gregor seemed flustered. 'I haven't even offered you a drink.'

'Don't worry, it's fine. I just had one . . .'

'I'll make coffee.' He rushed out.

The energy in the room, without Gregor, was completely different. Ruby put the violin away, and when she looked up she realised that Constance hadn't said anything for a long time. The quiet settled, both of them listening to the sound of Leonie shuffling here and there over the carpet.

'Thank you, little lady.' Ruby took the wooden brick that was offered. 'So, Constance.' Leonie shuffled across the length of the room. 'Where are you from, originally? You have an accent.'

Constance looked in the direction of the seascape print, and pointed. 'I'm from there.'

Ruby stood up to get a closer look at the image. There was no land in it, only water and sky, in different shades of gunmetal grey, green, and white on the tips of the waves. The ocean during a storm.

'Where was this taken?' asked Ruby. Thinking of the accent, she said, 'Somewhere in Scotland?'

Gregor came in holding a tray with three mugs and a cafetière.

'It's nice, isn't it? I bought it in an online auction, last year. Somewhere off Orkney, apparently. They get a lot of weather up there. Sideways rain.'

'It's a beautiful image. Are you from the island, Constance?' Ruby thought the picture was kind of bleak. She hadn't decided if she liked it or not.

There was a long pause before Constance said, 'Yes and no.'

Confused, Ruby looked at Gregor.

'It's a story,' he said, with a small dismissive gesture. 'But she tells it as if it's true.'

'It is true,' said Constance, offended. 'All of my stories are true.'

She sat back on the couch, suddenly bristling with anxiety, twisting the end of her plait faster and faster. At the edge of the room, Leonie stopped what she was doing, one hand frozen in the act of turning the page of a fabric book. She looked at her mother but she didn't move or make a sound. In that moment the child reminded Ruby of a startled bird, hoping that if it stays completely still it won't be noticed.

Gregor's face was suddenly full of regret. 'I'm sorry,

Constance. You go on. Of course, it's true, I was being insensitive.' He gave Ruby a look, then, apologetic, perhaps.

'All stories are true, in a sense,' said Ruby. Leonie relaxed as the tension in the room eased. She went on with her page-turning. Ruby turned to Constance. 'Tell me. I'd love to hear about where you're from.'

Constance looked away. 'I don't want to, now. Not with him here. He doesn't believe any of it, clearly.'

'Maybe I should leave,' said Gregor.

'No,' said Ruby. 'You don't have to.'

But Constance glared at him, triumphant. 'Maybe you should.'

Gregor picked up his cup of coffee, got up and headed for one of the bedrooms. 'I'm sorry, Connie. I didn't mean to upset you. Really.'

'But you don't really have to go, do you?' asked Ruby. She wasn't sure she wanted to be alone with Constance. Something about the woman's mood was making her uneasy.

Gregor glanced at the wall clock. 'Actually, I do have to make a call for work. It shouldn't take long. Sorry. I'll be a few minutes. Then I'll be back.'

After he'd gone, Ruby wondered about the office in the city, and why he wasn't there now. Maybe he worked from home sometimes. What did he even do for a living? The opportunity hadn't arisen, yet, to ask him. She felt suddenly unsafe, and stupid, not knowing why she'd come up here, to Gregor's flat, to these people about whom she knew so little, and this strange, glassy-eyed woman.

Leonie, having come to life, bum-shuffled towards her and handed her the book.

'Raf,' she said, pointing to the giraffe on the front page.

'Amazing! You're so clever!' Ruby clapped her hands in applause and Leonie laughed.

For a while, Ruby played with the baby, who would bring things to her, hand them over and name each one as she did so. Leonie knew the name of everything, even correctly identifying a tarantula in a nature book.

'She knows so many words,' said Ruby.

'Yes.'

'And she sings. I've never seen that before. Not that I see a lot of children this age. Usually they sing, but they don't really sing, you know? They just sort of yell.'

Constance turned her head, and smiled at Leonie. 'She's done it since she was tiny. I could sing a note, she could sing it back. She was only a baby in the cradle.'

'Tuss!' said Leonie.

'Tuss?'

'She means tortoise.'

'Tortoise! Of course.' Leonie went over to the toy box, and Ruby turned to Constance. 'So,' said Ruby. 'You're from Orkney?'

'Not Orkney. The island is West of there, in the Hebrides. He bought me that picture because it reminded me so much of the sea near where I was born. I look at it and I can see my family.'

'You have family out there still?'

She nodded. 'I have everything there. When I came here, I lost it all.' As she said this, they both looked over at Leonie, and Ruby was puzzled. How could she say she'd lost everything if she'd gained this astonishing child? The relationship with Gregor might not have worked out, but Leonie was something, wasn't she?

'Your family must visit, though? And you visit them?'

'No. They can't; they won't. Not after I left, the way I did.'

Ruby felt suddenly very sorry for Constance, for the predicament she found herself in. How on earth could she go back, if the agoraphobia was keeping her prisoner? Quite apart from the travelling required to get there, Ruby wondered how a person afraid of the outside would fare, living on an exposed island in the middle of nowhere. No wonder she was homesick. 'Tell me about them.'

Constance stared at Ruby, holding her gaze for the first time, for so long that Ruby felt sweat prickling on her forehead. It was the intensity of it that unsettled her. The woman radiated an unstable energy, nervous and full of something else, suppressed rage perhaps. She spoke, eventually, through a clenched jaw. 'I'm not sure you'd believe me, either.'

Ruby said, 'Try me,' and for a while Constance just continued to stare, distrust etched on her face.

Then she tipped her head, deciding. 'We're a community. Like a clan. We have our own island.'

Ruby thought it sounded wonderful. She imagined the women in long, rough-hewn dresses, waiting on the shore for the fishermen to return. 'Sort of like a hippy commune?'

'What? No . . .'

'I don't mean that offensively—'

'We are Roane,' said Constance.

Ruby didn't understand. 'Is that your surname?'

'How are you two getting on?' said Gregor, from the doorway. He looked from one to the other, then at Leonie, and down at the scattering of objects on the carpet around Ruby's legs. 'Making a mess, baby?' he said, tutting as he scooped up all of the offerings before taking them over to the toy box. 'Shall we tidy up?'

'Di-dee up!'

Ruby stood up. She needed to get away. 'Well, thanks for the coffee.' She picked up her violin. 'I should be going.'

'Of course, we mustn't keep you. You must have to practise for hours to be as good as you are,' said Gregor. 'I don't suppose . . .'

'What?'

'Well, I don't suppose you'd come and play for us again?'

Ruby wasn't sure if she wanted to or not. 'Um . . .'

'Only if you have time,' he said.

Ruby found herself looking into Constance's eyes. Then Leonie came towards her, and pulled on her trouser leg, using it to stand up. Ruby reached down and offered her a finger to hang on to instead. That black shock of hair, and the rosy cheeks.

'I could make time,' she said.

'Ba-ba,' said Leonie, waggling her hand like a balloon on a stick.

'Bye-bye,' replied Ruby, mirroring the action. Leonie laughed.

Gregor walked her down the stairs, out and across to her building, then without Ruby really knowing how it was happening, he was riding in the lift to her door. She fumbled with the keys, turned to say goodbye but somehow after that he was in her flat, pretending not to notice the state of the place, tactfully stepping through into the tiny kitchen while she bundled up her dirty washing into a corner, straightened the duvet, kicked a couple of used plates further under the bed. There wasn't much else she could do to improve things after that; the bare bulb in the bed-sitting room made everything seem cheap and ugly. Cheaper and uglier than it was already, anyway – nothing she had was expensive or beautiful, except for the violin. She tried turning the light off. It was completely dark. She turned it on again. Ruby wished she had a couple of lamps to soften the atmosphere.

'You really can see right into my place from here, can't you?' said Gregor, from the kitchen.

She went through and stood behind him, inhaled his smell. 'Yep. Sort of asking to be watched, aren't you?'

'I thought I was safe, actually. Until I saw your little head peeping out, and by then it was too late, my cover was blown.'

She wished he would stop mentioning it. So embarrassing. 'I'm sorry about that. I really didn't mean . . .'

'I'm not sorry,' said Gregor, turning quickly so that they were standing far too close together. 'It meant that we met, didn't it? I don't meet many people.'

'You don't?'

'No. Well, I sort of do, for work and so on. I don't usually like them.' He smiled, shy and unsure.

Ruby took a step backwards. It was dangerous being this close to him. He might be technically single, but he was tangled up in something nevertheless, with Constance, and the child. She didn't want to get involved. Despite this, her body responded to him. It had been so long since she'd been touched.

'Why don't you like them?' she asked, leading the way out

of the darkened kitchen and into the harsh, unforgiving light of the bed-sitting room.

He shrugged. 'Most people are paste, that's why.'

'Paste?'

'Oh, you know. Sort of grey and uninteresting. Or pretending to be something they're not.'

'Huh.'

'But you're not, Ruby. You shine.'

She blushed, and not knowing what to say, she said nothing. She didn't feel shiny. She felt, if she were honest, like paste. Ruby stood there awkwardly, leaning against the wall nearest the door. Gregor walked the few steps to the window and looked out.

'I've got a weird thing to ask. You can say "no".'

'Oh, OK. What is it?'

'I wanted to ask you, if you wouldn't mind . . . not talking about us to anyone?'

'Why would I talk to anyone about you?' she said, thinking, I don't really talk to anyone, about anything, right now.

He grew serious then. 'I meant about Constance, really. And Leonie. No one can know they're there with me.'

'Why not?'

'It's hard to explain, but because of her background . . . there are a few legal issues. To do with Leonie.'

'What?'

'Nothing bad. Only that, since Leonie came along I've been helping Constance manage her mental health. The agoraphobia, and the . . . other stuff.'

She thought of her own GP, the antidepressants she was supposed to be taking. That look in Constance's eye, the volatility she sensed, a firework about to blow. 'So, I'm assuming she hasn't seen anyone about it?'

He shook his head, no. 'If it got much worse, I'd have to think about it. But right now we're doing OK, I think. I don't want anyone getting involved. Doctors, social services, or whatever. You understand.'

'But if she's unwell, wouldn't it be better if she got treated?'

He sat down slowly on the edge of the bed, and stared at his hands. 'Would it though?'

'What do you mean?'

'I hear what you're saying. But once you start down that road . . . I just look at Leonie and I think, how terrible it is for a child to grow up without a mother.'

Gregor's back was hunched, his eyes in shadow. He drew in a breath and let it out slowly, but she could hear the slight tremor, the emotion in it.

Ruby went to him. She sat down next to him, not quite touching. His breathing was ragged. 'What is it, Gregor? What happened to you?' She reached for his hand but he drew it away.

'I know how these things end. Once someone is in the grip of mental illness, if you let them out of your sight, abandon them to strangers, to medics. They try to . . . leave.'

She barely dared ask, 'Did you lose someone?'

'I . . . just can't. Not yet. One day I'll tell you, I promise.'

He must have had some terrible experiences, to have become so cautious and mistrustful. That he would confide in her, this man who hardly let anyone in.

'I worry that I wouldn't be enough for Leonie. If we ended up alone.'

Ruby reached again for his hand. 'You're not alone.'

He looked at her, then, searched her face for meaning. 'But, Ruby, you barely know me.'

She thought of Leonie, that joyous child, that gleaming ball of potential. She thought of Constance, her strange, ethereal mother, who already seemed so faded and distant, as if she had one foot in another world. The two of them with many complex needs; such a heavy burden for one person to carry. She held his gaze. 'I know enough.'

He shook his head, perhaps in disbelief, but when he looked at her she saw deep gratitude in his eyes.

'Can I ask you a question, now?' said Ruby.

'Go on.'

'What's *Roane*?'

His brow furrowed. 'What did she tell you?'

'Nothing, just the name. She phrased it strangely, that's all. Made me wonder.'

'It's her family name. Her clan, if you like. But, Ruby, it's more to her than that. *Roane* is an old word meaning seal, or selkie.'

'Selkie? Isn't that like a mermaid?'

'Kind of. They're shape-shifters: seals in the water, humans on land. But because of it, she believes that she comes from the sea, that she's part of that myth.'

So, the significance of the name had gotten distorted in her mind somehow. Poor Constance. A disordered thought, looming larger than it should have done in her confusion about what was real and what wasn't.

Gregor said, 'So you won't say anything, about them living there with me?'

'I can tell you one thing: your downstairs neighbour doesn't know about them.'

'You haven't told her?'

'No. She thinks she knows all about you, of course, from when your mother died. But Constance and Leonie didn't come up in conversation, really. I'm not sure she even knows that I've been coming over after I see her. To be honest, she spends most of the time talking rather than listening.'

He took her hand. 'Thank you, Ruby. I knew I could trust you. And thanks for tonight. I know that Constance is quite . . . unusual, I suppose. It's partly that she doesn't see many people. Because of the illness.'

'She's not paste?'

He shook his head. 'No, she's not paste. She's special in her own way. One of a kind. And you, well. You've got skills, and passion. What you did to "Twinkle, Twinkle" . . .'

'Not me. Mozart.'

'But you played it. You interpreted it. And you could probably have written it.'

Ruby laughed, slightly hysterically. 'No, I couldn't.'

'But you do compose, don't you?'

Suddenly shy, she said, 'I don't, not really. I mean, I have done, but nothing any good. Nothing I would show to anyone. And nothing that could even touch Mozart with a hundred-foot pole.'

She thought he would laugh, then, but he remained serious.

'I want to hear it.'

'What?'

'Your music. The stuff that comes from you. That you wrote.'

'But it's not very—'

'Please, Ruby.'

'But I . . .'

He was at the door, opening it. 'Just think about it, yes?'

Before she could answer, he was gone.

CHAPTER SIXTEEN

NOW
Joanna

Saturday, 22 December

Gregor Franks was very good-looking, even unconscious. Not pretty-boy good-looking but old-school handsome, so that his three-day stubble only added to the effect of rugged, symmetrical masculinity. He had a substantial upper body with defined pectorals, slim waist, strong thighs; clearly a gym bunny. She hadn't noticed when they hauled him from the bath, but he was tall: his bare feet were right at the end of the bed, almost hanging off. The fit body made his presence here even more tragic. For all of his physical grace, the man lay motionless on the bed, his arms draped at his sides, his head encased in a protective foam helmet.

'There's really nothing you can do for him?'

When Joanna had arrived at the ICU, Doctor Locke had shown her into the patient's room, a private space separated from the rest of the unit.

'The team worked on him for almost four hours after he came in. We tried everything to get his blood pressure up, but nothing improved it.'

'What does that mean exactly?'

'It means unfortunately his blood pressure is so low as to be incompatible with a life expectancy of any more than a few hours.'

The oxygen mask on Gregor's face misted gently at the nostrils.

'What are the machines for? Is that a ventilator?'

'No, just oxygen. And the other one is monitoring his heart rate.'

'He's breathing on his own?'

'For now.'

'But you don't think he'll recover?'

'I'd say it's highly unlikely.'

A large, bearded nurse entered the room, picked up the chart at the end of the bed and made a note.

'Are you the next of kin?' he asked Joanna.

'No, I'm a police officer.'

The nurse flipped the pages up on the chart and frowned. 'Is there anything you can tell us about him?' he asked. 'All we've got is a name, and that hasn't actually been confirmed.'

Joanna reached into her satchel for a plastic bag containing Gregor's wallet. 'The ID we have for him is all in here.' The wallet and its contents had already been swabbed and dusted for prints by the CSI team. There wasn't much in it that could help them trace family; only cash, a single VISA bank card and the driver's licence. The nurse took the wallet out of the plastic bag and retrieved the licence. Jo looked from the photo to the man in the bed, to his slack, unconscious face, as smooth and unmoving as a marble statue, all the life that was present in the photograph gone.

'So, there was considerable brain damage, from being hit on the head?' said Jo.

'The head injury wasn't as bad as we thought. It was the drugs he ingested that have caused his system to shut down.'

'Drugs?'

'Everything points to opiates. There are no track marks, so not injected. Probably some kind of prescription drug. I couldn't say what at this point, only that it's too late to reverse the effect. None of the usual antidotes revived him.'

'What about the head injury? It felt pretty serious to me.' *Like his brain was coming out*, she thought, with a degree of revulsion.

'I agree it did look dramatic, but the CT scan showed only a large extracranial haematoma and some skin abrasions. If he hadn't ingested the drugs, I think the outlook would have been much more positive.'

Jo said, 'Any sense of how he might have been injured? There was an initial theory that he slipped and fell in the bath, hitting his head on the edge.'

The doctor was shaking her head before Joanna even finished the sentence. 'I don't think so. The bath wouldn't have broken the skin like that.'

'You won't mind if we have someone come in to examine him?' said Jo. 'One of our medical forensic people will need to see the injury, have access to the medical records and so on.'

'You're welcome to examine him. But I'm afraid, while he's alive, you would need his consent to get access to the medical records.'

Joanna looked at the still and silent patient, then at the doctor. 'How do you suggest I go about obtaining that?'

'That's your department. You might need to get a court order. I can't release the notes without one.'

Someone would come forward with information about this man soon. Young, good-looking chap like that, had to have friends and family. The phone would be the key, she thought. Scroll through to the most-called number, and bingo. It was locked with a password, but the tech boys could open anything, given enough time.

'So, what's the next step?' asked Jo.

'We're monitoring him. That's all we can do for now, apart from keeping him as comfortable as possible.'

The doctor approached the bed, where Gregor's head was supported by the padded helmet device and a small rubber-ring shaped pillow. 'This is to keep pressure off the wound. Tissue damage and so on.'

Jo said, 'Can I get a look at the scan?'

The nurse turned to a computer monitor that was mounted on the wall, made a few clicks and the scan appeared. Harper and the doctor stepped closer.

'You see this area, this sort of circular impression? That's the site of the injury.'

Jo could just make out the place she indicated, which was about the size of a tennis ball.

'But as you can see, there's no bleeding to the brain,' said the doctor. 'I'd say he was hit with something roundish. And heavy. Maybe a large hammer or a mallet. Something with a sharp edge or corner. Big swing from behind, *pow*. Or, could have been more than one blow, and that's why the skin was broken. But I'm not an expert in weapons.'

Pow, she'd said, and done the action to go with it, like an underhand shot in tennis. Jo had seen many people become desensitised to the horrific nature of their work. In the police it was more than commonplace. She felt it was important to remember that in both professions they dealt with extremes. In such a position you had to choose: try your best to keep a sense of perspective, or let the job turn you into the kind of person that looked at a man in a coma and found it interesting rather than shocking. She considered herself to have achieved a good balance, so far. She could look at Gregor Franks and feel terrible for him. Then she could put those feelings away and get on with the job.

Just then, an alarm sounded somewhere in the main ward.

'Excuse me,' said Doctor Locke, and was gone. The nurse followed, absenting himself with such swiftness that Jo stood there with her mouth open for a few seconds, her hand on the edge of the open door. There were sounds of feet running, trolleys being wheeled across, a cry of *clear!* And the unmistakable loud bleep and clang of the defibrillation machine. Jo turned back to Gregor, letting the door fall shut behind her, closing the noise out. She watched his chest barely moving as he breathed. Her mobile rang into the silence.

She prayed it wasn't Amy, her cheeks flushing in shame with the memory of the not-proposal. Then, for a moment she thought – hoped – it might have been Ruby, having turned her phone on when she awoke this morning and seen the missed calls. But no, neither. It was Atkinson.

'I thought I told you to go home.'

'We think we've found her. The woman and the kid who were staying in Gregor's flat. We've got a woman on CCTV leaving the building and heading straight across the forecourt, holding a child of about the right age. This was yesterday, in the morning. She's got her hood up, and she's hurrying. I can't say exactly what drew me to her but she just stood out from the crowd, you know?'

Jo did know. Copper's nose was real, and Atkinson had a good one.

He went on. 'So, we traced her movements. We've got images of her going to the train station and buying a ticket. The whole time, she's facing away from the cameras, as if she's avoiding them getting an image of her face.'

'Where did she travel to? Can you get hold of the train station ticket office people?'

'Not right now, boss. The ticket office is shut. Opens in an hour.'

'Well, shake them up, Constable. We need a good image of her.'

'Are you at the hospital?' asked Atkinson. 'How's Franks?'

'Not good. He's got a load of drugs in his system. They don't think he can survive.'

'Drugs? I didn't see anything at the flat, no packets or bottles or anything.'

'Me neither. Let's see if the CSI search turns up anything.'

'Maybe the person who attacked him also spiked him, just to make sure?'

'That's why I like you, Steve. Always striving to see the best in people.'

'I learned from the best, boss.'

She smiled grimly.

Atkinson said, 'It makes it even more urgent that we find this woman, though, if his condition is so critical. I think we need to do a media shout-out. Local radio, TV. Someone will have seen her face, even if the cameras didn't.'

Jo thought of Amy, and the time before they'd been a couple when she would have been the first person to call in this situation. Perhaps one day, that would be the case again.

'Good idea. I'll leave it with you, if you don't mind.'

'No problem.'

'After that go home, will you? You haven't slept.' She hung up before he could point out that she hadn't either.

Jo examined the X-rays for a while longer, then moved across, behind the head of the bed to stand near the emergency button, in case Gregor should start flatlining while the medics were otherwise engaged. She watched the machines closely for any sign of alarm, but nothing happened. Heart kept beating. Lungs kept inflating. The patient just lay there, eyes closed, splayed feet pointing to the corners of the ceiling. She moved to the other side of the bed, and glanced at the man's fingernails, at the white skin like wax, bloated and wrinkled from being so long in the water.

He was alive. But for how long? Despite what the doctor had said, she didn't want to believe there was no hope of recovery. Someone, somewhere, cared about this man, and would have been willing him to live if they'd known what was happening. Until those people were found, all he had was Joanna.

'Hold on, Gregor,' she said to him. 'If you can hear me. We're going to find the person who did this to you. So just hold on, OK?'

CHAPTER SEVENTEEN

THEN
Ruby

September

'Close your eyes and open your hands.'

Ruby did as he asked. Gregor placed something flat on her palm.

She opened her eyes. 'That's not my phone.'

'It is now.'

The model in her hand was top of the range. It probably cost several hundred pounds, maybe more.

'Do you like it?'

'I can't accept this.'

His face fell. 'Whyever not?'

'I mean, thank you so much for thinking of me but honestly, you really shouldn't have.'

'But it's your birthday, isn't it?'

Ruby was shocked; how could he have possibly known it was her birthday? 'Well, actually it was yesterday.'

Gregor burst out laughing at her surprised expression. 'I didn't know! That's so funny, I was going to say that as a joke. Was it really your birthday yesterday? How perfect! Oh, brilliant. What a coincidence. Well, you'll have to accept it now, won't you?'

It had been a little over a week since the phone had been lost, and for those few days Ruby's life seemed stripped back; simple, in a clean, uncomplicated way. She'd been to the library to find some Scottish folk tunes for Constance, and what time she hadn't spent practising she'd been using to develop her own piece. On her birthday, apart from playing her violin and working on her composition, she'd had a bath that lasted for two hours while she listened to *Tosca* on the second-hand record player she'd treated herself to. Perfection, added to by the fact that she didn't even need to actively ignore any annoying calls from Joanna and Marianne.

She turned the device over in her hand. It was sleek, and sophisticated. The kind of phone she would never have bought for herself, whether or not she could have afforded to, which she could not.

'I don't know what to say.' She certainly couldn't say she was enjoying life without the hassle of a smartphone. It would have sounded so ungrateful.

'You don't have to say anything.'

'I was going to get myself a phone, soon.' If only to prevent her family panicking, or, God forbid, trying to visit in person. 'But it wouldn't have been as fancy as this one. This must have cost a bomb.'

'It's a gift, Ruby. I bought it for you.'

'But—'

'No buts.'

She hesitated. 'This is a bit embarrassing, but the thing

is, I'm not sure I can afford the monthly fee. I wasn't paying the bills for my other phone. My parents were paying for it. Without my income from teaching at the moment, there's no way I could . . .'

'Don't worry. I've set you up on a really cheap deal. And, I've paid up for the first six months.'

'The first six months? It's too much.' She tried to give the phone back, but he put his hands behind him.

'The first three months were free if you bought the next three, that kind of thing. So, it barely cost me anything. I'm seeing it as a way to support the arts. My first deed as your patron.'

Ruby pressed a finger to the screen so it lit up. The wall-paper was a picture of him, pulling a silly grin.

'You can change that,' said Gregor. Then he looked at her and frowned. 'Did I do something wrong?'

Don't be so proud, she told herself. *He can afford it. He's only trying to be nice.*

'No,' she said. 'Of course not. It's very generous of you, Gregor. Thank you. I'll pay you back as soon as I can.'

He looked hurt. 'Don't be silly, Ruby. It's a gift.'

'Sorry, I didn't mean to . . .'

'And look,' he said, unlocking the phone and scrolling to the contacts page, where just one person was listed. 'You have my number already.'

She couldn't remember any of the other numbers she'd once had, apart from the home landline number, and Joanna's mobile. All the others – mostly friends from school, a few bad dates and a handful of ex-pupils – had been lost along with her phone. Gregor's gift made her feel pressure to get in touch with some of those people and ask for their numbers again. Then she had another thought. *Does it really matter that much?* The only people apart from Jo to ring regularly were Barbara at work, and Marianne, neither of whom she particularly wanted to talk to. She supposed she could put Mrs Stefanidis in there. And then there was Sam, who didn't even have a phone – his address had been stored in the other phone but she still had it written down on a sheet of paper back at the flat. So, with Gregor, Sarah Stefanidis and Joanna, that made a grand total of three contacts, four if you counted Sam. Was that beyond pathetic? When did her world get so small, she wondered.

Maybe it was fine. Maybe she didn't need anyone else, anyway.

'Come through,' said Gregor, leading the way further into the apartment. 'Leonie's asleep, I'm afraid. But Constance is here.'

He opened the door to the sitting room. 'We haven't had the best day, today, unfortunately.'

Constance was reclining, catlike, on the same couch as always. There were dark circles under her eyes; her gaze was dull, her hair loose and tangled.

'Is she OK?' asked Ruby.

'She will be. She's had a sedative. Sometimes things get a bit . . . too much.' He raised his voice. 'How are you feeling, Connie, any better?'

There was no response apart from a flicker of the dull eyes in Ruby's direction.

'Should I go?' asked Ruby.

'No, no. It'll help her to see you.' He lowered his voice to a whisper. 'She might not show it, but I think it was really therapeutic for her to hear you play last week.'

Ruby was unsure, but Gregor smiled encouragingly.

'Hey, Constance. I found you some songs,' she said, taking out her instrument, and the book she'd borrowed. '*Hebridean Ballads, Jigs and Reels*. Yes?' She started to play. It was a folk song, beautiful, ancient and solid, sounding very Scottish to Ruby, reminding her of the folk bar she and Sam went to whenever he was in town. When she got to the end of the first chorus, she fell silent. Constance hadn't moved, or made a sound.

'Maybe I should come back another time,' said Ruby.

'No, stay,' said Constance at last. There was a creak to her voice, as if she hadn't spoken for a long time. 'I know that one. It has words, doesn't it?'

'I don't know them. It's only the tune in the book.'

'Play, please.'

With effort, Constance moved to a sitting position, her thin arms straining against the cushions to push her upright. After a few bars, she started to sing, in Gaelic.

Chuir iad mise dh'eilean leam fhìn
Chuir iad mise dh'eilean leam fhìn
Chuir iad mise dh'eilean leam fhìn
Dh' eilean mara fada bho thìr

There was something terribly sad in the sounds, in the way she sang them. Gregor stood and stared at Constance, as if seeing her for the first time. It was the way he'd looked at Ruby when she'd played for them the week before. Ruby watched him, watching the mother of his child, and wondered what had passed between these two that they should have become so distant from one another. Something powerful remained, clearly, though the nature of it was far from obvious.

When the song was over, there was a silence in which nobody breathed. Ruby lowered her bow.

Gregor said, 'What's it about?'

Constance raised her eyes to him, slowly. They never quite reached his face. 'It's about being sent to an island, far away and all alone.'

Gregor looked from Constance to Ruby, and back again. 'You make such beautiful music together. I can't take it in.'

'Gregor,' said Constance. 'I'm thirsty. Can you . . .'

'Of course. I'll get water.'

'Something hot?' she said. 'Tea?'

When he left the room, Constance seemed to come to focus. She fixed Ruby with her eyes and hissed urgently across the gap between the couches. Ruby moved closer.

'He locked me in the bedroom today.'

The words were so surprising that Ruby could only stare. 'He *what*?'

'He locks me in so he can hide my coat. My sealskin. I need it so I can go home. He's a bad man, Ruby. You should stay away from him.'

'Your sealskin?' Ruby didn't know what to say. It was possibly the most peculiar thing she'd ever heard. Perhaps she meant *oilskin*, like a rain slicker. But then Ruby remembered the conversation with Gregor, about the name Roane linking to the shape-shifters, the seal-people: *she thinks she's part of the myth*. Constance's face was a tight grimace, with veins standing out on her forehead, shiny with sweat.

'I can't go outside without it. That's why I'm stuck here. It has to be with me. It has to . . .'

Gregor came back into the room. 'It's a yes for milk and no for sugar, right, Ruby?' he looked over at Constance and his face changed to one of concern. 'Oh, hon, you don't look well. Much worse than earlier on – sure you want tea? I can make lemon and honey? Or cocoa?'

She waved a dismissive hand and leaned into the cushions. 'I feel fine. A bit sleepy, maybe.'

'You should probably go to bed. Do you need any help getting up?'

Constance glared at him. 'I do not need anything from you,' she said. 'And neither does Ruby.' Her eyes drooped and closed; her hand went to her head.

'Let's get you to bed,' he said, taking Constance's hand.

She yanked it away. 'Don't touch me.'

'Ok, I'm sorry.' Gregor held his hands above his head, in a gesture of surrender. 'I won't if you don't want me to. But I'm right here, if you change your mind.' His voice had a tremor; he was upset, trying not to let it show.

Constance struggled to her feet, pushing herself up with effort. Whatever she'd taken was affecting her balance. 'Remember,' she said to Ruby, 'Everything he says to you is a lie. I tell the truth. I tell . . .' She trailed off, her eyes drifting almost closed. With the gait of a person fifty years older, the dark-haired woman walked slowly across to her room and went in, shutting the door behind her.

The room was mostly in darkness, lit only by the table

lamp, the pool of light not quite reaching the walls. Gregor handed Ruby her tea, then sat where Constance had been on the other couch. In the dimness, she couldn't see his eyes, but as he turned his head, there was a glint where tears were gathering.

'I'm so sorry about that,' he said.

Ruby wasn't sure how to respond. She said, 'It's not your fault. She seems so . . .'

'Paranoid?'

'I was going to say different, to last week.'

Gregor nodded slowly. 'When it's good, I think it will be good forever, that she's better. That maybe, she'll be able to live independently. But then, out of the blue, she'll wake up in the morning, and there will be a look in her eye. And I'll know.'

'Know what?'

Gregor seemed to struggle with what he was about to say. He winced, as if in pain. 'I think of it like a demon, now. When it's bad, it's like there's a demon inside her, controlling her. Not letting the real Constance speak.'

'Sounds like it's really hard for you.'

'Yes. For both of us. Though when she's better she often forgets what she's said.'

Ruby thought of Marianne, then, and how it was hard to understand how very different she was when she was bad, how far from her sober self. She had blackouts, too, though Ruby wasn't sure whether Marianne really forgot what had happened or blocked it out deliberately, because of the shame. That wasn't the same, though. To an extent Marianne could have helped herself. Constance couldn't do that.

'You're so good to take this on, Gregor.'

'Not really. It was my carelessness that got us both into this mess in the first place. I'm seeing to my responsibilities, that's all. Leonie, I mean, though she's more than just a responsibility.'

'Yes, but with Constance. I don't know anyone who would do what you've done.'

'That's just it. You don't know the half of it. There are things I've done, that I knew were wrong at the time. I thought I was helping her, I really did, that it was worth the sacrifice. And now it's too late to go back.'

'What things?'

'I'm not sure I should tell you. I don't want you to think I'm a bad person.'

She moved closer. 'I'd never think that.'

After a long pause, he began. 'I helped her hide the pregnancy. And the birth. When it came to the labour . . . we did it on our own.'

'Do you mean, you delivered Leonie? Without help? No midwife or anything?'

He nodded, his forehead crumpling.

'But anything could have happened . . .'

'I know that. Don't you think I know that? She was in so much pain, I begged her to let me call an ambulance. But then, it all happened so fast, and afterwards they both seemed to be fine. So I just . . . went along with it.'

'My God, Gregor.' She couldn't get her head around it. 'What did you do with the . . . umbilical cord? With the afterbirth?'

He shuddered, looked like he might throw up.

'I don't want to talk about it. Can we not?'

Gregor's head dropped into his hands. Ruby heard a soft sob. She went to him, put her arm around him as he cried.

'I loved her once, you know. I still do, as the mother of my child. But when someone's ill, and you become a carer . . . It can kill it dead, even if you don't want it to. That sounds awful, doesn't it?'

'No, it doesn't,' said Ruby. 'It's understandable. And nobody's fault.' She thought she understood, now, why he wanted Ruby to keep Constance and Leonie a secret: the birth was the first lie, and to cover it up he'd had to keep lying. It was illegal not to register a birth. Every day they went without declaring it would complicate things further, make explaining their actions ever more difficult. Could he go to prison? Could Constance? Perhaps that was what he was really scared of, not the mental illness.

'It is my fault though. I failed them both when I ended it between us. It doesn't matter that we didn't intend on having a baby. Leonie deserves two parents.'

'Of course. Two good parents, and she's got that. It doesn't mean they have to be a couple.' She thought of her own parents then, who were really her biological grandparents. They'd stayed together, and provided a stable enough environment for her early years, but the cracks were there even for them, growing wider with the secret amounts of vodka that Marianne poured in. As for her biological father, Ruby had no idea where he was now. He was just a name, without even a face attached. A teenage boy at the time of her conception, he'd probably forgotten Ruby even existed.

'And now all I want is for her to be happy, to be well again.

Because, despite everything, she's a brilliant mother. Or she would be, given the chance.'

'Yes,' said Ruby. 'And you're more than a brilliant father. You're having to take care of Constance, too.'

He turned towards her, looked into her eyes. 'Ruby. Can I ask you something?'

Her heart started racing. 'Of course.'

'When I was out of the room, what did she say to you?'

Ruby hesitated. 'Why?'

'I feel like I don't know what's going on in her head any more. I hate to have to ask you, but she barely speaks to me these days.'

'She said something about a coat. I didn't understand it. I think it was part of her delusion.' She remembered the horrible accusation then, and instinctively moved away from him. 'She also said you . . . locked her in the bedroom. Did you actually do that, Gregor? Because if so . . .'

'Oh, Jesus,' said Gregor. 'Oh, no. This is how it started last time. It's worse than I thought.'

'What?'

'Look, I'll show you.'

He took out his smartphone and pressed play on a video. It took Ruby a second to realise what she was looking at. There on the screen was the room they were sitting in, from above. She looked up, searching for a camera, but could see nothing. In the video the room was dishevelled, and there was a figure moving around it, frantically searching.

'A burglar?'

'Look closer.'

It was Constance. She was pulling the room apart, removing

139

cushions from the sofas and throwing them, tipping chairs, pushing over the coffee table. She disappeared from shot and the camera switched to the kitchen.

'Do you have cameras everywhere?'

He grimaced, nodded his head, yes. 'I have to. It's for everyone's safety.'

On the screen, in the kitchen, Constance opened the cupboards and threw everything on the floor, packets of food, jars, the lot. The kettle went flying, water splashing against the wall. Shards of smashed plates scattered. She climbed on top of the surface and searched above the cupboards, dislodging rolls of kitchen towel, bottles of bleach. The next moment her face filled the screen. There was no light in her eyes, only anguish, her lips pulled back, teeth bared. Then, she jumped off the kitchen counter and opened the fridge, scooping out the contents and throwing food, cartons of drink, everything on to the floor, liquids spilling in pools. After she'd rummaged inside it, she started to drag the fridge towards her, out of its alcove, her small form demonstrating surprising strength.

'What's she doing?' said Ruby. 'She looks like she's totally out of it.'

'She's looking for the coat.'

'What coat is it, Gregor?'

'The one she told you about, that I'm supposedly hiding from her. The one that doesn't exist.'

Constance returned to the main room. She tried one of the doors, but it wouldn't open. Though there was no sound on the film, Ruby could feel the scream of rage and frustration that escaped from her then, her back arching, mouth twisted, fingers like claws, ripping out handfuls of her own hair.

'That's my room. I have to keep it locked, or she'd tear it apart.'

On the screen, the woman dragged an armchair towards the locked door. She struggled with it for a few seconds. Then she picked it up above her head and threw it straight at the door. As she did so, the outline of the baby bump was clearly visible.

'She's pregnant in this video?'

'Yes.'

'But, Gregor, isn't this dangerous? For the baby? I mean, the stress and everything.' She thought about how small Leonie was, how she wasn't yet walking. The way she was alert to everything her mother did.

'This is why I started working from home. I realised I couldn't leave her for any amount of time. When she was pregnant she couldn't take anything to help, no meds, not even herbal things. She was talking about the coat all the time, and when I wasn't there, this would happen.'

'Why a coat? Is it significant in some way? Seems pretty random.'

'It's to do with her family, the place she grew up in. Did she tell you much about it?'

'She said they were from the Hebrides. That the community has their own island.'

'You could call it a community. But I say it's a cult.'

'A cult?'

'When we met, at the party on the beach, at first I thought it was wild. The drumming, the dancing. We had a great time. The best. But once I got her away from the crowd, she was babbling such nonsense to me. I thought she was on drugs, then, but it was just that she was so indoctrinated. She was malnourished and brainwashed, and when I took her back in the morning, they'd all gone without her. Good riddance, I said, but she was heartbroken, couldn't accept that they'd done that, that they didn't care about her and wouldn't wait for her. She had nothing but what she stood up in, and I swear nothing she was wearing would constitute a coat. Anyway, I brought her home, got her some proper clothes, fed her up. She seemed to get better. We were so happy, for a short while. When she was about three months pregnant, that's when the delusions took hold. She said I'd taken her coat, meaning her skin. It's got tangled up in her mind. She thinks she puts on her coat and *turns into an actual seal*, Ruby.'

There was so much to take in. 'So, her family . . . abandoned her there?'

He nodded. 'So cruel. It sent her mad, I think. She needs therapy, a kind of decompression, anti-brainwashing. She never had the chance for that.'

Ruby felt it like a gut punch. It explained why she was losing her mind. Constance's problems suddenly made Ruby's seem trivial.

'What about all the seal stuff, though? It can't just be about the name.'

He sighed. 'Within the community, cult, whatever – there are stories. They're all to do with seal worship. Their version of Bible stories, I suppose. And they have rituals. When they come of age, there's a ceremony. On the solstice or the equinox or whatever, they wrap a sealskin coat around themselves, throw themselves into the sea and swim until dawn. They're convinced, when they come ashore, that they've been seals all night long, catching fish in their teeth, sleeping on rocks, all of that. Hallucinations brought on by the exhaustion, probably.'

'Must be freezing, the sea up there.' Ruby wrapped her arms around herself, shivering at the thought of it.

'It is. And the thing is, they don't all come back.'

'You mean they drown?'

'Well, yes. But that's not how they see it. If they don't come back, to them it's because they've decided to live as seals for the rest of their lives. The tribe are actually happy when that happens. The parents do a special ceremony, with dancing and feasting, and so on.'

'Wow,' said Ruby. 'So, you lose your kid forever, and you're happy?'

'I know. The things some people believe.' Gregor stared into the middle distance. 'Do you know there are hundreds of unidentified bodies that wash up on beaches, in morgues up and down the country?'

'Hundreds?'

'I'm not saying they're all from the Roane clan. But those that don't return have to wash up somewhere. Healthy, young people. Throwing themselves into the sea, thinking they'll turn into seals. The police probably assume it's suicide, but really, in my view, it's murder.'

Ruby rubbed her temples.

'I can't believe you've been dealing with all of this on your own.'

'The tranquillisers I got for her help a little bit, but I don't like to give them to her. I only do it when I need to go out, for work, or to the shops.'

'You leave Leonie alone with her when she's in that state?'

His face was suddenly angry, defensive. But then his shoulders slumped and he nodded. 'It's never for long, and she would never harm the baby. Never. I don't know what else to do. I couldn't work if I had Leonie with me. I can't get anyone to help me, there's no one I trust enough to keep our secrets.'

'No one at all?' He seemed to miss the implication, *what about me?*

'I told you, Ruby, there are things I've done, that if anyone found out, I'd be arrested. We both would. The birth . . .' he shuddered. 'If I could go back, I'd do it all differently. But I can't. I have to deal with it.'

Ruby looked down at the video, still running, of Constance hurling herself at the bedroom door repeatedly. The baby bump was barely visible under a loose shirt.

'I'll do it.'

'What do you mean?'

'I said I'd help. I can keep them company. Then you won't need to give her any tranquillisers. I can make sure she's OK. I'm not talking about care, I couldn't do that. Just company. And if she gets really paranoid, I can call you. From my new phone.'

'You would do that for me?'

'Yes. For you, and for Leonie.' She nearly said, *For Constance, too*, but stopped herself, not quite understanding why she wanted to hide from him her quiet sympathy.

Ruby had an urge to get away, then. To be alone to process everything. She stood up. 'I should go. It's late.'

'Already?'

She patted her pocket. 'I'm just on the end of a phone.'

Ruby bent to pick up her violin. When she turned back,

he was right there, standing close to her. She could hear his breath.

'It's good to be able to talk to someone, finally. I think I've been lonely. I just didn't want to admit it.'

She raised her face. His hand caught hers, thumb gently stroking. *I should step away*, she thought. Her feet did not move.

'I didn't mean to spend all night talking about Constance, again.'

'Then stop,' she said, her fingertip tracing his knuckle.

'I don't want to take advantage of you,' he said, leaning closer, letting his lips brush hers.

Ruby's eyelids fluttered closed. Her lips parted. Gregor's hand encircled the back of her neck with gentle fingers.

Suddenly, she went cold, realising what she was about to do.

'No,' she said, grabbing his wrist. 'Stop.'

Gregor stepped away, looking shocked. 'What's wrong?'

'This is,' she said.

'I thought you . . . wanted to.'

She did. So badly. The hurt on his face cut her deeply, and she wished with everything she had, that things could be different.

'I'm sorry,' was all she could say.

Ruby let the door to the flat slam shut as she ran down the stairs, wondering if she'd done the right thing, if she should have just gone ahead and let it happen. He was so perfect. And yet. There was too much to lose here. She couldn't betray another woman in that way. If there was even a chance that, when Constance was better, she and Gregor might get back together, for Leonie's sake she didn't want to be in the middle of that. And even if there was no chance, he'd said himself that she wasn't the one who wanted to split. If Constance still held a candle for the father of her child, then Ruby wasn't going to be the one who destroyed that dream for her. She was better than that. She had to be.

CHAPTER EIGHTEEN

NOW
The Injured Man

He hears muffled sounds. Voices. Two or three people are speaking, but he can't make out what they're saying. They're not talking to him, only to each other. There is darkness, and the beeping of machines. He appears to be floating, weightless, unsure which way is up; the voices are all around, above and beneath him, as if he's suspended among them. Then, a sharp certainty about what this is: he's in hospital. He can smell it now; cleaning fluid and the faint stench of human waste. Someone leans over him; their voice is booming near his face and he tastes perfume, thick and chemical in the back of his throat. He doesn't understand the words, though they are being pronounced clearly enough; nonsense syllables. No, that's not right. They're just speaking in a language he doesn't understand. He can't think in a straight line, the links between ideas are broken, thoughts floating as freely as he is. Nearby, someone is unfolding a blanket or a sheet, and shaking it out. It swishes, plasticky, and then it's laid on top of him. He fades out.

CHAPTER NINETEEN

NOW
Joanna

Saturday, 22 December

The officers gathered in the incident room, seats pulled out into rows facing front, where Joanna stood before a whiteboard. Atkinson sat nearby, to the side, his arms crossed, feet planted.

'OK, folks, we have a critically injured male, age thirty-eight, who was found at his home on Friday night, unconscious with a suspicious head wound. We are treating this as attempted murder, and so far, we have no suspects in custody.'

She turned around and pinned a large photograph of the injury on the back of Gregor's head to the board. There were one or two indrawn breaths, but mostly no reaction. Every person in the room often saw much worse.

'Unfortunately, Gregor is not expected to recover. Apart from this injury, he is also suspected to have ingested a quantity of prescription drugs, which we are also treating as suspicious. The charge therefore is likely to become murder, so watch for updates. Our priority is finding the perpetrator or perpetrators, but also, any family. We know next to nothing about this guy. Clive, any movement on next of kin?'

An officer seated by the window shook his head. 'Not yet, boss. I'm working on it.'

'Keep looking. There must be someone. No one in his phone that you can ID?'

'The numbers don't seem to connect.'

'What do you mean, they don't connect?'

'I mean, where there is a number for Dave or whatever, it literally won't connect. Some of the numbers aren't even long enough to be phone numbers. It's weird, as if his phone is full of fake contacts.'

There was a ripple of interest in the room. Harper had never come across this before. Once they'd opened up a phone and retrieved the contacts, finding a next of kin was usually fairly straightforward.

'What about call history?'

'There's an app on the phone called Whypr. It deletes all information, cookies, searches etc, at least once an hour. There's no way of recovering any call history at our end. We could try to contact the makers of the app, but I doubt they are storing any data, what with the data protection laws.'

'Also, why would they store it if they're in the business of getting rid of it?' said Jo. 'Did you find any photos on the phone? What about social media? Email?'

'No photos, and emails were connected to the Whypr app too. And as for social media contacts, the few that we have for him aren't current. There are one or two old school friends, but he hasn't interacted with them for over three years. He doesn't seem to use his Facebook or Instagram accounts at all, or very rarely. From everything I've seen, I think he's a bit obsessed with online privacy.'

'It would seem so.'

'We can try to get the phone cleared for tracing, to see where he's been in the last few weeks, at least. We might even be able to get more from the phone company data.'

Joanna addressed the assembled officers. 'OK. Until then it's the old-fashioned way. We need to look at his post, knock on doors, question all the neighbours and try to find some family or associates from local knowledge. Someone will be missing this person, and they will want to know what's happened to him.'

She pinned another photograph to the board. In this one, Gregor Franks was shown face up, eyes shut, tubes bisecting his face, with attachments entering his nose. Harper put her fists on her hips and frowned at it. 'Don't we have a better image than this? Steve?'

'Sorry, boss, yes we do. We have his driver's licence. I'll get the headshot blown up.'

'What about profile pictures? He must have something up on Facebook even if he doesn't use it much.'

'The profile picture he uses for everything isn't actually of his face. It's there on the desk, I printed it.'

Harper found the printout, pinned it to the board. It was a picture of crossed feet on a poolside lounger, a bottle of beer gently condensing on a side table.

'Did you mine the data on this photo?'

Clive said, 'Yes, it was taken five years ago, in the South of France, but I don't think those are our victim's feet: I also did an image search. It pops up everywhere, almost like a stock photo. Been used for various things: holiday websites, blogs.'

'What does he do for a living? Something to do with finance?'

'Property development, and investments. He works alone, out of a laptop. Doesn't even have an office.'

'If he's buying property, he must know people. He's a land-lord, so what about tenants?'

'He uses an agency. Never met any of his tenants, as far as I can tell.'

'He has to have a solicitor. And an accountant, probably. Find out who it is, would you? And we've got his bank details, so can someone get the data from the bank, please? At the scene we have Forensics working on DNA and fingerprint evidence, with a report expected today on the print pro-files, and later this week for DNA. We are currently looking with priority urgency for a female who was seen leaving the area with a child on the day the neighbour reported a leak through the ceiling that turned out to be from the bathroom above. That was Friday.'

One of the officers put a hand up.

'Yes?'

'Do we know when the victim was last seen alive?'

'He's not dead, Louise. Keep up.'

Nervous laughter burst from several people in the room. Louise Reynolds, a young community support team officer, was shamefaced. 'Sorry, boss. When was he last seen, before the incident?'

'A good point, I don't have that information, perhaps you could find out. We did a door-to-door of the immediate neighbours last night, but we need to expand that now. Get that sorted, would you, this morning?'

'Yes, ma'am. Also . . .'

'Yes?'

'I did notice something. Might not be relevant.'

'Go on.'

'The window, on Gregor's flat. It's overlooked by the window of one of the West block flats. Is it worth asking the tenants if they've seen anything?'

'Good idea,' said Harper, concentrating on not glancing at Atkinson, whose eyes she could feel on the side of her face. 'You might need to knock on all of the seventh-floor flats . . .'

'I looked at a floor plan. I know which one it is. Flat 7b.'

Ruby's place. Of course it was. Harper could barely control the nervous tic in her cheek. It wouldn't be anything to do with Ruby, though. There was no need to mention the connection. Was there? She said, 'Great. I'll follow that up, then.'

'You will?' said Atkinson. She looked straight at him. He was frowning, probably because, as SIO, she should have assigned a junior officer to take a statement.

Joanna wasn't going to be questioned. 'Anything to add, Steve?'

It took him a couple of seconds to gather his thoughts. 'Um, yep. We've managed to get a good likeness of the woman we suspect was living in Franks' apartment with the child. This is a still, from the train station CCTV.'

The woman in the picture had her hood up, as she had in the footage from the estate, but her pale face had been captured, finally. The dark eyes seemed haunted.

'What's she looking at?' asked Jo. In the wide shot the woman stood away from the other passengers, holding the child tightly against her chest. She stared intensely into the middle distance, as if frightened of whatever it was that she could see. But there was nothing there.

'We've circulated the picture to news outlets, and this morning there will be an appeal for witnesses. At this point we're thinking child protection, mainly. We don't know the name or circumstances, but we need to find this woman and child, to check there's nothing amiss.'

Another young officer said, 'She's not a suspect?'

'We need to rule her out.'

Harper said, 'In terms of evidence, did anyone manage to find any images of this woman inside the actual building?'

'Not yet,' said Atkinson. 'But we got this a few minutes ago.'

He pressed a button and the video projector came to life. It showed footage from the ticket office, a high angle showing the woman buying a ticket. Audio had been recorded from the microphone intercom system.

'Single to Cleethorpes, please.' The woman's voice was muffled, but it was clear she didn't have a Sheffield accent.

The officer issued the receipt, but the woman didn't take it immediately. She turned and shouted for the child, who'd run away into the crowds. *Leonie, stop.*

Atkinson paused the tape and looked at Jo. 'It's the same name,' they said together.

'That's confirmation of a link to Gregor Franks. So let's comb the system. Any child with that first name of the right age, involved in any incident, child protection or not.'

'Worth a shot,' said Atkinson, opening up his laptop.

CHAPTER TWENTY

THEN
Ruby

October

The next day, Gregor didn't contact her at all. Ruby stared at the blank screen of the new phone and tried not to fret. Yes, she'd pushed him away, cut him off when he was at his most vulnerable. It might have even looked, to him, like an out-and-out rejection. But couldn't he tell that she would have kissed him, if things had been different? Didn't he understand that it wasn't him that had set her running, but the fact that to have let it happen would have complicated things too much, for both of them? She was sure that he'd got the wrong idea, and his silence confirmed it.

Sleeping was a challenge, as the new phone glowed brightly every few seconds so that she kept thinking there was a message. Eventually, to end the madness, she forced herself to turn it off.

The day after that, hope returned. Switching the phone on, she remembered how pleased he'd been when he gave it to her. She was ashamed that she'd felt so ungrateful.

After it had started up, silence. There were no notifications, no messages that had been sent while the phone was off. Clicking on Gregor's name, the chat box was empty. *Last seen at 3.42am*, read the header. Yoga time.

Before she could think it through too much, she'd typed out a message.

Hi Gregor, how's things?

The answer came forty-two anxious minutes later, though the app told her that he'd seen the message the second she sent it.

Yes, fine thanks. Busy! Leonie wants to see you, maybe you could come tomorrow? Bring the fiddle?

It had been three full days then when, as requested, she stood at the entrance to his building, thinking, *maybe I'll just leave it. Maybe I'd be better off without him in my life; without any of them.* She thought she might not press the buzzer, that she ought to turn and walk away. Last week, in that brief window of having no phone, her life had been so peaceful. There was no one but herself to worry about. Maybe that was what she needed, now, to focus on herself rather than get involved with these people. Even if they were, in turn, gorgeous, mysterious, and cute as hell. It was more than she could handle right now. The sensible thing – the healthy thing – would be to leave.

She could post the phone he'd given her into his mailbox. Imagine how freeing that would be. But despite the thoughts, her decision to go home, her feet didn't move. Then, just when she was willing herself to turn away, the door buzzed and clicked open. *The cameras*, she realised, as she went through and towards the lifts. *He must have been watching.*

Gregor beamed from the doorway, welcoming her, delighted to see that she'd brought the violin. It was as if nothing had happened, or – maybe better – that he'd forgiven her entirely and put aside his hurt feelings. He took her jacket, made her a drink, smiled warmly. While Constance rested in the bedroom, the two of them spent a delightful hour playing with Leonie, and when Constance appeared she seemed cheerful, asked if Ruby would like to help with bath time. Later, as Leonie settled down, Ruby played lullabies. When the child was asleep she played a soothing nocturne, mainly for Constance, who seemed tired by then but much calmer than before. As the bow moved across the strings, Gregor watched Ruby, his eyes full of admiration.

Finally, after Constance headed to bed, Ruby and Gregor were alone. Without the presence of either Constance or Leonie, Gregor's demeanour changed. The temperature in the room seemed to drop. She glanced at him, and caught a shadow of the awkwardness she'd seen the last time they were alone, right before she ran.

She sat next to him on the couch, cleared her throat. 'Are you OK?'

He moved infinitesimally further away. 'Why wouldn't I be?'

'I wanted to apologise for what happened the other night.'

'Nothing happened though, did it? So you've nothing to apologise for. Everything's fine.'

She swallowed. His body language had shifted, his hands clutched together in his lap.

'It's clearly not fine,' she said.

'I get it, OK? I've been friendship-zoned.'

'No . . .'

'Look,' he turned to her, softening, the warm smile returning. 'I understand, I really do. It's happened before. I know I'm not much of a catch. Too much baggage. Why would anyone want this?' he gestured to himself, to his handsome face, his strong, supple body, toned by hours of nocturnal yoga sessions and daily cardio. She frowned.

'Are you going to force me to compliment you?' He must have been aware of how he looked, of the effect he had on women. He was solvent, handsome, well-spoken, tall. Up until this point she would have said he was modest, but this outlandish display of self-deprecation simply didn't ring true.

He folded his arms. 'I wouldn't try that. I'd be waiting a long time.'

Ruby had had enough. 'Well, you can wait a bit longer, then.' She took a deep breath, stood up and gathered her bag and jacket.

'Please don't go,' he said. 'I'm sorry. I was being a dick.'

She walked towards the door.

'You're coming back though, right?' he said. 'Tomorrow?'

She stopped, but didn't turn. 'I don't know.'

'Leonie loves you,' he said. 'And Constance does too.'

'Constance loves me? Really? I doubt it.'

He paused. 'Well, she likes you. I can tell.'

'But what about us? I can't keep coming over if it's going to be awkward.'

'It won't be. I guess my pride was hurt a little. But I'll get over it.'

'It might be better if I stay away for a while.'

'No, please, Ruby. Even if it's only for the music. I think I'd die if I couldn't hear you play.'

Will that always be enough for you, though, she wondered. And for how long will it be enough for me?

As she walked out of the door, he called after her. 'You said you'd help me. Didn't you?'

Ruby turned to face him. 'Of course I'll help you. I just need some time. A day or so. Then I'll be back.'

Their eyes met and she hesitated as if she might go to him, embrace him, let it happen the way she both wanted it to, and didn't want it to. She took a breath, to strengthen her resolve. She left without another word.

CHAPTER TWENTY-ONE

NOW
The Social Worker

Sunday, 23 December

Diane is driving home from a job when she turns on the radio. It's the news.

> *A man has been found in a critical condition at his home in Sheffield. Police are appealing for witnesses. A woman, wanted for questioning by police, is missing, along with a child aged between eighteen months and two years. The pair were last seen boarding a train from Sheffield to Cleethorpes on Friday afternoon. If anyone has any information about their whereabouts they are asked to contact Greater Yorkshire Police on . . .*

Diane's first thought is, *I don't have time for this*. She keeps driving, grimly determined to go home, thinking that she deserves a bit of rest, now, despite whatever this is. Probably nothing, anyway. It's Sunday, and she's just removed three children from their mother, having been called in on her day off. The mother is a drug user but it's mostly her partner the children are being protected from: there's a legal order of no contact between the man and the children, but the mother seems as addicted to him as she is to the heroin. Diane took them early this morning with the help of specially trained enforcement officers. She unpeeled the middle one's fingers from the mother's scarred and unresisting wrist, carried her to the car. She delivered them to foster carers, all three children stunned and dirty and the little one screaming his head off. Diane is brewing a cold. She just wants a sit-down, and a cup of tea, and some more painkillers.

She turns off the radio, but she can still hear the announcer in her head, like an echo. *A missing woman, and a child aged between eighteen months and two years.* On Friday. In Cleethorpes. From Sheffield. Could be a coincidence, she thinks. It can't be the two she had in the police car, outside the shop, the nice woman, the big fuss over nothing. Constance and Leonie, the mother she spoke to, that she let go without so much as a background check. The little girl they found on the seafront, who turned out to be not abandoned, but simply lost. Surely not. And yet she is suddenly filled with the cold possibility that she's made a giant, career-derailing mistake.

She feels sick and giddy, and fears that she'll lose control of the car. She manages to pull up in a side street and turn off the engine. Closing her eyes, Diane takes one slow breath, and another.

She literally jumps in her seat when her phone starts ringing. It is Belinda, the Senior Social Worker for the area. Her voice is as harsh as dogs barking in Diane's ear.

'I've just had a call from Detective Sergeant Joanna Harper

at Greater Yorkshire Police. She says police officers attended a missing child incident of yours on Friday, and the mother is a person of interest in an inquiry into a serious assault. I can't find anything on the database.'

Diane doesn't say anything. She hears the blood rushing in her ears.

'Diane? Are you still there? What's the reference? Name of the mother? Maybe you made a mistake inputting the date.'

'No, it's not that. I didn't write it up yet.'

This time Belinda doesn't say anything. She clears her throat with such powerful passive-aggression that Diane shivers.

Diane goes on, 'I've got the notes. Handwritten. I . . .'

'Where are you?'

'It might not be the same people, I mean, this was only a lost child, not anything that needed our attention. The woman I saw was genuine. It was a genuine mistake. I was sure.'

'It is the same woman. The local police officers who were attending have already given a name and the description matches the person they're looking for. They said they left it to you to deal with the details.'

'I did deal with it, as far as I thought it was appropriate. I was sure it didn't require intervention. At the time. She seemed really normal. I didn't think . . . it can't be her. They must have made a mistake. Maybe there were two missing child incidents?'

'Oh, and two Diane Rathbones, I suppose? They've got your name in their report. They want to see yours. To cross-reference the details.'

'What's it got to do with the man they found in Sheffield? I don't see how it can be connected.'

Diane's head feels like it is being compressed in a vice. The cold she's had coming for days has laid itself down on her like a wet blanket over her face. She blows her nose and a palmful of green snot collects in the tissue, some of it escaping and running down the heel of her hand. She wipes it up as best she can. She feels like crying, but she knows she won't, it's just that she always feels like crying when she's talking to Belinda.

Belinda says, 'I don't need to tell you how badly you have screwed this up, Diane. You need to go in to the office now, and write up what you can, and explain to the police why your report is dated two days late.'

The phone goes dead.

When she arrives at the office, Belinda is waiting, arms folded, bum perched on Diane's desk. She is wearing a holly-green velvet dress with a silver tinsel trim around the bottom, but her face is far from festive.

'That DS is coming over to see you. She'll be here in about an hour.'

Diane nods. 'I'll be ready.'

'What were you thinking, Diane?'

'I was trying to see the good in people, all right? I'm always judging people, playing God with their lives. I just wanted to let everyone forget about it and get on with their day. How was I supposed to know she'd . . . done whatever it is she's supposed to have done? I can't know everything, can I?'

Belinda narrows her eyes.

'How long have you been in this job?'

'Sixteen years. Give or take. Why?'

'What made you think you didn't need to follow procedure in this case?'

I just couldn't face it, thinks Diane. The forms, the grief, the mother's inevitable protest. I wanted to be the good guy, for a change. That child was happy, she was sure of it. Absolutely certain.

'I decided there was no need for intervention. So the procedure was irrelevant. That's all.'

Belinda's voice is low, and dark. It cuts like tiny knives. 'The procedure was irrelevant? Not even an incident form, a statement from the mother?'

Hearing Belinda say it, she realises how very unprofessional it sounds. She sinks into her chair and rests her arms on the desk, allows her head to droop momentarily.

'I'm not very well, Belinda.' It comes out whiny, like a child declaring that she has a tummy-ache.

The other woman snorts, implying that Diane is pathetic. Fair enough, thinks Diane; what kind of an excuse is that, for a grown-up?

'Well, I hope you have the contact details at the very least.'

Diane presses a tissue to her streaming nose. 'Of course. I was going to pass them on to the service in Sheffield, when I had time.'

'I suppose that's something. Let me see.'

Belinda holds out her hand for the note, then takes it over to her desk. She types for a few seconds.

'Huh. Fake address. Haven't you checked it?'

'No, I told you. I've been snowed under.'

'Fake name, too, I'll bet.'

Diane's head throbs. She wonders again if it is too soon for another painkiller.

CHAPTER TWENTY-TWO

NOW
Joanna

Sunday, 23 December

On the motorway, Joanna mused on the particular tragedy of this year's Christmas, trying to look at the positives. Yes, Ruby had gone AWOL from their lives, and at this time of year it hurt more than usual. She'd been dreading Christmas Day without Ruby, the empty spot at the table sure to bring back memories of the fight the previous year. Marianne would be drunk, as usual, Dad would be struggling to keep up the pretence, as usual. Jo had hoped that the day after the fight, when Marianne sobered up and learned what her words and actions had done, she might seek help in earnest. Instead, she'd sunk further, had progressed from being drunk almost every day to being drunk every day, without fail, allowing herself to pour the first measure a fraction earlier each time. Joanna found it hard not to let her anger towards her mother show; whenever they were together, Jo fantasised about grabbing Marianne's frail shoulders and shaking her back to sobriety. So, on the upside, it was a relief to have an excuse to duck out.

Atkinson, in the passenger seat, sighed dramatically, breaking Harper's train of thought.

'Honestly, if people could just choose to try to top each other any other week, it would really help my personal life.'

'Ah, her at home not happy, I take it?'

'She's not. And, I was going to . . . never mind.'

'You were going to what?'

'Oh, it's just— I bought a ring.'

Without taking her eyes off the road, Jo let out a little whoop of joy, leaned over and slapped Atkinson on the knee. 'Congratulations!'

'I haven't actually asked her yet, don't jinx it.'

'Mate, she will say yes. I'm really happy for you.'

'Well, we'll see, won't we?'

'How could she not?'

'If you get me home before Christmas is over completely, then there might be a chance. A slim chance.'

Harper laughed, assuming he was joking. Atkinson grimaced, and looked out of the window at the traffic.

Whatever Felicia ended up saying to Steve in response to his proposal, it was unlikely to go as badly as it had for Joanna the previous morning. He'd planned it, for a start, bought a ring. He actually wanted to get married, too, wasn't just throwing it out as a pathetic attempt to hold onto something he wasn't even sure was the right thing. Jo still didn't know where Amy had gone, though she planned to try to find out later, to make sure things were OK between them. This morning, after a starfish sleep and a quick series of hill sprints, she had returned her road bike to its familiar place in the hallway, where the stacks of high-heeled shoes had been until very recently. The feeling was bittersweet.

Grimsby was suitably named. Although it was on the coast, the industrial town wasn't a typical tourist destination, dominated as it was by the fisheries and the seafood processing factories. It didn't look good, it didn't smell good. Cleethorpes, a couple of miles south with its famous beaches, was the place people were drawn to, but the bigger town of Grimsby was where the police and social services were based. Much of the older housing stock appeared neglected, and as they got closer to the centre the sky turned from grey to muddy brown with approaching rain.

So much for a white Christmas, thought Harper, turning up the radio for a bit of festive cheer in the face of Atkinson's persistent Scrooge-like countenance.

They parked on the street outside the concrete-and-glass municipal building where the social services were housed, and were soon shown into an interview room by a woman in an ill-fitting suit who said her name was Belinda Sumpter.

'I spoke to you on the phone, didn't I?' said Jo.

'That's right. Diane's the one who dealt with the case in question. She won't be long. She's just locating her notes. I'll let her know you're here.'

They followed Belinda past the main office, a large room with about fifteen desk booths. Only one of the booths was occupied, by a sweaty-looking woman, typing furiously. A few minutes later, very apologetic, she appeared at the door clutching a sheaf of printouts.

The social worker looked absolutely fucking terrible. Red nose, streaming eyes, skin almost grey.

'Thanks for making the time to see us. Have a seat. You know why we're here?'

Diane nodded.

'Just before we start, are you feeling OK?'

Diane tried to smile. Her eyes were small and red-rimmed. She withdrew a lump of damp tissue from her handbag, started trying to straighten it out. 'I've got a bit of a cold, that's all.'

Joanna took out some hand sanitiser and squeezed a blob into her palm, rubbed her hands together, feeling the alcohol evaporate, relaxing slightly as she imagined all those germs dying. The last thing she needed was to get ill herself. Beside her, Atkinson drew out a package of tissues and handed Diane a fresh one.

'Thanks, love.' There followed a great wet nose-blowing.

Jo said, 'Yesterday, my officers entered the apartment of a man called Gregor Franks, who lives in the New Park estate over in Sheffield. He's been quite badly injured and taken to hospital, and has yet to regain consciousness. We're trying to trace a woman who we suspect may be connected to the victim. She's travelling with a child. I believe, on Friday, you attended an incident along with some local officers, in which a woman and child of the right age were detained.'

'Initially, they were detained,' said Diane. 'It seemed to me that there wasn't a problem, so they were allowed to be on their way.'

Jo nodded. 'Just to confirm the details, what were their names?'

'The mother was called Constance Douglas. The girl was called Leonie Douglas.'

Atkinson made a note. 'Tell us what happened. From the beginning.'

'We had an emergency call from the police about a lone child, a toddler, who'd been found on the seafront. A shop-keeper had opened his door and she'd just wandered in. No adult to be seen anywhere nearby, and it was freezing. I went there expecting to do an emergency referral, but by the time I got there, the mother had turned up.'

'What did she say?'

'She explained that she'd lost sight of the child, who was a bolter, always running off. She said she'd been looking for her everywhere. It seemed fine. Genuine mistake. Tragedy averted.' Diane did a small, unconvincing 'ha ha'. Both police officers regarded her with stony faces.

Atkinson said, 'Did she say why she hadn't called the police? The 999 was from the shopkeeper.'

'She said she'd been frantically searching. And it hadn't been that long, either. The police must have got there very quickly.'

Harper checked her notes. 'Less than three minutes from the call to when the first officer arrived on scene. Impressive. I guess sometimes you're in the right place at the right time.'

Diane threw her hands in the air. 'Well, there you go. If the mother hadn't found her when she did, she most probably would have called 999. But she did find her, and she would have done whether the police had been involved or not. If the shopkeeper had waited a minute or so more, the situation would have resolved itself. But there was no harm done.'

Jo thought that Diane Rathbone's body language seemed overly defensive. She glanced at Atkinson, who gave a bland smile. To Joanna, his eyes conveyed his scepticism.

'What did you put in the report?' he said. 'Will there be any follow-up?'

'I was going to hand the details to Sheffield Social Services, so that they could do a routine check in six weeks' time.'

'You were going to? You didn't do it already? How long does it usually take?'

There was a tight pause. 'I've got a lot on. As you can imagine. I was going to do it, and then it was the weekend, so it was going to have to wait until tomorrow. And like I said, it wasn't a priority.'

'Was there anything on your database about them, the mother or the child? Any previous contact with social services?' asked Joanna.

Diane pursed her lips. 'I didn't check.'

'Oh?'

The social worker gave Jo a hard glare. 'I had to remove three children from their mother this morning. Two days before Christmas. Do you know what that feels like, Detective Sergeant?'

Joanna's voice was calm and pleasant when she said,

'Have you checked now?'

Diane mumbled something incoherent.

'What's that?'

'I said, Belinda did. Turns out the address the woman gave me was a false address.'

Harper left a pointed pause. She was starting to get very slightly annoyed by Diane Rathbone. 'What I don't understand, from what you're telling me, is why you decided it was nothing to worry about. What was it about Constance Douglas that made you think she wasn't a risk to the child?

She'd lost her, for a good amount of time, and not thought to call for help.'

'I had to make a judgement call. I assumed she just wasn't thinking.'

Jo had to assume that Diane wasn't thinking, either. She should have known better. As for suggesting the shopkeeper ought to have waited to call 999, no social worker worth their salt would recommend a delay in alerting the authorities if a child was found alone on the street in wintery conditions. The cold Diane was suffering from must have been brewing for days; perhaps it had skewed her judgement.

'OK, Diane. Let's see if we can start again. Our victim is named Gregor Franks, and there's a possibility that he is the father of the child. Let's assume that Leonie is the child's real first name. Can we try searching for the name Leonie Franks on the social services database? And maybe Constance Franks? Also, this address?' She gave Diane a piece of paper with Gregor's address on it. Then she turned to Atkinson. 'Can you . . .'

He was already opening his laptop. 'I'll search for the names Leonie and Constance Douglas on the police database, boss, right away.'

A few minutes later, they had each drawn a blank.

'So. Constance Douglas doesn't appear on the social services database. Nor Constance Franks, nor Leonie Douglas, Leonie Franks.'

Jo had to assume from now on that all the names were false. They were looking for an invisible mother, and an invisible child.

'But she seemed so normal,' said Diane. 'She seemed so

– and I know this sounds terrible – but she was middle-class. I don't see many like that. Very nice, you know?'

Jo squinted at Diane. The woman had lost all sense of perspective. She wouldn't be surprised if this case led to an internal investigation by the service, and even this person's suspension. That might not be such a bad thing for the vulnerable children of Grimsby. Diane could do with a rest, at the very least. She had the word *burnout* written all over her.

'There's one more thing we need you to help us with. I have a CCTV image of Constance in Sheffield train station on her way to Cleethorpes. Then the cameras catch her again leaving Cleethorpes station, but we can't find her returning, or getting on a train. She certainly never came back to Sheffield. We need to know where she went.'

'That doesn't make any sense. I know there's a camera opposite the entrance.'

'We didn't pick her up after she got off the train at Cleethorpes.'

'So, she never got on the train? She's still in Cleethorpes?'

'Possibly. Or she was covering her face when she went past the cameras. I've got an officer scouring the footage at the moment, but it's a slow process. Here's the image we have of her.'

She showed Diane the image on the police tablet. There was the woman, her hood pulled up, dark hair showing. Those haunted eyes. Diane's face creased in confusion.

'That's not her. That's not the woman I spoke to. I knew it. I knew there had to be a mix-up.'

'That's not Constance?'

'No. The woman I talked to wasn't as thin. She had different hair. Let me see it again.'

Harper watched as, if it were possible, even more colour drained from Diane's face.

'Oh, no. How can that . . .?'

'What is it?'

'That, without a doubt, is not the same woman I spoke to on Tuesday. But it's the same child. That's Leonie.'

'What?'

They all stared at the screen.

'What does this mean?' said Atkinson.

'It means,' said Jo, 'that whoever's got Leonie, it isn't the same woman who left the New Park estate on Tuesday, carrying her.'

'So, the woman I spoke to . . . wasn't her mother? Or was her mother? If . . . then . . . so who is this?' Diane grabbed her own head as if she was in sudden pain. Harper thought, yup, investigation, suspension.

'Could have been anyone,' said Joanna. 'And who knows where the real Constance has gone. If this woman is even really called Constance. Meanwhile, there's a seriously injured man lying comatose in a hospital bed, whose child may have been abducted.'

Joanna looked again at the image on the tablet. An invisible child, no records, no way of knowing that she even exists, except for this bit of footage. Well, thought Jo, she's not invisible to me.

She turned to Atkinson. 'We can do facial recognition with Leonie. We'll be able to track her that way, and find out where she's gone, and who with. Come on.'

They stood up and started to leave the room.

'Wait,' said Diane, 'let me see it one more time.'

Harper handed over the tablet.

'So strange,' said Diane.

'What is?' asked Harper.

'This woman, she's wearing exactly the same clothes as the woman I spoke to.'

'Really?'

'Yes, and she had the same bag, that changing bag.'

Very odd indeed, thought Jo.

'There is one difference, though.'

'What's that?'

'That leather holdall thing she's got. I never saw that.'

When they zoomed out, the item was clear to see. Strange that they hadn't noticed it before, wrapped across the woman's body exactly like a papoose. In the footage, while she held tightly on to the child with both arms, at all times one hand possessively gripped the edge of this papoose as if it contained something equally as precious.

CHAPTER TWENTY-THREE

THEN
Ruby

November

'Mamma Bee!'

Ruby lived for the sound of the little feet padding down the hallway in her direction. The baby had progressed this week, from bum-shuffling to running in a matter of days. Ruby wasn't worried about her development any more, she'd looked it up. Sometimes kids didn't walk until they were two, sometimes they talked non-stop from before the age of one. Leonie was a child of extremes, but she was certainly progressing within the wide range of 'normal'. It was like a miracle; you could watch this person growing almost in real time.

'Look, Mamma Bee, got socks!' Leonie pulled her socks off, one by one. 'Here go!'

'Thank you, honey.' As Ruby bent to take the socks, she caught an unmistakable odour coming from Leonie. 'Hey, you need a change, baby?' Ruby picked her up and took her through to the changing table in the bathroom. She was getting to be quite the expert at nappies, and feeding, and all the other things she'd been helping with recently. She pulled up the little girl's tights and set her back on her feet, let her lead the way through the door to where her mother was.

'All clean!' Leonie declared, thundering into the space, heading straight for the toy box.

In the living room, Constance was curled on the couch in her usual spot. Ruby tried to discreetly gauge how unfocused she was today, how vague she seemed, how distant. Sometimes it was as if the other woman couldn't keep her eyes open. Other times she didn't seem to be aware that Ruby was even there until she started playing her violin. Then, there were good days.

'Hi, Constance.'

It was a good day. Constance smiled. 'Hi, Bee.' Her eyes drifted across to the seascape, but they came right back to Ruby.

Gregor leaned in the kitchen doorway, arms crossed, still in his yoga pants. The two of them had fallen into an almost-easy friendship, punctuated with occasionally awkward moments when they accidentally touched, or she caught him gazing at her for a little too long. What had passed between them hadn't gone away, but she thought they'd found a balance, and that it was worth making the effort to keep it steady.

'Moosic, Mamma Bee. Pleeeese.' Leonie was tugging Ruby's violin case towards her so that she'd play all the tunes she loved to dance to. And Ruby loved to see it, the little hips swaying from side to side, arms pumping. Pure joy. She played 'Molly Malone', and Leonie's favourite, 'A Fox Went Out on a Chilly Night', bending the notes just like on the old American Bluegrass version she knew so well.

'I know a song,' said Constance.

She started to sing, a haunting melody, sad and moving.

Ionn da, ionn do ion da, od-ar, da

It made Ruby think of the ocean, and of the night sky; deep and mysterious. After a few times round, she joined in with her violin. Leonie swayed to the slow beat. Gregor didn't say anything. His face was strangely blank.

'Beautiful,' said Ruby. 'What's it called?'

'It's hard to translate,' said Constance. 'It's a cry of joy. "The Seal-Woman's Joy"? We sing it to each other. I mean, back home, they do. They did.'

Just then, Leonie tripped over her feet and fell, her head catching the corner of one of the wooden bricks. Constance sprang from the couch in an instant and scooped up the little girl, whose face was contorted with pain. Leonie inhaled for a long few seconds, then started to cry. Or, she looked as if she was crying, but she wasn't making any sound.

'Did you hurt yourself, baby? Don't cry,' said Constance. A lump was forming on Leonie's head. She continued to cry, but the only noise coming out between the girl's jerky inhalations was a high wheeze, like air escaping from a puncture.

'I'll get an ice pack.' Gregor went to the kitchen.

'What's wrong with her?' Ruby whispered to Constance. 'Why is she silent? Is she choking?'

'This is how she cries. Always. Barely a sound.'

'But that's not normal. You know that, right?'

A frown creased Constance's forehead as she stroked Leonie's hair. She tipped her head towards the kitchen. 'He doesn't like noise.'

'Dammit,' said Gregor, from the other room. 'No ice.'

Ruby thought she saw Leonie's small body tense up at the

sound of his voice. She curled closer to her mother, became very still.

'Hey, baby,' said Ruby, touching Leonie's arm. She flinched, and Ruby drew away. 'Daddy's not angry with you, don't worry.'

Constance's face was solemn, her eyes intense as she gazed at Ruby over her daughter's head.

By the time Gregor returned with a pack of frozen peas wrapped in a towel, Leonie had stopped the silent crying. She wriggled to be let down, had apparently forgotten that she'd even hurt herself, despite the half-egg sticking out of her forehead. Constance tried to put the cold pack on her forehead but the child batted it away and toddled off, bump and all, to carry on playing as if nothing had happened.

'So brave,' said Gregor. 'That's my girl.'

Later he walked Ruby to the door. 'Thanks for tonight. You're a good friend to us.'

'It's no trouble. I love coming over. And that song, wow. It's like a gift every time she teaches me something new.'

Their eyes met, and Ruby was suddenly aware that they were alone together. Gregor shuffled his feet awkwardly. 'Well, I'll see you next time, then.'

Ruby said, 'I wanted to ask you . . .'

'She's been better recently, Constance. Don't you think so?'

Ruby wasn't sure she agreed, in general. 'She's better today, sure. But Gregor, when Leonie was crying . . .'

'Oh, that. I've got used to it now. She's not like other kids, right? You don't need earplugs.' He laughed a little, then stopped when he realised she was serious.

'But why is she like that? Is there something wrong with her? Did you teach her not to cry?'

Gregor's eyes darkened. 'And how do you imagine I would teach a baby not to cry, precisely?'

'Well, I don't know, but Constance said . . .'

He hissed at her, angry now. 'Constance said? Didn't I explain what's going on with her? You can't trust anything she says, the woman's delusional.'

'Gregor, let go, you're hurting me.'

He looked down at where he'd grabbed her upper arm and immediately released her. Mouth open, he stared at his hand like he didn't recognise it.

'Ruby, I'm so sorry, I didn't mean . . .'

She backed away from him, rubbing her arm, a bruise forming. Then she looked at his face, and saw that he was about to cry.

'It's fine,' she said, though despite the pity she felt for him, it was not. 'No harm done.'

'Are you sure? Oh, God, I don't know why I did that. Seriously, I'm really sorry. Did I hurt you?'

He searched her face, but she couldn't quite meet his eye. 'Not really.'

'I'm such an idiot. Let me see . . .'

She drew further away, towards the door, as he reached out to try to touch her. 'No, honestly, I'm OK. But I should go, anyway.'

'Don't . . . I mean, you can leave, of course you can. And I would understand if you didn't want to come back, after what I just did.'

A tear slid from his eye. He hung his head, shoulders slumped.

'I'm sorry too,' said Ruby. Though for what, she wasn't entirely sure.

CHAPTER TWENTY-FOUR

NOW
Joanna

Sunday, 23 December

Joanna gathered the team together in the incident room. She brought up a grainy image, an enlarged section from the train station CCTV, of the little girl wearing her pink bobble hat.

'Priority number one is safeguarding this child. Leonie – assuming that's her real name – is not registered with any midwife or health visitor team, nor with social services or the NHS. Also, although we strongly believe that Leonie and her mother live or have lived recently in Gregor Franks' apartment, neither the electoral roll nor the council tax listing show anyone apart from Gregor at the address. As for the mother, all we have so far is this image.' She pointed to the photo from the station CCTV in Sheffield of the woman with dark hair buying a ticket.

'And this is where it gets interesting. Whoever this person is, it's not the same person who was allowed to leave with the child on Friday night. This is the reason facial recognition software didn't track where she went after she returned to the station, because she never did.'

One of the PCs said, 'I don't understand.'

'I can't explain it, either, Jade, but these are the facts we're working with.'

Harper stuck a silhouette of a woman's face next to the picture of the woman at the train station. It was a drawing, meant to represent the woman they didn't have an image of yet. It had a white question mark in the centre.

'Two different women, one name: Constance. I want to know, firstly, what happened to this one, the one who had the child first of all. And secondly,' she pointed to the silhouette, 'Who is this one, what does she look like, and where is she now? She was the one last seen with the child, and therefore she's the one we need to track as a priority. Any update on the media shout-out? Any leads?'

Clive said, 'We haven't had any useful calls from the public after the news bulletin. Maybe we should do another one.'

A young man knocked and was waved into the room. Dressed in civvies, tall and lanky, he looked like a member of the tech department, which was exactly what he was. 'Jo?'

'Yes, Eddie?'

'We found her. The second one.'

'Good work,' said Harper. 'From the Cleethorpes station cameras?'

'Yes. We loaded Leonie's face into the software and it pinged straight away. She might have told the Social that she was going back to Sheffield, but from the timecode on the ticket office camera you can see that she actually bought a ticket to Edinburgh.'

She's running, thought Joanna, and held out her hand for the A4 printout. When she looked at the photo, she immediately wanted to throw up. She tried not to react outwardly in any way, not in front of all these officers.

'I have a bigger image with more detail,' said Eddie. 'This one is a close-up of the face, but in the wider image she's waiting on the station, holding the child.'

'I think I need to see that one, if you don't mind.' Even Joanna could tell that her voice was uncharacteristically soft.

Eddie said, 'Sure, not a problem. Give me a few minutes.' He left the room.

How can it be her, thought Jo, as she turned slowly towards the whiteboard, still holding the image in both hands. It didn't make any sense.

Someone cleared their throat, and she realised she hadn't said anything for a weirdly long time.

'Um,' she said. 'This is our second person of interest. So.' She pinned the image up and took down the question-mark silhouette. As she faced the room, thirty inquisitive pairs of eyes studied her, every one trained to spot a liar. Joanna rubbed her palms together uncertainly. What did she just do? Why didn't she say anything? It wasn't if she could keep the truth from them forever. She needed to tell them. Now.

'That's it for now, folks. Get to work.'

Chairs scraped as they were pushed back and everyone got up to leave. Atkinson was staring at her. He waited until the room was clear before he spoke.

'You OK, boss?' he asked. 'You look like you've seen a ghost.'

For a second she considered telling him. In the corner of

her eye Ruby stared down at them from the board, so much older than she'd seemed last time Joanna had seen her. Apart from evident anxiety, Ruby's face was closed, expression indecipherable; holding on to her secrets, as always.

'Oh, nothing,' said Jo. 'I mean yes, fine. Sorry. I've just got a bit of . . . indigestion. I think I need a drink of water.' She pushed past him and out of the room before he could respond.

In the bathroom, she splashed water on her face and stared at herself in the mirror. She was pale as paper; her hands shook as she re-tied her blonde hair into its topknot. When she reached into her pocket for a tissue, her fingers touched the box containing the silver ring she'd been carrying around since Ruby's birthday, that she hadn't sent, that she'd hoped she would be able to give to Ruby in person. She took it out, slipped the tip of her finger inside it to feel the engraved inscription. Not simply a birthday present, the ring was an apology, a promise, and an olive branch, supposed to be the first step in healing the rift between them. She turned the ring in the light and the letters glinted. *Filia mea et soror mea et cor meum.* My sister, my daughter, my heart.

CHAPTER TWENTY-FIVE

NOW
The Injured Man

Dreams

He hears the faint slap-slap of a spinning rope, a pair of feet taking off and landing, over and over. The dark place has transformed into a hospital room, but it's not the muted white and grey tones of a normal hospital. The walls have no windows or doors, are twice as high as they should be, and they glow with lurid menace. The whole scene is wonky, over-saturated with colour. There is a girl in the corner, skipping.

> *Cinderella, dressed in yell-er,*
> *Went upstairs to kiss a fella*
> *By mistake, she kissed a snake*
> *How many doctors will it take?*
> *1, 2, 3, 4*

She's holding up her fingers with the numbers. When she gets to number four, the wooden handle falls from her hand. She comes closer, her bare and toughened feet shuffling along the vinyl, the rope trailing behind her. The man tries to move, to sit up, and finds that he cannot. The girl seems to know that he is trapped, a fly in her web. It's a dream, he tells himself, and she's been conjured by his imagination. Perhaps if he shuts his eyes, when he opens them, she'll be gone. He shuts his eyes tight, and waits.

When he opens his eyes she's right up in his face. He jumps, hard, and lets out a scream. All he sees is her wide, white-and-blue eyes, her grinning mouth, the black holes of her nostrils, her fringe hanging down. He smells her breath, sweet and foul with rot, but he can't turn his face away. She is sitting astride his chest, crouching there like an evil little imp. He tries to scream again, to make her move. But either she can't hear him, or she doesn't care.

Get off me get off help me someone please help

The grin grows slowly on her face as she sits up and regards him with a cold kind of interest, as if he is a specimen that she has collected. The fact that he's sure this is happening inside his head is no comfort. There's no escape. He is trapped there with this malevolent girl, who he thinks he knows and is sure hates him and he can't move or speak or get away, and it's not fair, why is this happening to him?

Then, the girl lifts her arm and fans out her fingers over his face. The pinkie is missing, cleaved off at the base. He remembers, then, who she is and how he knows her, and the knowledge of it makes him freeze with dread. He looks again, to make sure, but there's no mistake. It's his sister, Dora. She died in 1997, aged eight. He remembers, as a teenager, feeling angry with her, because after she died he was the only one there to help on the farm. Their parents barely spoke to him again, unless it was to talk about the search for his sister. They never found the body, and yet, here she is.

A drop of blood from the stump of the girl's little finger falls in his open eye, turning half of the world a grisly red. He screams. He fades out.

CHAPTER TWENTY-SIX

NOW
Joanna

Sunday, 23 December

Eddie looked at her over the top of his thin-framed spectacles. 'I got the image you wanted.'

This time, when he handed it over, she was ready. Atkinson was watching her carefully. She shot him a look, a kind of what-are-you-looking-at-exactly, and he shifted his eyes away, pretended he hadn't been looking.

Briskly, she pinned up the print. There was her baby girl, without question. The picture captured the way she held herself, her limbs and body shape, the way she inclined her head. Ruby's form was as individual to her as a fingerprint, and as familiar to Joanna as her own face in the mirror.

'This is great, Eddie, thanks.'

In the full-length image, Ruby was wearing the exact same clothes as the other woman had been: a long, hooded parka and knee-high boots. The jacket had a thin fur trim on the hood, the boots had a low heel. What was Ruby doing?

Who was the other woman? And the most important question of all: where the hell were they now?

'I don't get it,' said Atkinson. 'Why did they wear the same outfit?'

'They want to look the same,' said Joanna.

'Well, obviously, but . . .'

'Maybe it's so that if they get seen, witnesses only think there's one of them,' said Eddie.

'Hmm,' said Atkinson, 'not going to work in the age of CCTV though, is it?'

'Not for long, no. But maybe they didn't think they would be scrutinised this closely,' said Eddie.

'Maybe,' said Joanna, almost to herself, 'when they planned this, they weren't thinking of trying to avoid the police. Maybe it was a game.'

'Not much fun though, really,' said Steve.

She thought of Ruby's voice on the phone when she said she'd met some new friends. The way she sounded when she said the word *complicated*. The case was certainly that: she couldn't get a sense of what they were doing, what or who they were running from, or to.

No one spoke for a minute, their eyes on the photographs.

Atkinson pointed at the most recent image. 'What are we calling this one?'

Ruby appeared in her mouth like a prayer. 'B,' said Jo, swallowing the first part of the name. 'Constance B, because she was the second one we found. The other one is Constance A. Until we know better.'

'Better than Jane Doe. Suppose neither are called Constance?'

One of them definitely isn't, thought Harper, but she said, 'That's a possibility. But it's such an unusual choice for a pseudonym, don't you think? It must have some significance. Good to keep the name at the front of our minds.'

'We've been scouring the available CCTV, like you asked.' said Eddie. 'We tracked B to where she started her journey to Cleethorpes. She came from Sheffield, was caught on the same camera as Constance A, but a couple of hours earlier.'

He showed her another image of Ruby, head down into the wind, hands thrust in pockets, waiting at the tram stop near the New Park for the next one to take her to the interchange. She could just be identified in profile. She seemed cold, vulnerable. Joanna thought she looked lonely. What had she got herself into?

Atkinson looked at the data on the sheet of paper Eddie had given him. 'So, Constance B gets a train to Lincoln, where she waits for a connection to Grimsby that is due to get in at 15:34.'

'Right.'

'You know, she could easily be the one who attacked Gregor Franks.'

'No, I don't think so,' said Harper.

'Why not? There's no evidence to say otherwise. It would make more sense, actually, for it to be her, because Constance A had a kid to look after, which could be considered a deterrent. Maybe Constance B did him in, then a couple of hours later Constance A went round to his place and found him like that.'

'We don't even know if B was in Gregor's flat. She could have come from a different neighbourhood. We have her on camera at the tram stop but not in the actual estate, correct?'

'Yes,' said Eddie, 'but . . .'

'Whereas,' she said, turning to him, her face a picture of calm, 'we do have a positive ID for Constance A, from the neighbour. A was in the building. Not B.'

Atkinson said, 'The neighbour didn't ID Constance A, boss. She heard someone say the word *Leonie,* and that was days before the attack. Hardly hard evidence. She never *saw* either of them. She couldn't have done.'

'Well, no, but A is the one who carried the child from the block. The neighbour might not have seen her with Leonie but the camera on the estate did. And A is the one we have on camera getting the train at the later time. All we have on B, the lighter-haired one, is footage of her at the tram stop, showing that she's wearing similar clothes, and heading for the same place, albeit by a completely different route.'

'They're working together,' said Atkinson. 'The outfits prove it. The lighter-haired one is a person of interest, and should be a potential suspect. For the assault, and for child abduction. She was in the right place for the assault, and she definitely took that child. But we don't know why.'

'The outfits prove nothing. And, yes, she took the child. Maybe it's her child,' said Harper, trying to appear reasonable but sounding snippier than she would have liked, and surprising even herself at what she was suggesting. There was no way it was Ruby's child.

'Hang on, she can't belong to both of them. You were the one who prioritised the kid as high risk, boss, based on the assumption that it wasn't B's child. I thought that was still the working theory? Unless there's something you're not telling me?'

'Of course not,' she said, telling herself, stay calm, wondering again if it was time to come clean. No, not now, not with Eddie in the room. 'I'm just tired, sorry. Not much sleep last night. You're absolutely right, it could have been either or both of them. Or neither. We'll stick to the working theory. Until more evidence presents itself.'

She couldn't conceive of Ruby hurting anyone. Certainly not doing something like what happened to Franks. But then, did she really know Ruby at all? She hadn't seen her for so long. What the hell *was* she doing with that child?

'So,' said Harper, 'we know the movements of Constance B, after she left Sheffield and up to the point where she gets on the Edinburgh train with the kid. What about Constance A?'

'After she left the New Park in the afternoon she got a direct train, with the girl, from Sheffield to Cleethorpes. It stopped at Grimsby at 15:37,' said Eddie. 'I'm wondering if they were supposed to meet up at that point and travel to Cleethorpes together. Or, if A was going to hand the kid over to B and travel to Cleethorpes alone.'

'B only had a ticket to Grimsby, which backs up that theory,' said Atkinson. 'She had to buy another ticket to get to Cleethorpes. I suggest the plan didn't take into account the trains being delayed. Looks to me like the rendezvous should have happened at Grimsby station, and would have done if B's train had been on time.'

'I still don't get why A would abandon the kid though,' said Eddie. 'Why couldn't she have waited a few more minutes, if she was planning to hand her over to B all along?'

'I found footage of what happened at the seafront,' said

Eddie. 'Watch this.' He set a laptop on the table in front of them.

The woman in the image was waiting with the child. The camera picture was hazy, all in shades of green, darkening as the light drained from the day. Shot from above, both figures were foreshortened, but it was definitely the same pair that had travelled from Sheffield.

'They're there for quite a while. I'll forward it a bit.'

The sped-up Constance kept glancing at her wristwatch, and staring off-camera in the direction of the sea. 'She must be waiting for B,' said Jo. 'But what's she planning to do?'

'You'll see,' said Eddie.

On the screen, Constance held the little girl close, pressing her face into Leonie's hair. Then she put the child down, took a step away. Looked back at the little girl. Her hand went to her mouth.

Eddie said, 'She's hesitating. She doesn't want to do it.'

'Do what?' said Atkinson.

Then the child toddled towards a shop window and at the same time the woman disappeared out of shot.

'Where's she gone?'

'I can slow it down slightly, hang on.'

The split second in which the woman disappeared was like watching a sprinter shooting out of the blocks. One last look at the kid and she crouched, then ran in the direction of the sea.

'Is there no camera that covers the beach?'

Eddie shook his head, no.

Atkinson said, 'So she's running towards the water, right? For what? To drown herself?'

'What else could it be?' asked Eddie.

'Are we thinking that A wanted to kill herself, and B was trying to help her do it?'

Joanna said, 'B would never do that.' She blurted it, too fast and too loud. Both of the men looked at her, baffled. 'I mean, the evidence doesn't point to that. It makes no sense for that to be the reason. And let's say she did go into the water to drown herself. There would be a body washed up by now.'

'Not necessarily,' said Atkinson. 'It can take days, months, years. If she caught a riptide then the body might never wash up.' He gave her a look that said, are you feeling OK?

'What we do know for sure,' said Eddie, 'is that after this, A isn't seen again on any cameras we can find. She ran in the direction of the sea. And she never came back.'

They paused for a second to take this in.

'What about B?' said Jo. 'You say she got on a train to Edinburgh, can we track her from there?'

Eddie said, 'We're still looking. I'll let you know the moment I find something.'

After Eddie had left the room, Atkinson and Harper studied the laptop screen, where the child on camera, now completely alone, was fiddling with something on the ground. 'What is that?' said Jo.

'Her handbag. That's what the kid was found with.'

'Where is it now?'

'B has it. The police gave it to her, assumed it belonged to her. But Constance A is the one who carried it to the seafront.'

Harper shook her head. 'I can't understand how they missed that. I've read the report. B told the social worker that the kid must have run off carrying it. That child can barely pick it up.'

'If she'd stopped B then, or simply asked a few more questions, none of this would be happening.'

'That's a bit harsh, boss. Gregor Franks would still have been floating unconscious in his bath, whether or not they'd been apprehended at that point by social services.'

Harper could feel her professionalism slipping. She realised she hadn't been considering the terrible attack on Franks; she was only thinking about Ruby, about the trouble she was in and how she might be helped to get out of it. She told herself to focus on the task in hand. It shouldn't have mattered that she had connections to any person in this case; she should be able to do her job without prejudice, for the sake of equal justice for all. But at the same time she already knew what she was going to do, and it wasn't the most sensible plan.

She turned to Atkinson. 'We need to go and search the beach at Cleethorpes. See if there's anything we've missed.'

'OK, let's go.'

'You go. Take Jade if you like. I've got a few things to do. Let me know what you find.'

Atkinson stood up, but he didn't immediately leave the room.

'Boss, I just wanted to make sure . . .'

'What?'

'There's definitely nothing you're not telling me.'

'Don't be silly, Steve. On you go now.' She smiled tightly as she gathered up her stuff before pushing past him out of the room.

CHAPTER TWENTY-SEVEN

THEN
Ruby

December

Now that she had a spare key, Ruby had developed a technique of opening the door to the flat stealthily, like a burglar, making almost no sound. Then, when Leonie caught sight of her, she was even more delighted. Gregor usually knew she was there, of course, because of the motion sensors on the stairs. Today, it seemed he'd missed his phone alerting him to her approach. He and Constance were arguing.

Silently, she closed the front door behind her and stood in the hallway, listening. She reached inside her bag for the fruit snack she'd brought with her, the organic kind that Leonie loved, but her hand stopped when she heard his voice.

Gregor sounded agitated.

'She has everything she needs, right here. Why would you want to put her in danger like that?'

'It's not dangerous out there,' said Constance. 'It's a play-park. She should be allowed to play, like the other children.'

'If people around here see her, they'll start to ask questions.

And that can only end one way, with Leonie being taken away.'

'But she's our daughter. Why would anyone take her away from us?'

'We've been through this. They won't care about that. They'll say we've been neglectful. They'll ask for birth certificates, for proof of residency. Then, when you can't show them, you'll be thrown into a detention centre and she'll be put with a foster family.'

'That's not going to happen. Ruby knows how to be careful. Please, for Leonie, if not for me. You don't want to take her yourself, fine. Let Ruby take her out. I'll stay here. It's not as if I can go very far, is it? Not without my coat.'

'You realise how insane that makes you sound, don't you?'

Constance mumbled something that Ruby couldn't hear.

'I HAVEN'T GOT YOUR FUCKING COAT, FOR FUCK'S SAKE! IF YOU WANT TO LEAVE, GO AHEAD!'

'Gregor, please, you're hurting me. Leonie's upset, look at her.'

'If she's upset, it's because of you, not me. You're ranting again, you're so indoctrinated, you know that? I wish you'd just let it go.'

'I'm not going to let it go. I won't let anything go until you agree to let her go outside. I won't ever—'

There was the hard crack of a slap, skin on skin, then another.

He's hitting her. Ruby froze.

A thudding sound, a person collapsing to the floor. Then silence. At once Ruby wanted to storm into the room and shout at him to stop, but at the same time she was fixed to the spot, praying the door to the living space would remain almost shut, that Gregor wouldn't come out now and find her, listening; that he wouldn't do to her what he was doing to Constance.

'She should be in fucking bed. Why is she still up? It's your fault she saw that. If you'd put her to bed then she wouldn't have had to be here. You're a terrible mother. You made me do that, and you made her watch. You're sick. Maybe I should let the police know you're here, then I'd be rid of you. I'm sure they'd love to hear all about your weirdo relatives as well, how about it? They'd break that oddball cult up quick as you like, and prosecute half of them for all kinds of crimes. The child protection people would be over there like a shot. One phone call, that's all it would take.'

A mumble that she couldn't hear.

'Oh, you want to stay, do you? Well, I'll think about it.'

Ruby heard Leonie hiccup. She could imagine the anguish on her small face, the silent cry. So, this was the truth of the man. Why hadn't she seen it? Ruby's body trembled with the shock of it, her cheeks burned with humiliation at how she'd been fooled.

'Shh.' Constance's voice.

Ruby's hands formed fists.

Gregor sighed with irritation. 'She'll never sleep now. I'll give her some tonic.'

'No, Gregor, it's not for children.'

'Oh, it's fine, I'll give her a little bit less than what you have.'

'Really, I don't think you should—'

'Would you SHUT UP with your FUCKING WHINGEING?'

Another slap.

'See what you made me do? When are you going to learn to go along with things? You always have to argue.' Ruby heard him go through to the bathroom, the cabinet opening and shutting. When he returned, his voice had changed, softened slightly. 'Here, baby, open wide, medicine for you.'

'Please . . .'

'Well, hold her fucking head, would you? Hold her mouth open. Come ON.'

There was a gurgling sound, and Leonie started to cough and splutter. Ruby needed to go in there, right now. But the fear gripped her, rooted her, even as the shame of doing nothing crept into her stomach.

'That was too much, Gregor, you said—'

'It's fine. She spat most of it out on the carpet anyway, hasn't she? I'll have to clean that up now, won't I?'

Ruby hardly dared to breathe. Perhaps she ought to go outside and come in again, pretend she hadn't heard any of it. But that other part of her, the brave part, wanted to burst through the door and punch Gregor in the throat.

There was the sound of paper towels scrubbing on the rug.

'I'm sorry I shouted, baby.' It was as if a switch had been flipped. This was the voice of the Gregor she knew – gentle, considered.

'I'm sorry. I just get so angry when you ask me things that we can't do. It's for your safety, don't you see? This isn't easy for me, either, having you both cooped up here the whole time. I'm trying as hard as I can to find a way she can go outside safely.'

'But we could let her go out now, if it was with Ruby . . .'

There was a pause then, in which Ruby silently begged Constance not to bring that up again, because of how angry he got last time. But he didn't shout, only sighed. It seemed that the danger had passed, for now.

His voice was kind. 'It's too risky. Some nosy old neighbour would make the connection between Ruby and this flat, and then the social would come sniffing around. We'd no longer be safe here. And as for the coat, I wish you'd let it go. There was never a coat. You were all but naked when I found you, drugged up on something, don't you remember? I told you before, love. You must have dreamed it. The coat doesn't keep you in here. Your mind does that.'

His voice got louder as he approached the door where Ruby was standing but it was too late to make any kind of move. He opened it and stopped dead.

'Oh,' she said, 'Hello.' She tried to push the fear away, to look normal, not so panicked that her smile would seem fake. She could almost hear her heart pounding; perhaps he could too.

'Hello.' He narrowed his eyes at her, patted his pockets for his phone but didn't find it. 'How long have you been standing there?'

'Sorry, I just came in. Is everything all right?'

He pulled the door shut behind him, took her to one side, whispered in her ear, his breath moist against her skin. 'She's ranting about that coat again. Will you be OK, do you think? I need to go out for a few hours. Can you keep Constance company, and make sure nothing happens? Not that it would. But just in case.'

Her skin bristled in revulsion at the closeness. She wanted

to push him away; only a primitive kind of self-preservation prevented her. 'Sure.'

'You can ring me, if there's any need to.'

'Do you think there will be?'

'I don't know. Maybe.' He placed a gentle hand on each of her upper arms. She tried not to flinch away, not wanting him anywhere near her, not wanting him to know that was how she felt. 'I've been thinking, actually, that maybe you were right about treatment for Constance. Maybe it's too much for us to handle.'

'You think she ought to see someone?' Ruby felt a small rush of hope, then. If Constance could get to a doctor, maybe she could get away from Gregor.

'I found a residential treatment programme that might be right for her. It's a commitment, though. She'd have to go away for a few weeks and wouldn't be allowed contact with us.'

'Oh, I see. No contact at all? Not even with Leonie?' The hairs on her neck stood up.

He shook his head, the regret apparently genuine. His act was so convincing. 'The therapy is quite intense, but with her being as bad as she is now, I think it might be worth it.' It was as if he were a different creature entirely from the cruel and violent man from moments ago.

'Where is it, this therapy place?'

'It's going to be hard for all of us, not to contact her. So, I think it's best I don't tell you.'

She knew then, with a cold certainty, that if Constance went away, she wouldn't be coming back – he'd make sure of it. She felt as if her heart would pound out of her chest. 'H-how long would she be gone?'

'Until she's better, I guess.'

Ruby stared at him, trying to work out what he wanted her to say, how she ought to respond. If he could fake it, so could she. Outwardly, she managed to look relieved and hopeful. Inwardly, her guts churned with fear. 'OK,' she said.

'But would you – I mean, if it came to it, if I can get her on the programme – would you help me with the baby, when she's away? You'd come to stay?'

So, that was the plan. With Constance gone, he'd need a replacement there, to do the bulk of the childcare. She pretended to consider it. 'Just while she's away? I can do that, sure.'

He grinned with relief. 'Thank you, seriously, you don't know how much that means to me. You're so good with Leonie. She loves you more than she loves me, I think.'

Ruby forced herself to laugh, to show that she thought that was ridiculous. But it wasn't. It was the only true thing he'd said so far. There had always been caution in the way Leonie interacted with her father. She should have known there was something very wrong.

'I don't need an answer, now. But think about it, would you promise to do that? It's a lot to take on. Too much to ask, really.'

'I don't mind, honestly.'

'If it wasn't for you, I never would have considered sending her away, you know. But I think it's the right thing, now.'

'You do?'

He nodded. 'Don't you?'

Though she felt sick with dread, she forced her face into a smile and nodded that she agreed it would be best to send Constance away for treatment.

'I don't know how to thank you, Ruby. For everything.'

Ruby rolled her eyes, *it's nothing.*

He checked his phone screen. 'Is that the time? I've got to run. She might need her sleep tonic tonight, it's in the bathroom. Can you make sure she gets it? It's awful when she doesn't sleep.'

'Sleep tonic?'

'Yeah, it's just a herbal thing. Brown bottle. One spoonful is usually enough to do the trick, but tonight I think two would be better. She's a little antsy.'

Gregor kissed her on the cheek, grabbed his jacket and left. When the door clicked shut, she wiped the kiss away with the back of her hand.

In the living room, Leonie was asleep in Constance's lap, her arms and legs limp and splayed. As Ruby entered, Constance swiped at her eyes with her sleeve. Ruby expected bruises on the other woman's face, but there was no redness on the pale skin, no marks from the beating she'd endured. He must have hit her in places that didn't show. Always the long sleeves, the high-necked shirts. It made sense now. *Where does it hurt?* She wanted to ask. There was a carefulness in the way Constance held her head, and now that she looked, one ear was bright red and swollen at the lobe.

'Hey, Mamma Ruby. You're too late, she's all ready for bed.' Constance held the small girl close, studied her face and stroked it gently with a fingertip as she sang.

Ionn da, ionn do, ionn da, od-ar da

Ruby sang the answer.

Hi-o dan dao, hi-o dan dao, hi-o dan dao, od-ar da.

'You almost sound like one, when you sing it like that,' said

Constance. Her voice was low and resonant, so that Ruby struggled to catch the words.

'One what?' The air seemed electric, and Ruby felt light-headed. She didn't know if the feeling came from the long shadow of what had just happened, or from her worried anticipation of what Constance might be about to say.

Constance lowered her voice further and glanced from left to right, imparting a secret. 'One of the seals. From the old skerry.'

'They sing?'

'Of course. All the time.'

Ruby felt anxiety take hold at the strange look on Constance's face as she spoke, her grey eyes too large, too bright, the way she was when she was beginning to detach from reality. But there wasn't time to worry about Constance's delusions now. It was more important to get her away from there – they could deal with her mental health when they were in a safe place. A place that wasn't rigged with cameras and listening devices.

As Constance went to put the baby down for the night, Ruby switched the TV on and turned it up loud.

She laughed – then worried it sounded false – at Constance's confused expression when she came back into the room. They never usually watched TV. 'I love this one,' said Ruby – too loud? 'Let's watch it together.' It was one of those talent shows, all glitter and ballgowns. Constance looked sideways at her, questioning. Ruby turned it up even louder, and flicked her eyes at the ceiling. After that Constance seemed to understand. Almost without moving her lips, keeping her eyes trained on the screen, Ruby said,

'I heard what he did to you, just now.'

Ruby could almost feel Gregor watching them from the overhead cameras. Her head itched, though she didn't scratch. The bad feeling crept down her neck, spreading over her skin. Her whole body ached with the effort of not moving, not reacting, not trembling, though her heart was drumming so loudly she was sure it could be picked up by the hidden microphones.

Constance said nothing for a while. From the corner of her eye, Ruby saw a fat tear sliding down the other woman's cheek, changing colour in the light from the TV.

'Does he ever hit Leonie?'

She turned to look at Constance, who nodded, almost imperceptibly. Rage made Ruby's cheeks burn. Her fingers twitched, as if they would have grabbed something to hit him with, had he been there. She tried to breathe slowly.

'I can help you get away. You can't let her stay here any longer. You could go anywhere you like, another city – there are hostels for people like you, with small children.'

'No,' said Constance. 'I need to go home. Back to the island. The *skerry*. They'll come and get me, if I can get to the coast at the right time, on the solstice . . .'

'Are you sure that's where you want to go?' Of course it was home, to Constance, but everything she'd heard about the place was awful. The rituals, the strange beliefs that resulted in drownings. Although, Ruby realised, all of that had come from him. The man who, until recently, she'd trusted without question. Ruby hadn't listened properly to Constance, because Gregor had made her believe Constance was mad. But Gregor had lied about so much, from the very start. She had no idea who he even was.

Constance's eyes shone with tears. She muttered, 'I was happy before I met him.'

Ruby's phone beeped, then. Gregor. *Has she taken the tonic yet?*

Just doing it now, she replied.

'He says you need to take your medicine.'

'Good,' said Constance. 'At least I'll be unconscious for a while.' She went to the bathroom, and Ruby heard the cupboard opening and shutting, the clinking of a glass bottle. When she returned, Ruby spoke out of the side of her mouth, still aware of the camera overhead, hoping the sound of the TV was masking them completely.

'We need to think about the next steps,' she said. 'The plan, for getting you both out of here.'

'Not now,' said Constance. 'It's too much. Today I sleep.'

'But he said he might send you away, soon. I don't know how long we've got.'

'Send me away? Where?'

'For treatment. But you can't trust him . . .'

'I can't leave. Not without my coat.'

'Your coat?' Was it real, then, after all? Ruby decided that even if it wasn't, she had to pretend she believed in it if Constance was to trust her. 'Can't you get a new one?'

She shook her head, no. 'It's part of me. I was born in it.'

Ruby imagined the scene, a wind-blown stone cottage on an island, the mother in labour with nothing to cushion the baby from the packed earth floor but an old coat.

'But what if he's got rid of it?'

'I don't think he has. The man keeps things, forever if he can. I think he's planning to keep you too, Ruby, one way or another.' The tonic was starting to take effect, as Constance's speech slowed and she slumped deeper into the cushions.

Ruby felt her heart rate increase. They could go right now, if they were quick. But Constance was curled on the sofa, her eyelids starting to droop.

'Is it really worth staying here, for the sake of a coat?'

'I stay here *only* because of the coat. Otherwise don't you think I would have gone already?'

When she looked into Constance's eyes, she thought she understood, finally. The coat was a link to her past, to her real self, to everything Gregor had been keeping from her. It was more than a symbol, more than a possession. Ruby wanted so much to help Constance regain something of what she'd lost, something of her fragile sanity, her sense of self. But more than that, she needed to get them away.

When Gregor came back an hour later, Constance was fully asleep and snoring. She didn't even stir when he hauled her up into his arms, carried her to bed.

Ruby hid her fear, or she hoped she had. She yawned and stretched, started to get up to leave.

'You off?' he said.

'Yup. I'm not sleeping brilliantly at the moment. Bloody insomnia. I'm trying not to stay up too late. Get a bit of a routine back. Maybe I need some of your sleep tonic.'

He laughed. 'Maybe you do.'

'What's in it? Constance was out like a light after she had some.'

'Secret recipe,' said Gregor, tapping his nose. 'Well, I guess it's not that secret. Chamomile, essence of lavender. Valerian. And a tiny bit of alcohol, of course.'

Ruby had to stop herself from blurting, *Alcohol? And you gave that to the baby?* She covered her reaction with a cough and an interested smile.

'Help yourself. No more than half a spoonful though, if you're not used to it. It's pretty good stuff.'

In the bathroom, Ruby opened the cupboard above the sink. There was a brown bottle with a spoon beside it. She took out the bottle, unscrewed the cap and sniffed. It smelled sweet and chemical, not like alcohol at all. She poured a full spoon and swallowed. Bitter.

Before she even got home her legs were as heavy as concrete. She woke up fourteen hours later, face down on the carpet in her apartment, the front door ajar, unable to remember how she got there. Thankfully no one had robbed her. As she dragged herself to her knees, felt the roughness inside her mouth and the pain in her head, one thought surfaced, white-hot and shining with fury. He gave that fucking stuff to *Leonie*?

CHAPTER TWENTY-EIGHT

NOW
Joanna

Sunday, 23 December

On the way to the New Park estate, Joanna thought only of Ruby. There was so much she'd never said to her, that she thought perhaps she should have. It had never been the right moment, and now it might be too late. Rain started falling as she crossed the city, the sky blackening with her thoughts.

Jo had been so careful to avoid getting between her mother and Ruby in the early years that for most of Ruby's childhood she'd absented herself, keeping herself busy at first with school and college, after hours with her sports, and in later years with her police training. She'd learned to live with the nagging, aching feeling that she worked hard to suppress, knowing deep down that this was the urge to be a real mother, that she had not only been denied but actively denied herself. For all those years the family went from day to day, doing their thing, ignoring the reality of the adoption, ignoring their mother's alcoholism, ignoring Ruby's feelings of rejection and Joanna's of replacement. Right up until they couldn't ignore it any more. And Ruby had left them, taking half of Joanna's heart.

Immediately after the fight, Jo had been so angry that she'd decided she never wanted to see her mother again, either. But as the days went on, she realised the blame had to be shared. There was a kernel of truth in what had been said, as there always was in the most hurtful things: None of it would have happened if Joanna hadn't given birth to Ruby in the first place. It took a week for the worst of Joanna's anger to subside, and be replaced once more with pity. She'd persuaded Marianne to give Ruby the space and time she needed. Joanna was convinced that, if they did that, she would come home, she would forgive Marianne the way Jo had done. But it hadn't happened, in the twelve months they'd waited patiently. Ruby had just gotten further away.

As the looming apartment blocks appeared in her eyeline she wondered if it was too late to make any of it right. Ruby had always needed her, not just as a sister. Jo should have admitted that sooner, when her baby was still a child, when it mattered most of all. Now she felt like she was being given a chance to do something to show how much she cared. Whatever Ruby had done, whatever crime, Jo could forgive her. More than that, she knew how she could help her stay out of prison. It was her duty as a police officer to apprehend and arrest suspects, but her duty as a mother came first.

Joanna parked and approached the West block, glancing at the entrance to the North block only briefly. She knew that Gregor's flat had been sealed by the CSI team who would be back the next day to complete the work. They'd taken samples, fingerprints and photographs. Tomorrow, the search would get a bit more structural: one of the officers had noticed an area of plaster that was newly replaced, and had sought permission to open up the wall. For now, though, the entrance to the block looked as it always had done. There was no police tape, no officers guarding the building, no sign that anything untoward had happened there. Apart from one small thing. Someone walking by wouldn't notice, but Harper knew that if you looked carefully, there were still drops of Gregor's blood on the paving. She refused to imagine Ruby wielding the weapon that caused those injuries; the figure she pictured carrying out the crime was faceless, with a rope of jet-black hair. Whatever she imagined, she knew it was probable that Ruby had been in Gregor's flat very recently, and it was only a matter of waiting for CSI to analyse the DNA and fingerprints. If, or more likely when, they connected those samples to Ruby, it was a short step from Ruby to Jo. Joanna would find herself answering one or two awkward questions about withheld information and bias. She had to make the most of what little time she'd got.

At the entrance to the flats she pressed buzzers randomly until she got a response.

'Yes?'

'It's the police. I need access to this block.'

Whoever it was simply hung up on her, so she tried again, and the second person who answered was more amenable. She heard the buzz as the electric lock disengaged. She pushed open the door to the stairwell.

On the seventh floor she found Ruby's door and knocked loudly, announcing her name and rank, mostly for the benefit of the neighbours. She wasn't expecting an answer, and so there was barely a hesitation before she swung the bag containing the Enforcer off her shoulder onto the floor and unzipped it. She took out the heavy metal cylinder, positioned it, took aim at the lock.

'Step away from the door. I'm going to force the lock, in five, four, three, two—'

'What are you doing?'

She froze, looked to her left. It was Atkinson. Surprise turned quickly to anger.

'What am I doing? What are you doing? You're supposed to be searching the beach at Cleethorpes.'

'I ended up behind you in traffic. Then I saw you were coming in here and I . . . thought maybe you'd need help.'

'You followed me.'

'I called out, when you got out of the car. You didn't hear me. I didn't want to use the radio, in case . . . well, I didn't know what you were doing. Whether it was related to the case, or . . . personal.'

Harper lowered the Enforcer. She took a step towards Atkinson. 'Whatever you think you're seeing here, just forget it, OK? That's a direct order. Turn around and go.'

Atkinson took a step backwards. He seemed uncertain.

'Who lives in there, boss?'

For a few seconds she just stared at him.

He went on, 'It's 7b, isn't it? The flat that overlooks our victim's. You said you'd take the statement, but I guess they didn't answer?' He glanced at the Enforcer which she still held in one hand. When their eyes met she got the feeling he was nervous. He thought she'd gone rogue, that she wasn't in her right mind. She too looked down at the Enforcer and then at the door. Maybe she had, and maybe she wasn't.

'Do you trust me, Steve?'

A very slight hesitation, then: 'Yes, boss.'

'I feel like I could explain,' she said.

'Yeah?'

'But first I'm going to do this.'

Joanna turned, and in one fluid movement lifted the Enforcer and rammed it into the lock. The frame splintered, the lock gave and the door swung inwards, banging hard against the wall. Harper turned and glared at Atkinson.

'Now. As you can see, what I'm doing here isn't strictly by the book, so I'm going to give you two options. You can either keep your mouth shut, and stay above board. Turn around right now. Go and do the task you've been assigned to do.' She paused.

'Or? What's the alternative?' said Atkinson.

She met his eyes. 'The alternative is that you take that look off your face and help me find out where she's gone.'

CHAPTER TWENTY-NINE

The Injured Man

Remembers

He is following a man through the churchyard. The target is unaware of his presence, as he has been for the past month. As he follows, keeping a safe distance away, he copies exactly the target's gait, his way of running his fingers through his hair every few seconds. When the target stops walking to check something on his phone, he stops too, checks his own phone, mirroring the same stance. The target glances up at him, but he's not really looking, not really noticing. If he was, he might have thought it odd that the person he is looking at had the same haircut as he did, and the same shoes.

The target has no significant friends, though he is very rich. Only those who use the BDSM website the target frequents know him at all, and none of them know his real name. They wouldn't recognise his face, as the target is careful never to post selfies online. He keeps himself to himself, happy in his own company, though he shares his large apartment with his elderly mother, whom he is devoted to. The target probably enjoys the fact that the tenants in the block of flats that he owns don't even realise that he's the landlord, and that he lives above them. They don't know that he had the penthouse flat soundproofed thoroughly when it was being refurbished, so that he hardly ever has to leave the building. The target orders his entertainment in, easy as pizza, every Friday. His mother never hears a single thing. The person following him knows this, because he has been taking careful note. The person following has been watching from the opposite flat, the empty one in the social housing block that just happens to overlook it, that he has managed to keep empty for his own purposes by means of a little light hacking of the council housing portal. The person following has been waiting for the right time to strike, enjoying the wait, the game of it. And now, finally, he's decided the persona has been perfected. There's nothing more he can gain from allowing the target to continue. Tonight's the night. It couldn't be better.

He lets the target enter his building, and walks on for a few minutes before he uses his phone to log on to the BDSM website where he has set up a profile he is certain will appeal. In moments, they have a date.

He waits another thirty minutes before he presses the buzzer, is let into the block. He walks up the stairs, knocks on the door, watches it open. The two men exchange a matching slow smile. The target moves aside to let him in and he takes in the large living space, the tasteful decor, the high ceilings. *Nice place*, he thinks. *I think I'll be very happy here.*

The scene cuts to a few hours later, and the target is kneeling on the bed, naked except for a blue shirt. He's helpless, his eyes big and pleading, mouth swollen slightly, blood dripping from one corner. The handcuffs the target owns fit the wrists perfectly; they were made to measure. The soundproofing the target has had built into the fabric of the flat is excellent. No matter how much the target screams, no one outside the room or downstairs will hear it at all. The man turns and picks up an old green embroidered tie that he has found in a wardrobe. The target sees what the man has in mind, and as anticipated, begins to fight. As the tourniquet is tightened around the throat, the end of the tie becomes frayed where the target is scrabbling at it. Together they struggle, and together they fall, twisting slightly so that the target's head catches the corner of the bedframe badly on the way down, the sound of it a wet crack, and by the time they hit the floor those sparkling eyes have glazed over. He stands up and brushes himself down, watching with fascination as the pool of blood spreads blackly outwards like a pupil dilating in the darkness. It occurs to him that the rug on which the target lies will need to be replaced. Also, he's not sure about the wallpaper.

Now for the old lady, he thinks, wrapping the tie around his hands, noticing with irritation that he has pulled a muscle in his shoulder during the fight with the target. It's unlikely to affect his finishing the old lady, but there's a great deal of salt to be brought up, eight sacks of it, ready to deal with the bodies. He supposes it can wait a day or two, until he's at full strength again – there's all the boxing in and plastering to be done, too, after all, once they're finished. No particular hurry. He knows from experience that bodies don't ripen for at least a week if you keep the heating off.

He cracks open the bedroom door and peers into the living space. The old woman, seated facing away from him, jerks as if she's just woken up. She tries to look round but doesn't quite have the flexibility in her neck.

'Gregor?' she says. 'Is that you?'

CHAPTER THIRTY

NOW
Joanna

Sunday, 23 December

Jo took a few steps inside Ruby's flat and held up a hand for Atkinson to stop. They waited, listened. All was still; the place was empty. She flipped the lights on. The bare bulb dangling from the ceiling illuminated the bed-sitting room in a stark yellow light.

It was clear from the state of the apartment that the occupant was not a natural homemaker. It was a tip, by anyone's standards. Jo felt a pang of protectiveness, but also one of recognition. Her own place might have been bigger but it had looked similar before Amy moved in, with pictures still leaning on the wall where she'd not had time or inclination to hang them, washing drying on the radiators and piles of unopened post. It didn't seem right, somehow, that Ruby's place was so untidy, so uncared for. The Ruby that lived in Harper's head was the sort of person who liked order and neatness; her bedroom at home had always been pristine. Jo had pegged her as a neat freak. Another thing she'd been wrong about, by the looks of it.

What furniture there was in Ruby's place was well-worn, second-hand stuff: a small TV on a low table, a carton of tatty books. The bed, which had been made up with cotton sheets that showed their age, stood out as the only tidy corner of the room. By the door there was a tangle of dirty washing spilling from a plastic laundry sack. She picked up the familiar washed-out grey T-shirt featuring 'Last Splash' by The Breeders, that Ruby used to sleep in. She'd 'borrowed' it from Joanna probably fifteen years previously, when it was already a relic. Jo pressed the fabric briefly to her face. Her throat swelled up and she choked back tears. Ruby had kept this old thing for all this time, it must have meant something. But now it was screwed up in a dirty ball in this unloved apartment, and Ruby was missing.

'What's that?' asked Atkinson.

'Nothing,' said Jo. 'Just stuff. Doesn't matter.'

She tossed the shirt back with the rest of the washing. Atkinson was giving her that look again. It occurred to her that it wasn't usual to sniff things during a search. She ignored him.

Joanna wondered about practicalities: who had helped Ruby get the bed up here? Gregor? Someone else entirely? Why hadn't she bought nicer stuff, or more of it – she earned good enough money at the music service, or she had been doing when Jo last saw her. Ruby loved that job. Jo remembered her saying she'd been lucky to snag it without a teaching degree, that they'd taken her on audition and recommendation. It was only part-time, though, and when she lived with Marianne, Ruby would also teach from home to make up the shortfall. How was Ruby supplementing her income now? No student would want to come up here, to this.

Shame flooded Joanna, at the fact that she didn't know this much about her own . . . what was she? *Sister* had always felt wrong. Why hadn't she admitted that before now? *Hi, Sis*, she used to say when they met, but it wasn't sincere, hadn't been for years. *Sister* had become a kind of dark joke shared between them and in front of Marianne. The word stood in place of what they wanted to say to each other, a poor substitute, a thing they'd both been forced to accept.

Jo got down to search under the bed.

'Oh, no,' she said.

'What have you found?' said Atkinson, dropping to his knees to see.

She pulled it out and unzipped the case. Under a yellow duster that had never seen dust, had only ever been used to lovingly polish the instrument's curves, was the burnished form of Ruby's violin. Jo stared at it, letting the significance of it being here sink in.

Atkinson said, 'Are you OK?'

'She never leaves this thing anywhere,' she said. 'It's like a child to her.' *Or it used to be*, thought Joanna. Things must have gone really badly wrong for Ruby to abandon her violin.

'Are you going to tell me, then?'

'Tell you what?'

'Whose place this is? Or do I have to guess?'

'It's Ruby's place.'

'Your sister, Ruby?'

She looked at the carpet. Then she nodded.

In the kitchen, she and Atkinson stared across at the big

window on to Gregor's flat. It was dark in there, the open curtains offering nothing more than a vague impression of the plush living space they'd searched the day before.

'Can I ask you something, boss?'

'Sure,' said Joanna.

'Why haven't you told the DI that your sister lives here?'

'It's not relevant.'

'But the address is already part of the investigation. I can see now why you wanted to take the statement yourself, but there's nothing stopping one of the team looking up who lives here. Louise seemed keen to start digging.'

'Louise isn't going to make that link. Harper's a common enough name.'

'I think you're underestimating Louise. And me, actually.'

She looked at him. 'Fine, maybe it might be relevant to the case, but I want to find her first, talk to her. Give her a chance to explain.'

'Explain what?'

'Where she's gone. Why she left. She won't answer her phone, Steve, she won't talk to me. Hasn't for months. I think she's changed her number.'

'Hang on, this has been going on for months? How long has she been missing?'

'I didn't realise she was missing until today. I thought she was still avoiding me. There was a big family bust-up. I haven't spoken to her since October.'

'But she might be a witness in this case, Jo. You need to tell someone. If she's involved somehow . . .'

'She's not involved,' Jo snapped.

Atkinson raised an eyebrow. 'You can't know that. You're

too close to this. Maybe you should think about handing it to another SIO.'

'No. I need to be the one in charge, Steve.'

'Why?'

She stared at the floor, hating that she was having to discuss her private life with a colleague. She never mentioned anything to anyone at work that didn't involve sport, or jokes, or police work. She took a deep breath. 'Ruby. She's not my sister, not really, that's a . . . force of habit. She's my kid. But I didn't bring her up, my mother did. Does that explain it well enough?'

Atkinson paused before he said, 'It explains some things pretty well.'

They locked eyes.

'Are you here to help, or just to make snarky comments?

'Sorry. That must be hard for you. I didn't mean to be flip. Wow, I mean . . . I can see why you're so worried about her.'

'Yes, well. Now you know. Can we get on with searching the place? Or is this a therapy session?'

They moved back into the main space.

'What are we looking for, boss?'

'Anything that tells us where she might have gone. How about you start with the post. I'll look for devices.'

'Some of these aren't opened,' said Atkinson, holding up the letters.

She took them from him, tore each one open and handed them over. 'They look open to me.'

He stared at them, then at her, in disbelief. 'If we reported her missing, we could have done that legally.'

'Done what?' She raised her eyebrows in a challenge.

Atkinson shook his head, then started going through the contents of the envelopes.

Joanna pulled out a plastic box from under the bed. It contained mostly stationery. She rummaged and found a notepad and pen, a sheaf of envelopes with several missing. Ruby had been writing to someone. Harper held the pad up to the light, turning it this way and that, trying to read the jumble of illegible impressions left by the pen before the sheet above had been torn away. All she could make out were two words at the top of the page. *Dear Sam*. Sam Douglas, the fiddle-playing crusty from the folk music bar. Who lived on a boat, and made no secret of the fact that he hated technology, that he owned no phone or computer and never would. Sam made his living as a joiner getting jobs by word-of-mouth. He moved around all the time for work. If you wanted to hide, Sam Douglas would be the man to help you do it.

Dear Sam, she read, *Don't* . . . what? It was impossible to see. She would need to have it properly analysed. They'd decode it in seconds at the lab.

Frustrated, she tucked the pad and pen into an evidence bag and continued the search.

'There's no phone here. Not even a charger,' she said. 'No laptop, nothing.'

She went through to the kitchen again to see if she'd missed something in there. There was nothing plugged in, and nothing in the cupboards but a box of out-of-date cereal. When she opened up the fridge a puff of rotten air escaped and she shut it hastily.

'This place. It's not like there's anyone living here, not really. She's been sleeping here, maybe, but not much else.'

'Certainly looks that way,' said Atkinson. 'I think she must have come back regularly to check the post, though. There's nothing here older than a week.'

'Did you find anything interesting?'

'Only one thing, but I'm afraid it won't give us much to go on.'

Us, she thought, experiencing a begrudging little glow at the fact that Atkinson had thrown his lot in with her, despite the risk to himself if he went along with her off-the-record antics. He handed her a yellow envelope handwritten in blue ink. On the back, when she closed the flap, a capital S had been drawn where an old-fashioned seal might have been.

'What was in it?'

'Nothing. Just the envelope. But if you look closely there are some words on the inside where the ink has transferred.'

The postmark was smudged, impossible to read. 'I can get this to the lab. They'll be able to tell us more. And they'll be able to lift prints, hopefully.' She slipped it into an evidence bag and folded the flap closed.

'The lab?'

'Yes, the lab. You remember. Where we send things to have them analysed.'

'I know that. I just meant . . . how are you going to square that with Thrupp? What code are you going to use?'

All official evidence was coded with a catalogue number that indicated where it was found, at what time, and what case it related to. There were no exceptions: if the lab couldn't categorise it, they wouldn't process it. Joanna was well aware of the procedure. She'd planned to deal with that when she had to. Solutions would present themselves, she was sure of it.

'Leave that side of things to me, will you?'

'Look, I get why you'd want to protect your kid, but we should think about stopping before we go too far. Why don't you put it on the record? Then you can run as much evidence through the lab as you like. It's not too late to get the search authorised, if I vouch for you. Ruby's a potential witness. If a witness is reported missing, then we can throw everything at it. And there'd be no need to sneak around.'

'But if they find out I'm related to a witness, they'll take me off the case.'

'Maybe that wouldn't be such a bad thing.'

She stopped, turned. 'What?'

'I saw the way you reacted when Eddie gave you that picture of Constance B. It was a picture of Ruby, wasn't it?'

Jo couldn't react quickly enough; she fumbled for an answer. 'I . . .'

'You know she could be the one who attacked Gregor?'

'Nobody asked you to be here, did they? In fact, I recall asking you more than once to be somewhere else entirely.'

'I want to help you, Jo. I won't tell the DI. Just be straight with me, now and in future.'

Joanna studied her friend's face. After a while, she decided to trust him. 'If Ruby was involved in the attack on Franks, then she would have had a good reason. She's a good person, Steve. She helps people, she doesn't hurt them. She was helping the old woman, wasn't she?'

He nodded. 'I'm sure you're right. But if she's committed a crime, that changes things.'

'She hasn't. I know her. And if anyone asks you what happened here, you'll tell them. I broke the door down, I ordered the search. That is a direct order. Though you don't seem to be putting much store by those, today.'

Just then there was a sound in the hallway, and both of them froze. Harper crept to the spyhole and peeked out, caught a glimpse of a neighbour walking towards the lifts. The noise must have been their door closing. Had they noticed the broken lock? She knew they had to get out of there. Someone from work would see her car parked in the lot, then if they went to Gregor's flat and she wasn't in it they'd start to wonder. Even if they didn't notice her unmarked vehicle, Atkinson had come in a patrol car.

'Listen,' she said, her voice a controlled whisper, 'I only need a couple of days. If I can speak to Ruby, find out what's going on, then I'll put it all on record after that. Two days. Tops. Then if I haven't reported it, you can do it.'

'I can't blow the whistle on you. And you know it.'

Their eyes met. Then she nodded, pulled open the door onto the brightly lit corridor, and they went through.

CHAPTER THIRTY-ONE

THEN
Ruby

December

'Hurry up,' said Constance. 'He might come back.'

'Just a few more seconds,' said Ruby, 'I've nearly got it. There.'

The lock on the bedroom door finally turned. She left the hairpin where it was – sticking out of the keyhole – knowing she would have to perform the tricky operation of picking it the opposite way if she was going to avoid Gregor finding out what she'd been up to. She straightened up, took a deep breath. Then, she turned the handle and pushed.

Inside the bedroom it was dark. Ruby started to reach for the light switch, but Constance grabbed her arm. 'He'll probably have a tripwire or something. There'll be a booby-trap.'

Ruby didn't think so. Gregor can't have known about her lock-picking skills, which she'd learned one long summer from YouTube videos, quietly practising until she was able to open an old cupboard at her music school for which the key was lost. There was a rumour that inside was a treasure trove of baroque instruments, but when she finally got inside it was empty, apart from a dusty Hoover from the 1950s. It had been a fun challenge, though, and a useful skill to have.

In the days since Ruby had witnessed Gregor's violent, bullying nature, she and Constance had been biding their time. When he was there – and even when he wasn't – they made a show of maintaining their expected roles. Ruby was still the 'babysitter', looking after Leonie and helping Constance cope, making sure she took her medicine whenever Gregor hinted or texted that she needed it. In actual fact, Ruby was making sure she didn't take that stuff, tipping it one spoonful at a time down the sink. Constance pretended to be sleepy and vacant, when in truth, she was getting stronger and more focused every day. She still longed for home, though, and Ruby would catch her gazing wistfully at the seascape pictures, lost in thought.

Ruby played her violin for them, often, and they sang shanties, sea-songs, and lullabies from the old skerry, as Constance called her home. Gregor listened, his eyes gleaming. He loved the sound of the two of them as much as they loved it themselves, but when the songs were over, the women were careful to hide their affection. They made up complaints about each other to tell Gregor when the other wasn't in the room, so he didn't think they were too close. Constance said Ruby was a bossy, nosy, little busybody. Ruby complained that Constance was bad-tempered and uncommunicative. So far, the plan was working. Maybe a little too well.

On his way out that evening he'd pulled Ruby aside.

'You're an angel for staying,' he said. 'I've told her she needs to stop being such a bitch to you, when you do so much to help us out.'

'I don't mind,' Ruby said, 'I know she doesn't really mean it. Some of the stuff she says to me when you're not here can be hurtful, sure, but it's nothing I can't handle. But I'm not here for her, not really. I'm here for Leonie.'

'I've seen the kind of things she says to you, on the cameras. You shouldn't have to put up with that. Not with everything you do for her, and for us.'

It was good to know that the occasional spats they staged for him were being noted, and having the desired effect.

'We don't fight the whole time, you know.'

'No, I know. Sometimes you watch TV.'

'You watch us doing that?'

He laughed. 'No, I don't have time for that. I just . . . check in sometimes. That's all. You don't mind, do you? Too stalkery?' He laughed, didn't wait for her to answer. 'She's out of order, picking on you. I could have another word with her. Make her stop.'

She stroked his arm, attempting a distraction. 'Honestly, it's not needed. I think you're being over-zealous.'

He caught her hand, pulled her towards him. 'Have you thought about us, recently?'

'It's all I've thought about.'

He kissed her, then, before she could pull away. He held her arms as she struggled to free herself, keeping her there a little too long. The strength of him. If he'd wanted to do anything to her, she wouldn't have been able to stop him. She stilled herself with every ounce of strength, fighting the urge to fight him, to push him away. He smelled of cloves; his tongue darted past her teeth, sweet and poisonous.

'Gregor,' she hissed, fear coursing through her, making her

tremble. She hoped he assumed it was because she wanted him so badly. 'We can't, I told you before. It wouldn't be right.'

'I'm sorry,' he said. He studied her face, his lips parted. She tried to gaze at him with the longing she had once felt, that had now turned to ash. 'I find it so difficult to be near you at the moment.' He pulled her into a too-tight hug, the hard muscles of his arms bruising her cheekbone. 'Can I come and see you, later? At your place, I mean.'

No, never, she thought. *I don't want to be alone with you even for a moment*.

'At my place?'

'I want to hear your piece. I haven't heard it for so long. The opening section has been in my head all day.' He hummed the theme, the tritone that spanned the first bars, setting the mood for the rest.

'You don't need to come over, Gregor. I can bring my violin, play it for all of you. I'll bring it tomorrow, yes?'

He gave her a long look. 'I suppose.'

She stopped, then, blinking to cover the widening of her eyes, pulling him in for a second hug as she tried not to show her reaction, her skin prickling all over, events slowing with her breath as every single hair on her body stood up. Despite the heat in the apartment she felt suddenly ice cold, her jaw clenched.

I have never played him that piece. How does he know it? There was only one possibility. He was spying on her. There were listening devices, and maybe even cameras, over in Ruby's flat, too.

It was important that Gregor thought she was still in love with him, only denying herself because of Constance and

Leonie. So it was useful, now, that the fear looked so much like desire. Standing there with her pupils dilating, tongue wetting her lips, trembling, she must have looked to him like a fruit ripe for the picking.

They had to get out, and soon. Tonight they would act. As she'd watched him disappear into the stairwell, she'd known they would need to search fast. If she and Constance were going to access his private space without him knowing, it had to be after he'd set off in the car and before he arrived at wherever he was headed, because he couldn't be watching them and driving at the same time. They didn't know how far he was going, or therefore how long they had. The moment his car started to move she'd given the thumbs-up to Constance, who stuck a piece of masking tape over the tiny camera lens in the light fitting so that Ruby could pick the lock without it being recorded.

They checked all around the door for traps and wires, but could find nothing, not even the tell-tale bore hole of a hidden camera.

'I think it's safe.'

Ruby walked into Gregor's scrupulously neat and clean bedroom, flipping the light switch as she went. The bed was covered in a white cotton top sheet, folded back to reveal a white cotton duvet. Crisp white pillows were perfectly symmetrical. There was a white chest of drawers, a matching wardrobe. The painted walls were bare. Ruby got a feeling of blank nothingness. Like a hotel room, but with even less character.

Having been reluctant to enter the room, Constance suddenly pushed past her and flung open the wardrobe doors. She shoved aside the shirts, dragged the bottom drawer open.

'It's not in here,' she said. 'It has to be somewhere. Where's he hidden it?'

Ruby opened the top drawer of the bedside cabinet and found nothing, not even dust. In the second drawer, also nothing, but when she shut it she heard a soft metallic sound and opened it up again. There at the back of the empty drawer was a small silver key. She picked it up, looked at it. A serial number was marked on it, but nothing else. She replaced the key where she'd found it and closed the drawer.

Constance moved fretfully around the room, looking for more places to search. She looked under the bed and made a grunt of frustration.

'Nothing here.'

Inside the open wardrobe, Ruby could see Gregor's shirts arranged in colour order, a row of shoes neatly placed. She moved towards it and started straightening them out where Constance had rummaged.

'What are you doing?' said Constance, still on the carpet, feeling the underside of the bed for hidden pockets. 'Help me look, will you? There's nothing in there, I checked.'

'We need to tidy, though. We've got to leave it all the way we find it. Otherwise he'll know we've been in here snooping.'

Constance got up and wrenched open every drawer in the chest, her search becoming more frantic. 'Maybe I don't care if he knows. Maybe he needs to know.' By the end of the sentence she'd lost her conviction. She stared down at the mess she'd made, the bundle of underwear she'd thrown to the floor. She dropped to her knees and gathered it all up, folded the items carefully, replaced them with shaking hands.

She started straightening out the rest of the drawers. 'This was a mistake. We should get out of here, Ruby. It's not in here.'

'Yes,' said Ruby, 'First let me sort these shirts.' She placed each hanger equidistant from the next, then ran a hand down each front and back to smooth them. Soon the wardrobe looked the way it had when Constance first opened it. She was about to close it up when she noticed a wrinkle in one of the middle shirts. This time when she ran her hands down the fabric, her fingers grazed something at the back of the wardrobe. Parting the shirts carefully, she bent to look.

'What is it?' said Constance. 'What have you found?'

'I don't know.'

She pulled gently and the box came towards her. It was about the size of a shoebox, made of metal, painted black and fastened with a small, gold-coloured padlock.

'The coat won't be in that,' said Constance. 'It's not big enough.'

Ruby tried to prise the lid off. As she did so, there was a noise from the front door.

'Is that him?' They listened.

There was the sound of a key sliding into place. Gregor's key.

'Quick!' said Constance. 'Put it away. I'll get the tape off the camera.'

Ruby shoved the box back where she'd found it and slammed the wardrobe doors. Scanning the room for things out of place, she blanked, couldn't tell. She hoped there was nothing; she'd no time for anything more than hope. Constance was outside the bedroom; Ruby could hear her panicked breathing. She stepped out, flicked the light off, closed the door. Just the lock to turn now. From behind her, an urgent whisper. 'Come on, Ruby. He's coming in.'

She turned the pin too hard at first; she thought it was going to snap. But then, as the front door opened, she wiggled the lock, the cylinder turned, she wrenched the hairpin free and took a step away from the bedroom door.

'What's going on here?' said Gregor.

'Oh,' said Ruby, realising how suspicious they must look. 'We weren't expecting you.'

He stared hard at each of them in turn. 'What are you doing, though?'

'We were exercising,' said Constance.

'We . . . were?' said Ruby. 'That's right. You weren't watching, were you? That would be embarrassing.' Both of them were red-faced, breathing hard and sweating. It was the perfect lie.

'No, of course not.'

Gregor walked through to the kitchen with the shopping bag he was holding. 'Glad to hear it, though, about the exercise,' he said. 'You need to shift a bit of that baby weight, right, Connie?' He stuck his head out of the door. 'Oh, hang on, if you're planning to get in shape, should I not have bought these cakes, then?'

Ruby had pulled herself together, though her cheeks still burned. 'Don't be silly. She can eat whatever she likes. She's barely there.'

'I'm not sure that's true,' he said. 'You can overcompensate. She's not fat now, but everyone's only a few calories a day away from weight gain. Even me.'

'I don't even like cake,' muttered Constance. 'You can eat them, Ruby.'

'Are you staying for dinner?' said Ruby to Gregor. 'I thought you were working tonight?'

'I'm not staying. I still need to go to Liverpool tonight. Business. I just popped in to drop off some shopping. In fact, do you think you could stop over again, Ruby?'

'You don't need to,' said Constance, to Ruby. 'We'll be fine.'

'I'd be really happy to,' she said.

'That's settled, then.'

When he'd gone, they waited, the way they should have waited the first time. Constance checked on Leonie and found her awake in the cot, needing to be soothed. She brought the sleepy tot through into the living room where they all watched half an hour of mindless kid's TV, Ruby taking none of it in. Then they waited a bit more. Ruby got up and made sure that Gregor's car wasn't in its space before she dared to relax even slightly. They had to pray that he really was going to Liverpool; if it was true, they had about two hours to search before he stopped the car and checked the cameras from his phone. If it wasn't true, and he suspected them, then Ruby reasoned that they were already fucked so it didn't matter what they did.

Ruby stuck the tape over the camera in the ceiling light.

'Maybe we should leave it off,' said Constance. 'If he checks the camera and can't see a picture he'll know we're up to something.'

'Better that he sees nothing than what we're actually doing,' said Ruby, fishing the hairpin from the pocket where she'd shoved it.

Picking the lock was easier the second time. She knew what to feel for, where the pressure needed to be applied and when to be gentle. Soon the lock gave and she was inside, where she went straight to the wardrobe and pulled out the black metal box. After a moment's thought, she went to the bedside unit and fetched the small silver key. Back in the living room, the key slid easily into the padlock, which opened with a satisfying click. More proof that Gregor trusted they wouldn't go in his room, if all there was to find in there was a padlock and the key that opened it. Something tugged at her mind, though, a quiet warning. It seemed a bit too easy. She pulled at the tightly fitted lid until it came free, swinging open on its hinge.

Constance was on the sofa, feeding Leonie a cup of warm milk. 'What's in there?'

'Bills,' said Ruby, leafing through the file folders as she pulled them from the box and placed them one by one on the coffee table. 'Papers, certificates, boring stuff. The deeds for this place. You'd think he would have a proper filing system.' She pulled out his birth certificate, looked at the dates, the name of the Royal Infirmary Hospital. 'Funny,' she said, 'According to this, he's thirty-eight.'

'And?'

'Don't you think he looks younger than that?' She thought about his voice, then. Born in Sheffield. Gregor's accent was carefully neutral, which he'd explained by the fact that he went to a fee-paying school. But sometimes his long vowels shortened unexpectedly, and he sounded almost Bristolian to Ruby.

Underneath the last file was something she recognised.

'Oh my God,' she said, picking up the phone that she'd lost, that she thought had been stolen, or thrown away. Her old phone, containing all of her numbers, her text message conversations, her passwords. Gregor had had it all along. Her whole life was on there, or her life before she met him, anyway. She turned it on, not expecting, after all this time, that the thing would have any power, but it chimed into life, the battery at 75 per cent. Ruby was halted by the chilling knowledge that not only had he been keeping the phone, he'd been regularly charging it up. She saw that there were no unread notifications. Gregor had been reading them all. But why? In the calls menu there were hundreds of missed calls, mostly from Marianne, but some from Joanna, too. Her breath caught, and she felt sick with guilt and regret for ignoring them, for not contacting and telling them she'd changed numbers. Scrolling through, she saw that every Sunday, Marianne would start calling in the morning, then continue every hour or so until the early hours of Monday morning. Drink-and-dial, her speciality. She immediately stopped feeling guilty. If Ruby had answered any of those desperate calls, she would have spoken to a person still ruled by drink.

She switched the phone off again, pushing thoughts of Marianne and Joanna away, no time for that now. Also in the box was a black device almost the size and shape of a mobile phone, but unlike any make or model she'd seen before. She turned it over, found the ON button, pressed it. The word TRAX flashed up in blue and disappeared before the screen filled with a map. It took a few seconds for her to realise what it was she was looking at.

'It's a tracking device,' said Ruby.

Constance leaned over to look. She pointed at the flag icon in the centre. 'Is that the apartment?'

Sure enough, the map was recognisably of the local

area, centred on the New Park estate, shown from above. The flag was in the North block.

'Must be,' said Ruby. 'I don't get it, though. What's it tracking, itself? Is that like a "Home" flag?'

'No,' said Constance. 'Look, there're two flags, but they're really close together. There'll be a locator device, a small thing. He told me once he had one for his car, in case it ever got stolen.'

Ruby ran to the window, panicking that he'd come back again. The space was still empty. 'His car isn't here, though.'

'Is the locator in the box?'

Ruby turned the box upside down. Nothing. She felt in the corners. 'Not in here.'

'Maybe it's faulty.'

Ruby scrolled through the menu. She clicked on 'locate at close range', and the screen changed to a set of concentric circles pulsating from a blue central dot. The word in the dot was 'Receiver'.

'This must be the receiver, then,' she said. Next to the receiver dot was a smaller, red dot, labelled with the word 'locator'. At the bottom of the screen, the words, *less than 0.5m.*

'That means it's here somewhere. In the room. You're sure it's not in the box? Have a good look, might be stuck on. They're magnetic, probably.'

Constance ran her hands over the box, inside and out. Nothing. They both looked around them. Ruby lifted the cushions on the sofa. 'How big is the locator, do you think? Did you ever see the one on his car?' She got up and walked across to the bathroom, went inside and began to feel along the top of the cabinet.

'Ruby,' said Constance. 'It moved.'

'What?' she went back into the main room and walked across to where Constance was sitting.

'Stop,' she said, and Ruby stopped. Constance's eyes flicked between her and the screen of the tracking device. 'OK, go again.'

She'd only taken three steps when Constance said, 'It's you.'

'It's me? What do you mean?'

'When you went to the bathroom. The dot moved with you. It's on you somewhere. What have you got in your pockets?'

'Only my phone.' She reached into her pocket and pulled out the phone. 'But it's turned off.'

'Here,' said Constance, taking the phone and handing her the tracker. 'Watch the dots.'

Constance walked towards the bathroom. The locator dot moved. The distance marker went up as she got further away, *less than 1.5m, less than 2.5m, less than 3.5m.*

Ruby threw the tracker down and grabbed the phone from Constance. She unclipped the back and took the battery out. There was a flat, black circle underneath it that she'd never seen before.

Gregor was tracking her. He'd given her a phone that meant he could follow her every move. She'd been carrying it around, not knowing that, at any given moment, Gregor knew exactly where she was. The few times he'd phoned her when she'd been in town, she'd always been at the bus stop by the police station. Not a coincidence, then, as she'd thought; he didn't fully trust her, suspected she might have been about to betray him to the authorities.

Quickly she bundled everything into the box, hoping she'd

got it all in the right order. She wedged the lid on, fastened the padlock, replaced the box exactly where she'd found it hidden in the wardrobe. Finally, she wiped the padlock and the wardrobe door where her prints might be found. Paranoid, perhaps, but she'd seen just how far Gregor would go to keep tabs on them. The idea of him routinely dusting for prints seemed perfectly plausible, now.

CHAPTER THIRTY-TWO

The Injured Man

Remembers

The girl is running ahead of him through a field of maize, her small form disappearing into the high stalks, reappearing again in flashes of white cotton and yellow hair. It's a game: he's laughing as he chases her. She ducks to the left and disappears. He stops to search the rows. He can't find where she's gone, but then he steps forward and sees a foot quickly drawn away under the low leaves. He creeps along. He can feel himself grinning, the sun on his back, stalking his prey, the thrill of a good chase. She's hiding, perfectly still. She thinks he can't see her. Then, the crops shudder as she realises he's there and takes off, running chaotically, here and there like a startled rabbit, and he's after her. She's an arm's length away and he reaches for her, grabbing her wrist and turning her to face him. She stares at him, her mouth wide in a scream. Up close, the white dress she wears has uneven red spots. She struggles to get away, so he goes to take hold of her with his other hand but can't because he's holding something already. He opens up his palm to reveal a severed finger, and in that moment she twists and slips out of his grasp.

Next, he is standing at the edge of a deep hole, looking down. There on the distant bottom, the girl's limbs make a star, still and pale with a fan of yellow hair in an angel's aurora around her head. She stares in his direction, but the eyes no longer see.

He is pushing the front door open, heading to the kitchen for a glass of water.

His mother is saying, 'Where's your sister?'

He turns, looks her in the eye. 'I haven't seen Dora all day.' As he leaves the room he slips his hands in his pockets. His left hand grips his penknife that he knows he must wash. His right hand caresses the nestled finger, a gruesome treasure, his first and his best.

CHAPTER THIRTY-THREE

NOW
Joanna

Sunday, 23 December

Streetlights spread weak orange light on the paving between the apartment buildings. Jo followed Atkinson to where the cars were parked, her breath billowing in puffs of vapour, though she didn't feel cold. When she reached the car, she paused in the act of unlocking it.

Across the top of the car, Atkinson followed her eyes to the seventh floor of the North block.

'You're not thinking what I think you're thinking, are you?'

'I just want a quick look.'

'You can't go in there now; they've sealed it up to preserve the evidence.'

'I had no idea Ruby was involved when we went in before. There might be something I missed.' Jo pocketed her keys and started towards the brightly lit lobby of Gregor's building. 'Go home, Steve,' she said, but when she reached the door and he was right behind her, she was secretly pleased.

At the apartment door she ripped the yellow police tape

from the frame and pushed the key into the lock. As she did so she noticed that the utilities cupboard in the corridor to the right of the door was ajar. There was a padlock lying open on the floor, its key still inserted. Inside the cupboard there was nothing but the water stopcock, the energy meters, and a space underneath with a gap in the dust as if something that had been there for a long time had been recently removed.

Not knowing what or if this meant anything, she tucked the information away, cataloguing it along with the other scraps she had, none of which seemed to her to be connected yet, though she knew they had to be. Cases came together for Harper all at once like illusions, puzzle pieces falling randomly until she took a step in a different direction and suddenly it would come to her: the links, the gaps, shining a light on it all so she could see the way through. She turned each fact over, searching for the kinks, the points at which each one joined the rest: first, a child abandoned on the seafront; a mysterious woman disappearing; Ruby convincing the social services to let her take the woman's child; disappearing herself. The state of Ruby's flat. The last phone call they'd had, Ruby's tone of voice when talking about the people she'd met. The neighbour, who thought Gregor lived alone. The invisible child, with no records, slipping through the cracks. The invisible mother, Constance. Where did Ruby fit in to the picture? Something in Franks' flat might tell her. But she had to be quick. Atkinson was on her side but the fingerprint evidence would point the investigation at the name Ruby Harper soon enough, no matter how hard she tried to obstruct it.

Jo stepped into the flat, with Atkinson close behind. She went into the first bedroom, the one with the crib in it. She started opening drawers, slamming them when she found nothing but women's clothes, kid's clothes, toiletries. In the box under the bed there were shells of varying sizes and colours, the larger ones with intricate, ear-like curves on the inside, shining pinkly, almost glowing. Jo weighed one in her hand. It was heavy, like a rock, its edges sharp and brittle.

In the other bedroom, it seemed at first that there was even less to find, until she opened the wardrobe and pushed aside the shirts. There was a metal box, padlocked shut. For a split second she paused, considering the consequences of what she was about to do. Tampering with evidence, ignoring direct orders, interfering with an investigation. Together it spelled court order, disciplinary, maybe even gross misconduct. Then, she thought of Ruby's expression in the photograph from the train station. So far away, so lost and alone. Up until recently Jo had assumed Ruby was fine, but she had to admit that it was a convenient assumption – if Ruby was fine then Jo didn't have to do anything. She realised now that it wasn't just the past few months: assuming that Ruby was fine had been her default position ever since the baby was born and handed to Marianne. Well, she couldn't use that excuse now, or ever again. Ruby was in trouble, and the only person in a position to help was Joanna. She loved her job, she'd dedicated her life to it. But if it came to a choice, there was only one way to go. In that moment it didn't even feel like a difficult decision.

She took a pair of bolt cutters from her satchel and set them at an angle on the flimsy padlock bar, squeezing only slightly before the lock came apart with a metallic pinging sound and she opened the box.

Underneath a sheaf of legal paperwork, at the bottom of

the box, her hand closed around a black device, which on closer inspection turned out to be the receiver part of a high-end tracking device of the kind used by undercover operations.

Placing the device on the bed, she returned her attention to the box. There was a phone in there, the same make and model that Ruby had owned, before the number changed. Was it Ruby's? Too risky to leave it here, just in case. She pocketed the phone at the same time as she noticed: the metal box was much deeper, by two or more inches, from the outside than from the inside. There was a secret compartment.

'Jo? Have you found anything?' Atkinson's voice floated through from the living space.

She felt in the bottom of the metal box, found a small ring attached to a chain and pulled. The false bottom came away.

'Maybe. I'm not sure.'

'I heard on the radio, they're sending a patrol to check the apartment. We need to scarper.'

She stared at the items revealed in the secret compartment, picked one of them up, flipped it open.

Atkinson came into the room, where Harper was sitting on the bed, still with the metal box open on her lap, the bolt cutters and the broken padlock lying beside her.

'Did you cut that?' said Atkinson, pointing at the lock.

She ignored him. 'Did we check Gregor Franks on the police computer?'

'Of course we did. I ran his details myself. He has a clean record, but I don't see how—'

'Did we check his prints, I meant?'

'The prints from this place matched the ones we took from Franks at the hospital, yes.'

'But did anyone check the prints against the records on the police computer? To see if they matched any unsolved crimes?'

'No, of course not. I just told you, we checked his name and he had a clean record. We're not investigating Franks, we're trying to find out who attempted to kill him. Franks is our victim, Jo.'

'He's a victim, sure,' said Harper, 'But whether or not he's actually who we think he is, that's another matter.'

She handed over the passport that she'd found in the bottom of the box. The name was right: Gregor Christopher Franks. But the photo was of a different man entirely.

'I don't understand,' said Atkinson.

'Whoever that man in the hospital is,' said Harper, 'he's not Gregor Franks. And look,' she said, indicating the other item lying in the bottom of the box. It looked like a rolled-up handkerchief, edged in blue stitching, a posy of embroidered flowers at one corner. The white cotton was stained with something dark.

'Is that . . .'

'Yes,' said Harper, 'I think it's blood.'

With a gloved hand, she picked up the handkerchief and unwrapped it. Lying in her palm was a curl of something that looked like tree bark, but on closer inspection had a fingernail. A child's pinkie finger, brown from age, dried up, mummified, and stored in the bottom of a box as if it were a keepsake.

CHAPTER THIRTY-FOUR

On a fine summer's evening, an inhabitant of Unst happened
to be walking along the sandy margin of a voe. The moon was
risen, and by her light he discerned at some distance before
him a number of the sea-people, who were dancing with great
vigour on the smooth sand. Near them he saw lying on the
ground several seal-skins.

THOMAS KEIGHTLEY, 'The Mermaid Wife', 1870

The Injured Man

Remembers

The man has travelled to the coast to inspect some property
he is thinking of buying with the money he has now that he
is Gregor. It's the second night of the trip. After he's gone
to bed, he hears drumming coming from the beach, and is
curious enough to get dressed and head out there. Might be
a party, someone to play with. It's been so long since he's had
the urge for a girl. He grabs a bottle of wine and leaves the
rented cottage barefoot.

The half-moon swims and flickers on the waves in multiple
versions of itself. There is a soft lapping at the shore, but

otherwise the sea moves silently, gleaming and swelling under a matt sky pierced with stars. It's too dark to see properly, but he feels his feet sinking into the wet beach as he walks, the water occasionally sucking at the sand beneath his soles. He likes the idea that as he makes his way towards the gathering of people at the bonfire, whatever impressions his bare feet leave behind will be erased by the sea as quickly as they are made.

From far out in the darkness, a scream. He stops and listens, straining his eyes in the direction of the horizon for the source of it. He glances further up the beach at the dancers around the fire but the drumming doesn't falter, the silhouettes of the moving bodies keep the steady rhythm; they haven't heard it. Their laughter drifts towards him on a soft breeze. Gregor knows that he ought to run, to call out for their help with whoever is screaming. He wouldn't go into the water himself; he isn't a particularly strong swimmer. But maybe someone at the party has lifeguard training, or knows of someone who does. He's not at all concerned for the person who may be in trouble in the water. His worry is that people will expect him to do something about it, and that he will be obliged to make the effort to appear as if he is concerned. He stands on tiptoes, listening, watching the dancers.

The scream, when it comes again, pushes him down onto his heels. The breath he is holding comes out in a sigh. Not a human cry; it's a seal. Moonlight falls on the animal's pointed face as it nods in the inky darkness, whiskers dripping with salt water, before disappearing under the surface.

Of course it was a seal, how ridiculous. He wishes he has someone to laugh at him then, that he'd brought a friend along after all. But then, he doesn't have any friends, not really. He hardly ever thinks of this, and even now, as he examines the fact, he doesn't feel anything about it. Not even a numbness, merely an absence.

He's close enough now that they will see him the moment they turn to look. He hovers in the shadows, waiting to see what will happen, whether he'll be welcomed, if it is that sort of a party. There are twelve or thirteen of them around the fire. None of them immediately turn in his direction, and he thinks about clearing his throat to draw their attention but he does not. He's content, for the moment, to watch without being observed himself. A young woman is playing a hand drum that hangs from a strap over her shoulder, and next to her a young man sits on a crate that he hits with a stick on the off-beats. Three girls dance and the remainder, young men and women both, are around and about, talking, leaning on each other, making patterns in the beach with sticks and pebbles.

And that is when he sees her. Her hair is braided into ropes, her skin patched with sand. The curve of her arm is perfect, how the muscles move, and the collarbone dipped in shadow scooping up to an exquisite jawline.

Beautiful creature, he thinks. And a second later, how different from me. She won't want me. Not at first, anyway. But then she will. They always do, eventually.

From where she crouches, drawing with a driftwood pencil in the packed sand at her feet, she raises her eyes to his and there is something between them, as quick as that. He feels the vibrations of it, and he sees it in her eyes too, like a chime bar striking the same note within them both.

You're mine, he thinks, but her eyes dart away, to the

old woman he hasn't noticed, seated on a crate behind the drummers. The young woman's eyes dart back to meet his, a look of panic. Slowly the older one stands, a big woman, wide and square, and the drums falter, then stop. The old one's face is closed up hard, a warning. Gregor sees this but he can't take his eyes from the younger one for long. She's twitchy, like a woodland creature caught in a beam of electric light. *What's she so scared of*, he wonders.

Gregor walks forward into the circle of firelight. He shrugs and smiles, friendly, unthreatening. 'Hi,' he says.

'Can I help you?' says the big woman, her voice deep and resonant. Even as she says it, she seems to relax slightly. It's the smile he is wearing. It melts people.

'I was just passing,' says Gregor. 'Looks like a party.'

He shines the smile around the circle, and brings his bottle of wine out to show them. There are murmurings. One or two of the women appraise him openly, their eyes roaming slowly up and down his body, their hands rising to cover their mouths. He can tell they are whispering to each other. His attention drifts back to her, to the young woman he has connected with, but she's made eye contact with the big woman, something passing between them. Then, the big woman glances over at him and her face has changed. She doesn't smile, but the accusation is gone. She returns her eyes to the young woman and he thinks – no, he's sure, though it's almost imperceptible, that she nods. Then, she sits down, and the drumming starts up again. The scene resumes as before, the dancers beginning to move to the beat. Gregor sits cross-legged on the sand and opens his screw-top bottle.

From the ocean the seal calls once more, and the sound is terrible.

By the time she makes her way over to him, as he knows that she will, he is almost enjoying the rhythms, letting the drumming and the movement lull him as he waits for her. When she sits down at his side and takes the bottle from his hand, he notices a young man on the other side of the fire get up and walk away. This young man throws one last glance at them before he disappears into the shadows. Gregor thinks he detects bitterness in the other man's expression.

'Who's that guy?' says Gregor.

She stares after the young man for a moment, then draws her eyes away. 'You English?'

Up close, he is struck by her facial features, her wide-set eyes and the high cheekbones. She has a strong nose and full lips. He can't tell, in this light, exactly the colour of her eyes nor the shade of her hair, other than that both are dark, and the hair hasn't been brushed for a long time. He expected, when she was this close, that he would smell the tang of unwashed body that you often get with these hippie types, but he can detect only a faint hint of sea water, salt and fresh fish. The smell of her makes his stomach rumble and his mouth water, though he is not hungry. Still, he wants to taste her.

'I'm English, yes. I'm from the north.'

She jerks her head sideways to look at him. 'How north?'

'Yorkshire.'

'Pfft,' she says, 'That is not north. We're from the north. From the islands.'

He laughs. 'You win then, I guess. What are you doing here?'

'It's tradition. On the summer solstice we party on the beach. Every year. Different place each time.'

'Long way to travel, though, isn't it? All the way to Cleethorpes?'

'We always travel. That is also tradition.'

He takes the bottle and drinks deeply.

She moves up close to him, brushes some sand away from the skin on his thigh.

'You know what else is tradition, on this night?'

He looks down at where her hand is still on him, light and easy. He shakes his head, no.

'We girls get to play with whoever we want.'

A grin spreads on his face. 'I like that tradition. Very much.'

When the wine is gone, he rises and reaches for her hand. 'I've got a place we can go to. It's not far.'

'I don't have long,' she says. 'We swim with the tides.'

'Swim?' he looks out to sea. There's nothing there, not for miles.

Her face twitches, very slightly. 'I meant sail. We sail with the tides.'

'I don't see a boat.'

She's already walking away, a dark-coloured coat thrown over one shoulder. 'Do you want to, or not?'

At the rented cottage, he offers her a drink. Only half an hour after that she is out cold. He hauls her unconscious body into the boot of his car. He drives through the night, back to the soundproofed apartment. He has plans for the beach-find girl. It's going to be fun.

CHAPTER THIRTY-FIVE

THEN
Ruby

Thursday, 20 December

Ruby no longer felt safe, anywhere. She carried the phone he'd given her even though it felt wrong to do so, now that she knew it was tracking her. The night she'd realised he was listening to her in her flat she'd stopped spending time there alone. It was better when she slept over at Gregor's on the sofa. Something about the fact that they all knew the cameras were there made it less sinister. Occasionally she would wake, sweating, in the small hours, stare up at the light fitting and think about phoning Joanna, telling her everything, asking her to come rescue them. But then she'd remember, she couldn't do that without him knowing, and if he found out he'd been betrayed, then what? He was clearly capable of violence. He had her old phone, with all her contacts – did he therefore realise who Joanna was, that she was a police officer? No, she was just listed as Joanna, so there was no reason he would know that. The idea that she still had secrets from Gregor was a comfort. Something she could use against him, if it came to it.

She thought of the Yoga Man days, when she would spy on him in the dark, convinced she was being so secretive, watching him when he didn't know. But he did know, he'd always known. At the time she'd enjoyed the fantasy that he was performing for her, but now the thought of it made her shudder. She'd started to take sleeping pills again, and several times found herself dosing up on beta blockers during the day for the anxiety.

It had been a week since they went looking for the coat and found the box. Ruby had repeatedly tried and failed to make Constance leave without it. Time was running out – Gregor's words still rang in her head, the idea that he might be getting ready to send her to a 'residential treatment programme'. She didn't believe that was his plan, not for a moment. It was too awful to try to imagine what his actual plan might be.

Perhaps she couldn't save them both. She'd decided she would try once more, and then if Constance wouldn't come, she would simply take Leonie. It was monstrous to allow Gregor – and Constance – to continue to keep the child here. Ruby was prepared for a fight; a physical one, if it came to it. Leonie had to come first. None of the needs of the adults were as important as that kid's safety. She was even prepared to phone Joanna, to let the police deal with it if her hand were forced. Anything was better than this. And if, as a result, the child was taken into care, then so be it. At least if Leonie were in care, she'd get to go outside.

Ruby opened the door to the flat with her key. Leonie

was seated in the living room cross-legged on the rug, facing the big screen with headphones concealing her ears. *Peppa Pig* was on. Ruby kissed her on the head but she was too engrossed to respond. Gregor wasn't there; she could tell from the atmosphere. When he was in the flat it thrummed with a certain kind of palpable tension, even if he was in the bedroom with the door shut. When it was just mother and daughter, there was a much more pleasant vibe. But there was nevertheless a background hum of vigilance, of awareness that they were being watched at every moment. That feeling never fully went away. Every word she spoke out loud was for the benefit of Gregor, to reinforce the things they wanted him to hear, and to hide the things they didn't.

Ruby could hear the shower shutting off in the bathroom, the sound of the glass door opening and shutting. 'I got your shopping,' she called, going through and unpacking the bag in the kitchen. 'They didn't have the rice you like.'

After a short while, Constance appeared in the doorframe, her long hair wetting the shoulders of her top. She came into the kitchen and flicked the switch on the extractor fan, another trick allowing them to speak more freely.

'I found it.'

Ruby's eyes reacted before she could think. She wanted to jump up and down, but stopped herself. If she'd found the coat, they could leave right now. 'Where? How? You've looked everywhere.'

'Everywhere inside, yes, many times. But he went out yesterday, and he didn't lock the door. Come.'

They were silent as they stepped outside onto the landing.

Ruby listened hard for movement from below. Constance reached up to stick a piece of tape over the tiny lens of the camera that covered the doorway.

To the side of the door there was a utilities cabinet set into the wall. Constance held up a small key. 'This was in the kitchen. I never knew what it was for, until now.' She unlocked the padlock and opened the door, then quickly drew out something that looked like a swathe of grey fabric and bundled it into her arms. She hurried back inside. Ruby bent to close the cabinet, and as she did, Leonie came running out of the door, laughing, heading for the stairwell.

'Leonie, come back here!' Ruby grabbed the small girl and carried her inside the flat, just as a door closed softly on the floor below. Sarah. She had to try to check in on Mrs Stefanidis before they went, make sure she had everything she needed for a few weeks. It was possible Ruby wouldn't be coming back for a long time.

Once in the living room, Ruby stuck another piece of tape over the pin-head camera in the light fitting.

Leonie started to fuss, trying to get to the front door again, restrained by Constance.

'Here you go, honey,' said Ruby, handing her half a peeled banana. It seemed to do the trick for the moment. The child went back to watch her TV programme.

Constance sat with the old leather coat draped on her knees. It was dark grey in colour and looked dry and cracked, like it hadn't been cared for.

'That's it?'

'Yes.' She stroked it tenderly, as if it were a second child of hers.

255

'It's kind of . . . tatty, isn't it?'

'Yes,' she said, letting her tears fall on the rough surface of the leather.

Where the salt tears fell, circles of the cloth became luminescent. Constance rubbed at it with her thumbs in sweeping motions, spreading the moisture across the garment. As she did, more tears fell, and as the circles of gleaming, anthracite-grey grew on the surface, they met and joined together, spreading across the coat until it shone. Soon it was completely transformed.

'It's so beautiful.' Ruby watched as Constance ran her hands over the skin, a strange light seeming to come from within it, illuminating Constance's face. But no, now that she looked closely; the glow was coming from Constance, too.

Ruby couldn't believe what she was seeing. How were the tears having such an effect on the fabric? It was as if each one, as it splashed and spread across the coat, were capable of rehydrating much more surface area than one tiny droplet ought to have been. *It's like magic*, she thought, swiftly followed by: *Don't be ridiculous*.

Then she caught sight of something else that made her pause. 'Your hands,' said Ruby, and Constance quickly hid them under the coat. 'Let me see them. I never noticed before but . . .' Was she imagining it?

Constance stayed very still for a long time, looking down at her lap. Then she brought out one fist and uncurled it slowly. The skin in between her fingers was webbed.

'Have you always had that?'

Constance nodded.

'Why didn't I see it?'

She shrugged. 'People only notice the things they expect to be there.'

'Can I . . .' Ruby reached for the shining pelt, but Constance yanked the thing away from her.

'No, don't touch it.'

Ruby withdrew, slightly hurt. 'I wasn't going to do anything.'

'If you touch it, something is lost. And I've already lost so much. Do you understand?'

Constance's wide eyes were bright with hope, shiny with tears.

'I'm so sorry,' said Ruby. 'I didn't believe it was real. Or if it was real, I didn't think he would have kept it. I thought you were crazy to stay here, just for that.'

'He had no choice but to keep it, if he wanted me alive. It would be like asking me to live without a head.'

Ruby thought she knew what Constance meant; she felt that way about her violin. More recently, she'd started to feel the same way about Leonie.

From beneath the coat, Constance brought out a white comb, carved from a shell. Ruby couldn't understand where the comb had been hidden; the coat didn't appear to have any pockets, or even any arms. It was more like a cloak, or a long, unfilled pillowcase. Constance turned the comb over in her hand, held it out for Ruby to take.

'It's exquisite,' said Ruby, and tried to hand it back, aware of the strange impulse she'd had to touch the coat, to possess it. Constance indicated that it was OK this time, that she should keep it.

'There's only one like that. After I go home, that's how you'll find me.'

Ruby looked at the teeth of the comb, so finely crafted she was scared they might snap if she touched them; at the shape of it, how it fitted into her palm. On the edge of it, the maker had created an intricate, intertwining mermaid pattern. It must have taken weeks of work.

'I don't understand what you mean.'

'Don't worry. You'll understand, when you need to.'

Ruby felt light-headed. The way the coat had transformed before her eyes from a cracked old thing to a soft, rippling fabric somewhere between leather and suede. She'd never seen anything like it. What kind of fabric did that? She held the comb in one hand, but she couldn't take her eyes from the coat. Once again she could feel the draw of the garment. She wanted more than anything to take it in her hands, to stroke it, to hold it to her face. Constance caught her looking, must have seen the covetous gleam in Ruby because she held it closer to her, crossed her arms over it and leaned away. Ruby held out her hand; she couldn't help it.

'Just let me touch it. Please.' Her fingertips reached out, trembling. Constance was saying something but the words weren't quite clear . . . she reached a little further. If she could only hold it, feel it for a second—

A sharp pain seared Ruby's knuckles and she jumped back, shouting out with surprise. Constance had slapped her hand, hard.

'What did you do that for? It really hurt.'

'You weren't listening to me. You were under its spell.'

The coat had gone; she'd put it away somewhere out of sight, and without the presence of it, Ruby felt shame at what she'd tried to do. This is what Gregor must have felt, though he wouldn't for a moment have thought to fight it. He saw it, liked it, and took it for himself. The way he'd been planning to do with Ruby. He'd hidden her phone, put a tracker on her. Would he have gone as far as to keep her violin? No, he hadn't needed to. Leonie was the reason she couldn't stay away. She saw then how – and why – he'd offered Leonie up to her in pieces, like bait. All the small things he'd encouraged her to do for the baby over the past few weeks, the nappies, the feeding when Constance wasn't able, the babysitting of both mother and child. It was real, the trust they shared, the bond. But it did exactly that: she was bonded, now, and it felt unbreakable, love and confinement in one, like sweet shackles.

Ruby was so glad the coat existed, that it was as wonderful as Constance had hinted at. For all this time she'd thought Constance was delusional. Turned out she was telling the truth about it all along, though what she'd seen only a few moments ago, as the coat transformed, already seemed like a strange kind of dream. It ought to make sense, and yet it did not. There wasn't time for reflection; for now, the fact that it was real was enough. She thought back to what else Gregor must have lied about, and concluded that it was in fact everything. He breathed lies with every word he spoke. There was no cult, only a community with very particular ways. He'd taken Constance, and kept her here, it was as simple as that. All the seal-talk was unusual, sure, but Constance was under extreme pressure, and to her, the stories were true. The stories were part of their way of life. And poor Leonie, living her small life within these walls, never imagining the size of the world outside. It wasn't too late for the child, Ruby realised. Not by a long shot.

'You've been looking for the coat all this time. And you've finally found it.'

'Yes,' said Constance. She didn't look happy. Not at all. Her eyes followed Leonie as she made her way around the room, chatting to herself, picking things up, exploring.

'So, you can finally leave. If that's what you want to do?'

'More than anything.'

'Constance. Why are you crying?'

'I want to go home.'

'Then go. Gregor's not here – he might not be back for days. There's enough time, you can contact your family, they can come and get you. Right?'

She nodded slowly. 'They will come and get me. Now I've got my skin.'

My skin. What a strange way of putting it. 'That's right. So, you should get ready. All of Leonie's stuff will need packing. I can help you.' Ruby started to walk to where the shopping bags were kept. There were no suitcases that she knew of; shopping bags would have to do.

'Wait, you don't understand. They will come and get *me*. But they won't take Leonie.'

Ruby paused. She turned slowly. 'Why can't they take Leonie?'

'Because she wasn't born in the skin, like I was. She doesn't have a coat.'

'Can't they give her one when she gets there?'

Constance shook her head. 'It doesn't work like that.'

Ruby said, 'Can't they make an exception? She's your baby. Your parents' grandchild. They'll be thrilled. Won't they?'

Constance was shaking her head. 'No. They won't be

thrilled. They'll be disappointed. They might even reject me, too, when they find out about her.'

'But . . . how? Why?'

'When he took me . . . I was supposed to be married to someone else the next day. On the island, babies outside marriage simply don't happen. I went with him because it was part of my rite, the way that we – how can I put it – strengthen the blood-line? But children, whether conceived on the wedding night or during the *wandering* night before, must be born into wedlock. Otherwise, they don't exist, not in the eyes of the elders.'

'That's bloody ridiculous. It's the twenty-first century.'

'It doesn't matter. Tradition, and the old ways, are what we live by. They are like your laws.'

'Well, why would you want to go back, then? If you can't take her with you?'

There was a pause, and Ruby thought perhaps Constance would change her mind, see how unreasonable she was being. But she shook her head. 'It's my home. They're my family. I have to go.'

Ruby stared at her. She didn't think she would have to say it. The silence stretched out, and it became apparent that she would. 'But, Constance. Leonie's your family, too.'

Constance blinked. She gazed at Leonie while she spoke. 'I must persuade them. But it would mean going back without her, first of all.' She turned to Ruby. 'I need your help. I can't do it without you. I can't leave her with him and I . . .'

'I'll do it,' said Ruby, although she had no idea what it was she was being asked to do. All she knew was that she would do it, whatever it was. Because she loved Constance, but mostly because she loved Leonie. And the little mite had no one else.

They worked out what they had to do, what false trails they could set to throw Gregor off. Ruby would get a train to Lincoln, where she would take the tracking device out of her phone and put it on a train heading south. They would dress the same as each other so that when Gregor tried to follow, if he asked anyone whether they had seen either of them the stories would be confusing. Constance would take Leonie and meet Ruby at Grimsby, where Ruby would take the baby so that Constance could meet her family at the beach.

'So they'll come for you in a boat, to the beach at Cleethorpes? Why there? Why not the docks at Grimsby?'

Constance's face twitched slightly before she answered. 'That is where they last saw me. They come and look for the lost, every solstice, in the place they were lost. It's a tradition.'

'They won't have forgotten you? Or assumed that you'd run away?'

Constance looked stricken. 'I hope not. If so, then I'm lost forever.'

They straightened out the rest of the plan. After the hand-over, Ruby and Leonie would get on a train with a ticket to Scotland but get off somewhere else and hide out for a few days, just in case Gregor had somehow managed to track them that far. After that, Ruby would make her way to a secluded beach on a tiny island in the Hebrides, by any means possible and without being detected. Constance would meet them there, having persuaded the elders to take Leonie in. Then, Constance and Leonie would start their new life together, on the old skerry, where they belonged.

'What will you do, though?' asked Constance. 'Once we're gone?'

Ruby thought of her broken family, the increasingly desper- ate missed calls and messages from Marianne every Sunday night; the last, brief phone call she'd allowed herself with Joanna. Once she was done with this, perhaps she'd be strong enough to deal with all of that.

'I'll be free of him. We both will. I can start my life again.'

'How will you? He won't stop searching for me and Leonie. My family will protect me from him. But you? You won't be free of him until he's dead.'

Ruby hoped it wouldn't come to that. Gregor was away, not expected back until the evening of the next day. By then they'd be long gone, and impossible to track.

CHAPTER THIRTY-SIX

NOW
Joanna

Monday, 24 December

'There's been no change in his condition,' said Dr Locke. 'To be honest, I'm surprised there hasn't been a deterioration.'

'But you said on the phone that you needed me to attend. If there's been no change, did I really have to come all the way down here?'

Joanna had been expecting to find Gregor awake. She'd wanted to ask him so many questions.

'I need your help to proceed. You may be interested to learn that a colleague of mine has selected Mr Franks for a medical trial involving a functional MRI scan.'

'I don't know what that is.'

'Essentially, it's a scan where you can view the brain in real time, and see different parts lighting up in response to different stimuli.'

'Like, you poke him with a needle and see if he feels pain?'

'That's amongst the things they may do, yes. Another is to ask him questions.'

'But if he's a vegetable . . .'

'Well, that's kind of the point of the trial. To find out if he has any brain function, any consciousness remaining.'

'I can ask him questions?'

The doctor's eyebrows shot up. 'You?'

'I can sit in on the scan, right? Isn't that why you asked me to attend?'

'I suppose you could. But the reason I needed to see you was because we would need to obtain permissions to go ahead. There's an ethical procedure we have to follow.'

'I can OK it. Where do I sign?'

'I was hoping you'd obtained that court order, in the absence of next of kin?'

'I don't need one,' said Jo. 'Not if it's part of a police inquiry, and in the public interest. As the SIO I can authorise it for the purposes of assisting the current investigation.'

'But the study isn't part of the investigation, Detective.'

'It will be, if you let me sit in the control room.'

'I honestly don't see how . . .'

Joanna pointed at the still form of the man that until recently she thought was called Gregor Franks, lying on his back in the hospital bed. 'He *knows* things. If I can gauge his reaction to some questions I have, it might make the difference between finding the little girl we're looking for and not finding her.'

The doctor paused, considering.

'I need to make some calls first. And it'll take a while to get the patient ready for the scan and have him brought up from the ward. I hope you're not in a hurry.'

After the doctor had left, Joanna walked up to the bedside

and stood next to the man who had been living as Gregor Franks. She watched his motionless face. 'Soon I'll be able to speak to you, and see how you react,' she said. There was no reaction. She bent closer. 'You won't be able to hide for much longer, whoever you are. I'm going to see right inside your brain.'

While she waited in the control room of the MRI, Joanna dialled Ruby's number and listened again to the bot reciting the phone-switched-off message. She pulled out the phone she'd taken from Gregor's flat and looked at it. It couldn't tell her anything more than it had done when she'd gone through it the night before – it was Ruby's old phone, and it hadn't been used since September. The missed calls page made her sad, but not as sad as the gallery, where she found only one photo of herself, grimacing, trying to avoid being captured. She remembered Ruby taking it, laughing at Joanna's camera-phobia, how Jo had held up a hand to try to block the lens. She wished, now, that she'd simply smiled, like a normal person.

The door opened and Atkinson entered.

'Jo. What the hell are you doing?'

'How come you're here, Steve?'

'I came to find you. Someone from the hospital contacted me to confirm we were OK to go ahead with some kind of fancy scan on Franks. Apparently, you've said it's part of the investigation.'

'Well, it is. They can look inside his brain. I'm going to see how he reacts to certain things.'

'But he can't answer.'

'I have a plan, don't worry. His reaction will be enough. Unless Dr Locke's right, and the bugger's brain-dead.'

'They said that because it was part of the police investigation, some of the cost should come from the police budget. Do you know what fifty per cent of an FMRI scan costs?'

'Oh. Does Thrupp know?'

'He will soon. And then he'll wonder why I didn't tell him.'

'Ah.'

Atkinson sank heavily down into a chair.

'Jo. What we did last night was stupid. And dangerous. We've got information the investigation needs, but we can't tell anyone because of how we got it. That passport, and the finger, for fuck's sake. The fact that Gregor isn't who we think he is.'

'Relax, Steve. We were one step in front, that's all. CSI will be opening up that box as we speak. They'll find the passport and then they'll know everything we know, and they'll start running checks on Mr Mysterious immediately. And then there's this scan. If I ask him a question and his brain lights up in response, we'll be able to work out where Ruby has gone.'

'Oh, so you're planning to stake your reputation on a highly expensive version of the YES/NO game, with no guarantee that it will even work?'

'It will work. You'll see.'

'Even if it does work, we'll still be in trouble. You think Thrupp's going to overlook the fact that we broke into a suspect's property and then carried out an unrecorded search of the victim's place?'

'We won't be in trouble if we get the results. Plus, he's not going to find out about either of those things.'

'You broke the lock on Ruby's apartment.'

'After you left, I went back and fixed it. Good as new.'

'You cut that padlock on the box in Gregor's wardrobe.'

'I replaced the padlock, too. It was only a cheap model. Anyway, they already catalogued the key, so they'll have to cut it themselves if they want to get inside quickly.'

Atkinson rubbed his temples and made a low frustrated groan.

There was a tense silence, in which they both stared through the glass into the MRI scan room at the huge, space-age machine.

'This is too risky, boss. I think you should—'

'I'm only going to ask a few routine questions.'

'Of a man who can't consent to being asked. The ethics of this are all over the shop.'

The door to the control room opened and a technician entered, along with Dr Locke and a short, bald man who introduced himself as Mr Cunningham, the consultant radiologist in charge of the trial.

On the other side of the large glass screen, the patient was wheeled into the white-walled scan room by a porter. A moment later a team of staff entered and transferred the man's limp body to the platform that would feed him into the cylinder at the centre of the MRI. One nurse remained in the room and began to place straps on the patient. Through the speakers they could hear her talking to him as she worked.

'I'm just getting you ready for the scanner, Greg, OK? It'll be almost the same routine as last time, with the CT. Don't try to move while you're in there, it can distort the results.'

Joanna found it touching that the nurse talked to the patient as if he could hear. She wasn't writing him off as brain-dead, then.

The technician in the control room started adjusting the

equipment, switching on every screen on the bank of monitors in front of them. She pointed out the microphone, where Jo would need to speak into so that Gregor would hear her questions.

'What should I be looking out for on the scan?'

The radiologist brought up a recorded scan of another patient.

'This area here,' he pointed with a pen, 'is the hippocampus. Associated with emotions and memory. That's the bit you need to keep an eye on. I'd expect it to light up at anything personally meaningful.'

The scan video showed splashes of red and yellow appearing and dissipating on the screen.

'We're obviously presenting the patient with stimuli here. The darker colours represent increased activity.'

'And was this patient as outwardly unresponsive as Mr Franks is now?'

He nodded. 'Every patient in this trial has been selected due to the fact that they have been diagnosed with persistent vegetative state due to infection, or drug overdose. The head injury Mr Franks has sustained complicates things slightly, but he's still eligible. A bonus of the scan is that, if the head injury turns out to be more significant than the CT showed, we'll be able to consider further treatment.'

Jo was only half listening, thinking about the things she was going to ask. *Do you know where Ruby is*, was the first question. She could already picture the bloom of orange and purple caused by the reaction that question would get. *Who does that finger we found belong to?* The screen would light up like a firework display. She'd need to think carefully about how to frame the questions, if this was actually going to help in any specific way beyond confirming her suspicions. All she would see is emotional response. Perhaps she would need to take a very methodical approach, listing every major UK city Ruby might have gone to until she got a response. It could take a very long time.

'How long have I got to question him?'

'We generally scan for about ten minutes.'

'Can I have longer if I need it?'

'No,' said Mr Cunningham.

'Ready,' said the nurse, her voice metallic through the speakers. She left the patient alone in the room. The technician pressed a button and the platform started to draw the man's body into the machine.

From the angle Joanna was looking from, the patient's face was obscured by the foam helmet as he was slowly inserted into the aperture. She hadn't noticed when she stood next to his bed earlier on, but his body seemed different. Thinner than when she'd inspected him on Saturday. Perhaps a couple of days on a liquid-only diet will do that to you.

Once the man was fully inside the scanner, the doctor leant forward and pressed the button on the intercom microphone.

'Mr Franks, in a moment we're going to ask you a few questions. If you're able to, just think of the answer for me. We'll be able to pick up any brain activity on the scan. If you can hear me, this is your chance to communicate with us, OK?'

The patient started to cough and splutter. He was coming round. Joanna stood up. She could see his feet kicking in the restraints.

'Oh, shit,' said the doctor, scanning the readouts on the heart monitor. 'That's not right.'

'What's happening? Is he waking up?'

'We need to get him out. Right now.'

The technician pushed the button to slide the platform from the machine. The doctor left the control room and appeared a moment later in the scan room, followed by two nurses.

'He's fitting,' shouted the doctor. 'Let's get him back on the trolley.'

As more staff entered the room to transfer the patient, Harper and Atkinson stared through the glass at the carefully managed emergency happening the other side of it. Someone pressed the resuscitation alarm. Blood dripped from the patient's head as he was lifted across. And Joanna saw a strand of hair peeping from the foam helmet, the wrong colour, the wrong length. The man was too skinny. His legs didn't reach the end of the hospital bed. She wrenched open the control room door and ran around to the scan room, but she didn't need to get a good look at the much younger man lying there. She knew already.

'That's not him.'

'What?' said Atkinson. 'But, how?'

Jo started running in the direction of the exit, but there were too many options. The hospital was huge. It had about forty exits. She raised her radio and pressed to connect, summoning assistance to help with the search, still running down corridors and flights of stairs, with no sense of where she should run to, knowing that it was useless because she was looking for a man in a porter's uniform, a man well-practised at disappearing, who could move through the hospital – and through the world – without being seen by anyone.

CHAPTER THIRTY-SEVEN

NOW
Joanna

Monday, 24 December

The hospital lift security tape made grim viewing. Thrupp joined Harper and Atkinson in the CCTV monitoring station, the DI having made his way across town on blue lights the moment he heard what had happened.

The first part of the footage showed an apparently unconscious patient being wheeled into the lift by the porter. The porter then stood facing away from his charge, so that he didn't see the patient's fist uncurl, revealing what he had stolen from the trolley, unaware of the length of tubing being unravelled until it was looped around his neck and pulled tight. During the struggle, 'Gregor' managed to use an elbow to press the emergency stop button to halt the lift between floors. The porter collapsed, lifeless, and the next moment, the patient grabbed the smaller man under the arms, dragged his limp body up on to the hospital bed and started removing his clothes.

'I've never seen anything like it,' said Thrupp.

'How long do you think he's been lying there, pretending to be in a coma?' said Joanna. She knew then that when she'd spoken to him that morning, he would have heard every word. *I'm going to see right inside your brain*, she'd said. Her face had been inches from his.

On the screen, now wearing the porter's uniform, 'Gregor' had removed the protective helmet he'd been wearing and was fitting it on to the porter. He took the other man's glasses and used them to inspect his reflection, tidying his hair under the uniform cap before putting the glasses on as a final touch, then releasing the emergency stop mechanism. A moment later the lift doors opened and he manoeuvred the bed out confidently, as if that were his job all along.

Thrupp turned to Jo. 'He can't have gone very far. I've mobilised all the patrol vehicles and officers we can spare. Let's hope he collapses from blood loss – after all, the man's got a head wound.'

Joanna said, 'I think he's stronger than we imagine, sir. You saw what he did with that porter. He's cunning, too.'

'More than you know,' said Thrupp. 'I've got a confession to make, in fact.'

'Oh? What's that, sir?' Jo and Atkinson exchanged a microglance.

'First thing this morning, one of the CSI's found evidence in Franks' flat that the victim might not be called Franks at all. There was a passport, with a different photograph. We showed it to the agent who deals with Franks' rental property and he identified the man in the passport picture as Franks. The photo of our patient on the driver's licence, however, turns out to be a fake. The agent didn't recognise our man at all.

Apparently, they've been doing business entirely over email for the past three years. Haven't even spoken on the phone.'

Atkinson said, 'What? He's stolen another man's identity? Oh my God.' Harper wanted to kick him for his terrible acting.

Thrupp carried on, oblivious. 'We checked his fingerprints against unsolved cases in the system. Should have done that to start with, but there was no reason to suspect the man.'

'What did you find?' asked Jo.

'A few years ago there was a spate of burglaries, all with the same fingerprint evidence, but we never found the perpetrator. Our man's fingerprints were a match.'

'I don't understand, sir. You said you had a confession to make,' said Harper. 'I don't see what you could have done wrong.'

'I made a judgement call. First thing this morning I knew this man had committed a crime in stealing Gregor Franks' identity, but I decided not to organise a guard for him, because he was in a coma at the time of discovery. Why would a man in a coma need security? And now this has happened. So I have to take some of the responsibility for the injury to that poor porter.'

Atkinson was apparently studying his own shoes, in detail.

'The burglary offences connected to this man weren't of a violent nature,' said Jo.

'No.'

'Therefore you had no reason to believe he was a danger.'

'I suppose.'

'And, like you say, we'll find him soon enough. He's not going to get far, the state he's in. Me and Steve can join the search.'

'No. You need to concentrate on finding the girl, and the two women. We've still no leads on that. I'll see you back at the station.'

'Yes, sir.'

'Oh, and I'd appreciate it if you used your discretion, with what I've told you. No obligation, of course, you're both upstanding officers. I don't want a cover-up, just for you to keep it under your hats for the time being. Gossip, you know. I'll be making a full report, detailing my decision-making process. Hopefully the Chief Constable will see fit to accept my reasoning.'

'Of course, sir, no problem,' said Atkinson.

'Don't beat yourself up about it, sir,' said Joanna. 'Any one of us would have done the same.'

'One last thing,' said the DI, fixing Joanna with a steely eyeball. 'Don't try to charge my investigation with any more MRI scans. Unless you want to pay for it yourself.'

'Yes, sir. Sorry, sir.'

She drove back to the police station, the police radio turned up so she could monitor the search. By the time she'd parked and made her way to the incident room, she was feeling despondent about their chances of catching him. There'd been no sightings whatsoever since he'd escaped from the ward. It was as if he was the Invisible Man.

In the incident room, Eddie was waiting with news of the search for Constance B and Leonie. Like the doctor, he'd been up most of the night, and it showed.

'Hi, Eddie. Did you find them?' Joanna struggled to control the slight tremor in her voice. If they'd found Ruby and

Leonie, at least she'd have a chance at getting to them first, at keeping them safe from the fugitive.

'We checked CCTV at Edinburgh train station, where their journey was supposed to end. There's nothing. She didn't get off there. So, we've had to search cameras at every stop on the line, but I'm afraid to say it's not a straightforward process. Some of the systems are still analogue. We've been uploading all the tapes and programming the face-recognition software to search. It all takes time. As a result, we don't have anything yet, I'm afraid.'

'How long until you do?' said Harper.

'Maybe another couple of days.'

'Can't you make it happen quicker?'

'I'm afraid not. Today we're having the tapes couriered over, but getting them into our system is a bit of a laborious task, as you can imagine. We have to convert them to digital in real time, and then—'

'Well, get some more people on it, can't you?'

'There isn't anyone. And I'm going home.'

'Can't you stay? Do a bit of overtime?'

'No,' said Eddie. 'In case you haven't noticed, I've done ten hours' overtime already. And tomorrow's Christmas. My annual leave started yesterday; I should be at home, relaxing, by now.'

She thought about ramping up the pressure, letting him know just how urgent it was. Maybe she could try yelling at him. But there was no point burning bridges that might be useful in future, if she could help it.

'Fine,' she said, 'you go home, have a break, you deserve it. But if you could do one small, tiny favour for me before you do . . .'

'What is it?'

'I need you to set up email alerts for any mobile phone or data usage that happens on this number.' She wrote down Ruby's new phone number and handed it to him. 'Now, I realise we're not supposed to have alerts going to personal emails, but this phone belongs to a suspect and I'm sure you understand the need for urgency on this case. I wouldn't ask you, but it's Christmas Day tomorrow, there won't be anyone manning the surveillance system and if the person turns the phone on to contact family, for instance, then there'll be an opportunity there that we don't want to miss . . .'

'You'll need the DI to authorise that.'

'I will, of course, but he's not in right now and if you want to get home quickly . . . It's on my head, shall we say.'

'Right, fine. I'll do it. But then I'm out of here.' He hurried away, clutching the paper with Ruby's number on it.

'Thank you, Eddie,' she said. 'I love you, Eddie.'

She thought she heard him mutter, 'Yeah, right,' before he disappeared from view.

CHAPTER THIRTY-EIGHT

It happened that one of the children, in the course of his play, found concealed beneath a stack of corn a seal's skin. Her eyes glistened with rapture – she gazed upon it as her own – as the means by which she could pass through the ocean that led to her native home. She burst into an ecstasy of joy, which was only moderated when she beheld her children, whom she was now about to leave; and after hastily embracing them, she fled with all speed towards the seaside.

CHARLES JOHN TIBBETS, 'The Mermaid Wife,' 1889

Constance

Friday, 21 December
Early morning

There are only a few hours until she will be gone from this place forever. Ruby has left – she went last night so that she could start her journey in a different place to Constance, to make the tracks they leave behind them as confusing as possible. Soon Ruby will set off to catch the first train, south, and later they will meet up to make the switch. Constance couldn't have chosen a better guardian for Leonie; Ruby is a true friend. A saviour. Without her, none of this would be possible. She stares at the hands of the clock, willing them to go faster.

When she hears it, she instantly remembers the tape. The small pieces of masking tape she put on the cameras, that she forgot to remove. He's looked on the camera feed, he's seen that some of the cameras are obscured. He's come back, and he's angry enough to make a noise loud enough to alert her. She gathers Leonie into her arms, runs and hides, as quickly as she can. He'll kill her if he finds her trying to leave. She knows this in her bones.

The conch shell rests on the side of the bath. Heavy and curved, with delicate white edges and a polished interior, it sits just as it has since Gregor bought it from the gift shop in the seaside town where he first met Constance. Until this moment, the shell has always been an ornament, something to look at.

This should not be happening. They had expected him to be gone the entire night, and the next day, too. She eyes the conch shell as she crouches behind the door, an idea forming in the split second before his footsteps slow to a stop outside the room.

'Are you in there?'

She doesn't answer. Silently, she slips her hand inside the shell. It is cool and smooth, hard and heavy as a rock. The weight of it, hugged to her belly, comforts her.

There is a soft whimper from the bundle of towels under the sink, and she reaches to stroke the child, to quiet her. It won't be long. Only a few seconds more. Then it will all be over.

He speaks through the door. 'Leonie? It's Daddy. Don't worry, sweetie, I'm coming in. Don't be scared, OK? There's going to be a big bang.'

But before he can charge at the door, she unlocks it. The sound of the bolt being drawn makes him pause. He waits, perhaps to see if she'll come out. For a while nothing happens. Then, he opens the door and steps inside.

The shell flies through the air, her hand inside it, a deadly knuckle-duster, connecting with the man's skull with such force that the shell is cracked. The man is felled; he drops quickly, though to her it seems in slow motion, a building demolished by dynamite. In the silence that follows, she turns to check Leonie didn't see anything. The bundle of towels is shaking, but it's still intact. She lets go of the shell and picks up the girl, holding her head so she can't see, taking her away from the slowly growing pool of blood and into the bedroom.

'Wait here, baby girl.'

She lays Leonie in the cradle. Her silent cry contorts her face, but Constance can't comfort her, not now – the job isn't finished.

Constance takes the brown bottle from the bathroom cabinet, and goes through to the other bathroom where Gregor is starting to stir. He is trying to sit up. He eyes her with confusion.

'Gregor!' she cries. 'What's happened? Don't try to get up too fast. Here, let me help you.'

She grabs an arm as the man tries to stand up. He slips on the blood, and Constance only needs to push him a little to help him fall backwards into the tub, where he hits his head again and lies still.

She kneels, using towels so that she doesn't get covered in his blood, and drips the brown liquid from the bottle into his mouth. She squeezes his nostrils shut to make him swallow. When he's had the whole lot, she stops.

Constance wonders if it's going to be enough. She wonders if he's going to die. She hopes he does, and then she hopes he doesn't, because Ruby will be the one left behind. She'll be the one they try to blame.

Either way it's too late now. His breathing slows, becomes steady, until she almost can't tell whether he's breathing or not. It's better for Ruby if he's dead. It's better for all of them.

Constance chews her thumb and stares at the man, bent and broken-looking in the empty tub, a towel bunched at his feet.

Later, when she's dressed and ready, Constance returns to the bathroom and turns on the bath taps. She takes a pair of scissors and cuts off his clothes, to make it look like an accident, as if he was alone, that he has slipped and fallen badly. He groans when she shifts his body to get the clothes out from under and she jumps back, afraid he will rise up and attack her, the way he has so many times before. His eyes don't open. He settles, grows still, but the fear doesn't leave her. She pulls forward his head, hits him again with the conch shell, in the same place as before. This time, the blow lands with a squelch. Constance doesn't notice the small piece of the shell's lip that breaks off and lands on the tiles. She bundles up the cut clothes; she'll drop them in a litter bin somewhere in the city.

She locks the bathroom from the outside, using a teaspoon wedged in the groove of the bolt to turn it. She wraps her coat across her body, picks up Leonie in one arm and swings the changing bag over a shoulder. Time to go. Tonight she'll return to her old life, but even as she feels the joy and anticipation of that, she is broken-hearted. Because it means letting go of everything she has in this life, including her baby girl.

CHAPTER THIRTY-NINE

NOW
Ruby

Monday, 24 December

The cold clamped itself around Ruby's head and made the inside of her ears hurt. She zipped up Leonie's jacket and pulled the hood over. Then she tried to fasten her own coat, letting go of Leonie for a second. Almost in the same moment, her arm shot out to grab the child again as she got ready to run off. Ruby hauled her up to eye level.

'Baby girl? Please don't do that. You scared me so much.'

Leonie stared blankly at Ruby as if she didn't understand. Then she laughed and started wriggling to be let down. Ruby had to hold the little hand tightly to stop Leonie wrenching it away. With her free hand Ruby struggled to jam a beanie hat on her own head, tried to hold her jacket closed with frozen fingers as they made their way down the platform and out onto the streets of York.

They'd spent the past two nights holed up in bed and breakfasts, one in Leicester, the other on the outskirts of Leeds. The landlady this morning had served fizzy orange in a wineglass in lieu of bucks fizz to mark the season, but she'd also folded her arms and looked at her watch, anxious for her unwanted guests to leave. The woman had made no secret of the fact that Ruby and Leonie were inconveniencing her when they'd turned up late the previous night ('I never open on the twenty-third, I'm afraid you'll have to go elsewhere.'). Ruby's distraught face had softened her slightly, but it was Leonie's silent weeping when she saw Ruby was upset that had swung it in the end. ('Fine, stay the night. But you'll have to change the sheets yourself.') On their way out, the woman had half-heartedly asked Ruby where she was going for Christmas, though as she spoke she was opening the front door and ushering them through it as if to make sure they definitely were going somewhere and she didn't really care where exactly that was.

'Don't worry about us,' Ruby had said, thinking, *as if you would*. 'We're going to see an old friend.'

'Oh, good,' said the landlady, seemingly relieved to be let off the hook after being such a Scrooge. 'You have a lovely Christmas, now, won't you?'

Ruby worried now that she'd said too much. If Gregor somehow found out that they'd been at that B&B and questioned the owner, would 'an old friend' give him anything to go on? She couldn't recall ever mentioning Sam to him. Not that Ruby would have talked about Sam in any great detail, to anyone. The pair had a patchy history, had shared a fair few dark moments. They'd helped each other when they'd been at their lowest points; those stories were no one else's business. She also knew, deep down, that Sam was in love with her. But she couldn't recall every single thing she'd spoken about to Gregor, especially in the time before she knew what he was.

The taxi driver was wearing a Santa hat, but his face was thin and pinched. 'It's double time, today, love.'

'Merry bloody Christmas,' she muttered as they pulled away.

When the cab arrived at the wharf car park, the night was closing in around them. Only a few windows were lit in the barges that wintered there. Leonie was almost asleep again, and had to be carried. The moment they'd paid and got out, the taxi reversed away at speed, leaving them alone, standing under the single streetlamp that burned at the edge of the water.

In the silence she watched the gentle bobbing of the tethered boats, wondering where Sam might have moored.

'Hey, matey. How was your trip?'

'Jeez, Sam. You made me jump.'

She hadn't seen him sitting there on the old lock in the gathering dark. They both laughed, and Sam stood up and came close. He'd grown his beard longer, but the eyes were the same, wide and kind. When he put his arms around her and around Leonie, Ruby tried not to cry.

He gave them a long squeeze. Then he stepped back a little. 'So. This must be Leonie.'

'You're sure it's OK for the baby to stay too? We don't have anywhere else to go. We stayed in this B&B last night and the woman was really mean . . .'

'Hey, hey. You're here now. It's OK. I love kids.' He rubbed Ruby on the back. She leaned into him, into the familiar feel of his wiry frame, his strong arms. Finally, she was safe.

Arriving at Sam's, she thought it might have been the closest thing she'd ever felt to coming home.

The boat was just the way she remembered it. She carried Leonie down the steps into the cosy warmth, the smell of liquorice tea and woodsmoke. After the bed and breakfasts, which she had chosen on the basis that they were clearly run-down, ask-no-questions type establishments, she felt she could finally relax.

'Nice boots,' said Sam, with a smile in his voice. On her feet were a pair of ex-army boots she'd found in a charity shop. 'Not really you, though, are they? And what's with the hair?'

Still holding Leonie, Ruby twirled a strand of her newly orange hair in her fingers. Yesterday she'd bleached it, tinted it and cut it herself into a rough bob. (She knew she ought to feel bad about the mess she'd made of that landlady's sink. But she didn't. Not even a bit.) This morning she'd teamed the hairstyle with heavy eyeliner and a tweed jacket that was a size too small. The steampunk get-up was her third disguise this week, and not her favourite if she was honest. She looked at her friend for a moment without speaking.

'It's so good to see you, Sammy. I can't tell you how much I've missed you.' And she cried, then, letting her head fall into the padding on the shoulder of Leonie's thick coat.

Sam sat next to Ruby on the narrow bench. Leonie's eyes were open and she sat up, started patting Ruby on the head. 'Mamma Bee sad,' she said, 'No sad, Mamma Bee.' Her little hand stroked the orange hair, a little bit too roughly. 'Ahhhh,' she said. 'Ahhhh.'

Ruby laughed through the tears. She pulled the little girl into a hug. 'Thank you, baby. I'm happy now.'

'She's lovely, isn't she?' said Sam. 'Very caring.'

'Yes, she is,' said Ruby, 'I'm really lucky.'

'Milk,' said Leonie, 'I want milk, Mamma Bee.'

She looked at Sam. 'Can I heat some milk for her? She'll sleep then.'

Sam heated milk in a pan and she drank it from the sippy cup that Ruby had brought. Then Ruby said, 'Can I borrow your fiddle?'

She sat Leonie on Sam's knee and played 'The Seal-Woman's Joy', singing the words at the same time.

Ionn da, ionn do . . .

'What is that?' he said. 'I don't think I've heard it before. Is it Orcadian?'

It was rare for Sam to hear a tune he didn't know at all. The music filled the boat with calm. Rich and sonorous, the fiddle and the lullaby worked their magic on the baby, who gave a huge yawn.

'Do you like it on the boat, tiddler?' said Sam, stroking Leonie on the cheek with a knuckle. 'She's beautiful. Aren't you, honey?'

Leonie gave a tired smile from around the sides of her thumb.

'She's sleepy,' said Ruby. 'I might put her down.'

Sam arranged a purple corduroy bean bag on the floor of the boat, and Ruby laid Leonie in it. She curled up on her side, her thumb wedged firmly in her mouth, and her breath came and went, long and slow.

'Now,' said Sam, after a moment's silence. 'There is a fuck of a lot to tell me, I think you'll agree.'

Ruby held her head in her hands for a while. Then she said, 'I'm not sure where to start.'

'Let's start with whose child this is, and go from there.'

She shut her eyes. 'She's mine. Like I said in the letter.'

'Is it an adoption?'

'Yes, exactly.'

'An official one? I thought it took ages. That you had to own your own house, have a steady job, all of that.'

'Mmm,' she said. Her eyes ached.

He waited until she looked up at him. Then he tipped his head to the side, gave her a knowing look. 'Come on, Roo. Tell me the truth.'

Ruby shifted her eyes away, to where the stove glowed red and gold, a blackened log at its centre, turning to ash. He could always see the truth; it was stupid trying to pretend. Other people could never tell when she lied to them, but Sam saw through it every time. Though, it may have been that she didn't want to hide things from him. With most people, Ruby wanted them to leave her alone. With Sam, she wanted him to see her properly. But in that moment, it was too much for her to think about trying to explain it all to him.

'Not now,' she said, 'I just need to sleep now.'

'Fine,' he said. 'But if it turns out you've stolen someone's kid, then I'm not sure I can help you with that.'

'I haven't. I promise you. The mother knows about it. She asked me. And I'm like a mother to her anyway, you saw how she is with me.'

Sam nodded slowly. He didn't say anything for a minute or two. He passed her a cold bottle of beer. A short while later he inhaled as if he was about to speak, then made an indecisive *mmm* sound that could have been a yawn. She felt him observing her, which made her feel awkward in the unfamiliar clothes she was still wearing, and when she glanced up in the dim light she could tell he was frowning.

'I'll tell you in the morning, I promise.'

'Is that going to be my Christmas present, you answering all my questions?'

'Oh, mate. Christmas present? Yeah, I guess it'll have to be.'

'Don't feel bad. I didn't get you anything either.'

They both looked at the sleeping form of Leonie.

'I should have done something for her, though,' said Sam.

'No, don't worry. She's too young to be aware. Christmas is overrated, anyway. In my house it's been a sham for the past few years, my mother drunk all day, everyone pretending things are normal, that we're the perfect family. I know they tried their best, but even as a kid I never felt like I belonged. Not properly.'

She caught Sam's eye. He hadn't stopped watching her. 'You belong here, though. So, you can forget all that, can't you.'

'I can try. Christmas is like fucking Groundhog day. The same songs, the same shit in the shops. The same food.' She looked up. 'Oh, I just thought; you didn't get a turkey, did you?'

'Of course not, you tit. I'm a vegetarian. I was going to do curry.'

'Well, thank goodness for that. I can't stand the stuff. And gravy granules make me hurl.'

'No danger of turkey. Or Christmas telly, of course, because I haven't got one. And looks like no presents, either.'

She smiled. 'Sounds completely perfect.'

'We can all pretend it's not even Christmas Day.' He inclined his head at Leonie. 'Then we can have curry and secrets for lunch.'

She stopped smiling, and stared at her knees for a while. 'I'm not keeping secrets from you, Sam. I won't, not anymore. It's a long story, that's all. Let's get some sleep first.' Her exhausted eyes were starting to close on their own. She forced them open. 'Just so you know: she wakes up early.'

'That's fine, so do I. Up with the dawn.'

They shared a few more minutes of companionable silence. After a while he disappeared into the back of the boat, returning with two military-style blankets that he handed to her. He closed up the fire and made his way to the cabin, where he shut the partition door with a small click.

Ruby took a swig of her beer, which had gone warm in the heat from the fire. She let her body relax for the first time in days, so that when the tears came they were a raging wave that closed her throat and made her clap a hand over her mouth to stop the sobs from waking the baby.

CHAPTER FORTY

NOW
Joanna

Monday, 24 December

The moment Thrupp entered the department he made a bee-line for Joanna. He was holding a sheaf of paper, and had a strange look on his face.

'Jo. How are you?'

Harper looked sideways at her superior. She couldn't remember a single other occasion on which he had asked her how she was.

'I'm fine, sir.'

'This morning was quite shocking, wasn't it?'

'Well, yes. Just another workday, right? How are you?' She couldn't remember ever having asked him that question either. Neither of them were small-talk people.

'Oh, good, thanks,' said Thrupp. There was an awkward pause. 'Shall we go somewhere a bit more private?'

'Sure.' Every fibre of Joanna's body screamed that something was very wrong. They went through into her office and shut the door.

'Forensics just sent me this,' said Thrupp. 'It's the finger-print report for Franks' flat.'

The alarm bells that had already started ringing in her head got suddenly more urgent.

'Thanks, sir.' She held out her hand for the report but he didn't hand it over. She swallowed. 'What does it say?' She thought she could guess what it said.

'Well, it's very . . . revealing. It details four separate profiles. One is the fugitive. One is the child, from the size of them. The other two are, presumably, the two women we are searching for. So one of those will be, or might be, called Constance. And the other is this person.'

He opened up the report and placed it on the desk in front of her. He pointed at a name: Ruby Harper.

Harper stared at the report. She cleared her throat a couple of times.

Thrupp took his finger away and crossed his arms. 'Relation of yours, by any chance?'

'Harper's a pretty common name, sir.'

'How long have we known each other, Jo?'

The memory hit her like a slap for being so stupid. Of course. Ruby had met the DI at the Police Local Heroes awards ceremony four years ago. Only for a few seconds, but still. They'd shaken hands. How could she have forgotten? Thrupp clearly hadn't.

Quietly, she asked, 'When did you realise?'

'Oh, I didn't. Terrible memory for faces, unfortunately. That young Community Support Officer, Louise, made the connection. She saw the name on the lease on the flat opposite Mr Franks, then had a quick look at social media when she couldn't get access for a statement. Ruby doesn't have a profile on Twitter or Facebook, but there are ways of finding people, as you well know.'

Anger coloured Joanna's cheeks. *I told Louise I was going to follow that up myself. The snitching little . . .*

Thrupp went on, 'In fact it was very easy indeed to identify Ruby Harper as your relation. There's a photo of you together. On your social media. Several, actually.'

Jo wanted to cry. She forced the feeling downwards, into the pit of her stomach where it sat, hard and heavy, waiting to come back up.

'You knew it was her from the start,' said Thrupp. 'The photograph on the station platform. You'd have known immediately. Why didn't you tell me?'

'I can explain.'

Thrupp held up his hand. 'Actually, there's no need. I know you can get a bit . . . emotional sometimes. When family's involved. Hell, we all do. So, I'm not going to bollock you. But I'm transferring you, for now. With a note of caution.'

Jo was so surprised that she couldn't speak at first. Where was the almighty tirade, the lecture about holding up an investigation? Why wasn't he angrier? What she'd done – and this was only the parts he knew about – could have been a sacking offence. 'You're not punishing me?'

'Not this time. I've spoken to PC Atkinson. He explained that Ruby is your, um . . . well, he said the situation was complicated. That you're going through the wringer right now, with family stuff. You're not getting away with it completely – there will be a level of monitoring for the next few months.'

'Please don't take me off the case.' She needed to be on the case. Nobody cared as much about the safety of these people as she did, and that could only be a good thing, surely.

'It's unethical for it to continue. You know that.'

'Why is it?'

'I shouldn't need to spell this out for you: it's unethical because one of the suspects in the case is related to the investigating officer. It makes you biased.'

'She's not a suspect yet. There's no evidence to suggest she did anything to that man. Ruby would never do anything to hurt anyone. She's a loving, gentle person. And anyway, he deserved it.'

He threw up his hands. 'My point exactly. You can't be objective.'

'But, sir, I—'

'Fred West was someone's little boy, you know. Ted Bundy's mother said he was the perfect son.'

'This is nothing like that, why are you—'

'No arguments. You know what's right, Jo. Don't force me to suspend you, because if it comes to it, I won't need much persuading.'

'Couldn't I be kept on as an adviser? Even unofficially? I've got more of a chance of talking her round. For instance, she'd hand the kid to me, if it came to it.'

He hardened his expression, ignoring what she'd said. 'I'll send you your new case in a day or two. Why don't you take a couple of days off? Have a nice rest, a Christmas break. Gather your thoughts.'

'But—'

He held up his hand, his palm facing her. 'Stop talking. Get your stuff. Go home.'

She crossed her arms. 'Did you tell the Chief Constable yet, about what happened this morning, when your delay in communication meant that man could assault that porter?'

The DI stepped towards her and waggled a finger in her face. 'Don't threaten me, Joanna. I can guarantee it will not end well for you.'

They locked eyes for a tense few seconds.

'Fine. I'll go.' She grabbed her jacket and picked up her satchel. 'Who are you putting in charge?'

'Steve Atkinson can hold the fort for now. I'll keep a close eye on proceedings. Don't worry. We'll find the fugitive.'

'Before he finds Ruby and Leonie? How can you be so sure? You saw what he did.'

'It's not your concern any more. You need to leave it to us now. Go home.'

'Not my concern?'

'Would you like to speak to a family liaison officer?'

Harper didn't trust herself to speak. She stalked from the room without another word.

CHAPTER FORTY-ONE

NOW
Ruby

Tuesday, 25 December

At first light, Ruby was woken by a scream. She opened her eyes to find Leonie standing by the wood burner, her hand in front of her face, mouth wide, eyes wide, shock and pain and outrage all at once. The child inhaled quickly and began crying her silent cry, in which the only noise came from snatched breaths in between each soundless sob. Ruby jumped from the narrow bed and picked her up, held the small hand and turned it over, looking for what was wrong.

'Did you touch the stove, honey? Did you burn yourself?'

Sam thundered from the other end of the boat, topless and sleep-drunk. 'What's going on? Is she hurt?'

'She burned her hand, I think.' There was a red rectangle on the toddler's palm. 'Is it hot? Does it burn, sweetie?'

Leonie bawled and the tears came down, those not wiped away by Ruby disappearing into her collar. If there had been sound, it would have been deafening. Mouth wide open, teeth bared, she nodded her head in slow motion, yes, it's hot, it hurts.

Ruby said, 'I'm so stupid – I should have realised. She's never seen a stove, she won't have known it could hurt her. I'm sorry, lovely, it's OK.'

Between sobs, Leonie whispered, 'Mamma? Where Mamma? Want Mamma.' She took a deep breath and screwed up her face, shaking with the force of the soundless cry.

'I know,' said Ruby, stroking her back. 'I know.' And her heart was breaking then, for although she loved Leonie like she was her own child, to Leonie, Constance was irreplaceable. And she wasn't here.

'What's she doing? Why isn't she making any noise?' Sam frowned in confusion.

'Can you get some cold water?'

He filled the washing-up bowl from the tap and brought it over, but Leonie's hand stayed rigid, arm outstretched, and she couldn't be persuaded to bend it at the elbow. Ruby picked her up bodily and dunked the hand in, held it there. When she instinctively took it out again, Ruby grabbed it and forced it in.

'I'm sorry, sweetie, but this will help to cool it down.'

The girl just cried and cried, her face a mask of pain and terror, and all without any noise at all but a high squeak, air being let out from a balloon.

Sam was wringing his hands and shifting from foot to foot, causing the boat to rock slightly 'What's wrong with her voice, Ruby? Should we take her to the hospital?'

She looked at him. He saw her hesitate, and frowned. If Leonie was badly burned, then they wouldn't have a choice, of course, but the hospital would need names, addresses, background checks. And then, when they didn't find Leonie on the system . . . it was too risky. Ruby brought the child's hand out of the bowl. It was a little pink, now, but there was no blistering. Tentatively, she touched the top of the stove with her own finger. Hot, but not burning. Perhaps they wouldn't need to go.

'That's just how she cries. I don't know why. She's always been like that.'

'But she talks fine. She screamed *silently*.'

Ruby felt shame for what she was about to say, even though she had nothing to do with it. When she met Leonie, she never cried. It was many weeks before she realised what happened when she did.

'I don't think there's anything physically wrong. I think it's learned behaviour.'

'Learned how?'

'I . . . oh, she's fine now, look at her.'

Leonie had stopped crying, though there were tears still wetting her cheeks. She was splashing in the bowl of water with her other hand. Soon, she dragged the injured hand away from Ruby and started to play in the water with both hands. Sam found a beaker to fill up and pour, and Leonie went towards him to get it. As she toddled over, apparently perfectly happy now, the hood of her top brushed the wood burner and Ruby drew in a sharp breath. 'I think we might need a fireguard, though.'

He nodded. 'I'll make one. We won't light the stove again until it's done.'

Later he crouched in the tiny space next to the table, picked up a spoon and handed it to Leonie, who tried to add it to a pile of three other spoons. The pile fell over.

'Upsadaisy,' said Leonie.

'How old are you, honey?' said Sam.

'Spoon,' said Leonie.

Sam turned his head towards Ruby. 'How old is she? Two?'

'Nearly.'

'And I dropped you off at the New Park when, February? How long have you known her?'

'OK, I'm sorry. I should've told you the whole story. I planned to.'

Sam heaved himself up from the floor to sit on the bench. 'Hit me.'

So, Ruby told him everything. How she'd met them when she was struggling with her own personal stuff, the way she'd felt about Gregor and the lies he'd told to reel her in. He listened to her account of everything Gregor said about Constance being mentally ill, and how she'd fallen in love with little Leonie, and eventually become friends with Constance.

As she spoke, the child was roaming the boat, looking for things to explore. Ruby pulled out a notepad and pen from her bag, handed it to Leonie who held the Biro in her fist and concentrated on drawing spirals of scribble on all of the available space.

Ruby told of the moment she'd learned the truth about Gregor, and how she'd promised to help Constance escape by looking after Leonie until she could persuade her folks to let them live together.

'We waited until Gregor was out. And we just ran.'

Leonie toddled over and handed the pen to Sam. 'Thank you, sweetie.' A second later, she took it back with a 'Taaank-yoo!' and resumed drawing, scribbling over what she'd done already.

'She said she lived on an island in the Hebrides. A skerry. So that's where we're heading.' The song came to her then, the folk tune she'd found in the book and learned for Constance. 'Can I play your fiddle again?'

Ruby played, and Sam listened. Afterwards he said, 'I know that one, I think.'

'I can't pronounce the Gaelic name. In English it's called *They sent me to an island by myself.*'

'I learned it as "The Song of the Seals". Here.' He took the violin and played the tune, slower this time.

'It's different. The chorus is different.'

Sam said, 'Yes, the man who taught it to me said it's the actual tune the seals sing to each other.'

'Do you think that's true?'

He laughed. 'It's only a story. Seals don't sing.'

'Play that bit again. It's beautiful.'

As he played, Leonie became still, and started to hum along. Ruby watched her, swaying slightly, for a moment transported.

'It's a lament, I think,' said Sam, putting the violin away. 'Kind of sad.'

'Not to me,' said Ruby. 'I think it's full of hope.'

Sam looked at Leonie, who had stopped singing and gone back to scribbling. 'Musical bones, that one.'

'Yes.'

He sighed. 'How could her mother just go off and leave her?'

'It was terrible, Sammy. But she must have been so

desperate. I was late for the handover, and she went anyway. When I got there, the police had the kid.'

'The police? You were lucky to both get away then.'

'I know. It was close. But I wasn't going to let the social take her. Her mother might have abandoned her, but I would never.'

'What did you do? How come they let you have her, when her mother had left her?'

'I told them I was Constance.'

Sam sat up straight, then. There was the sound of Leonie dropping the pen on the floor. 'Oopsadaisy,' she said.

'The woman's name is Constance? Not Constance Douglas?'

'How do you know . . . I mean, that's the name I gave them, but how—'

'Have you heard the news the past two days?'

'No. Why?'

Sam was scrabbling for the radio, turning it on, looking for a news station. There was nothing but static, and Christmas pop songs.

'Stupid bloody thing. Do you have your phone?'

'Yes, but I turned it off, so that I can't be traced. You taught me that.'

'Turn it on.'

'Really? Here?' She looked at him, still unsure. He'd said so many times that he didn't want the boat contaminated with mobile signals.

'Yes. Do it now. There's something you have to see.' He said it with a grim determination, so that she grabbed her bag and found the phone, pressed the button to start it up. Sam took a step backwards, away from it, as if it might explode.

'What am I searching for?' she said.

'The name should do it. Constance Douglas.'

She typed it in. The first result was a national newspaper website headline, dated 22 December:

WOMAN AND CHILD MISSING IN RELATION TO MURDER ATTEMPT

A man was found badly injured and unconscious at his home in Sheffield yesterday. He is currently in a critical condition, being treated at Sheffield Royal Infirmary. It is not known whether he will recover. A woman, going by the name of Constance Douglas, is missing, wanted by police for questioning in relation to their inquiries. She is travelling with a child, a female around 2 years old. If you have any information, please contact . . .

'You used my name,' said Sam.

Ruby couldn't speak. She stared at the phone, re-read the article. There was no photograph, and the details were vague. But the name they had was the same made-up name she'd given to the social worker in Cleethorpes on Friday. What else did they know, now?

She wanted to look for more information, but Sam took the phone from her, took the battery and dropped the separate bits into her bag.

'Did you try to kill that man, Ruby?'

'I had no idea he was injured. He must have come home early. I left before Constance did, so she must have . . .'

She could imagine how frightened Constance would have

been when Gregor appeared. The desperation that would have caused her to defend herself so violently. She left him for dead. Part of her was horrified. Another part was deeply impressed. Constance surely meant to tell Ruby when they met up. But then, they never did.

'So he's in hospital? In a coma?'

She'd been terrified. The idea that the man was in a critical condition gave her a sick kind of hope.

'He might not be looking for you, but the police are. But they have eyes everywhere. It's only a matter of time. They'll have you on camera, on the streets, in the estate. Especially if you've been to a train station.'

And if Joanna's seen the footage, thought Ruby, then the game's up.

'What should I do, Sammy?'

'Go outside,' he said, 'get the rope in. We're moving. Now. We'll think about what to do when we're on our way.'

'Everything I did, I did to help Leonie.'

'They don't know that, do they? It doesn't matter to them, either, if it fits the story they're telling themselves. Come on, we need to get going. This friend of yours, she knows how to drop you in it, doesn't she?'

Within five minutes Ruby had released the ropes, Sam had fired up the engine and they were travelling. Although they weren't going very quickly, she felt safer on the move, in the boat, with her old friend. As they chugged serenely along the waterways, her heart slowed, and she smiled a little to herself. She realised she was in the strange position of being relieved that the police were after her. Compared to the fear she'd had over the past few days, the terrible knowledge that Gregor would surely track her down, being wanted by the police was frankly a much lesser threat. She'd witnessed what that man was capable of, how strong he was, how relentless. And, worse: how charming, how plausible. Her relief was cautious, however. Now that she'd tricked him and wronged him, and helped to take away both Constance and his precious daughter, she was in no doubt: whether discovered unconscious or not, if Gregor was still alive, one day he'd find a way to get to her.

CHAPTER FORTY-TWO

NOW
Joanna

Tuesday, 25 December

She'd messaged ahead of time, but Marianne still pretended not to understand the situation when Jo arrived.

'What, you're not staying?'

'No, Mum. I told you. I've got to work.'

It was just after 9 a.m. Her mother had opened the front door holding a champagne glass that she sipped at anxiously. Today was supposed to be the one day of the year on which morning drinking was acceptable, yet Joanna couldn't help but glance judgementally at the beverage. Her mother noticed her looking, and smiled. 'Would you like a drink? Little festive drinkie-poo?'

'No, thanks, Mum. I can't turn up smelling of booze. Even today.'

'Champagne is not booze, sweetie. It's virtually pop.'

Jo tried not to make any comment, but she was aware that her lips were pressed together in irritation. Marianne took a sip of the pale liquid and looked around as if she'd forgotten something. 'Where's lovely Amy?'

'We're on a break.'

'Oh, darling,' said her mother. 'I'm so sorry.'

Her mother didn't look sorry, not in the slightest. She'd never fully approved of Amy. Joanna remembered the time her mother had complained that Amy laughed too loudly.

'What's wrong with that?' Jo had asked.

'Well, if you like that sort of thing, it's fine,' her mother had replied. 'Seems a little . . . I don't know. Brash.'

Jo hadn't forgotten that comment – probably never would – but Marianne had, almost instantly. The conversation had taken place rather too late at night, and although her mother was adept at hiding how drunk she was, especially on the phone, Joanna had had years of training in spotting the signs. That had been a two-pints-of-vodka sort of an evening. Sober Marianne would absolutely never have made such a remark, but knowing that didn't make it any easier to forgive her.

Marianne turned towards the kitchen. 'Did you hear this, Phillip? Joanna isn't coming for lunch. So it's just you and me. No children this year. No children! On Christmas Day.' She turned off the hallway, stumbling slightly as she disappeared from sight into the lounge. Jo would have bet her life that the champagne glass her mother was sipping from had been given a good fortification from the vodka bottle.

In the kitchen, her father was intent on a huge half-cooked bird, peering through steamed-up glasses, doing something with juices. 'What a shame you can't join us, we'll have so much left over. Plenty for four, and now only the two of us. Oh well. Did something come up?'

The turkey was wedged into the biggest oven tray her parents owned. Plenty for a hundred and four, more like.

'Sorry, Dad. I know you've made a real effort. What time did you have to wake up to get this beast in the oven?'

'Oh, not too early. Sixish. I'd have been up anyway,' he said, waving away her apologies. 'What's happened with Amy? You haven't broken up, have you? I liked her.'

Dad actually had liked Amy, and Amy adored Phillip. They'd bonded over a game of sevens and a mutual love of true crime podcasts. Joanna felt sad all over again, that the two of them wouldn't get to hang out any more. Then she felt relieved all over again, that she wouldn't have to force Amy to endure any more visits with her mother.

'It's fine, Dad. We're spending some time apart. You know what I'm like. Hard to take, sometimes. I don't blame her.'

'You're lovely, Joanna. Just a little bit . . . independent, perhaps. For a girl like Amy. She's a bit of a homebody, maybe.'

'You don't have to say that, Daddy. I screwed it up, that's the truth. She deserves better.'

'No, no, I don't believe that. She was a darling, but not right for you. You need someone a bit more outdoorsy.'

Joanna filled the kettle and set it to boil.

'Maybe.'

'It must be a big case for you to go in today, right? Can you tell me about it?'

'Oof, it's a bit messy. Do you really want to know?'

'Of course.'

She spooned coffee into mugs, added milk and boiling water. There was no need to ask what her dad was drinking, because it was always the same. Instant coffee, black, a mug of it on the go constantly until twelve noon. Then, tea with milk until bedtime. Never alcohol. That was Marianne's department.

'We found a man in a bit of a bad way. He'd been attacked. We weren't altogether sure he was going to make it, actually, but then he woke up.'

'Oh, that's good, right?'

'Yes and no. When he woke up he attacked a porter, and now he's on the run.'

'Ah.'

'Then there's this missing woman and child, who may or may not be involved.' Jo tried to deliver this information without emotion. She couldn't let on that Ruby was involved, not yet. Her dad wouldn't be able to sleep for worrying.

'Oh, I think I heard about it on the news. Terrible business.'

'We put something out today, too, on the radio channels and the TV. Did you see it?'

'No one listens to the news on Christmas Day. Too busy cooking.'

As if to demonstrate, he got up and tipped a sack of potatoes into the sink, turned on the tap.

'Still,' said Jo, 'someone has to be at the office just in case. It's the baby we're most concerned about. Can't really stop until we know she's safe.'

Her father opened the oven and with a great deal of clanging and swearing, jammed the turkey inside. Then he turned and looked at her. 'Sometimes I don't know how you carry on, the things you have to deal with. How are you so strong?' He pulled her into a hug, still wearing the oven mitts. 'I'm so proud of you, Jo-Jo. Always.'

You wouldn't be so proud if you knew the truth, she

thought. If she dared to go into the office today, she'd probably be given a formal warning for disobeying orders. Her actual plan was to drive straight to her flat and spend the day listening in to the response team on her radio, in case they found 'Gregor'. And she might go for a run in the woods down by the hospital, no harm in that, was there? If she happened to find the fugitive herself, well so be it.

Marianne called through from the living room. 'Are you coming in here, darling?'

'In a minute, Mum.'

'Bring a fresh bottle of pop, would you? Get yourself a glass.'

Of course, Marianne had forgotten what Jo had said about not wanting any. Standard. 'I'll be right through.'

She met her father's eyes.

'Don't be angry, sweetie. She can't help it.'

'How can you say that? There's help available. Why doesn't she—'

'She knows she's got a problem. She's promised to deal with it, after today. I thought I'd let her, you know, do whatever she needs to do, to get through Christmas. Especially since what happened last year. Bad memories, you know.'

She looked at him properly, then. He'd lost a little weight. The strain was showing in the deep lines around his eyes, in the slight tremor in his voice. But he was strong, he always had been. Reliable. A rock for Marianne, for all of them. None of this was fair on him.

'You haven't heard from Ruby, then?' she asked.

'No. Nothing at all.' After a moment he said, 'What about you? Usually she'll speak to you.'

'Not this time. I've tried ringing. I went to her flat. She doesn't answer the door if she knows it's me knocking.'

'What about that boyfriend you said she told you about? She hasn't said anything more about that?'

Jo deeply regretted mentioning that conversation to her parents. The information had slipped out and Dad had clung to it, probably because there'd been nothing else.

'I still don't know anything more. She hasn't rung me, I told you.'

'You're not just saying that because she's asked you to pretend?'

'No, Dad. I wish I were.'

'It's good that she's found someone though, isn't it?'

'I keep telling you, Dad, it's not a boyfriend. She just said she'd met some new friends, and that one of them was a man.'

The driver's licence in the name of Gregor Franks came to mind, the face of the fugitive staring out. It occurred to her that they needed to add Gregor, the real Gregor, to the list of people they had to find. The list of people this invisible man had caused to disappear.

'Don't be like that, Joanna. It's a comfort to know that she's not on her own. Since last year we haven't known who she's with, whether she's eating properly, nothing at all. Only the updates we get from you. I like to imagine he's a lovely man, that she's happy and settled.'

She took a deep breath before she said, 'Her phone is switched off. Has been for a couple of weeks.'

'Oh, no. Don't tell your mother that, will you?'

'I'm not sure she'd remember if I did.'

'Marianne wants to give her something, a Christmas gift. She missed her terribly on her birthday. We never sent anything because we were hoping she'd come home. I hope it didn't make things worse.'

Jo thought things couldn't be much worse.

'If you see her, could you pass it on? Even if it's only the card.'

'You're not listening to me, Dad. She won't see me, either.'

He was facing away from her, his hands rummaging in the sink for potatoes. When he turned, his face had crumpled in a way she'd never seen before, that made her heart lurch with pity. She caught him in a tight hug, because it seemed as if he might collapse right there on the kitchen floor. Joanna held her father up as he cried, and thought about the fact we never really leave our childhood selves behind. The little boy that grew to be her father still lived inside him, just as the little girl she'd once been lived in her. It was the little girl part of Ruby, too, that was hurting now.

'Why does she hate us, Joanna? We tried to do the right thing. I loved her like a daughter. I still do. Exactly the way I love you. Maybe even more, because of who she is.'

Me too, thought Jo. 'I don't know what she's thinking, Daddy,' she said.

He turned back to the potatoes. 'Your mother and I tried to catch her at work last week.'

'Oh, Dad. What happened?'

'Well, I was starting to think maybe she doesn't work there anymore. Once or twice, I've sat outside that music service building, when the schools finish. Just on the off chance, you know, because she told me once that she runs the after-school orchestra on a Wednesday. I've never seen her. And then last week, she wasn't there either. One of the other tutors told us – and I had to really lay it on thick because they gave me all this data protection bullshit – that she's off sick. Your mother was so upset.'

Harper felt a surge of anger at Ruby, then. If she was in some kind of trouble, why didn't she ask for help? If she was sick, she needed her family around her. 'I didn't think it would go on for this long. If I had, I would have tried to do something much sooner. After everything you've done for her – for both of us. I don't know how she could just cut you off. Mum, I can understand, but you?'

Dad looked at his slippers. He dried his hands on a tea towel and placed it on the side. 'Well, that's the problem, isn't it? She thinks what we did – what we all did – was the wrong thing to do.'

'If she can't see that—'

'Shh, Joanna. Don't get upset. Your mother doesn't need it today.'

There was a sound then, from her mobile phone, still in the pocket of her coat in the hallway. The distinctive *boing* of an email notification.

'I better go, Dad. Work's calling.'

'Proud of you, sweetheart. Making the world a better place. Come round later for some leftovers, won't you? Please?'

In the living room, her mother was sitting very straight in her chair, facing the telly.

'Bye, Mum. I'll try to drop by later.' Joanna knew that she probably wouldn't.

Marianne smiled thinly and tipped her head at the

Christmas tree in the corner, decorated with paper angels. The familiar sight of them tugged at Jo. She remembered making them with a six-year-old Ruby, gluing the silver foil, cutting sprigs of tinsel to make the crowns. Under the tree were two piles of beautifully decorated presents, ten or more in each pile with a card on top.

'Don't forget your gifts, darling,' said her mother. 'And Phillip said you wouldn't mind passing on little Ruby's presents when you see her?'

One card said *Joanna*. The other said *Ruby*. Tears pricked at the corners of Jo's eyes. She bent and picked up Ruby's card. It was thick, probably with cash. Marianne rose and stood behind her daughter, both of them facing the decorated tree. The anger she felt towards her mother was still there, but it had faded into the background, replaced by pity.

'Mum, I don't think I'll see her today.'

'Tomorrow, perhaps?'

'I . . . maybe.'

The next thing her mother said was almost a whisper. 'I know she's gone, Joanna. I know we've lost her. I lost her.' The words were flat, emotionless. But repeated in the reflection on every bauble, Harper could see the tears rolling down her mother's face.

'She hasn't gone, don't say that. I can't take the presents, but I'll give her the card, Mum. I'll find her. I'll make sure she gets it. Then she'll come over and you can give her the presents yourself.'

She gave her mother a quick hug, then walked out of the front door and climbed into her car, pushing the envelope into the zipped pocket of her satchel. She took out her phone and checked her email, hoping to see a message from the automated mobile phone signal detection service that Eddie had set up for her, which would ping whenever Ruby's phone number was used. It was a spam email from a sports drink company. She set off for home.

CHAPTER FORTY-THREE

NOW
Ruby

Tuesday, 25 December

They travelled all day, not even stopping for their lunch of the promised curry: Ruby heated it up and took the tiller while Sam ate and watched Leonie. It was a bizarre situation; here they were, on the run from the police and social services, with a child that didn't belong to them. Yet there was a sense of peace as they cruised along the canals and rivers. It was a different world from the one Ruby usually inhabited, that of cities and buildings, roads and vehicles. There was only the water, which meandered through farmland, and the boat, gently churning up the surface as they escaped almost comically slowly, at a leisurely walking pace. It was too serene to get stressed, though when she thought of the news article her stomach tightened. She wanted to turn her phone on and search for more information about the case, specifically, which DS was working it. Did Joanna know already that it wasn't Constance but Ruby at the seafront?

The fact that it was Christmas Day made her think about

what happened last year, and the many missed calls she'd seen on her old phone. She realised she wasn't angry any more, only homesick. Joanna hadn't done anything wrong, not really. As for Marianne, she probably couldn't even remember what she'd said. In the end it didn't make much difference whether Ruby forgave her or not, the woman barely remembered anything from one day to the next. Forgiveness wasn't about the other person, though. It was about drawing a line under something, and moving on. What Ruby had realised since knowing Leonie was that, once there was a child in your life, you no longer had the luxury of deciding whether or not to forgive. What you did, you did for them. Her mother – both of her mothers – had sacrificed a lot for her, perhaps more than she would ever know. And they did it, not from a sense of duty, but because they chose to. Joanna chose to carry her to term; Marianne chose to bring her up. Neither was forced into anything. Constance, in contrast, hadn't been given a choice at all.

That night, they moored on a deserted stretch of canal bank, between two derelict working boats. Sam let Ruby steer as he jumped on to the towpath with the rope, guiding them in, using the light from his powerful head torch. Leonie was already asleep on the bean bag underneath the table, her thumb in her mouth.

In the frozen dark, Ruby helped him to tie the boat up, then they both went aboard, down into the saloon, and shut the doors behind them. The heat enveloped her, like an embrace. After a while they sat together to eat another delightfully unfestive meal of canned spaghetti on toast washed down with fizzy orange.

'We should go on the run every year,' she said, 'It's kind of nice.'

He grew serious then. 'Don't make the mistake of letting yourself feel safe.' He stood up to pull closed an infinitesimal gap in one of the blinds. 'That's when they'll get you.'

Sam started to list all the ways in which she had to modify her behaviour if she wanted to stay free. Avoid cities, train stations, buses. Don't call anyone. Don't turn on your mobile phone.

'You can't take any money out, either. Not from cashpoints.'

'What? How are we supposed to eat? And I need some toiletries, moisturiser, lip balm, you know.'

'You can't be thinking about beauty stuff now, Ruby—'

'It's not for me. It's for her. She's got sore lips. The cold weather isn't good for sensitive skin.' She looked at the baby, nestled on the beanbag like a little pup in the warm glow from the fire. There was a patch of skin on her chin that she couldn't seem to stop licking, that by the end of the day was sometimes bleeding. Ruby's own skin was sore too. Her cheeks were tight from the extreme changes in temperature from outside to inside. Her cracked lips cried out for relief. But it was the baby she wanted the balm for, first and foremost. Her priorities had shifted, without her really noticing.

'We'll be able to get some money,' said Sam, 'There are ways to do it without them finding us. We'll be OK, but you might need to give me your bank card, for security. You'll get it back.'

'Why can't we just go and get some money out ourselves?'

'Because they will have set up an alert on your account.'

'They don't know it's me, Sam. They're looking for someone called Constance.'

'If you're on camera with Leonie, then someone is going to recognise you eventually, and people love to snitch.'

He was right. It was likely they would have made the connection by now. It was safest to behave as if they had.

Ruby checked her wallet. There was a ten-pound note and a few coins. 'There'll be a corner shop in one of the villages. I'll go there tomorrow.'

'But you can't go, Ruby. I'll go.'

'Surely it's safe to go to some random village shop?'

He shook his head, no. 'That's how they get you. You can't go in any shops. Not if you really want to avoid the hunters.'

'The hunters?'

'That's what they are, the police. Professional hunters. They think they've got the upper hand, too, with all their equipment and tracking technology. But it's not foolproof. We can beat it, if we're careful.'

It seemed so far from them, this danger. Thinking about it hurt her brain. She looked at the sleeping child, felt the heat of the fire, the sensation of floating on the river, the occasional pull of the ropes in the mooring when the wind took them.

'You're not listening. Ruby? What did I just say?'

She jolted back to the conversation.

'Sorry, Sam. I guess I'm too tired.'

'We both need to get some rest if we're going to stay one step ahead of them.'

Sam went into the tiny bathroom. She heard him brushing his teeth. When he came out, she said, 'Why are you helping me?'

'What's that supposed to mean? Why wouldn't I help you? I'm your friend. Why do you even need to ask?'

'Only because it must look really bad. I'm here with some-one else's kid, being chased by the police after a man has been attacked. And you, without even really asking many questions, you just accept it.'

'Yes. Because I trust you.'

'You could get into trouble.'

'I don't care. Anyway, where else are you going to go?'

'I just don't know if I'd be able to do the same. If the tables were turned.'

He narrowed his eyes in the dim light. Then he sighed. 'I suppose it's a good job that you won't have to, then, because I'm never going to get into the kind of trouble you can create. Not anymore. And when I needed you, you were there. This is payback.'

'Payback?'

'For saving my life.'

They held each other's gaze. 'It was nothing.'

'No,' said Sam. 'I know we joke about it, but in all serious-ness, if you hadn't picked me up off the street that night, I would have died.'

'Someone else would have come along.'

'No, they wouldn't,' said Sam. 'I don't know if I would have done that myself, either.'

Ruby considered for a minute. Then she nodded. 'OK. But then we're square. We don't owe each other anything.'

Sam's expression changed, as if he had more to say. But then he tilted his head, smiled slightly and went through into the cabin.

The tip of the narrowboat nosed through the thin ice on the surface of the river, driving a dark path up the middle and leaving floating white islands drifting in its wake. She and Leonie were dressed in their gloves, hats and coats, huddled low in the bow against the cold wind, their heads sticking up over the side. Sam was at the stern, holding the tiller with one hand, only his eyes visible between his woolly hat and the scarf he'd wrapped over his face. Leonie was pointing at birds in the winter trees as they passed, calling, 'Wobin!' whenever she spotted anything remotely winged. The proximity of the water, combined with the toddler's complete obliviousness to any danger, made Ruby nervous. She kept one hand wound tightly in the fabric of the little girl's coat.

Since the incident with the stove, Leonie hadn't mentioned her mother. She'd been fully engaged with discovering everything new about the world she found herself in. Having been confined for the entirety of her life so far, Ruby was impressed with the way she took everything in her stride, delighted in everything, laughed and charged about all day with an energy she hadn't seemed to have when in the apartment. But minding a tiny human with no sense of danger was a full-time occupation. By 6 p.m. both of them were exhausted. Leonie slept for twelve hours every night, her little brain soaking up all of the newness and assimilating it, ready for her to leap up in the wee hours and begin all over again. Ruby had to be ready for anything, and although she found it difficult to be on duty so unrelentingly, the rewards were huge. She was seeing everything through Leonie's eyes, as if it were new to her, too. And it was wonderful.

Ruby was about to suggest to Leonie that they go indoors, get warm by the fire, when the sun came out in glorious ribbons of gold, and the way it caught the ice crystals that had formed on the branches of the trees gave the scene an achingly festive, greetings-card beauty. 'Look, baby, there's a sparrow.'

'Wobin!' shouted Leonie, pointing at the small brown bird.

Sam cut the engine. The boat edged towards the towpath, where he jumped ashore and banged in a mooring pin with a mallet, securing the stern. 'Throw us the rope,' he called, and he did the same with the bow end. They'd stopped by a small gate in the hedge which led to a farmer's field.

'Let's go for a leg-stretch,' he said. 'There's a village just down there.'

They set off at toddler's pace, the path cutting straight through the fields to a weighted kissing-gate at the far perimeter of the second one. It would have been a few minutes' walk, but for the fact that every couple of metres, Leonie found something to stop and look at. She would examine it, hold it up for approval. 'Look, Mamma Bee, stick!' 'Look, Mamma Bee, stone!'

After about twenty minutes of this they'd barely made it past the first field and were only halfway to the gate. Sam said, 'I'm going to go ahead. I've got a few things to do, OK? I'll meet you at the boat in an hour.'

'What are you doing? I thought we were keeping out of sight?'

'Should be fine, as long as you don't draw attention to yourself. Try not to talk to anyone, don't go into any establishments. You'll just look like a tourist. I need to make a phone call. I think there's still a call box here – there was last year.'

'Who are you calling?'

'We need some money. I'm going to get us some.'

'But, Sam—'

'Don't worry about it. I'll see you soon.'

As Sam paced ahead and disappeared, Ruby took hold of Leonie's hand and steered her towards the gate. On the other side of it, there was a street of old stone cottages leading towards a village green, at the centre of which, a picture-perfect duck pond. 'Ducks!' shouted Leonie, and set off running.

'Wait,' said Ruby.

In slow motion, Ruby saw it play out, but she was slightly too far away to stop it happening: Leonie's welly made contact with the kerbstone, she toppled like a domino, the hat came off her head, her head connected with a sharp piece of gravel on the ground, all in one short second that seemed to last forever. As she went down, Ruby's fingers barely brushed the edge of the girl's coat, her hand grabbed at nothing. The blood came before the screaming, running down her face and into her eyes and mouth, turning her baby teeth pink. A dark bruise formed quickly at the site of the injury, a lump started to swell there. Ruby picked her up and held her, searched for a clean tissue to press to the cut. All the while, she was trying to contain her emotion. Because for the first time, Leonie was crying out loud.

And she wanted to say, *please don't cry*, but she also wanted to tell that sweet baby she could cry whenever she liked, as loud as she liked, for as long as she liked.

Don't draw attention to yourself. So much for that. As the baby screamed at full volume into her ear – such a joyous moment, the fact that she finally felt safe enough to, but why did it have to be now? – Ruby rubbed Leonie's back in soothing circles. She stood up and looked around to see if she could tell where Sam had gone. There was no phone box nearby that she could see. A curtain twitched in one of the houses and she turned to retrace her steps, but as she passed the entrance to the pub at the edge of the green a large woman dressed in chef's whites and a stripy apron appeared at the open door. 'Are you OK, love?'

'Yes, fine, don't worry. It's only a scratch. She's just making a fuss. It's nothing.'

The woman came close. She lifted up Leonie's fringe. 'Doesn't look like nothing to me. Might need stitches. I'd go to hospital with that. Are you local?'

'No. Yes.' What was the best thing to say? Ruby just wanted to get away.

The woman frowned, and examined them both a bit more closely. This was a village, where everyone was bound to know everyone else. Ruby laughed, a simulation of amusement that felt flat even to her. 'Sorry, that doesn't make sense, does it? I'm not local, but I'm hoping to be. We're looking at a house this afternoon, getting a feel for the village.'

'Oh, you're looking at the Simonsens' place?'

'Yes,' said Ruby, then, 'I think so. It's a lovely building. Lovely area. Lovely.' *Stop, Ruby, you sound manic.*

'I see,' said the woman, narrowing her eyes. 'Well, hope this hasn't put you off. The hospital is a few miles down the main road. I can give you the postcode, to put in your phone?'

Leonie had stopped crying. Ruby was always impressed with how quickly she got over things. The girl leaned into

Ruby's chest, sucking her thumb and gazing at the chef with her big eyes. The woman covered her face with her hands for a second. 'Boo,' she said, opening her hands wide and grinning in a silly way. Leonie laughed.

'Thanks,' said Ruby, 'but I think she just needs a plaster.'

'What?' said the chef, frowning slightly. 'You're not going to take her? Looks pretty deep to me.'

'I'm a nurse,' said Ruby, rather too defensively. 'I think it's superficial. Don't suppose you have a first-aid kit in your kitchen?'

The first-aid kit contained steri-strips, which Ruby used to close the cut after she'd cleaned it. The chef was right, the cut was deep and probably should have needed stitches, but of course there was no question of going to the hospital.

'How old is she?'

Leonie had been handed a bottle of apple juice with a straw sticking out of it, and she sat, dangling her legs on the stainless-steel kitchen counter, slurping the sweet liquid and humming.

'Nearly two,' said Ruby, thinking, *why did I come in here?* She needed to get away, return to the boat. Every second she spent here, every bit of information she gave to this woman, would put them in danger of being caught.

Just then there were footsteps on the stairs above them. It was too early for the pub to have any customers yet. They both looked up. 'That's the landlord,' said the chef. 'What's your name, lovely?'

'Lonie!' shouted Leonie.

'Ha ha,' said Ruby, picking her up and making for the door. 'I don't know why she says that. Her name's Anna, actually.

Funny, the things they come out with, isn't it? Better be off, thanks for the first-aid kit.'

Ruby hurried through the bar. As she did so, she caught sight of the TV, where a news anchor was delivering her report: *Police are still searching for a man who escaped from hospital after seriously assaulting a member of staff. The man, who was using the name Gregor Franks, until recently, was in a coma after being found unconscious on Friday. The public are being asked to help search for a woman in relation to the inquiry, who was last seen travelling with a young child who may answer to the name of Leonie . . .*

The chef followed Ruby's eyes to the TV, and then looked at the child. Ruby saw her frown, look again at the TV, again at Ruby.

'Which house did you say you were looking at, love? The Simonsens'? Maybe I could put in a word for you.' But her face had changed. She wasn't friendly any more, she was suspicious.

Without saying another word, Ruby backed into the swing door and went through. It was bad enough that the police were after her, that she might have given away their location by talking to this person. But the thing making her heart pound was the other part. Gregor was no longer in hospital. He was on the run, and he'd be coming for her. She needed to get moving, as quickly as possible.

'Hey!' shouted the chef, as Ruby held Leonie close and started to run across the green and back to the gate.

CHAPTER FORTY-FOUR

NOW
The Injured Man

From the bench at the edge of the green, the man watches the gate bang shut, the woman and child disappear into the furrowed field beyond. Standing in the doorway of the pub, the chef looks over at him and raises a hand, but she frowns slightly, as if she can't quite place him. He flashes a reassuring smile, and the chef smiles back. The trace of suspicion is gone, just like that. Villages like this, they always clock an outsider, but the injured man has taken steps to appear as if he ought to belong, and that's the most important thing. Dressed in a tweed jacket and walking boots, he knows that he looks the epitome of a middle-class, higher-income-bracket, older man, taking a rest after a morning stroll. The chef steps inside and shuts the pub door, no doubt forgetting she even saw him, her mind moving on to the next thing. She can't have guessed that the man has taken the jacket and boots he is wearing from the unlocked boot room of a large house ten miles south, that he's been walking the canal path, searching for the boat he knows was, until recently, moored at a wharf near York. She can't have guessed that the flat cap covers up an almost circular injury on the back of the man's head, or that his hands bear small wounds where he ripped out his drip.

The man leaves the bench and makes a slow circuit of the village green, standing for a while to admire the ducks on the pond. No one is watching him, as far as he can tell, but it's worth a little stroll around to make sure, if there are curtain-twitchers in the vicinity, that he isn't considered suspicious. After a minute or so he climbs into his stolen car and sets off at a leisurely pace in the direction of the Ripon terminal, knowing he'll have more than enough time to change both his vehicle and his appearance before *Nessie* has travelled even halfway there.

CHAPTER FORTY-FIVE

NOW
Joanna

Thursday, 27 December

Joanna was awoken by the soft *boing* of her email alert.

Ruby had turned her phone on, and the system had sent her the location. She knew there was a time lag, but when she saw exactly when the phone had been turned on, she swore. It was forty-eight hours ago; time she'd spent listening in to the police radios and conducting her own ground searches of local wooded areas, using the hospital as a mid-point. There had been no sign of the fugitive. She'd been crossing her fingers that he'd be found dead in a ditch, but after what she'd seen she knew better than to underestimate him. Jo scrambled out of bed and into the car.

It took the best part of three hours to drive through the heavy back-to-work traffic to where Ruby's new mobile phone had pinged, a small canal wharf in the middle of nowhere, north of York. The data contained in the email stated that the phone had activated the nearby mast on Christmas Day. Therefore it was unlikely she was still going to be there, but at least it was a starting point.

At the wharf she parked and started walking towards the first narrowboat in the row, where she knocked on a window, three sharp raps. The afternoon was crisp and cold, frost laced on the edges of leaves, floating islands of ice on the river. The craft's curtains were drawn, but she knocked once more anyway. There was no answer.

Jo glanced at the chimney of the next boat, from which she could see a curl of smoke escaping. When she knocked this time, a curtain twitched, and a few minutes later, a woman's head appeared out of the hatch. Her white hair was messed up, and she had a face brown and wrinkled like a walnut. Clouds of steamy breath filled the space between them.

The woman squinted into the bright slanting sun. 'Yes?'

'I'm from the police,' said Harper. 'I'm looking for a young woman called Ruby. She's travelling with a little girl called Leonie, about eighteen months to two years old.'

The woman climbed from the hatch onto the small deck where the tiller was, dragging a blanket that she wrapped around herself tightly in the cold. 'No one here by that name, not that I know of.'

'What about a man called Sam Douglas?'

'*Nessie*? Yes, he was here.'

'Nessie?'

'That's the boat,' said the woman.

'When was he here?'

'Day before yesterday. I saw her leave, oh, late morning, I'd say.'

'Her? I thought you said there wasn't a woman?'

'I was talking about the boat.'

Joanna was holding it together, but the boat woman was

starting to annoy her very much. At times like these she did well to remember the tips she'd picked up at the two politeness training sessions she been obliged to attend as part of her CPD.

'Just to be clear,' said Joanna, 'Sam Douglas, the man, not the boat. He plays the violin. Do you know him?'

'Yes. He built my kitchen. It's very good. Are you looking for a handyman? Or a violinist?'

'No. I'm looking for a woman called Ruby, and a little girl. I know they've been here, because we had a mobile phone alert from the area. You're sure you haven't seen them?'

'You know, there was something strange that happened. Sam's a real loner. I've never seen him with anyone before, so I suppose I wasn't expecting it. But the other morning, we heard a scream, coming from over there, where he was moored. I thought it must have been someone passing by, a gongoozler. We get families walking on the towpath all the time. Especially on Christmas Day. Morning walk with the family, you know. It's like Paddington bloody station round here.'

'You heard a scream?'

'Yes. Very high-pitched scream. I never imagined it could be from Sam's boat. I didn't get a chance to ask him whether or not he'd heard it too, because later, he'd gone, which in itself isn't unusual. Anyway, I didn't connect the two things. But now that you're here, maybe it does make sense. What's he done, run off with someone's wife?' The woman seemed strangely delighted by the prospect. Bent over, wrapped in her blanket, Harper couldn't help thinking she was just like the witch in so many of the fairy tales she read as a child.

'Who do you think was screaming?'

'I don't know. I got the impression it was a child, from the pitch of it.'

'Not an adult?'

'Well, could have been a woman, I suppose. Do you think he was strangling her? Is that why you're looking for them? Is it a murder inquiry?'

Jo kept her face completely still.

'You say that Sam's boat left on Christmas Day. Do you know which way he went?'

'That way,' said the woman, pointing to one of only two routes out of the wharf. 'North. Very itchy feet, that one. Always on the go. I never thought he might be a criminal, though.'

Joanna noticed the boarding ramp from the woman's boat, which rested on the towpath. There was grass growing all around it. 'You don't move, though?'

'Not me. I pay for this mooring, so I don't have to. Some boat people like to be able to move. That's part of why they choose to live onboard. Very small world though, especially in the winter. I've seen Sam here a few times. He's not one for farewells. Or hellos, actually. And he's not a terribly festive chap; no decorations or anything.'

She fingered the wrinkled berries on the holly wreath adorning her cabin door. 'It's always the quiet ones, isn't it? I never took him for a violent man.'

'Can you show me exactly where he was moored?'

'Just across there,' said the woman, indicating the other side of the wharf, which had space enough for about fifteen boats. 'And I wouldn't bother knocking on any of those other boats. No one's in. Mostly holiday craft.'

Joanna gave a tight smile. 'Thank you for your time, madam. We might be in touch again.'

As she started to move away, the woman shouted after her, 'Hey, this isn't about that missing woman with the girl, is it? I heard it on the news.'

Well, I did mention that it was about a woman and a child, thought Joanna. 'Oh?'

'Only, if it is, I did find something on the towpath. Thought it was an interesting coincidence, that someone would drop one so similar. Maybe it wasn't a coincidence at all. Look, I hung it on the fence, just down there. It looks like the hat they were talking about on the news, doesn't it?'

Jo walked towards where the woman was pointing, and there on the fence was a scrap of pink something. Harper picked it up and brushed the ice off. It was a woollen hat, with two bobbles like a bear's ears. Identical to the one Leonie had been wearing in the images from the train station. She tucked it into a plastic evidence bag.

Just then, Jo's phone rang. It was Atkinson.

'Hello, boss,' he said.

'Hello, Steve. Have you found the fugitive yet? Any leads?'

'Where are you?'

'I'm . . . at home.'

'No you're not. I'm standing outside your place right now. Your car's gone.'

'What, are you checking up on me now?'

'I came over to tell you that the surveillance system recorded a location flag from a number that I didn't recognise, that I hadn't keyed in. I couldn't get in touch with Eddie, but I assumed it was something to do with you. Something to do with the case that you are not supposed to be investigating anymore.'

'You'd be right about that, *Detective*. It's Ruby's number. I got an email notification about it this morning.'

'Is that where you are now? I could have come with you, if you'd said.'

'Probably best you stay away from me, Steve. You're in charge of the operation, and you don't want to chuck that opportunity away. Could be great for you, career-wise. It's different for me. It's personal.'

'There's more to this case than your daughter disappearing, Jo. I had that preserved finger we found fast-tracked by Forensics. It was a child's, like you thought it might be. Around eight to ten years old.'

'Can they tell if it's from a male or a female? When was it severed?'

'They couldn't say much more than the fact it wasn't recent. They're running DNA, but Thrupp is also talking about opening several linked inquiries.'

'Several?'

'One for each victim. They opened up the wall yesterday. There were two bodies inside. A female and a male.'

Harper felt her blood run cold. She thought of Gregor's mother, how she'd disappeared so suddenly just after they moved in. And how, when the neighbour had knocked to ask about it, 'Gregor' seemed to have forgotten who the neighbour was.

'I've been inside the apartment. We both have. There was no smell, no sign . . .'

'No. There wouldn't have been. The bodies had been

preserved, much like the finger was. They're trying to work out what the process was. It might help us identify the killer.'

Preservation. A deliberate act. The murderer had really thought things through.

'Can you identify them?'

'Forensics are working on it. They say they should be able to reconstruct the face of the male, make a computer simulation and compare it with the passport image we found, but I have a strong suspicion . . .'

'It's Gregor Franks. The real one.'

Joanna walked a little way down the path in the direction the boat she suspected Ruby was aboard had gone. The silence out here was unnerving, especially for a city girl.

Atkinson said, 'One more thing. They found a bottle with traces of . . . hang on, I'll read out the description. "A cocktail of liquid paracetamol, diamorphine, Valium and GHB." This was in an unmarked bottle in the bathroom. Take a spoon of that, you'd be out for a week. Take two or three, you might not wake up.'

'Do you think that's what he'd taken?'

'I'd say it's likely. Though I don't know if he took it on purpose.'

Joanna could see that she'd been right all along. If Ruby had given the man a head injury – and if she'd dosed him up with that stuff – then it was for a very good reason indeed.

'You're not safe up there, boss, not with him on the loose. This man is a killer. There are two bodies already, and the finger, the drugs – all indicating further crimes. And there's Constance, throwing herself into the sea – I know we haven't found her body, but it looks most likely that she drowned herself just to get away from him. That kind of man wouldn't think twice about attacking a police officer.'

'He wouldn't think twice about attacking a woman and a little girl, Steve. I have to keep looking for Ruby and Leonie.'

'You can't do it on your own. It's too dangerous.'

She ended the call.

Joanna stood on the towpath in the fading daylight and found a map of the waterways on her smartphone. There were only thirty miles of canal left in that direction, until it ended in the terminus at Ripon. She eyed the sign sticking out of the reeds that stated the speed limit was 4 mph. She could probably catch them up if she'd had her bike with her. Or she could borrow a boat. *Nessie* couldn't have gone anywhere especially difficult to find, confined as she was to the waterway. On the other hand, thirty miles was a huge search area, and checking every boat in the dark would take hours.

'There's a quicker way to find them, you know,' said a voice from behind her. It was the woman she'd spoken to earlier. 'If you were interested.'

'Go on.'

'All of the boats are registered, and the men from the Canal and River Trust monitor where you are. It all goes on a database.'

'They monitor where you are? How?'

'Man on a bike. They go up and down, note down the registration numbers, make sure you've moved far enough if you're a continuous cruiser. They're a bit like traffic wardens.'

'How often do they do that?'

'Not sure, actually. They're quite secretive. I suppose they don't want people to cheat the system. But I saw him go by yesterday, as a matter of fact. Might be worth checking with them?'

Jo searched for the number and pressed to connect, held the phone to her ear.

'No answer,' she said to the boatwoman.

'Office hours, dummy,' said the old woman, rolling her eyes. 'Try in the morning.'

Jo called Atkinson back.

'You hung up on me,' he said.

'I'm really sorry about that, Steve. It turns out I do need your help.'

CHAPTER FORTY-SIX

NOW
The Injured Man

26–27 December

The boat rests, in the dark; its engine is ticking as it cools. The water is completely still, disturbed only by the occasional movements from inside the boat, rocking the vessel slightly, causing small ripples.

The man is crouching, his body hidden by the brambles and by the darkness. He is cold, but he doesn't move at all.

In one of the nearby houses, there is a shrill voice complaining.

'You need to move that boat,' it screeches. 'You can't moor here, you know. I'll call the authorities. They'll be along to move you.'

It's true there are no other boats moored here, only the ancient hull of a pleasure boat, and a speedboat, covered with canvas and pulled up on to the bank for the winter.

A man with greying hair and a scruffy beard sticks his head out of the top of the boat. The injured man can see him, lit from below by the light coming from the boat's cabin. He knows that the man is called Sam. He first became aware of Sam almost a year ago, when the cameras he'd installed in the empty flat opposite his window were triggered by the girl moving in. He'd had a plan in place for this eventuality – that was why he'd set up the cameras in the first place. The idea was that, when someone moved in, he would contain the problem by first observing and then eliminating the tenant – he'd even stockpiled several sacks of salt to deal with the body, as it had worked so well the other time. But through the listening devices he'd heard her playing, and it was like a siren song, urging him to change his plan, attempt something new for once, despite the risks. He realises now that this was the decision that changed everything, the point where things had started to get complicated for the injured man. He should have gone ahead and done what he'd always intended. The injured man doesn't like things to be untidy. And things, as they stand, are very untidy indeed.

To befriend Ruby had seemed like the perfect solution, at first, and for a while he'd thought that the two women could remain under control indefinitely. Ruby kept Constance and Leonie entertained. She was lonely – he knew from her phone history that she had no friends nearby or family to interfere. And she had seemed so trusting, so pliable. Even when she rejected his advances, he saw it as a victory, understood it was because of the story he'd told her about Constance still being in love with him.

He should have anticipated that it couldn't stay that way forever, though. The child had started walking, and Constance had begun whining about letting it go outside. Ruby appeared to feel strongly for the child, in a way she didn't feel for him. Those kinds of feelings made people unreliable. There was a point when he realised the whole set-up could easily spiral out of his control, and for that reason it had to be scrapped. He had it all planned out, would pick them off one by one, Constance first, telling Ruby she was going for treatment. He'd just finished getting everything ready when they betrayed him. Thinking of the things he has prepared, the man is annoyed that he has wasted his time, that his efforts will amount to nothing. A few miles away from the apartment in an abandoned warehouse, behind a secure door, there are three bathtubs standing ready, the salt sacks leaning against the wall, next to the shovel.

'I'm sorry, we're not staying long,' says Sam to the screechy person, and he shuts the cover and zips it.

We're not staying long, that's what Sam said. So, Ruby is still aboard. The man doesn't want to be seen by her, but the fact that he hasn't laid eyes on Ruby or Leonie since the village green is worrying him slightly. Recently she's shown a talent for deception of which he was previously unaware. Right up until the day they attacked him and stole themselves away, he'd thought Ruby was at least partly on his side. No matter. He can get the upper hand again. He already considers himself to be one step ahead of her. The tracker being taken from the phone and placed on the train as a decoy would have been a cunning move, if he hadn't been able to visit the warehouse after leaving the hospital, where he picked up the cloned phone he uses to track her online life, such as it is. It's inconvenient that he can no longer track her physically, but he can watch, in real time, whenever she uses the internet to try to evade him. The first escape may have taken him by surprise, but he knows what she's been planning, this time. He was watching as she booked the tickets yesterday. His first thought was that he ought to go there and wait for her, but all of Ruby's lies have undermined his confidence in predicting what she's going to do next. If she's somehow guessed he has access to her search history, there's a risk that the tickets themselves are a decoy, intended to send him hundreds of miles in the wrong direction.

Part of him wonders if he ought to draw a line under it all. Finish the three of them on the boat now, and move on permanently, let Constance go. 'Gregor' has become rather tedious, and although he has enjoyed spending all of that rental money, one can get too comfortable. It will be fun to take on another challenge, another persona. He's done his research, he just needs to take the leap, start again in the new life he knows is waiting for him – once he's dealt with the man currently living it. A surge of anger turns his thoughts around. The rage he feels now is caused by his humiliation, the injustice of it. He's been made a fool of, and he no longer wants to finish Constance but punish her. Killing Ruby and Leonie is part of that, but if he does it here and now, she'll never know.

The screechy person cuts through his thoughts. Apparently they have lots to say, but it seems to be all along the same lines. The injured man stops listening.

Many hours pass, but the man does not fall asleep. He waits, to see what will occur. Ruby should come out at any moment, he thinks. He imagines her passing by in front of him, unaware that he's hiding there, waiting to follow her wherever she goes.

And then, when the winter night is at its darkest, the injured man can't bear the suspense any longer. He creeps from the shadows and places silent fingers on the zip of the boat's rain cover.

CHAPTER FORTY-SEVEN

NOW
Joanna

Thursday, 27 December

Jo broke the speed limit twice on the way to Ripon, where Atkinson had found out was the last recorded location for Sam's boat. She followed satnav directions to the canal terminus, parked hastily next to the water and got out. The sky was completely dark, but the canal was illuminated by a handful of streetlights scattered around the almost-deserted basin. A single narrowboat floated in darkness, moored a short distance from where the waterway came to a dead end.

As she approached the black-and-red painted craft, Harper read the name on a plank propped in the window, hand-drawn letters picked out in white on a blue background.

Nessie.

From above her, a harsh, disembodied voice yelled, 'Is that boat anything to do with you?' and Joanna looked up to see a person leaning from the window of one of the houses backing onto the canal side where *Nessie* was moored. 'There's no overnight mooring here. So you better move it, or I'll get it moved for you.'

'I'm a police officer,' said Harper.

'Oh, good. Are you going to tow it? I'm sick of looking at the scruffy old thing.'

'How long has it been here?'

'More than twenty-four hours now. The Canal Trust man came by, left them a fixed penalty notice, serves them right. Since then I've been keeping an eye out.'

'You haven't seen anyone on board?'

'A man, yesterday. He didn't say much, refused to move. I'm glad the police are interested, finally. When I rang up, they didn't seem to care. They said it was a civil matter.'

'Just a man? No one else? What did he look like?'

'White guy. Straggly beard. Looked like they all do. Boat-dwellers.'

'Thank you, madam, go inside now. I'll deal with it.'

Once the person had shut the window and drawn the curtain across, Jo turned back to the boat.

No light burned in any of the windows, but when she put her hand on the chimney she found that it was very slightly warm. The fire had been lit, perhaps this morning, and allowed to burn out. She knocked on the side. No sounds.

There was a waterproof shelter attached to the deck, a kind of awning that had been left unzipped. She pushed it aside and stepped on board, seeing that the hatch was ajar. Quickly she descended the steps into the saloon, and there, by the light of the torch on her phone, she saw the form of a man, slumped and bloody on the floor of the small galley.

'Sam Douglas?' He was face down, his body twisted, one

343

arm at an unnatural angle. She crouched and put her fingers at the side of his neck. A pulse, but very weak.

Joanna looked around the inside of the boat. There were books thrown everywhere, cushions on the floor, everything turned out of the drawers and cupboards. There wasn't anything Harper could see that belonged to Ruby. Except . . . she reached out and pulled on a small, furry thing sticking out from under a heap of papers. She held up the child's teddy bear in the shaft of light from her phone. They'd been here, she was sure. But so had Gregor.

Harper's mind was racing. Had he taken them? Were they injured, dead?

From the floor of the boat, the man let out a soft groan.

'Sam? Can you hear me?' She knelt over him, willed him to look at her. His eyelids flickered open.

'Jo?' The voice was breathy, almost inaudible. The fact that he recognised her was a good sign, though; they hadn't seen each other in years.

'Who did this to you, Sam?'

Sam started to cough, so that she thought he might choke. He spat out a mouthful of blood.

'Listen. Don't try to talk. Just blink once for yes, twice for no. Was Ruby here when this happened?'

Sam blinked, twice.

Joanna felt a wave of relief. She hadn't been caught. But how long ago had she left? And where was she headed to?

Blood had dried on the floorboards and cupboards where it had splashed. The attack on Sam must have been many hours ago.

'Do you know where she is now?'

One blink.

'And did you tell him where she was going?'

Two blinks. A tear ran down his cheek. He tried to say something, but it was so quiet that she couldn't hear what it was. She leaned closer, and could barely make out the words:

'He already knew.'

CHAPTER FORTY-EIGHT

NOW
The Injured Man

The man stands at the window, feeling the great rumble of the boat's engine beneath his feet, watching as the lights of Castlebay, gleaming like flecks of white gold in the distance, draw slowly closer. The winter night fell hours ago, and now it is as if they sail through space; the thick dark of the sea can be distinguished from that of the sky only by the occasional streak of white foam at the top of a wave, and the way the heaving swell catches the reflection from the ferry's lights at a certain angle.

He is light-headed, delirious from the pain that has been getting steadily worse since he boarded. The fight with Sam in the early hours was more difficult than it ought to have been. When he'd seen that Ruby and Leonie had already gone, he'd been too angry to react efficiently. He must have made a noise that woke Sam, who'd managed to get a few good punches in before things were properly under control. All that time wasted waiting to follow them, when he hadn't even needed to. Imagine if he'd left it any longer – he might have missed the ferry altogether.

The drive up in the car he'd stolen at Ripon had been calming, the landscape through the Scottish lochs and valleys soothingly dramatic, but something about being at sea seemed to disagree with him. The moment he was on the ferry he'd slipped into the first bathroom he'd come across, knowing that Ruby and Leonie were somewhere nearby. The choice of hiding place was rather appropriate, it turned out, because only minutes after the boat set sail he'd been overcome with the worst seasickness he'd ever experienced. The force of the first great expulsion of vomit was too much for his injured head: he'd blacked out.

In the darkness, the dreams returned. Constance was standing in front of him, her gaze steady. She had big, sad eyes, and a baby in her arms. She opened her mouth to speak, but all that came out was a terrible scream, a high-pitched, barely human shriek. It had the ocean in it somehow; it sounded exactly like the seals on the night he took her. As he watched, her eyes became entirely black, the whites disappearing. Her mouth grew bigger, her nose became elongated, her skin darkening to grey. She was half-seal, now, a horrific chimera, with a human's legs and torso but a thick neck and the head of a seal, and she was screaming that awful scream. He wanted to cover his ears but he couldn't seem to move his arms. She put the baby down on top of him and turned away, and he wanted to shout, *Don't leave it here. I can't have it, it's not mine. What have you done? Where are you going? She's your baby, come back for her.*

But no sound came from his lips, and she kept moving away. Now the baby, another half-seal, Leonie but not-Leonie, was looking at him with its big dark eyes, but even if he could have picked it up he wouldn't have done so. He was repelled by it. He shouted, *Come back, Constance, and do your duty,* and he knew that if she didn't then the thing was going to die. He experienced the thought in a matter-of-fact sort of way, because he couldn't, wouldn't – and what is more didn't want to – look after it, not in a million years. And even though there was no sign that she would come back, somewhere in the depths of his brain he knew that she wouldn't just walk away from Leonie. He had started to feel angry. She was messing with him. She'd turn around in a minute. And yet she kept getting smaller and smaller as she receded into the distance, and she didn't look around, not once. Her legs were gone then, replaced by a seal's tail. The last he saw of her, she was diving in a perfect arc, disappearing into the black. The baby opened its mouth and started to scream, and the sound was just like the mother's: distant, soulful, and so terribly loud.

Someone was shouting, then, and there was a loud knocking sound. The man had opened his eyes and remembered where he was.

'Are you all right in there? Do I need to get the doctor?'

'No,' he'd managed, trying to sound convincing. His voice cracked, and he said it again, more forcefully. 'No, thank you. I just feel a bit sick. I'm not used to boats.'

'Well,' said the voice, 'if you're sure.'

'I'm sure. Thank you. I'll be fine.'

'You've been in here for half an hour.'

'I'm . . .' he cut himself off with another wave of nausea, head down into the bowl, his whole body clenched. Matter rose up from his stomach and splattered into the toilet.

'I'll check again in a bit,' said the person, and went away.

With every heave, the pain in his head intensified, and with each bright burst of it he pictured Constance coming towards him with the rock or whatever it was that she'd used to bash his head in. This picture was not a memory; he'd been hit from behind, he hadn't even known she was there. After Ruby had led him to Constance, the first thing he was going to do was make her pay for that.

The man had ventured from the bathroom a couple of hours into the journey, but he hadn't been able to go far. He kept needing to dash back and hold himself over the toilet, though after a while mostly he'd been dry-heaving. When he first saw the lights of the island he'd been convinced it was a mirage, but as they got closer, he saw that there were streetlights, and a few lit windows punched out of the dark, seemingly set into the dense blackness of rock. When the moon broke through the clouds for a moment the island loomed from the sea, both bigger and smaller than he had expected, like the hump of an impossibly large whale; an ancient, tree-less mound with the edges of cottage roofs silhouetted against the sky like giant limpets.

The boat tips very slightly and he loses balance, his stomach turning with the movement but there is nothing left to come up. Leaning with one hand on the cool glass, the man hears the sound of the child's – unmistakably Leonie's – chatter behind him, and discreetly moves away to the other side of the ferry. The child's noise is like an early warning system; he can hear them coming and get out of the way before they spot him. There had been only one moment, about an hour ago, when he'd realised that Ruby was coming towards him, heading for the toilets without Leonie, and he'd had to duck sideways into the bar area to get away. There, he saw that Leonie was asleep under a coat on one of the benches at the edge of the room. He watched her for a minute, until he realised he too was being watched, by the bartender. When their eyes met, the man smiled but the bartender did not. He just stared back, steadily, continuing to polish a glass with a cloth.

'You feeling all right, mate?'

The man was on the verge of replying that he was fine, when he realised he was about to be sick again and ran for the gents with a hand clamped over his mouth. As the door swung shut he could hear the bartender's soft chuckle and his comment to a colleague. 'First-timer, that guy. You can spot them a mile off.'

As the ferry docks, most of the people on board begin to gather near the stairs to the car deck. The man hangs back – as a foot passenger he will be exiting the same way as Ruby and Leonie, but he doesn't want to risk being seen at this crucial point. He keeps his eye on them. In Ruby's arms, the child is almost asleep, her head on the woman's shoulder. He lets them go in front, with another six or seven people between them. Leonie's eyes are just closing when she spots him. He looks straight at her for a split second, then bends quickly, pretending to tie a shoelace. Shit. He was so close. It couldn't be spoiled, not when he'd come so far.

'Mamma Bee?' he hears Leonie say, talking around her thumb so that the words aren't quite clear.

'Yeah, baby?' says Ruby.

'Daddy there.'

He holds his breath. It isn't a question, but Ruby answers it as if it is. 'No, honey, Daddy's not here.'

When he peeks above the heads of the other people, he sees that Ruby has whirled around and is searching the crowd, standing on tiptoes, scrutinising every face. He ducks in the nick of time.

'I seen him,' says Leonie. 'Daddy there.'

Perhaps aware of listening ears, or wary of frightening the girl, Ruby merely says shhh, and Leonie stops talking. Hemmed in by the crowd, Ruby faces the front and rocks the child gently, though he can tell from the way she holds her shoulders that she's tense. The man moves so that he isn't directly in Leonie's eyeline before he checks again, and sees that she is asleep.

The bow door clanks open, and he stands aside to allow everyone to get off before him so that he can put as much distance between him and Ruby as possible. Gingerly he pulls down the baseball cap that covers his wound, and wraps the fisherman's jacket tightly around himself as he disembarks. By the time he walks slowly up the freezing dock, the two of them have gone, into the nearby hotel; he can see them through the window as Ruby speaks with the receptionist. It's too late, too dark to try to find Constance now. They'll be planning a daytime rendezvous, and he needs to be ready in the morning, the moment they set off.

He waits until all the locals have dispersed before he starts trying the doors of the cars parked in the street that leads from the bay. He has his pick. No one here locks their car, it would seem. The first in the row is a Mini, too small for him really, so he tries the next, a large BMW. The door opens. He slips into the back seat, curls up and falls quickly into an untroubled sleep, lulled by the sound of the waves against the nearby shore.

CHAPTER FORTY-NINE

NOW
Joanna

Thursday, 27 December

Heavy footsteps on the towpath outside alerted her. Sam lay on the floor of the boat, so Joanna crouched in a position from which she could defend them both. Silently she grabbed a broken bottle and gripped it, ready to strike.

'Boss?'

She relaxed. 'Steve. You scared me.'

Atkinson thumped down the stairs into the saloon, shining a heavy-duty torch around the trashed inside of the boat.

'I guess the fugitive beat us to it,' he said. 'Did you find Ruby and the girl?'

'No, but I know where they are. On a ferry in the middle of the sea.'

Sam groaned softly.

'Is he all right?'

'Not really.'

Once Sam had been attended to and taken away by the paramedics, Harper and Atkinson climbed into the patrol car and started driving north, heading for the port at Oban. As they joined the motorway, Steve wordlessly handed her his phone, on the screen of which was an email from the mobile phone surveillance system informing them that Ruby had turned her phone on again, and that it was located off the coast, en route to the Western Isles. Such a remote place – why did it have to be there? The alert was from only an hour ago. Jo took out her own phone and tried Ruby's number, and this time, it connected. She listened to it ring three times, four, imagining her daughter holding the phone in her hand, thinking about whether or not she should answer. Then, she did.

'Joanna?'

'Ruby.'

There was a pause, as they both choked into tears. Harper searched in her bag for a tissue, ended up wiping her nose on the back of a hand. The distance between Jo and Ruby was huge: six hours' driving, six hours on the ferry. It was as if they were on separate planets. Yet just hearing that voice, Joanna felt closer than she had in years.

'Are you OK?'

'Yes,' said Ruby, 'I'm in trouble though. I need to tell you—'

'It doesn't matter.'

'Joanna, don't. I'm trying to explain.'

'You don't have to explain. I know already.'

'What do you think you know?'

'That you took that child, that you pretended to be someone else.'

'You make it sound like I committed a crime.'

'Technically, you did. But that's not what I meant, Ruby, honey. Can we start over?' How come they always ended up

354

here, no matter how much Jo tried not to? Atkinson side-eyed her. This was no time for an argument. Don't make her hang up and turn off the phone again. Jo took a slow breath and tried again. 'I'm not . . . blaming you. I know why you did it, Ruby. And we're not going to arrest you—'

'We? You mean, the police? But, Jo, I thought I was talking to you. As a person, not as a copper.' She sounded hurt, then angry. 'Nothing ever changes, does it?'

'Please, Ruby. I'm sorry. Is Leonie OK?'

'Yes, she's fine. She's the best thing in the world, actually. She's asleep right now.'

'And you're on the boat?'

'Yes. We should dock soon.'

'I need to ask, have you seen Gregor anywhere?'

Suddenly Ruby's voice was panicked. 'Why would I have seen him? Is he in Scotland? I know he escaped from the hospital, but I hoped, because of the injury, maybe he wouldn't have got very far.'

'He went to see your friend Sam—'

'Sam? Is Sam OK? What did he do?'

'He'll be fine. But Gregor . . . he knows where you're going. He's trying to find you, and maybe hurt you. He's angry. Perhaps he wants to take his daughter back. And he's ahead of us, though we're coming as fast as we can.'

'But I'm on a ferry.' Ruby sounded shaken. 'I've been on it for nearly five hours, and he's definitely not here. I haven't seen him. Although . . .'

'What?'

'It's nothing. Only, Leonie said something about seeing him. But she was half asleep at the time.'

Joanna stiffened in fear. 'You're sure? You checked he wasn't there?'

'Yes. I'm sure.'

There was a tremor in her voice, though, that neither of them acknowledged. She must be terrified. And the little girl; surely she was traumatised, too. No wonder she was seeing that man around every corner.

'That's great,' said Jo. 'He must have missed it, like we thought. He might try to get on it tomorrow, but we'll be there in time to stop him. We won't let him get to you.'

'If he catches me, I don't know what he'll do.'

'I know, honey. I know what he's capable of. I know why you had to defend yourself. Just a shame you didn't hit him harder.'

'Me? You think that was me? I didn't even know about it until I saw it on the news.'

Jo exhaled. 'I knew it couldn't be you.'

'But if you think I'm a criminal—'

'What are you even doing up there, Ruby? What's on the island you so desperately need to get to?'

'Leonie's mother, Constance. She asked me to bring her. So, I'm keeping my promise.'

'Constance? But we don't know if she's still alive. She ran into the sea, Ruby. She didn't even have a wetsuit.'

When Ruby spoke again her voice was full of doubt. 'But she said she'd be here. For Leonie.'

Ruby was so far away. If only she'd told Joanna what she was planning, she could have talked sense into her before it was too late. Constance had clearly been a woman with a severely troubled mind. Jo gave a frustrated groan.

'Even if she is there, after what she did, abandoning her child on the seafront, do you really think she's a fit mother?'

Ruby went quiet. Then,

'That is fucking rich, coming from you.'

Click.

'Ruby. Ruby? Oh, shit.'

'Did she hang up?' said Atkinson.

'Yeah.'

'Huh.'

'I always say the wrong thing. I don't know why I can't just keep my stupid mouth shut.'

A few seconds later, Atkinson's phone rang through the speakers of the car. It was DI Thrupp.

Steve put his finger to his lips as he pressed to allow the call.

'What do you mean, you're going to the Outer Hebrides?' Thrupp wasn't quite yelling.

Atkinson said, 'Like I said, that's where Ruby's gone, with Leonie. I just spoke to her, she's about to disembark from the ferry at Barra.'

'What state of mind is she in? Is there any risk to the child?'

'No, of course not,' said Joanna, interrupting. 'None whatsoever.'

Atkinson grimaced. He mouthed, *shut up*.

'Who is that? Steve? Who just spoke? DS Harper, is that you?'

'Yes, sir.'

Thrupp's voice rose a half-octave. 'What do you think you're doing? Can someone explain what is going on?'

'Well, sir—'

'Not you, Jo. I don't want to hear from you, after what

you've done. In the morning I'm meeting with Hetherington to discuss what's happening, but I wouldn't be surprised if he recommends a suspension—'

'But, sir . . .'

'But nothing. Stop talking. Learn to follow an instruction, would you? Steve, I want you back here as soon as possible.'

'But what about the little girl? Don't we need to bring her home?'

'She's not our priority right now, neither of them are. Yes, it's important that we locate the child and bring her back, of course it is. I'm going to liaise with Highlands and Islands Police, and get them to help by directing some manpower. They can pick up Ruby, and Leonie. But our team only has so many resources, and at the moment all of our focus needs to be on finding this man.'

'But that's who we're chasing, sir. He's attacked Sam Douglas, and he's gone after Ruby. We're right behind him.'

There was a short silence. 'He's on the island now, too?'

'No, we don't think so,' said Atkinson. 'It would have been tight for him to catch the ferry, and Ruby wasn't aware of him on the boat during the crossing.'

'We need to get an officer to the island, as quickly as possible. Can you fly, from Glasgow?'

'Me?' asked Joanna.

'One of you. The other one needs to go to the port, in case he's waiting for the next crossing.'

'So I'm back on the case?' said Jo.

'For the moment. You said you'd spoken to Ruby?'

'Yes, but she hung up on me. I put my foot in it, slightly.'

Harper could almost hear the sound of Thrupp hitting his

forehead with a palm in frustration. 'Jo. If you weren't the only copper available for this, I would . . .'

During the pause, Harper and Atkinson exchanged a glance.

'Fine,' said Thrupp, 'I mean, it's not fine, but I don't have much choice in the matter, do I? Jo, get the plane. Steve, go to the ferry port, intercept him if you can, arrest him. I'll send backup, but it might take a while. Keep me updated.'

The call ended. They drove in silence for a few minutes.

'What do you think that man's planning to do to them? To Ruby and Leonie, I mean.'

'The guy's a psychopath,' said Jo. 'Who knows what he's thinking? One thing in our favour though: he's got quite a severe head injury to contend with, and Sam said he managed to land a few blows before he was overpowered. Hopefully that will slow him down enough for us to catch him.'

'Yeah,' said Atkinson, though to Jo he sounded far from certain.

CHAPTER FIFTY

NOW
The Injured Man

Dora is kneeling on his chest, holding his eyelids shut. *Get off me, you little shit*, he tries to say, but his mouth seems full of cotton wool, his tongue too thick to move properly.

I won't let you do it, says Dora. *You've done enough, now. Just leave them alone, won't you?*

It's a dream. He knows it's a dream, yet he can't shake it off. He can't shake her off; he bucks his body but she clings to him like a goblin. *You're dead*, he tries to say, *you can't stop me doing anything.*

Dora lets go of one of the man's eyelids and reaches behind her. When she brings her hand around, she's holding a pen-knife that he recognises. It's the one he used, to take off her finger, just before he . . . just before she fell, so tragically.

You pushed me, she says, as though she can read his thoughts. Then, she plunges the blade of the penknife into the soft part at the back of his head, and the pain explodes like a grenade.

With the pain, clarity returns. He stops struggling and lies still. *This is not real*, he thinks. *You're not real. It's all in my head.*

Dora stops what she's doing. For a moment she seems unsure. Then she glances to her right, and Constance is there, floating beside them, her bottom half a fish, top half human. The man tries to say, *This isn't fair*, because now there are two of them, and he still can't move. *You're just a dream, both of you*, he thinks. Then he sees that behind Constance is an old woman, and next to the old woman, though it takes him a while to place him, is the man whose name he took. *Now this is getting ridiculous*, he thinks. Both Gregor and the old woman are laughing at him. *I don't see why you're laughing*, he thinks. *I killed you.*

It's because we know what's coming next, says the old woman. *And I don't think you're going to like it very much.*

Constance comes near.

What are you? she asks. *You're not a man. You took my skin. You kept it.*

You're not real, he tries to scream. *None of you are real.*

Dora's still crouching above him, her hand on the knife sticking out of his wound. Her lip curls, like a shrug. *Real is relative*, she says, twisting the knife, and the pain he feels is real, excruciating. The last thing he sees before he blacks out is Constance, swimming away into the distance, to the sound of Dora, Gregor, and Gregor's mother laughing.

He awakes into darkness, remembering where he is, that he's in a car and he needs to get out before anyone sees him there. His head throbs violently, and when he reaches up to feel it, he realises he has been resting his head on the seatbelt connector. He must have jerked his head in his sleep, and that is what has stabbed him. Dora, you crazy little hallucination, he thinks, smiling bitterly. But still, his pulse races with the memory of the vicious apparitions, and he can't shake off the uneasy feeling for some time.

The woman at the hotel crosses her arms. 'I'm sorry,' she says, 'We have no one of that description staying here, I'm afraid.'

'Look,' says the man, 'I know she might have told you not to let me know where she is, but I'm her husband. It was just a little fight, honestly. I only want to talk to her.'

'I don't know who you're talking about.'

'But I saw her come in here last night. You were serving her. You must remember.'

The woman shrugs.

'I'm worried about her, that's all. And my daughter. She's such a daddy's girl. She'll be missing me.'

The shy smile, that beautiful smile, and the bashful eyes. It never fails. He smiles it right at her, and the woman cannot look away. She takes a deep breath, visibly softening. 'She only came in to ask for a taxi. She didn't stay.'

Well, why didn't you say that first off, thinks the man. He smiles again, not completely hiding the irritation that he feels. 'Do you know where she went in the taxi?'

'Nope.' How can that be true? The second smile hasn't been as effective, clearly. She stares at him, daring him to ask again.

'Ah,' says the man. 'Well, thanks for your time, I suppose.' He turns to leave.

'Not many places she could have gone though.'

'Oh?'

'Only three other hotels on the island, and one of them is shut for the winter.'

'Thanks,' says the man, pulling open the door.

'This is a small place,' says the woman, with a warning tone. 'There are eyes everywhere, you know. No police, but eyes everywhere.'

This is interesting. 'No police?'

'There was one, once. But he tried to arrest one of ours so we locked him in his own cells. We police ourselves, these days. Have done for twenty years. And we are very, very, good at it.' She folds her arms and lowers her chin to look at him from under her brow.

The man sits on his rage. He takes a slow, deep breath. Then he holds up a hand in farewell, leaves the hotel and goes down the steps to the road.

CHAPTER FIFTY-ONE

NOW
Ruby

Friday, 28 December

It was pitch-dark outside. In winter, this far north, the hours of daylight were limited to the middle part of the day; in summer, the opposite was true, with only a few hours of darkness. When Ruby drew open the curtains she could barely make out the expanse of the beach that she knew stretched out in front of them, and to the right of that, the ocean. The hotel boasted the best view of any of the three hotels on the island. She'd chosen it because of the location, close enough to where she needed to be but not so close that anyone would see what she was doing, or try to interfere with the plan.

Leonie was sleeping, her chest gently rising and falling in the light from the bathroom door. Ruby had an idea that she might just slip out, leave the comb where Constance had said to and be back before the toddler awoke, but almost as soon as the thought had surfaced she dismissed it. Leonie was coming with her, of course she was. It was unthinkable that the child would wake up alone, and think she'd been abandoned again. By the time Ruby had dressed herself, the little girl was rubbing her eyes and sitting up.

They made their way to the front door of the hotel, avoiding the restaurant where the smell of breakfast wafted tantalisingly towards them.

'I mungry, Mamma Bee,' said Leonie as the door swung closed and Ruby began walking fast along the coast road, heading north, with the child strapped to her back.

'We'll eat soon, baby,' she said over her shoulder. 'Just got to do one thing. Then it's brekky, OK?'

'Yay! Brekky.'

As she hiked around a corner, the landscape rolled out in front of them and she almost had to stop to get her breath. Even in the weak, pre-dawn light, with the freezing wind whipping her face, the harsh beauty of it floored her. The road was cut into the rock, which stretched craggily down to meet the sea, that heaving, blue-black, infinite thing. The island curved to one side, with coves and crevasses breaking up the flat edges of the machair, falling away to beaches with sand that shone white as if they held the light inside them for times such as these.

Ruby pressed on, shushing Leonie as she complained of being cold, heading for the outcrop that Constance had described, the barren, exposed peninsula with a single, half-derelict cottage on it. It was further away than it looked at first. Leonie started to moan softly, and wriggled against the scarves that Ruby had used to wrap and secure her on her back.

'Just a few more minutes, baby. Don't worry. Nearly there.'

Up close, the cottage was even more of a wreck than she'd thought. The windows were boarded, the door rotten in the corners with only a few flakes of paint left on its surface. It was clear to Ruby that it was abandoned, had been for years. She screwed her eyes shut against the wind that was causing tears to sting her face, and leaned close to the wall, hoping for a little shelter, finding none; the wind whipped the house on all four sides. It was a mystery as to why it had been built. No one could live here. No one would want to. She went to the door and knocked, not expecting a response. Sure enough, all she could hear was the crashing of the sea, the whistling of the wind. Then she kicked the door, feeling the planks give way a little against the toe of her boot. Finally, she tried the doorknob, and it turned.

They stumbled into the cottage, grateful to get out of the weather. The only furniture in the single room was a rickety table pushed up against a wall. On the table, a large and beautiful conch shell, much bigger than any she'd seen before; twice the size of the one that had been in the bathroom at Gregor's. The table on which it stood was thick with dust, but the shell itself was spotless. Something shifted in Ruby and she let out a sob, steadied herself against the damp stone wall. She realised that until she saw the conch, part of her hadn't believed it was real.

'It dark, don't like it,' said Leonie.

'Don't worry, only a minute more,' said Ruby. She took the carved white comb from her zipped pocket and placed it inside the conch shell. It made a small, musical clanging sound as it slipped out of view, into the pinkish interior. She stood there, breathing, wondering if this was really going to work; if someone from Constance's family really came and checked the conch every day, the way Constance had described when they were planning how to meet up again. The family had no phones, no other way of communicating.

'We've people on the big island,' Constance had said. 'Some of our children, cousins who weren't born in the skin, who can't live where we do. Like you, my lovely.' She'd kissed Leonie on the head as she slept in her mother's arms. 'When the comb's in the shell, we come across to the beach at Seal Bay. It's a message. This one, they'll recognise. I carved it myself.'

'Want get down, Mamma Bee,' said Leonie, wriggling and kicking. Instinctively, Ruby started to bounce on her heels and sing. *Ionn da, ionn do . . .*

So far away from anyone, in this remote spot at the edge of the world was the last place she expected thoughts of Joanna to find her. Nevertheless, as she backed out of the dark room, into the wind on the headland, pulling the door shut behind them, Joanna was who she yearned for. Leonie had taught her what it was to put someone else's needs before your own. She realised then that perhaps Joanna had been trying to do that, all those years ago. Jo hadn't abandoned Ruby. She'd sacrificed the chance to be a mother, the gift of experiencing the joy and the fear that came with being the provider of unconditional love. Alone on the rock with Leonie, Ruby wanted to find her mother, Joanna, and say she was sorry, that she was forgiven – and that there was nothing to forgive, really, because she understood everything now. Most of all, she wanted to hold her, be held by her, and to say that she loved her.

Seagulls circled above them as she hiked over the rocks, then over the machair to the road. Soon they would be back in the warm hotel, eating breakfast and waiting until it was time.

CHAPTER FIFTY-TWO

NOW
Joanna

Friday, 28 December

The flight from Glasgow to Barra, which lasted a little more than an hour, wasn't the kind of flight you could sit back and enjoy. Joanna watched her knuckles turning white as she gripped the seat in front, and prayed for it to be over.

She supposed she had been warned, up to a point. 'It's a wee bit windy today,' the man she'd bought the ticket from had said. 'Keep your eye on the board for a delay, or a cancellation.'

'Is it likely to be cancelled?' There was only one scheduled flight a day. A cancellation would be unthinkable.

The man tipped his head in thought. 'They fly in a force eight. But they won't fly in a force nine.'

'What's the gale force now?' she'd asked. Outside, trees were bent sideways. People leaned at unlikely angles, clutching their coats to them, hair battened to scalps by the driving might of the wind and rain.

'Eight point three.' The man laughed at her. 'Don't look so worried.'

She shut her mouth.

The plane circled back on itself, and if Harper hadn't been gripped by the certainty that she was going to die she might have appreciated the moment when they broke through the cloud cover and the island came into view. There was no airport, no runway that she could see. She tapped on the newspaper of the man next to her, who lowered it and raised an inquiring eyebrow.

'Where do we land?' she asked, trying to keep her voice steady. When the man answered, she was sure she'd heard him wrong, that the accent had somehow made her mistake his meaning. The second time he said it, she understood, with a kind of sinking feeling, that she'd heard it correctly the first time.

'On the beach,' he said, nodding out of the window as the aircraft tipped to make a turn. She could see a long stretch of sand between two needles of rock. 'Only at low tide, mind. In a couple of hours, all that'll be underwater.' He grinned at her before returning to his paper. A second later he lowered it again. 'First time, I assume?'

She nodded. 'Last time, too, I think.'

He laughed, low and phlegmy.

To distract herself, she looked out of the window, and almost forgot she was scared. The sun had come out, turning the sea a translucent blue-green, the ripples on the water sparkling silver. The sand was pure white at the edges of the island. It reminded her of the colours of the Caribbean. The island itself was unspoiled, almost devoid of civilisation, apart from the airport building, itself a stark reminder that humans had conquered this place, even if the tide was still in control of the flight times. From what she could see of the coastline, apart from the huge white beach that served as a runway there were no accessible beaches on this side of the island. With probably sixty or more miles of coastline on the eight-mile-wide island, she wondered how she was going to find Ruby. There was no way of ringing. Straight after the badly judged conversation yesterday, Ruby had switched off her phone.

As the plane made its descent she turned again to the newspaper-reading man. 'Do you know where I can hire a vehicle?'

He folded his paper, finally. The plane was low now, the engines loud as it got ready to land.

'Sure,' he said, 'I'll show you if you like.'

'Maybe you have a number?' She pulled her phone out of her pocket, and saw that there was no signal.

The man chuckled gently. 'Who's your service provider?'

She told him, and he shook his head. 'Nay chance wi them, lassie.'

Joanna's hope wilted a little more. Even if Ruby did turn her phone on, there would still be no way of connecting.

The plane touched down on the sand, and Harper had to hold on tight to stop herself bouncing around as the brakes roared, came to a mighty crescendo, and died away. Finally, the aircraft was still.

'I wonder, can you also tell me where the local police station is?'

The man chuckled again.

'No police on Barra,' he said, standing to retrieve his bag from the overhead locker. He turned and looked her in the eye. 'No need. No crime to speak of.'

'That can't be true,' said Harper.

'Well, not entirely. But nobody really likes police, do they?'

When he grinned knowingly at her then, she raised her eyebrows. 'How did you know I was police?'

'Apologies,' he said, 'didn't mean to hurt your feelings. Just saying. What are you here for, anyway? Can't be anything big, I'd have heard about it.'

'I'm here to find my daughter.'

And she realised, then, that she'd stopped thinking and speaking of Ruby as her sister altogether. She was a mother, and her child needed her. Perhaps for the first time, she knew she would be there, no matter what; she was the only person who could do it. And it felt completely right.

CHAPTER FIFTY-THREE

I am a man upo' the lan'
An' I am a silkie in the sea:
And when I'm far and far frae lan',
My dwelling is in Sule Skerrie.

> 'The Great Silkie of Sule Skerrie',
> SCOTTISH: TRADITIONAL

Ruby

Friday, 28 December

The sun was bright as she hiked across the machair to the beach, with Leonie tied to her back once again in the makeshift sling, and Sam's violin strapped across her front. Ruby heard the sea before she saw it, the hiss and tumble of the waves against the sand, and the screeching of the seabirds above them. As the horizon came in sight, she spied the old cottage they had visited that morning, hunched and lonely on the headland.

Constance had entered the sea in a very different spot, so many miles away at Cleethorpes, on a freezing winter's night. Did she ever meet her family? If only Ruby could have caught a glimpse of them as they left. The way Constance expressed herself in fanciful tales of ancient lore, stolen skins and an island where seals danced on the beach as humans – the metaphors were so tantalising, and being here made Ruby see how you could grow up believing the stories were true. In the moment of helping Constance escape, Ruby had been convinced she was sending her into the arms of her family. But in recent days she'd become less and less certain that she hadn't simply helped a madwoman to her death. Coming to Barra had been a decision taken in desperation; she'd seriously doubted that Constance would be here, but it seemed as good a place as any to hide from Gregor. But the conch, that beautiful shining shell. That had been the proof that she'd needed to carry on. There *was* a colony, a secret island clan. They existed, and Constance was among them. Ruby was so close now, to what she'd come to do, to return the baby to her mother and her people so that they could live freely in the traditional way, away from prying eyes.

The deserted bay was pristine. White sand led to the ocean, clear blue-green in the bright wintry sunlight. Shaped like a perfect crescent, the beach was surrounded by rocky outcrops. Ruby turned towards the water, the wind coming straight off the sea and flattening her hair to her head, whistling past her ears. Right in front of them, about a hundred metres out, was a large rock, its edges washed by hundreds of tiny waves.

With Leonie still secured in the sling, Ruby took out the violin and began to play. First she played the folk song, *Chuir iad mise dh'eilean leam fhìn*. When she got to the chorus she played the part Sam had taught her, that he learned as 'The

Song of the Seals'. In that moment, she could see how the song could be sung both ways. She felt as if she'd been sent to an island, but it wasn't in exile. She'd come here for a reason. And as she played, a seal lifted its head, appearing as if out of nowhere on the rock in the bay. Of course, it had been there all along, just camouflaged, and sitting very still. She smiled, imagined it thinking, *Who's that playing our song?*

Leonie started to sing along. The song transported Ruby back to the folk bar where she'd first heard it, and from there to the dark interior of the flat on the New Park that she hoped never to see again. Playing it here washed all of that away. She knew from now on that the song would forever make her think of this beach, this perfect morning.

The wind should have whisked the notes from them, but the music seemed to echo in the bay. When she finished, the wind dropped and she felt the sun on her face. She put the instrument under her chin again and played 'The Seal-Woman's Joy'. All of the tension she'd been holding in her body drained away. Leonie relaxed against her, singing quietly the words, *Ionn da, ionn do . . .*

The final note quietly faded away. For a while she could hear only the wind, the sea, and the birds. Something screamed, then, and she jumped.

'What that, Bee?' said Leonie, wriggling in the wrappings that bound her to Ruby's back.

'It's a seal, honey. Can you see it?'

Once she'd seen one, her eyes adjusted, and she perceived three large grey seals, all of them watching Ruby and Leonie on the beach. One opened its mouth and made the noise again, but this time it didn't sound like a scream; more like a yelp, or a cry of recognition; perhaps even of joy. The seal heaved itself off the rock into the water, where only its head could be seen above the waves for a moment before it disappeared.

Ruby unwrapped Leonie and let her down, so that she ran with arms open wide towards the ocean, stopping just short of the lapping waves. She bent and tried to touch the edge of a wave, laughed when it disappeared, started to chase another as it withdrew and was only saved from a soaking by Ruby, who scooped her up and ran back to the dry sand. More games of 'touch the waves' followed. The child was looking down, so she didn't see the seal's head pop up, much closer now, before disappearing again.

Soon the two of them were sitting on a rock, Ruby drying the child's hands on one of the scarves, doing the counting rhyme, one-little-piggy, both of them laughing when the little one went wee-wee-wee all the way home. As she tickled her under the chin, Ruby suddenly realised that when the Roane arrived, when she handed her back, Ruby wouldn't be doing any of this anymore. Constance would take her daughter with her to wherever she lived now, and Ruby might never see them again. Of course it was the right thing for Leonie to be with her mother, and her other relatives. Ruby was never intending to keep her, that wasn't the plan. Only, now she wished it was. She squinted into the sunlight, scanning the beach for signs of Constance. *Maybe she won't come*, she thought.

Leonie, now with her gloves on, trotted down towards the water to look for shells. Ruby followed. The wind dropped to a light breeze; the sea was flat and calm. A chill crept up her spine and she whirled around, sure that she was being watched.

'Constance?'

But there was no one there, only the empty sand dunes, the seagulls, and out there in the ocean, the seals. Would she be in a boat, or a vehicle? If the colony lived on an island then it would be a boat, but she didn't see any craft in the bay. Perhaps there was a causeway, just out of sight somewhere. She shaded her eyes and searched the horizon. Two of the three seals she'd seen were still on the rock. The other one was nowhere.

'Mummy!' cried Leonie, and started running along the sand. There was Constance, at the edge of the sea, barefoot, glowing, and smiling, and running towards her daughter with her arms out ready to catch her. The sight of it filled Ruby up with joy, and yet pierced her heart at the same time. Mother and daughter, reunited. Just the way it should be.

The girl reached her mother and fell into her arms. Constance lifted her up in the air, both of them whooping. The woman's hair was loose down her back, threaded through with small shells, and she was wearing a sleeveless dress made of a patchwork of fabrics roughly sewn. Just behind her, on the rocks, Ruby saw that she'd placed her sealskin coat, which seemed good as new, shining like polished pewter in the sun. Constance balanced Leonie on a hip, walked towards Ruby. As she did so Ruby could see the difference that a few days with her people had made. Constance seemed truly alive, for the first time, in a way Ruby had never seen; her eyes sparkled, her skin was illuminated. Whatever had been missing back at the New Park estate had been returned. Leonie lay her head on her mother's bare shoulder; apart from the dress, she wasn't wearing anything. Ruby shivered, wondering how Constance could stand the cold.

'You came,' said Constance.

'Of course. I promised.'

'Thank you for coming, for bringing her.'

When Constance moved forward to embrace her, Ruby jerked away.

'What is it?' said Constance, finally seeing Ruby properly, how her expression had darkened.

'Where were you?' said Ruby, her voice sharpened by anger. How could she look so happy, after everything she'd done? 'At Cleethorpes. You left her on her own. How could you do that?'

'I didn't want to.' Constance set Leonie on the sand, straightened up and looked at Ruby. 'I had no choice.'

The wind had picked up. Ruby's words were being whipped away as it took her breath and stung her eyes. But she didn't feel it. 'Of course you had a choice. You could have chosen to keep her safe. You could have chosen not to leave her all alone.'

'I would have died if I'd stayed there. You know that.'

'You? *She* might have died because of what you did. How could you leave her – how could you choose yourself over your daughter, what kind of mother does that?'

'If it's a choice between my daughter or death, then it's not a choice. What use am I to her, without my own life?'

'Some people might say that it's your duty to sacrifice yourself for your child.'

Constance grimaced. 'I thought you understood. Clearly I was wrong. I don't have to explain myself again.'

'Right. And I don't have to do anything to help you, or your kid. You treat me like I'm an idiot. Just like everyone does.'

'You can choose whatever path you feel is right, Ruby. That's always been the case.'

'You asked me to help you.'

'You didn't have to say yes.'

Leonie looked from one to the other. Her bottom lip had started to stick out. 'No shouting,' she said, and a tear escaped from her eye. Both of them rushed towards her. Ruby got there first.

For a second she thought the child would reject her, reach for her mother. But she snuggled there, sucking a thumb, watching Constance with big eyes.

'I'm sorry, baby,' said Ruby. 'We won't shout anymore.'

Constance reached out a hand to rub her daughter's back. Her arm was shiny with seawater. Sand clung to her elbow and her bare shoulder.

'Aren't you cold?'

'I'm used to it. I like it.'

Ruby noticed that Constance's hair was wet. 'Surely you didn't swim from the island?'

She nodded. 'It's the quickest way. It's not too far.'

'But I didn't see you coming.'

'I know how to stay hidden.' Constance shifted her eyes towards the sea. 'You can't really see the island from here – look, see that rock just beyond there?'

Ruby looked where she was pointing. There was a rock, quite far out, disappearing behind the edge of the island they stood on. Waves were crashing against it.

'Not that one there? That's miles out.'

'It's only part of where we live. I'll show you, one day.'

'Will I have to swim there?'

Constance smiled.

'Mummy Mummy Mummy,' said Leonie, and Constance took her from Ruby. 'Down,' she demanded immediately, so Constance squeezed her, kissed her, set her on her feet where she squatted down to inspect a small stone.

'You can't swim back, though, can you?' said Ruby. 'Not with Leonie.'

Constance looked at her steadily. 'No,' she said. 'I can't.'

'Look, Mummy, look,' said Leonie, holding up a shell for Constance to see.

'Yes, baby, I see. It's beautiful.'

Constance looked back at Ruby. 'I can't keep her,' she said. And although Ruby expected to see tears glistening on Constance's cheeks, there were none. 'She can't come home with me. She wasn't born in the skin. She has to live on the land. With you.'

Born in the skin, that phrase again. Ruby didn't think it was literal, despite her notion that the sealskin coats might once have been used to catch the newborns. She'd assumed it was an expression meaning *born to the harsh island life*. She glanced again at the sleek sealskin behind Constance, and then over at the rock in the middle of the bay from where the grey seals watched them.

So many questions crowded her mind. 'But . . .'

Both seals called, loud and sharp, a warning bark.

Ruby heard a sound behind her, and she turned. Constance gasped. Ruby's throat closed.

The man they knew as Gregor was only a few metres away from them, where the beach became the machair. The sight of him chilled Ruby so that for an instant she couldn't move or

379

speak. He was dirty, unshaven, dressed in unfamiliar clothes. His lips were cracked, there was dried blood on his neck, but that wasn't the most terrifying thing. It was that finally, he wasn't trying to hide who he really was; she looked into his eyes and saw that the Gregor she had known was gone, if he'd ever been there at all. The creature standing in front of them was made only of spite, and hate. He looked as if he wanted to kill her, and not only that, but he was quite looking forward to it.

'Daddy,' said Leonie, and she was too far away to catch before she started running towards him.

Constance set off sprinting. Her fingers grazed Leonie's coat as the man picked up the child and took several steps backwards.

'Give her to me,' said Constance, and Ruby could tell she was making a huge effort to keep her voice steady.

The man laughed, a harsh, percussive sound. 'What, so you can leave her alone on the seafront again? Not likely. You're not fit to be a mother.'

'Fine, give her to Ruby, then.'

'Ruby? She'll run off with her, and I'll never see her again. My own kid! What were you planning to do, anyway, Constance? Take her away to your backwards little sect? To live like a bloody scavenger? I don't think so.'

'You don't care about her, Gregor. You never have. Just let her go.'

'You thought you were so clever, didn't you? Sneaking up on me, spiking me when I couldn't defend myself. But you can't win at this. I'm in charge here. She belongs to me. And so do you.'

The man was holding Leonie too tightly. 'Daddy, ow! Let go!' But he wouldn't.

'Don't, you're hurting her,' said Ruby.

He looked at Ruby as if he'd only just realised she were there. 'I'll do whatever the hell I like with her. And I'll have you know, for the record, that I could have done whatever the hell I liked with you, too, at any time. You were nothing to me. A game that got boring.'

'I won't say anything,' said Ruby. 'I'll take her far away, we'll start a new life, new names, everything. You won't need to worry about us. I've got as much to lose as you, Gregor, if the police catch up with me.'

He narrowed his eyes at her in disbelief. 'Firstly, I can't believe a word you say, honey, not after what you did to me. And secondly, I won't need to worry about you saying anything to the police, because pretty soon you won't be saying anything to anyone, ever again. But kudos for trying, I suppose.' He turned to Constance. 'You ready to come home?'

'Never.'

'Hmm.' He shrugged. 'I really wanted to make you sorry for what you did. But actually, this might be better. Makes things simple for me. No loose ends, shall we say.'

Still clutching the small girl, he turned and walked away from them, striding over the rocks, up the steep part at the edge of the bay. Ruby felt her arms twitch with the urge to fight him for the baby. Both women followed, gasping when he stumbled and nearly dropped the child, scared to go too close for fear of what he might do to Leonie if they did. At the top of the cliff he turned to face them. Leonie had gone limp, was whimpering silently, her eyes red with tears. *You've silenced her again, you bastard.*

Ruby stepped towards them, but Constance held out a hand to stop her. The man took another step backwards, edging closer to where the ground fell away to a deep crevasse.

'OK, so, kid first, I guess?' He grabbed a fistful of Leonie's coat and held her out over the edge.

'No,' shouted Constance and Ruby together.

They were fifty feet above the sea, perhaps more. A few steps away from a long drop into deep water, with needles of rock sticking up like teeth.

He took another step, held the child out at arm's length.

Ruby shrieked, tried to run towards him, but again Constance stopped her.

'He'll kill you,' she said.

'I don't care,' Ruby struggled with Constance to get away, 'I'd rather die than let him do that.'

'There are two of us and one of him,' said Constance, shouting so that Gregor could hear. 'If he throws her, we'll both go for him.' She turned towards him, his laughing face, mocking them and their panic.

'You're weak,' he said. 'I'm not afraid of you.'

'If you hurt her . . .' said Ruby.

Constance said, 'Gregor, if you do anything to Leonie we're both going to take you down.'

His smile faltered as he glanced over the cliff at the rocks. He looked at each of them in turn, seeming to weigh things up. Then he drew back his arm as if to throw the child.

'Maybe I'll risk it anyway.'

'Leonie!' Ruby shouted. But she was too far away to stop him.

'I'll come with you,' said Constance, and he hesitated, the arm holding Leonie dropping to his side so that she dangled there like luggage.

'Come with me?' he glanced again behind him at the crashing waves.

'Not like that. I'll come back with you.' She was holding out the sealskin coat. 'If you let her live.' Her face was set like stone.

His eyes narrowed, as if he might believe her. Then he laughed. 'Nice try. It's a trick.'

Leonie squealed and wriggled. Ruby felt like her heart would burst out of her chest. They were so close to the edge now. 'Stay still, Leonie. Please. Just for a minute. For me.' She held eye contact with Leonie, who stopped struggling, seeming to understand. 'Good girl.'

Constance stepped forward, holding out the coat. 'Take the coat. I can't go anywhere without it, you know that. Here.' She dropped it on the ground between them and it lay there, gleaming and still, seeming almost alive.

He grinned, his perfect white teeth glinting in the sun.

'Told you I'd win.'

Constance said, 'I'll count to three. We'll switch. Let her go, Gregor.'

He rolled his eyes, as if completely bored with the whole situation. 'Well, if you want her that much.' Ruby couldn't allow herself to believe that he was going to let her and Leonie go. He was toying with them, the way he'd been doing all along, since the yoga, since before that even, when he'd bugged the flat. She and Leonie were dispensable, now, and there was no predicting what he might be about to do. He might have been waiting for her to pick up the child so he could shove them both together over the cliff. Gregor eyed Ruby as she stood there, his tongue darting out like a snake's every few seconds. If she could get a bit closer, she would be able to touch Leonie, maybe even save her.

I dare you, he seemed to be saying.

Slowly he set Leonie on the ground but kept tight hold of one of her arms. With the other hand, he reached for the coat that Constance had left on the ground. His fingers brushed it as Ruby rushed forward for Leonie. She grabbed her, then nearly overbalanced as she changed direction, sensed the man's fingers almost touch her neck where he tried to get hold of her and she twisted away, feeling the sting of pain as he tore out a fistful of her hair.

'Stop, police!'

Ruby dropped to the ground and rolled away from the edge of the cliff, Leonie held tightly in her arms. As she did so she turned her head to see who had shouted. There was Joanna, running across the machair towards the rocks, cupping her hands to shout, 'Stop!' once more. What was she doing here?

'No,' she shouted, though the wind took her words away. 'Stay back.'

Gregor had picked up the sealskin. 'Oh, look, Ruby. It's your mummy. Come to save you.' He started to laugh, as if it was the funniest thing he'd ever heard. Ruby tried to signal to Joanna again to stop, that she was making things worse, that she might be putting herself in danger, too. She could feel Leonie's slack body against her, shaking softly with the silent cry.

'Come on then,' said the man, and Ruby felt him take hold of her upper arm, drag her to her feet. 'Looks like the three of you will have to go together, after all. Don't worry, Mummy will be with you soon, Ruby.'

What happened next can't have taken more than a split second. She saw a flash of dark hair as Constance swooped her head down, her mouth open, teeth bared. She bit the man on the wrist where he held Ruby's arm, and he let go with a yelp, blood from the wound arcing out, specks of it landing on her face. Ruby stumbled away with Leonie, protecting her, comforting her as she cried and cried, the noise no more than a breath of air but the shuddering of her body shaking them both. Joanna was there. She put her arms around Ruby, blocking out the wind, blocking out the world with her words, *Don't worry, you're safe, I've got you.*

Over Ruby's shoulder, Jo saw something that made her gasp, and Ruby turned just in time to see them fall. Constance went head-first as if in a dive, her hand gripping the man they had known as Gregor's arm tightly as his other arm windmilled, his eyes huge with shock. Time slowed: for a moment his body seemed suspended, feet cartoonishly scrabbling, first at grass, then rock, then nothing. His mouth opened in a scream.

As quickly as it started, the scream was cut off. Far below, the waves crashed against the rocks.

Leonie was wide-eyed.

'Mummy Daddy gone.'

A seal called, from somewhere far offshore. Another, much closer, answered. The sound was loud and terrible.

CHAPTER FIFTY-FOUR

Joanna

Within an hour of the pair falling from the clifftop, a team of specialist officers from the mainland arrived on the island by helicopter. With direction from the coastguard, Joanna offered to help organise the search parties. Rescue boats worked alongside local fishermen to comb the surrounding areas for the bodies overnight, but found nothing. At around 5 a.m., the pair of them freezing, huddled together in the old police station waiting for news, the sergeant turned to Jo. 'You get to the hotel, get some rest. If we find anything, I'll call you.'

The call came with the morning, yanking her from a flimsy slumber. It was fortunate that she'd been too exhausted to get undressed; she levered herself upright and into her boots in minutes.

A body had been found floating not far off the coast, and been towed in to shore by a fishing boat. Jo hiked over to where it lay, spread-eagled face down on the sand, surrounded by the fishermen who had found it, the scene lit red and orange by the dawn.

Two of them turned the body on its back, one arm flopping

wetly and splashing her shoes. 'This him?' asked one of the fishermen.

'Yes,' said Joanna. Jo felt nothing that he was dead, except frustration. In the hospital she'd spent too long staring at this same slack face and wondering. So many unanswered questions. Now, not only would she never have the chance to question him, he would never face justice for what he'd done. Not in this life, at least.

The fishermen shuffled their feet. 'Right then, lads,' said a big bearded one, who appeared to be the skipper. 'We'll be off.' Waders squeaking, all four men started for the row-boat they'd pulled into the shallows. The fishing vessel was anchored a little way offshore.

'Hang on,' said Joanna, 'you're still going to help search, right?'

'Search for what?' said the skipper, continuing to walk away. 'We found your man.'

'There's another body to find. The woman, Constance.'

They stopped walking. One exchanged a glance with another. 'Ah, but she's Roane, isn't she?' said the youngest of the group. The bearded one punched him on the upper arm; the others shushed him.

'Whoever she is, she's still missing. We can't call off the search yet.'

The skipper stared at her, his face unreadable. 'You won't find that one, Detective. Be a waste of our time, and yours.' He turned and waded into the surf, the other three men following.

She turned to the officer in charge. 'You just going to let them all go home?'

He shrugged, embarrassed. 'They're volunteers. And fishermen, you know. A law unto themselves.'

'But what about the rest of the search? What about Constance?'

They both looked out to sea, where the coastguard's boat was no more than a speck on the horizon. 'She's dead, Harper. We can't spend any more money looking for a body, not when there are live cases to deal with.'

She stared at him. 'I can't believe . . .'

'I've seen a lot of these,' said the officer in charge. 'When the sea's done with her, she'll give her back. It's just a case of waiting.'

Joanna thought of the little girl, not even two years old, now an orphan. Her parents had plunged to their deaths together in this bleakly beautiful place, right in front of her. That kind of thing left a mark, even if Leonie might not remember it consciously. Echoes of trauma would cascade down the generations, seeping into corners that love should have filled. Unless of course she was lucky, and the love got there first.

At the hotel, Joanna watched Leonie carefully for signs of distress, but all she saw was a sunny, happy girl, playing with Ruby, who she adored. Mamma Bee. They seemed so happy together, so natural. The bond was obvious.

'What's wrong, Joanna?' asked Ruby. 'You seem troubled. Not like you.'

'Oh, nothing, Just tired.'

How could she tell Ruby that in a matter of hours, Leonie would be taken away, perhaps forever? That safeguarding systems and social services would be even now deciding what was best for the child, and while they did that, they would almost definitely take her into local authority care? Unless . . . the parents were dead, but that didn't mean the whole family were.

'I need to see if I can find the family, this Roane lot,' she said, and headed out once more.

Jo went door to door. At every house, the same response; folded arms, closed faces. As the short time she had started running out, she became more desperate.

'There's a community, on an island, nearby. You haven't heard of it? What about the name Roane? Mean anything to you?' Each person feigned an unconvincing denial. One man said, 'Oh, you mean the selkies?' but his wife dragged him away before he could say any more. At the Castlebay Hotel, a strange expression crossed the face of the woman who ran it. Her words declared that she'd never heard of the secretive clan; her face and body language said the opposite.

She returned to the beach just as the helicopter landed, come to pick up Ruby, Leonie and Joanna. As the island drifted out of sight, Jo looked at the little girl – excited to be so high up, her head too small for her ear defenders – and felt sad that if it was true her mother was from here, this might be her only visit. Whatever her family set-up looked like after this, Leonie would be changed by it, like the roots of a sapling encountering a rock, and growing differently for ever after. But maybe that was just life; maybe that's how we all grow.

EPILOGUE

THREE MONTHS LATER
Joanna

The two bodies in the wall of the penthouse apartment were eventually proved to be that of Gregor Christopher Franks, a local property developer, and his elderly mother, Eva. Forensic examination of the bodies suggested they had been killed at around the same time as each other and sealed in the wall for at least three years. The murderer had gone to great lengths to make sure they didn't rot, using salting processes that the pathologist described as 'more usually applied to the making of serrano ham'.

The pathologist was oddly chirpy, as Joanna found that pathologists often were when they came across something out of the ordinary. 'He would have needed to salt them for a few months. I imagine he needed sacks of the stuff – the bodies would have been covered completely. In the bath, probably. To get all the moisture out, you see. The Ancient Egyptians did something similar, with mummification.'

'So he mummified them? Why?'

'I imagine it was so that the bodies didn't start to smell and give themselves away. Ingenious, really.'

'I'm not sure I'd go that far. Sick, certainly.'

Both bodies were devoid of innards, hanging upside down from butcher's hooks in the well-ventilated cavity, so that they had slowly dried out completely, finishing the job the salting had begun.

As for the man who'd killed them and stolen Franks' identity, while it took a lot of detective work to determine exactly who he was, assigning him to crimes he'd committed was initially a much simpler affair. As well as the many unsolved crimes which could be matched to him from the national police database, his DNA and fingerprints were found all over a disused industrial building on the edge of town, owned by Gregor Franks. From the equipment he'd been stockpiling, it looked as if he'd been planning to use the building to dispose of a number of bodies, three in total. Or three, to start with. Joanna hadn't been part of the team who searched the building, and no one would tell her what exactly they'd found, but her imagination filled in the blanks. It made Jo angry all over again that he was dead, because that meant she couldn't kill him herself.

'What do you think he was doing, when he left us alone all those nights?' said Ruby.

Jo knew exactly what he'd been doing, from the information that had been found on his various phones and devices. When he hadn't been building his body-disposal unit, he'd been stalking single gay men in neighbouring cities, using online dating apps. He'd met several of them, but others he'd simply been watching, researching, finding out everything he could. He was hunting for his next persona, planning to jump from 'Gregor' and into another lonely life via a little light murdering.

'I don't know,' said Joanna. 'Bad things, probably.'

'The worst thing is,' said Ruby, 'that he knew I was there, from the moment I moved in.'

Joanna was cooking for the two of them in her flat. She thought it was hard to choose what the worst thing was, but that this was certainly amongst the top five.

'But he didn't speak to me until August. I'd been there since February.'

Jo nodded. 'He was watching you. Two years before you were given the flat, around the same time he took over Franks' life, he hacked into the council system to prevent anyone from renting it. He must have known that the housing people would notice the glitch eventually. So at some point in those two years he fitted the spyware. I suppose, if a random stranger was going to be in a position to be observing him, he wanted to be watching them first.' Or maybe, and Joanna thought this more likely, he did it initially to amuse himself. One thing she knew from the many psychopaths she'd encountered over the years was that they tended to get bored easily. The crimes they committed had to get steadily more disturbing each time, ramping up the level of violence or deviance in order to achieve the same thrill.

'All those hours of practice, when I thought no one was listening. I never realised until he mentioned a piece I'd written that I'd played in the flat but never played him. After that I spotted three tiny cameras. There was even one in the bathroom.'

'Don't think about it too much. You'll drive yourself mad.'

Ruby's hand flew to her mouth. 'Oh, Jo, no one from the police had to look at that, did they? You didn't . . .'

Joanna shook her head. 'You don't have to worry. We've destroyed the footage.'

'What really puzzles me, though, was that he knew so much about classical music. We talked for hours about the vagaries of Brahms, or which was our favourite Schubert lieder.'

'I guess he was genuinely a fan,' said Joanna.

'I don't know if he was genuinely anything. He'd certainly done his homework, but there was this Mozart thing that he thought I'd written . . . Doesn't mean much. I guess I'm just going over everything he said to me in the early days, and wondering how I fell for it.'

Jo opened a bottle of red to let it breathe. 'I shouldn't tell you this, but we've found his fingerprints at crime scenes in almost every county. Mostly house burglaries, dating back ten years. One or two very odd ones, though . . .'

The frightened look on Ruby's face made her stop, then, before she got into the story behind the preserved finger from the metal box and how it led them to discover the dead man's identity. As she poured the wine, Jo kicked herself for over-sharing; she ought to keep in mind that gory details are not for everyone. In a similar way to the psychopaths, she'd become immune to horror: over the years it took ever more violence and deviance to shock her. This, however, was out of the ordinary, a case she would remember for a long time, and one she thought she would never cease to be sickened by.

What she didn't say to Ruby was that familial DNA testing had proved that the finger belonged to a sibling of the man who had stolen Gregor's identity, and from there it was a short step to scouring records, first of murdered children with missing fingers, and then of missing children whose bodies were never recovered, of whom no one could know the state of their fingers. Thankfully both categories of crime were few and far between. They found who they thought was the right person almost immediately. Joanna had studied all the newspaper clippings before heading to the village with Atkinson to confirm it.

Eight-year-old Dora Jones had lived on a remote farm in rural Wales with her family. She had disappeared in 1997 on a sunny day, after going out to play in the fields. Hope of finding her alive started to wane after a week. Police scaled back the search after two months, but the family and the community continued to search for Dora every day for half a year before they were forced to call it off due to the harsh winter that had set in. Dora's parents never stopped looking for her, though it would turn out they didn't have much time left to search.

The deaths of both parents two years later were recorded as accidental carbon monoxide poisoning, though many in the area assumed when they heard the news that it was a double suicide, brought on by the guilt and grief of losing Dora. The couple were dead before they ate their sausages, having sat down to eat in a very enclosed kitchen space with a new, but faulty, gas heater. Only the older brother, Daffyd, survived, what with being away that night, sent by his father to tend the furrowing sows, and therefore missing dinner. He came home late to find them with their faces in the mashed potatoes. When questioned by Joanna, it seemed that no one in the small rural community had seen or heard of Daffyd since the funeral. A cold fish, was the most she could get out of anyone who'd met him. Everyone remembered Dora, but some had forgotten she even had a brother. Not everyone: one retired schoolteacher shuddered in alarmed recognition at the sound of his name. She looked at a photograph of the dead man and confirmed it, providing old school portraits that proved it without a doubt. At the time of Dora's death, Daffyd would have been fifteen years old. His sister's body had never been found, but the finger was buried with her parents at the family plot in a ceremony attended by those who had known her.

One day, Ruby might want to know the extent of the man's crimes. But for now, it could wait.

Joanna looked at her daughter. Her cheeks were pinkly flushed. 'You look good, Ruby. Healthy. Sam must be feeding you well.' Since what had happened, Ruby had moved back onto the boat with Sam to help him recover. The relationship had developed, too: they were officially a couple, had been for almost three months.

'Yeah, right. He's a terrible cook.' She looked away, hesitated.

'What is it?'

'I know what you're going to say, OK? But just let me speak.'

'Go ahead.'

'Me and Sam, we're thinking about adoption.'

'Whoa, Ruby. That's a bit fast, isn't it? You've only just moved in together.'

'See? I knew that's what you'd say. We've known each other for years, you realise. Nine years, Jo. I think that's long enough to know if it's going to work.'

Jo moved to the hob, started throwing chopped vegetables into the wok. Ruby sat on a stool at the breakfast bar.

'But . . . children?' said Jo. 'Do you really want to tie yourself down, at this stage in your career? Now that you've got that soloist role . . .'

'It's a local operatic society. Hardly the RPO.'

'No but it's a step in the right direction. And the boat – it's not exactly brilliant for kids, is it?'

Ruby waved a hand in the air as if the words were a bad smell. 'That's just details. We can get a bigger boat. But we've got to do it soon because she's two now. Time goes so quickly when they're little, don't you think?'

Joanna turned the hob off. She came around the counter and took Ruby's hand, led her to the couch, made her sit.

'You're talking about Leonie, aren't you?'

'Of course I am. Who else would I be talking about?'

'Honey, I'm so sorry. I was going to tell you, but I never got the chance, it was never the right time.'

'What is it? What's happened to her, is she all right?'

'She's fine, sweetie. But she was placed for adoption, a month ago. With the foster family that she's been with since the start. It turns out there might be a family connection: the mother says her great-aunt was from the *Roane* clan...' she trailed off when she saw Ruby's reaction.

Ruby seemed so angry that Jo thought she might be about to hit her, and braced herself for the blow by closing her eyes. When she opened them again, Ruby was sobbing.

'Why didn't you tell me?'

Jo felt that her heart might burst. The guilt, the powerlessness. In that moment she would have done anything to swap places with her daughter, to take some of that pain from her. 'I'm sorry. I'm so sorry.'

'I loved her so much.'

Jo held Ruby as she cried. She'd been expecting something like this for a while. Ruby had started talking about trying to apply for permission to see Leonie and wouldn't understand that there was little chance, as an unrelated person, that the child protection order would allow it. Adoption by Ruby and Sam would have been entirely out of the question. Things simply didn't work that way.

'When you're ready,' said Jo, 'I have some photographs. I've been keeping them for you. If it's too much, then I can . . .'

'Let me see them. Please.'

In each photo, Leonie was happy. They had mostly been taken in a large and wild back garden full of play equipment, where she laughed as she went down a slide, smiled as she marvelled at some frogspawn, giggled as she was pushed on a swing by an older girl.

'That's her new sister, there, with the red hair,' said Jo. 'She's one of four, now.'

'So many children to play with,' said Ruby. 'She really looks happy, doesn't she?'

'She really does.'

'So why do I feel so sad?' Fresh tears spilt on to Ruby's knees. 'How did you do it, Joanna?'

'Do what?'

'How did you let me go the way you did? I only knew Leonie for a few months. I didn't give birth to her. How do people do these things? And Constance. I'll never understand the choice she made at Cleethorpes.'

'I understand why Constance did what she did. And although it's hard, I understand why you're going to let Leonie go, too. Because the choice you have is almost the same one Constance faced. To keep her, and sacrifice everything that you have, or to let her go, so that she can be happy elsewhere – so that you can live. That's not a choice, is it? Constance would have been kept by that man her whole life if she'd stayed. At least she got a few days with her family, before . . . she fell.'

'But I could have taken care of her. I promised Constance that I would.'

'You would have been battling the system for years, unable to get on with your life. Leonie wouldn't have been free, either. Look at her.'

In the photograph, Leonie was about to blow out the candles on a huge cake in the shape of a number two. Just behind her, a cheeky boy had been caught in the act of trying to blow them out for her, and the big sister was policing the situation by grabbing him, a fierce look on her face.

'I see that it's the right thing for her,' said Ruby. 'I see it and yet . . . I want her with me. I miss her. It hurts.'

'And this is why I'm so grateful for what Marianne did for us.'

'Marianne?'

'I never had to let you go, Ruby. You were right there, all the time. She stepped in and allowed us both to live.'

For a minute Ruby was silent. 'How is she?'

'She's good. She's been off the booze for a few months. She misses you, though.'

'I miss her too. I think I'm going to go and see her. Do you think she'd like that?'

'I think she'd be the happiest mother in the whole world. And I think I would, too.'

ONE YEAR LATER
Ruby

It felt like a pilgrimage, to come back. Seal Bay was exactly as she remembered it. The gleaming white sand, the sharp wind, the machair. Across the unspoiled landscape she hiked to the cottage and pushed open the door, was amazed to see that the conch was still there, spotless in the centre of the dusty table. The comb she placed inside was a cheap plastic one from Boots, but it was all she had. She'd been here before, with the same thoughts in her head; Constance had gone, but there was no body, no way of proving she was dead. Every day since she'd last visited the clifftop she'd thought about her friend, and wondered about what had happened, until finally she had to come back. Had Constance drowned? She'd been such a strong swimmer, but if she'd landed on rocks, she wouldn't have had a chance. Ruby hesitated before reaching into her pocket for the photographs she'd brought with her. The print she chose was dog-eared, one of the three precious images that she owned. There was Leonie, happy in the big garden, blowing out the candles on the cake. *What if she doesn't come?* The photo would mean nothing to other members of the Roane, but to Constance, it would mean the world. She kissed the photograph, then placed it carefully into the conch shell. As she returned the remaining photos to her pocket, her fingers brushed the edges of the small brown envelope she'd been given at the hospital the week before. Her face broke out in a smile but she didn't need to look again at what was inside; the black-and-white scan, that coiled spring of new life, sucking its thumb. The shape of it, like a miraculous bean with new shoots of limbs, was imprinted on her brain.

Back on the beach, Ruby sat down and took out her violin. As she started to play the tune she'd learned from her strange friend, the rock in the middle of the bay came alive. She saw five, six, seven grey seals raise their heads and start to call. One of them dropped into the water and disappeared. A flip, then, inside her, and she cried out with surprise, with joy. A tiny fish turning over, the first time she'd felt it, her little acrobat.

With one hand resting low on her belly, Ruby waited where the ocean met the land, to see what might happen. She caught sight of the head of the grey seal as it appeared once more, and wondered what was happening in that other world, just beneath the surface.

AUTHOR'S NOTE

Folktales live all around us. If you look hard enough, you can find one in the bones of every story, every bit of gossip, every film you watch, every book you read. The seed of this book sprouted when I read a folktale about a selkie, but the story may well have been waiting there in my mind all along, ready for me to water it, so that it could grow into the novel you have just read.

The folktale in question is called 'The Mermaid Wife', which is said to be from the isle of Unst, the most northerly island in Shetland, and therefore the British Isles. Unst is at the edge of one of the few places in the world where, in autumn, the sky is fleetingly lit with the mysterious and astonishing Northern Lights. Strange happenings and odd things coming from the sea there are not unusual, and the story goes that one evening, a very long time ago, a local man came across a group of selkie women dancing on the sand. He found their sealskins lying nearby and took one, so that when the selkies saw him and fled, slipping into their skins as they ran for the surf, one of them was stranded. In the way of many fairy tales, the selkie-woman's beauty worked against her: although the man saw that she was heartbroken, he could not bring himself to free her by giving her back her skin, dressing her instead in human clothes and taking the weeping woman home with him. Having no other choice, the woman lived with him for many years, and had several children. According to the story, she eventually seemed content, though it is noted that she often spent hours gazing out to sea. One day, while the man was out at work, the children came across an old sealskin hidden in the barn. They brought it to their mother, who fell upon it with joy, hugged her children one last time, and ran down to the water where she dressed in her skin and swam away.

This story chimed in a particular way with me. I felt the reason could be found in childhood, in the stories many of us share, in a kind of sub-conscious half-remembered collective knowledge that draws people towards such things. Folktales are retold in different versions the world over. As children, the music of story is sung to us so often that sometimes, we don't even realise that the story we are telling has been told before, time and time again.

Selkies exist in the folklore of Ireland, England, Scotland and Iceland, as well as the Scandinavian countries whose shores border that particular area of the globe. They are related to Finfolk, and perhaps to Swan-Maidens, as well as other creatures of myth and legend the world over who transform from animals to human form, and back again. Like 'The Mermaid Wife', many versions of the selkie stories tell of a magical creature trapped by a human man, forced to marry him and bear his children. She sometimes appears happy with her lot until she finds her stolen skin, the means to return home. At this point she escapes, often gleefully, into the sea, with only a passing, regretful glance back at her earth-born children. I was excited by this aspect of the legend, because it seemed so taboo: a woman who leaves her children? Shocking. But is it? Should it be? If that woman has been captured and kept for years against her will? And would it be shocking if a man did the same? Constance didn't choose to get pregnant or give birth, but she does love her daughter. She has this in common with generations of women the world over: her story is their story. It is my story, and the story of my ancestors.

There's no way of knowing, but I like to imagine that the selkie legend has roots in real events. Imagine a fishing and farming community on a remote island, centuries ago. One day a woman emerges from the waves, wearing sealskins, speaking a language no one can understand. Those big grey seals, their intelligent eyes, always watching from a nearby skerry. The onlooker glances from the seals to the woman and makes the connection, sees the evidence: She is a seal. Modern, logical minds might suggest that there is a more earthly explanation, perhaps the onlooker has missed the fact that the woman has come from a shipwreck, that she was always human. Nevertheless, the rest of the story is the same: she cries when her sealskin is taken away. She reluctantly becomes a wife. He hides her skin, naturally assuming that she would try to return to the ocean if he let her have it, despite her love for her children, that anchors her to him, and to the land. Perhaps she would. The question is, would you blame her?

ACKNOWLEDGEMENTS

Thanks go to the following people, without whom the book would not exist.

Madeleine Milburn, for her unwavering support, brilliant advice and so much more. Many thanks also to the wonderful, talented team at the MM agency.

For their excellent guidance and supremely wise editorial input, and for steering the book towards the market with such passion and professionalism: Manpreet Grewal and the team at HQ; Jennifer Lambert and all at HarperCollins Canada; Chelsey Emmelhainz for her early input; Matt, Melissa and the entire team at Crooked Lane Books.

To my first readers: Jennifer Usher, Mel Sellors, Chloë Kempton, Kitty Fordham, Alison Dunne, Mary Reddaway. Big kisses to all of you wonderful people. To Jenny Parsons, for medical advice and guidance. All omissions, mistakes and examples of wilful misrepresentation are my own.

To my supervisors at Bath Spa: Fay Weldon, C J Skuse and most especially Tracy Brain. Your input was invaluable: wise, crucial and transformative.

To my children, who are the absolute best.

To Jonathan Golding, who is always there, ready to listen to all of my nonsense.

EPIGRAPHS AND SOURCES FOR FURTHER RESEARCH

Chapter One

Excerpt of 'The Forsaken Merman' by

Arnold, M. (1897) *The poetical works of Matthew Arnold.*
Boston and New York: Thomas Y Crowel and co. Available
at: https://en.wikisource.org/wiki/The_poetical_works_of_
Matthew_Arnold/The_Forsaken_Merman

Chapter Six

Quotation from 'The Goodman of Wastness' in

Black, G.F. and Thomas, N.W. (1903) *Examples of printed
folk-lore concerning the Orkney & Shetland islands.*
London: The Folklore Society. Available at: https://www.
alternatewars.com/Mythology/Example_FL_Orkneys_
Excerpt.htm

Chapter Eight
Excerpt of 'The Fisherman and the Merman' in
Douglas, G. (1901) *Scottish fairy and folk tales*. New York:
Dover Publications. Available at: https://www.sacred-texts.
com/neu/celt/sfft/sfft57.htm

Chapter Eleven
Excerpt of 'The Silkie Wife' in
Kennedy, P (1891) *Legendary Fictions of the Irish Celts*.
London and New York: Macmillan. Available at https://
www.sacred-texts.com/neu/celt/lfic/lfic028.htm

Chapter Thirty-four
Excerpt of 'The Mermaid Wife' in
Keightley, T (1870) *The Fairy Mythology Illustrative
of the Romance and Superstition of Various Countries*.
London: Whittaker, Treacher & co. Available at: https://
www.sacred-texts.com/neu/celt/tfm/tfm063.htm

Chapter Thirty-eight
Excerpt of 'The Mermaid Wife' in
Tibbits, C (1889) *Folk-lore and Legends: Scotland*. London:
W.W. Gibbings. Available at: https://www.worldoftales.
com/European_folktales/Scottish_folktale_16.html#gsc.
tab=0

Chapter Fifty-three

Quotation from 'The Great Silkie of Sule Skerrie' in Thomas, Capt. F. W. L. (1855) *Proceedings of the Society of Antiquaries of Scotland Vol 1* p 86-89. Available at: https://books.google.co.uk/books?id=4t84AQAAMAAJ&pg=PA88&redir_esc=y#v=onepage&q&f=false

Song lyrics

'Chuir iad mise dh'eilean leam fhìn' *(They sent me to an island by myself)*

Traditional Gaelic song, perhaps connected with Uist. Additional source notes can be found here: https://thesession.org/tunes/4468

'The Sealwoman's Sea-Joy' *(Ionn-da, ionn-do)*

This song is popular among choirs and has been variously attributed to Icelandic, Scandinavian and Scottish cultures. The version I know is transcribed in David Thomson's *The People of the Sea*, first published in 1954, in which he ponders whether the seals themselves wrote the song and taught it to the islanders on Uist.

Turn the page for an exclusive extract from *Little Darlings*,
the bestselling debut novel from Melanie Golding

Available to buy now!

August 18th
Peak District, UK

DS Joanna Harper stood on the viaduct with the other police officers. On the far bank, across the great expanse of the reservoir, a woman paused at the water's edge, about to go in, her twin baby boys held tightly in her arms.

Harper turned to the DI. 'How close are the officers on that side?'

Dense woodland surrounded the scrap of shore where the woman stood. Even at this distance, Harper could see that her legs were scarlet with blood from the thorns.

'Not close enough,' said Thrupp. 'They can't find a way to get to her.'

In a fury of thudding, the helicopter flew over their heads, disturbing the surface of the reservoir, bellowing its command: *Step away from the water*. It loomed above the tiny figure of the mother, deafening and relentless, but the officers on board wouldn't be able to stop her. There was nowhere in the valley where the craft could make a safe landing, or get low enough to drop the winch.

Through the binoculars, Harper saw the woman collapse into a sitting position on the dried-out silt, her face turned to the sky, still clutching the babies. Perhaps she wouldn't do it, after all.

A memory surfaced then, of what the old lady had said to her:

'She'll have to put them in the water, if she wants her own babies back . . . Right under the water. Hold 'em down.'

The woman wasn't sitting at the water's edge anymore; she was knee-deep, and wading further in. The DS kicked off her shoes, climbed up on the rail and prepared to dive.

Chapter 1

The child is not mine as the first was,
I cannot sing it to rest,
I cannot lift it up fatherly
And bliss it upon my breast;
Yet it lies in my little one's cradle
And sits in my little one's chair,
And the light of the heaven she's gone to
Transfigures its golden hair.

FROM *The Changeling*
BY JAMES RUSSELL LOWELL

July 13th
8.10 p.m.

All she cared about was that the pain had been taken away. With it, the fear, and the certainty that she would die, all gone in the space of a few miraculous seconds. She wanted to drift off, but then Patrick's worried face appeared, topped by a green hospital cap, and she remembered: I'm having my babies. The spinal injection she'd been given didn't just signal the end of the horrendous contractions, but the beginning of a forceps extraction procedure that could still go wrong. The first baby was stuck in the birth canal. So, instead of allowing herself to sink inside her glorious, warm cocoon of numbness and fall asleep – which she hadn't done for thirty-six hours – she tried to concentrate on what was happening.

The doctor's face appeared, near to Lauren's own, the mask pulled down revealing her mouth and most of her chin. The woman's lips were moving as if untethered to her words. It was the drugs, and the exhaustion; the world had slowed right down. Lauren frowned. The doctor was looking at her, but she seemed so far away. She's talking to me, thought Lauren. I should listen.

'OK, Mrs Tranter, because of the spinal, you won't be able to tell when you have a contraction – so I'll tell you when to push, OK?'

Lauren's mouth formed an 'o', but the doctor had already gone.

'Push.'

She felt the force of the doctor pulling and her entire body slid down the bed with it. She couldn't tell if she was pushing or not. She made an effort to arrange her face in an expression of straining and tensed her neck muscles, but somewhere in her head a voice said: Why bother? They won't be able to tell if I don't push, will they? Maybe I could just have a little sleep.

She shut her eyes.

'Push now.'

The doctor pulled again and the dreaminess dispersed as the first one came out. Lauren opened her eyes and everything was back in focus, events running at the right speed, or perhaps slightly too quickly now. She held her breath, waiting for the sound of crying. When it finally came – that sound, thin and reedy, the weakened protest of something traumatised – she cried too. The tears seemed projectile, they were so pent-up. Patrick squeezed her hand.

'Let me see,' she said, and that was when the baby was placed on his mother's chest, but on his back, arse-to-chin with Lauren so that all she could see were his folded froggy legs and a tiny arm, flailing in the air. Patrick bent over them both, squinting at the baby, laughing, then crying and pressing his finger into one little palm.

'Can't you turn him around?' she said, but nobody did. Then she was barely aware of the doctor saying, 'push' again, and another pull. The boy was whisked away and the second one placed there.

This time she could reach up and turn the baby to face her. She held him in a cradle made of her two arms and studied his face, the baby studying her at the same time, his little mouth in a trumpeter's pout, no white visible in his half-open eyes but a deep, thoughtful blue. Although the babies were genetically identical, she and Patrick had expected that there would be slight differences. They're individuals. Two bonnie boys, she thought with a degree of slightly forced joviality, at the same time as: Could I just go to sleep now? Would anyone notice, really?

'Riley,' said Patrick, with one hand gently touching Lauren's face and one finger stroking the baby's. 'Yes?'

Lauren felt pressured. She thought they might leave naming them for a few days until they got to know them properly. Such a major decision – what if they got it wrong?

'Riley?' she said. 'I suppose . . . '

Patrick straightened up, his phone in his hand already.

'What about the other one? Rupert?'

Rupert? That wasn't even on the list. It was like he was trying to get names past her while she was distracted, having been pumped full of drugs and laid out flat, paralysed from the chest down, vulnerable to suggestion. Not fair.

'No,' she said, a little bit too loudly. 'He's called Morgan.'

Patrick's brow creased. He glanced in the direction of possibly-Morgan, who was being checked over by the paediatrician. 'Really?' He put his phone back in his pocket.

'You can't stay long,' said the nurse-midwife to Patrick, as the bed finally rolled into place. Sea-green curtains were whisked out of the way. Lauren wanted to protest: she'd hoped there would be some time to properly settle in with the babies before they threw her husband out of the ward.

The trip from theatre to the maternity ward involved hundreds of metres of corridor. Thousands of metres, maybe. Patrick had been wheeling the trolley containing one of the twins, while the nurse drove the bed containing Lauren, who was holding the other one. The small procession clanked wordlessly along the route through the yellow-lit corridors. At first Lauren thought that Patrick could have offered to swap with the nurse and take the heavier burden, but she soon became glad she hadn't mentioned it. As they approached the ward it was clear the woman knew what she was doing. This nurse, who was half Patrick's height just about, had used her entire bodyweight to counter-balance as the bed swung around a corner and into the bay, then, impressively, she'd stepped up and ridden it like a sailboard into one of the four empty cubicles, the one by the window. There was a single soft 'clang' as the head of the bed gently touched the wall. Patrick would only have crashed them into something expensive.

The nurse operated the brake and gave a brisk, 'Here we are!' before delivering her warning to Patrick, indicating the clock on the wall opposite. 'Fifteen minutes,' she said.

Her shoes squeaked away up the ward. Lauren and Patrick looked at the babies.

'Which one have you got?' asked Patrick.

She turned the little name tag on the delicate wrist of the sleeping child in her arms. The words *Baby Tranter #1* were written on it in blue sharpie.

'Morgan,' said Lauren.

Patrick bent over the trolley containing the other one. Later, everyone would say that the twins looked like their father, but at this moment she couldn't see a single similarity between the fully grown man and the scrunched-up bud of a baby. The boys certainly resembled each other – two peas popped from the same pod, or the same pea, twice. Riley had the same wrinkled little face as his brother, the same long fingers and uncannily perfect fingernails. They made the same expression when they yawned. Slightly irritatingly, someone in theatre had dressed them in identical white sleep suits, taken from the bag Lauren and Patrick had brought with them, though there had been other colours available. She had intended to dress one of them in yellow. Without the name tags they could easily have been mistaken for each other and how would anyone ever know? Thank goodness for the name tags, then. In her arms, Morgan moved his head from side to side and half-opened his eyes. She watched them slowly close.

They'd been given a single trolley for both babies to sleep in. Riley was lying under Patrick's gaze in the clear plastic cot-tray bolted to the top of the trolley. Underneath the baby there was a firm, tightly fitting mattress, and folded at either end of this were two blankets printed with the name of the hospital. The cot was the wrong shape for its cargo. The plastic tray and the mattress were unforgivingly flat, and the baby was a ball. A woodlouse in your palm, one that curls up when frightened. Patrick moved the trolley slightly, abruptly, and Riley's little arms and legs flew out, a five-pointed star. He curled up slowly, at the same speed as his brother's closing eyes. Back in a ball, he came to rest slightly on his side. To hold a baby, it ought to be bowl-shaped, a little nest. Why had no one thought of that before?

'Hello, Riley,' said Patrick in an odd, squeaky voice. He straightened up. 'It sounds weird, saying that.'

Lauren reached out and drew the trolley closer to her bed, carefully, trying to prevent the little ball from rolling. She used her one free hand to tuck a blanket over him and down the sides of the mattress, to hold him in place.

'Hello, Riley,' she said. 'Yeah, it does a bit. I think that's normal, though. We'll get used to it.' She turned her face to the child in her arms. 'Hello, Morgan,' she said. She was still waiting for the rush of love. That one you feel, all at once the second they're born, like nothing you've ever experienced before. The rush of love that people with children always go on about. She'd been looking forward to it. It worried her that she hadn't felt it yet.

She handed Morgan to Patrick, who held him as if he were a delicate antique pot he'd just been told was worth more than the house, desperate to put him down, unsure where, terrified something might happen. Lauren found it both funny and concerning. When the baby – who could probably sense these things – started to cry, Patrick froze, a face of nearly cartoon panic. Morgan's crying caused Riley to wake up and cry, too.

'Put him in there, next to Riley,' said Lauren. The twins had been together all their lives. She wondered what that would mean for them, later on. They'd been with her, growing inside her, for nine months, the three of them together every second of every day for the whole of their existence so far. She felt relief that they were no longer in there, and guilt at feeling that relief, and a great loss that they had taken the first step away from her, the first of all the subsequent, inevitable steps away from her. Was that the love, that guilty feeling? That sense of loss? Surely not.

Patrick placed the squalling package face to face with his double, and, a miracle, the crying ceased. They both reached out, wrapping miniature arms around each other's downy heads, Morgan holding onto Riley's ear. All was calm. From above, they looked like an illusion. An impossibility. Lauren checked again, but as far as she could tell the rush of love still had not arrived.

The fierce nurse squeaked back down the ward at just after nine and began to shoo Patrick away home, which would leave Lauren, still numb in the legs and unable to move, alone to deal with every need and desire of the two newborn babies.

'You can't leave me,' said Lauren.

'You can't stay,' said the nurse.

'I'll be back,' said Patrick, 'first thing. As soon as they open the doors. Don't worry.'

He kissed her head, and both babies. He walked away a little too quickly.

ONE PLACE. MANY STORIES

Bold, innovative and
empowering publishing.

FOLLOW US ON:

@HQStories